ALSO BY SARA FLANNERY MURPHY

The Possessions

GIRL ONE

SARA FLANNERY MURPHY

GIRL ONE

MCD FARRAR, STRAUS AND GIROUX NEW YORK

MCD

Farrar, Straus and Giroux

120 Broadway, New York 10271

Title page and chapter opener illustrations by Na Kim

Library of Congress Cataloging-in-Publication Data

Names: Murphy, Sara Flannery, author.

Title: Girl one / Sara Flannery Murphy.

Description: First edition. | New York : MCD / Farrar, Straus and Giroux, 2021.

Identifiers: LCCN 2020056718 | ISBN 9780374601744 (hardcover)

Classification: LCC PS3613.U7549 G57 2021 | DDC 813/.6—dc23

LC record available at https://lccn.loc.gov/2020056718

Designed by Abby Kagan

www.mcdbooks.com • www.fsgbooks.com

Follow us on Twitter, Facebook, and Instagram at @mcdbooks

10 9 8 7 6 5 4 3 2 1

To my parents, for everything, for always

GIRL ONE

1

April 24, 1972

My dearest Josephine,

I've just taken a call from President Nixon, who asked me to pass on his fondest birthday regards to you. Right now, I'm in my hotel room in New York City. (The Pierre, can you imagine? Last time I was in the city, I stayed in a closet and counted roaches scuttling across the ceiling.) Strangers have stopped me on the sidewalk to ask that I wish you a happy first birthday. Yet all I want right now is to be with you, little one. Back in Vermont, surrounded by wilderness, the two of us picking wild marigolds and watching the clouds.

Every proud papa believes his child is singular and astonishing, but in my case, it's the truth. Your birthday will forever be remembered as the anniversary of humanity's greatest scientific breakthrough. I'm ever so sorry to miss our big day, but I hope you will instead accept this letter, scribbled on this beautiful hotel stationery in my clumsy handwriting. So many words will be written about the two of us over the years, by so many people, but today I want you to have something private. Just for you.

Tonight, I will dine with the very men of science who used to snub me, and they will toast me. Us. One day, you'll understand just how bitterly I fought for your mere existence. But no words of praise can ever be as sweet to me as the sight of you. Ten fingers and ten toes, each one miraculous. Happy Birthday, Girl One.

Your loving father always,
Joseph Bellanger

2

April 15, 1994

I learned about my mother's disappearance from the evening news. I looked up from my textbook when I overheard my surname and recognized the exact cypress tree that grew outside my bedroom window. From that point on, my life turned into a stream of simple equations. How long my mother had been missing (one day). How long since I'd had an actual conversation with her (just over a year). The cost of a bus ticket back to Coeur du Lac, my adopted hometown ($15). The amount left in my bank account after spending fifteen dollars ($110.67). How doomed I would be if I abandoned Chicago for longer than three nights (very: I had four exams looming within the next few weeks).

For a while I lost myself in these calculations and the illusion of stability they offered. This was my standard coping mechanism: turn everything into problems on a checklist to be neatly solved, then filed away. If I pulled it off just right, I could focus on the question of how many pairs of jeans to pack (three) and keep my growing panic at bay.

But when I arrived back in Coeur du Lac, Illinois—*Heart of the Lake*, with no lake and no discernible heart—I stood in front of the shell of my childhood home in the balmy twilight and everything in me crumpled. *Something bad had happened here.* Something bad had happened *again*, and this time it involved my mother.

The footage on the news and the photos in the papers hadn't prepared me. The wreaths of yellow caution tape around the porch railings looked weirdly festive, like an interrupted birthday party. The porch still stood, but a narrow gash through the living room wall exposed blackened brick, hanging guts of insulation, snaky wires. The rest of the house looked more or less the same. That was almost worse: the untouched parts. I took a deep, shuddering breath.

The house felt both totally vulnerable and like a fortress. Thanks to my mother's long-standing paranoia, there was no spare key hidden near my home. I went around to the side door and tried the knob. Locked, of course. A small window was set into the door. My mother kept the glass panes covered with a frilly gingham curtain, more for the privacy than for any kind of aesthetic value. She'd hated that window, always eye-balling the distance between the pane and the doorknob, forever imagining a fist smashed through the glass, a hand reaching for the lock. I'd dutifully shared the fear as a little kid, but as a teenager I'd finally snapped. "Who even wants to get in here, Margaret?" I'd demanded, world-weary, contemptuous. "There's never anything going on in this house."

I stepped back now and examined the wilderness at the sides of the house, looking for a likely candidate, my pulse already surging with what I was about to do. Everything was weedy and overgrown, thistles blooming to calf-height. I grabbed a large rock, tested its weight in my palm with a few quick bounces. Good enough. Feeling wild, like I was inside a dream, I brought the rock hard against the glass: once, twice, watching the glass splinter into a spiderweb of cracks. The glass was cheap and brittle, hadn't been replaced since we'd moved in seventeen years ago. It shattered with a satisfying clatter. Then I sobered up, looking around. The block was dark and empty in the rapidly spreading dusk. Our street had always been lonely, occupied by a steady stream of short-term renters, our two-person household the only stubborn fixture.

I snaked my arm through the hole, avoiding the jagged crust at the edges. For a second the realization that I was vandalizing my own house hit me with a lurch of guilt. I was doing exactly what my mother had worried about, all those years. But screw it. The whole house was so ravaged that this broken pane didn't matter. I'd replace it for my mother myself. I'd replace every window in the house if I just found her safe.

Grappling for the doorknob, I felt the familiar wedge of the lock and twisted it. So many times I'd clicked that lock into place before bedtime, double-checking it to quell my mother's nervousness. With-drawing my arm, I stepped into my house, glass crunching under my soles.

I'd wasted too much money on newspapers at the bus station, driven by both a need for the facts and my growing dread, snatching everything from tabloids to the *Chicago Tribune*. My mother stared up at me, over and over again. Several shots from her Homestead days, hair waist-length and eyebrows unplucked. One candid shot had been snapped on the last day I'd seen her in person, taken just as I was about to drive away, heading into my bright new future without her. Both our smiles were uncomfort-able, obviously fake. I remembered the exact blouse my mother was wear-ing, even the precise depth of the dark circles under her eyes. She hadn't been sleeping much back then, the tension in our house so thick that it was hard to relax. The months between that day and this one collapsed as I hunched over the newspaper, worrying a fingernail, barely caring how I looked to the other bus passengers.

From the papers, I pieced together more of the story. The fire had started overnight. It was three in the morning before the bright shadow of the flames finally woke the closest neighbors, so a quarter of my child-hood home had burned before the fire department made an appear-ance. Afterward, the police searched the dark, dripping rooms, unable to find any real trace of my mother. Her purse left behind. Her car still there.

The tiny details stung the most. The fact that none of the neighbors could comment on her whereabouts because my mother had been even more of a hermit than usual. Mail piling up, the lawn piebald with brown patches, the windows darkened at all hours. She'd apparently quit her job at the library a month ago.

It was that last fact that nearly made me rip up the paper, as if de-stroying the words could make them untrue. My mother had loved her job. The public library had been her only refuge when the two of us came blowing into town in 1977, fear-struck, hair singed, unable to sleep at night without the flames chasing us in our dreams. Nobody else had wanted anything to do with a couple of cult escapees, our faces plastered all over newspapers beneath doomy headlines. My mother thanked the librarians who took a chance on her by efficiently working her way from reshelving books to the circulation desk, the farthest she could go without a degree. And now I tried to imagine my mother confined at home, shuffling, unwashed, vacant and alone.

I'd done that to her. I'd left my mother, and she'd become exactly who I worried she'd be without me.

Most of the newspapers jumped at the chance to resurrect the whole grim tale of the Homestead. It was like a game of telephone: every time our story reappeared, another name was misspelled or a date was off by a week, another false bit of gossip was recycled (this time, the claim that our mothers had hosted pill-fueled orgies). One paper included a list of the surviving members, all eight mother-daughter pairs arranged by birth order. It was the original taxonomy that we'd fall into forever, giving each other context though we hadn't been together in years.

The New York Times ran a full-color photograph of me and my mother in January 1973. It was a photo I'd seen a thousand times, reprinted so often it should've been faded by all the eyes on it. My mother stood next to Dr. Bellanger with me propped on her hip, Bellanger's arm around her. Toddler-me craned my neck to look at him, chubby-cheeked and beaming. The quintessential family portrait. My father (in a way). My mother (in every way). And me. I was the oldest Girl by a full two years, often selected for photographs and interviews, so the three of us—Bellanger, my mother, and me—had become a trio. Set apart in a way the others weren't.

Sitting on the bus this morning, I hadn't been prepared to see that photo again; I experienced the quick throb of grief and love I felt whenever I saw Bellanger's face. Usually, when I looked at this photo, my mother barely stood out. When I was a kid, her face in this photo was just a younger version of the one I saw as she tucked me into bed every night. As I grew up, it become an older version of the face I saw in the mirror. So totally familiar it was uninteresting. Now she grabbed my gaze with a stab of worry. I pressed a finger over Bellanger's face, then over my mother's, until I was the only one left.

Each year of my life revolved around two particular dates, an emotional arc as fixed in my head as the rotation of the earth around the sun. The first came on April 24, the anniversary of one of the most controversial scientific breakthroughs in the twentieth century: my birthday. A date that'd become a question in Trivial Pursuit and the title of a little-known song by the Clash.

The second date landed in June. The anniversary of the fire that'd taken everything from me. Together, those two formed the simple punch line of my origin story: it might've been birth that put us on the map, but it was death that kept us there.

Since first grade, I could recite my personal history on command, and often did for anybody who'd listen. In the year 1970, the shiny start of a new decade, a visionary named Joseph Bellanger put out the call for young women to become part of a risky reproductive experiment. Between 1971 and 1975, nine women gave birth to baby girls. There were no fathers. Not genetically, not biologically. Only eggs dividing, impossibly, without the influence of spermatozoa.

The nine of us, swiftly dubbed the "Miracle Babies," launched Bellanger from crackpot obscurity to global fame. For six bright years, there were photo shoots, interviews, limited-edition baby dolls; conference presentations, sponsorships, endless editorials. Bellanger stayed with us at the Homestead as much as possible, doing his best to protect us from both the shine of the spotlight and the inevitable darkness that collected at its edges.

By my sixth birthday, the darkness started to overwhelm the shine. The people who opposed our very existence got louder, more aggressive. Our most prominent critic was a man named Ricky Peters, an ersatz preacher whose fame grew alongside ours. But Ricky wasn't the only one. Politicians publicly promised that, if elected, they'd make parthenogenesis illegal. Ministers and priests took to the pulpits to remind the world that we were born pre-damned. Petri dish abominations, our eternal souls only half formed when we were conceived without fathers.

In 1977, everything fell apart, one disaster after another. Lily-Anne, Mother Nine, the last to give birth, was the first to die. She left her two-year-old daughter, Fiona, orphaned in every sense of the word. Doctors around the globe snagged TV appearances and front-page spots to argue that Bellanger's methods were clearly dangerous, illicit, and untested. Some Mothers fled the Homestead, taking their Miracle Babies with them. Our makeshift family fractured and scattered until barely any of us were left. And then—then the fire.

On June 22, 1977, a fire blazed overnight at the Homestead. When the smoke cleared, two bodies were among the wreckage, barely recognizable. One was Fiona, Girl Nine, always fatherless and newly motherless. The other was Dr. Joseph Bellanger. The secrets of parthenogenesis went with him, his research consumed in the flames.

For most people, the story ended with the fire. In 1978, after a well-publicized trial, Ricky Peters was found guilty of arson and two counts of first-degree murder, sentenced to life in prison without parole. The surviving Mothers and Girls sank into an uneasy infamy, becoming *Jeopardy* clues and textbook footnotes.

For me, though, the fire was only the beginning. My story began when my mother transplanted us to Illinois and tried to forge a quiet life out of the ashes, as if we could just disappear into normalcy. It became painfully obvious that wasn't an option for me when a group of seventh-grade boys surrounded me, asking if I even had a pussy or if my crotch was as smooth and blank as a Barbie's. My mother devoted herself to pretending our history never happened, forcing me to patch together the story on my own. I memorized each of the precious letters that Bellanger had written for me. Six of them, one for each of my birthdays before he'd died. I'd returned again and again to the line where Bellanger called me his *first and favorite daughter* and felt that love and protection still surrounding me, glowing in my DNA.

Of all the Girls, you're the most like me, Josephine. You have that same spark in you. That same curiosity. You see the world through my eyes.

In high school biology, I cut into a frog's slick, pale belly and a flood of memories returned. Helping Bellanger in his lab at the Homestead. The way it felt to sit with him for hours, being so patient, barely moving, watching him work. Handing him his instruments. In that muggy high school lab, I was the first of my classmates to identify the ovaries, the oviduct, those delicate, springy coils. Looking around, I knew it was different for me. I was drawn to this secret, interior world, brimming over with the potential to change everything.

That initial spark grew and grew until I appreciated what it actually meant: That I should be the one to pick up the loose thread that had started with my conception. Who better than me, Girl One, born with Bellanger's curious eyes and hungry brain? Before his death, Bellanger had described a world where any woman could achieve parthenogenesis with his help. I was tired of sitting by and watching his legacy shrink a little more every year, my birth becoming a weird hiccup in the timeline of human reproduction instead of a bold turning point.

And so I'd done everything I could to make Bellanger proud. I went to school in Carbondale, majoring in biology, commuting from home. A two-hour round trip every weekday, followed by the late shift at Coeur du Lac's all-night diner. I was saving money living at home with my mom, but there was a growing chilliness between us that made it increasingly uncomfortable. We had less and less to talk about. I couldn't really chat with her about my courses. It wasn't just that she was uninterested, it was the growing hum of disapproval, like an electrical appliance on the fritz, nagging at first and then piercing and unignorable.

It all led up to last year, when I'd finally left Coeur du Lac behind to attend medical school, stepping out of our quiet, careful life and into the waiting world.

The stench of smoke hit as soon as I stepped inside my mother's kitchen, sticking to the back of my throat. I panicked immediately, chest tightening as I reached for the edge of the counter. Had she been home when it happened? I imagined my mother coughing, crawling on her stomach beneath the heavy layer of smoke—

No. I couldn't let myself get caught up in this overwhelming fear. I had to focus. Find her. Figure out where she'd gone, get her back, return to my own life. I straightened, took a steadying breath.

The light switch next to the doorway clicked uselessly. I felt my way to the storage closet and reached for the highest shelf, groping for the sturdy stem of the flashlight my mother kept there. Never candles. Only this ancient, heavy Maglite, which I pulled down now and tapped against my palm. After a flicker, a watery beam spilled out. It hadn't been used in a while.

The ruined living room lay just beyond the kitchen. I stopped in the doorway and swept the beam slowly. Dense scabs of black ran along the walls, tufts of grimy insulation poking from the ceiling like stalactites. The TV set was a gnarled clump of plastic. The couch was half-scorched, the darkness lying over it delicately as a drop cloth. I swallowed hard, fighting down my nerves. There was an explanation for all this.

I walked through the hallway. Something felt off. Some layer beneath the obvious, gut-punch wrongness of the burned house. Everything looked just a little different. The pictures that had once lined the hallway—portraits of me, all taken by my mother, framed in cheap plastic—had been removed entirely, or knocked crooked. The baseboards were furry with dust; a chair was toppled in the hallway, legs sticking up like a dead insect. The place looked abandoned. I wandered down the hall, catching the staleness that drifted under the sharp scent of smoke. Mounds of neglected laundry moldering along the baseboards. I caught a flicker of movement and jumped, stifled a yelp. A cockroach, huge and shiny, stuttered across the hall and vanished under a vent. I swallowed hard.

I made my way to the garage, where our unreliable old Chevy still sat surrounded by musty boxes. My mother's purse was on the front seat, hanging open. Goose bumps rose along my arms. Maybe she hadn't actually vanished, but she was doing a damn good impression of it.

Yanking open the creaking Chevy door, I fished around in the purse and plucked loose the keys. I slipped them into my pocket, the pulse of worry growing stronger. How the hell could she have left town without the Chevy? I dumped the contents of her purse onto the seat. Her wallet was gone; I wasn't sure whether she'd taken it, or if it was at the police station, abandoned in a plastic baggie. Only trivial junk was left for me now. A piece of mint gum, stale-smelling. A thick hair elastic. A local gas station receipt from months back. A yellow Post-it note, the adhesive strip gray with dust and lint. Her handwriting was quick and sloppy. T.A.—KCT. Then a string of ten numbers, randomly spaced. Maybe a phone number? The letters didn't mean anything to me. I stuck the note into my pocket anyway. Even a tiny clue was helpful at this point.

I felt a sudden hopelessness, bottoming out beneath the frustration. I was worried for my mother; I was furious at her. This wasn't supposed to be happening. All the time I'd been in Chicago, my mother's place in Coeur du Lac had been a given. She'd scarcely ventured beyond the county lines since we'd landed here in 1977. I'd been safe in the knowledge I could walk back into our house and find her absorbed in a library book, looking up and reminding me to lock the door behind me: *You're too trusting, Josie.* I might've been identical to my mother in every other way, but on the inside we were opposites. Her ironbound caution, my restless curiosity. She was the one who stayed. I was the one who left.

Walking back through the kitchen, I caught the muffled sound of an engine from outside. The cops? Gawkers? A news van drawn to the hot scent of scandal? I dropped into a half crouch as I went down the hall, hoping my flashlight beam wasn't visible through the windows. I couldn't let anyone find me here. I had wanted to get in, get out, get my mother, not end up as a tabloid headline myself.

My bedroom was a wreck. I had to quash the sudden sense of betrayal. It wasn't like my mother had any obligation to keep my bedroom intact, with its outdated Popples pillowcase, my Rubik's Cube one spin from being solved, the stack of ratty thirdhand textbooks from my undergrad courses. But I hadn't expected her to tear the room apart. My mattress bare and sagging against a wall, my dresser pushed aside haphazardly. Strangest of all, the books and the papers. My whole collection, I realized. Scattered all over the floor, a chaotic layer of Homestead headlines and titles and photos. The entire fucking timeline of research that I had painstakingly put together on my own, now rooted from the top shelf of my closet and spread everywhere, some of the pages ripped, some with big squares cut out. My gaze landed on a photo of me and my mom, taken when I was a toddler. Our heads had been sliced out, replaced by a bare rectangle that showed the ugly green carpet pushing through.

I left my bedroom with my heart hammering. "What the hell?" I said, and it kept repeating. *What the hell, what the hell.* A mantra blaring through my head in the eerie silence. Somebody had been going through my things. Digging up the Homestead.

Moving on the balls of my feet, like someone would overhear, I made my way up the narrow staircase. In my mother's small, angled bedroom, the feeling of weirdness grew even stronger, dizzying. My mother had been tidy. Not a neat freak—neither of us were—but I'd never seen this level of chaos. Books and notebooks and papers scattered everywhere. A half-full coffee cup growing lily pads of mold.

My mother hadn't taken many clothes, wherever she'd gone. Most of her blouses and pants had been kicked to the floor of the closet in ungainly heaps. In the bathroom, her hairbrush was curled through with dark brown strands that matched mine, but threaded with gray. A preview of what my own follicles would do in another twenty-three years. The jar of coconut oil she used as moisturizer sitting half-open, releasing its warm, nutty smell. Her smell. But the trash can was overflowing, and the shower curtain was removed, and the grout was darkened into stark outlines between the tiles.

I breathed in, out, shut my eyes. I'd find her. Our DNA was identical. Our heartbeats once synced up. Our menstrual cycles, too, much to my adolescent embarrassment. Maybe our mindsets would finally match as well.

My eyes landed on the clock, and I hesitated. The clock was as big as a dinner plate and broken, a cheap plastic thing perpetually stuck at a quarter past four. I started toward it, stopped. It couldn't be that easy—

I lifted it off the wall. My mother used to stash things inside the clock's interior. A hiding spot I'd discovered when I'd peeked inside to see if I could replace the batteries, back in May of '82. That time, I'd discovered the letter inviting us to the Homestead reunion, already a month late, our chance long gone. Later, in sixth grade, I'd retrieved a packet of fruit-flavored Nicorette pellets, even though I'd never once seen my mother with a cigarette.

The last time she'd hidden anything inside the clock, I was in seventh grade, maybe eighth. I'd retrieved a letter. Urgent loops of handwriting. Like a love letter—*I think about you all the time*—but devolving into sudden fury—*You can't ignore me forever.* The only signature a letter *T.* My mother had never dated, barely even had friends, so it must've come from one of our stalkers, those lonely strangers who loved us and hated us with the same unearned intimacy. Why had she kept it? Fascinated, I reread the letter again and again until my mother caught me one night, crouched in front of the disemboweled clock. She tore up the letter without a word, flushing the torn confetti down the toilet. Since then, she'd stopped hiding anything where I could find it. And I'd searched everywhere. Even pulled out a floorboard looking for secret crawl spaces.

My mother's refusal to acknowledge our past had chafed between us for years. Our twin resentments, forever at odds. She hated my constant need to know-know-know. I hated that she couldn't embrace the world-changing history that she'd—*we'd*—been part of. The letters from Bellanger were my only direct lifeline to the Homestead, and sometimes I wondered what I'd have done without them. With only my mother in my life, would I have forgotten that I was a scientific milestone in the flesh? My own memories were fading around the edges, a little fuzzier every time I handled them. I couldn't even get a pure image of Bellanger's face in my mind anymore. Just a vague sense of height and warmth, leaning over me.

I stared down at the clock now. Why not? Using the tip of the car key, I maneuvered the screws out of the flimsy plastic and then lifted the backing away. My heart jumped, that old thrill of illicit discovery. A smallish marble-cover composition notebook had been tucked next to the battery compartment. Bingo.

My hands shook as I flipped through the pages, tucking the Maglite under my chin. The pages were full of cutouts, clippings, tattered edges, and taped-down corners. Familiar headlines about Bellanger's death, Fiona's death, Lily-Anne's death. Notes scattered in the margins. Some in pencil. Some in pen. One note seemed to be in crayon or smudged eyeliner. This wasn't like my mother, whose fastidious handwriting had been passed down to me. For a moment I couldn't make sense of anything. I was holding a scrapbook of the very things she'd forbidden me from exploring my entire life. Even in these circumstances, I couldn't help feeling betrayed.

I paused at a page near the front. The edges were embroidered with notes. Numbers, the word *REDBUD*. My attention settled on the list at the center of the page.

Trish/Isabelle (VT)
Tonya/Catherine (AR?)
Angela/Gina (?)
Tami/Emily (KS)
Vera/Delilah (??)
Debbie/Bonnie (MN)
Barb/Helen (?)
Lily-Anne/Fiona (deceased)

I sat back on my heels, my mind whirring over the other Homesteaders, heart racing in my throat. My mother had been listing us, in our forever order, documenting our last known locations. Seeing the names in her handwriting was so intimate that it took my breath away.

This was the most attention I'd seen my mom give the other Homesteaders. Ever. She'd barely spoken their names when I was growing up. I'd tried to tease revelations out of her, traps I had to set ahead of time, catching her after a long weekend shift at the library and plying her with her favorite tea (orange pekoe). My mother would soak her legs in Epsom salts while I crouched on the other side of the shower curtain. If I played my cards right, the dim bathroom became a time capsule where my mother's usual reservations didn't apply.

What were they like, Mom?

Drowsy splashing. *Who?*

You know. The Mothers. The other ones.

Each grudging glimpse into our lives at the Homestead was precious. My mother's memories were more detailed than mine, sharper and fuller. Tonya Bower's love of fresh apples. Patricia Bishop's habit of stealing cigarettes. Bellanger's favorite cologne: Eau Sauvage. I'd mouthed those alien syllables at night until they were imprinted on my tongue.

Well. I'd come back home looking for a puzzle, some clues to my mother's disappearance. I thought that if I could get the pieces back into place just right—*click*—she'd emerge safe and sound. I'd found a puzzle, all right. Not so much the names themselves, but the fact that my mother—Margaret Morrow—had been documenting the women she'd been avoiding for the past seventeen years. The scattered articles and chopped-up photos in my old bedroom hadn't been the work of an intruder; it'd been my mother.

My pulse pounded in my ears, a surge of excitement, curiosity, fear.

That noise of the engine outside was still itching at me. Setting the notebook aside for a moment, I crept to the dark window. A car idled across the street. A maroon sedan. I couldn't make out the interior from here. The taillights were dull blobs against the growing dusk, the license plate obscured. I tried to pinpoint exactly when I'd first noticed the sound. Five minutes ago? Maybe ten? Did someone know I was here?

Stupid—stupid and reckless. I hadn't told most of my professors and classmates why I was leaving or where I was going, figuring I'd be back in Chicago before they had time to wonder. But the inescapable reality of the house had me spooked. My mother was gone: really and truly gone, her absence telegraphed from every corner. Her favorite armchair reduced down to the stark lines of the frame, padded with a nest of blackened upholstery. The house was a strange, abandoned wreck. Something had been going on for a long time before this fire brought it all bursting to the surface. That car outside: Were they looking for my mother? For me? Whoever was after Mother One could be after Girl One too. We were a matching set, whether we liked it or not.

For a second I fantasized about running out there, ripping the car door open, demanding answers. But I thought of Bonnie Clarkson and was gripped with a well-worn fear. Girl Seven, attacked in 1982 when she was barely eight years old. Five years after the fire, just when we'd started to breathe again. The assault happened right on the heels of the much-televised reunion between the Homesteaders. As my mother and I had huddled silently in front of the news, I'd known exactly what she was thinking. That she'd been smart to avoid the reunion. That it had been a red flag waved in front of the bitter, seething masses who still listened to Ricky Peters's proselytizing from his prison cell.

When I glanced out the window a few minutes later, I saw taillights vanishing around the corner. My heartbeat dipped with relief. But it was a reminder that I couldn't hide here all night. I had to figure out my next step.

I went back down to my bedroom, pausing for a moment before going inside. Knowing that my mother had been the one ransacking my things made the room feel unnerving. Like I'd just missed her; like she was about to step out from the corner. Kneeling, I looked again at the butchered bylines, the sliced-up photos, all of which had apparently gone into my vanished mother's creepy scrapbook.

I shifted the papers around with my fingertips. "What were you doing, Mom?" I whispered. So many faces I hadn't seen since I was a little kid, my sort-of sisters. Some of us had been better than others about staying out of the public eye. The Kims and the Grassis hadn't been heard from for years. Others—like the Clarksons—were right there in the spotlight. I paused at an image of Emily French, Girl Five, her solemn eyes and wispy bangs. It was a piece from six months ago, last October, when Tami French died in a car crash. I remembered seeing Emily's face staring up at me from a discarded newspaper in the dining commons. The haunted and unmistakable look of a girl who'd lost her mother.

I pulled the paper closer. The story was in the *Kansas City Telegraph*, a publication that wouldn't have caught my attention normally. But now everything was covered in the layer of significance my mother had left behind as strongly as her fingerprints. I checked the byline. Thomas Abbott. *Kansas City Telegraph*. I fished in my pocket for the Post-it note, smoothed it out. *T.A.—KCT.* The phone number. Voilà.

For a second my excitement over figuring out the code overshadowed the actual implications: Why would my mother—a woman who wouldn't even talk about the past with her own daughter—keep the name and number of a reporter?

The phone lines in the house were down. I looked around before venturing back out of my shell of a house, making sure there were no strange cars lingering. The street was dark and empty. I hurried out, sticking to the shadows, mentally tracing the way to the nearest convenience store. I was so focused on keeping a low profile that I didn't notice it until I stepped on it: a crunch underfoot. I backed away. It was a bird, belly-down, eye filmy, lying near the overgrown rhododendron. The bird—a robin, maybe?—looked almost as if it could fly away, but one outstretched wing was scorched and blackened. As if the little bird had dipped a single wing into the fire. I wasn't sure what it meant, but my stomach twisted, and I hurried away from the little body, clutching the Post-it in my hand as if it would fix everything.

3

"Yeah, hello?"

"Is this Thomas Abbott?" I asked. "From the *Kansas City Telegraph?*" My brain was buzzing as I huddled between the convenience store restrooms, staring at the half-scrubbed shadow of a Sharpied obscenity on the wall.

"Most people call me Tom. Who's speaking?" A youngish voice, neutral, like he was expecting a sales pitch and was already distancing himself. I wasn't sure what I'd been expecting. Some weirdness about him right off the bat that would tip me in the right direction.

I leaned in closer to the pay phone, my warm, travel-soured breath curling back on me. Now that I had him on the line, I wasn't sure what to say. I opted for bluntness. "I'm calling about Margaret Morrow. Why did she have your number? Where is she?" Because I couldn't help myself, and because I had another living, breathing person to talk to, I added: "Do you know anything about the fire?"

"Whoa. Okay, slow down." Call-Me-Tom's voice turned more serious. "One question at a time. Yes, I know about the fire. Everyone in Kansas knows by now." A shift of voices, muted and tinny. A newscaster in the background. I imagined the phone receiver held up to the TV: . . . *with any information about Morrow is encouraged to come forward.* "Second question: No." Tom's voice arrived back in my ear. "I don't know where Margaret is. Trust me, I wish I did." A pause. "Can I ask a question now? Who is this?"

"Why was she in touch with you in the first place?" I persisted. "I once watched my mom chase a journalist off our porch in her bathrobe. She nearly took his head off with a flowerpot."

A much longer pause. "Your mom? Margaret's your—" Something adjusted on the other end, a restructuring of attention. Tom's voice brightened with a barely suppressed excitement. "That means you're Josephine Morrow."

"The one and only."

"Holy shit. I didn't ever expect to hear from you. Girl One."

"Usually I make guys wait for the third date to call me that," I said, a reflexive joke that came out before I could stop it.

A distracted laugh. "How do you even have this number? Did your mother—did Margaret tell you to get in touch with me?"

"I found your number with her things. In her burned-down house. Which is why I'd appreciate you telling me what's going on." The pause went on too long. "Now."

"Josie, I'm sorry, I don't know what to say here. Your mother was very clear that I shouldn't get in touch with you. I don't want to disrespect her wishes. You understand."

"No, I absolutely don't understand." Abandoning the ghostly FUCK U on the wall, I turned to face the display of Butterfingers and Funyuns, bright packaging turned sickly under the fluorescent lights. My mother had mentioned me to this guy. Warned him away from me. I was electrified in spite of myself. "Listen. I don't know who the hell you are. My mother's missing, and I found your number with her things. You'd better tell me what's going on."

He didn't answer. The pay phone was going to ask for another quarter in a minute or two. I bit down my impatience.

"You found my number with her things," he said at last. "Does that mean you're actually in Coeur du Lac?"

"Of course."

A pause. "I just figured you'd stay in Chicago."

"What, and miss my own mother's disappearance?" I deadpanned. But it stung. Whatever my mother had said to this stranger, she must've made it clear that I wasn't exactly the type to come home and visit.

"Listen, how long'll you be there? Can you stay for another . . ." A creak. "Can you stay for tonight? It's not a long drive to Coeur du Lac. Three hours, tops. We need to talk this over in person."

It only took two hours for Thomas Abbott to reach me. I was waiting just inside the front door—shaky, excited, nervous, everything in me switched on. The scrawled line I'd just found in the notebook had me jumpier than anything that'd happened so far.

The man who got out of the car—an older-model Volvo, butter-colored, pockmarked with dents—was tall and wiry. The lenses of his glasses caught a few slivers of moonlight; his pale hair was pulled back in a loose ponytail. I watched him through the window. He came toward the house, quick and confident at first, then slowing as he took in the damage. His face slackened with that same shock I'd felt earlier, sobered by the concrete proof that something *bad* had happened here.

Call-Me-Tom came up the steps cautiously, testing the weight. He wore a camera around his neck like a goofy tourist. I watched him pause to lift the camera, aiming it at the front door.

I opened the door, stepped out onto the porch. "What was my mother like when you talked to her?" I asked. "Was she upset? Was she scared?"

He startled, the camera smacking back against his chest. "Jesus," he said. "Give a guy a little warning. Josie, I presume?" Tom crossed the porch in one long stride, held out his hand like we were making introductions at a grad school mixer. "It's great to finally meet you. I'm only sorry it's not under better circumstances—"

"What was she like?" I repeated, ignoring his hand, which wavered.

"Uh. She was—she was determined. That's the best word. Very focused."

"Focused on Fiona?" I asked, and he let his hand drop. I held out the notebook, pointed the Maglite's beam at the words so that they floated there, isolated against the darkness. A note scribbled beneath a clipping about the '77 fire, right next to a photograph of Fiona, coppery-haired and round-eyed. *Tell the world about Fiona. Girl Nine.* The very youngest, linked to Bellanger in a way the rest of us could never match—not even me, not even his favorite. If the other eight of us were attached to Bellanger through birth, Fiona was bound to him through death.

"Why was my mother interested in Fiona?"

Tom sighed. "I don't know," he admitted. "I was hoping you would."

"Your mother called me out of the blue." Tom paced near the edge of the burned living room, just skirting its ruined flooring and charred wallpaper. "This was probably . . . a month ago? Yeah, back in March. I thought it was a prank. Margaret Morrow has a reputation. She never grants interviews, much less sets one up."

I lingered near the front door, arms crossed, ready to make a run for it if necessary.

"Your mother said she wanted to talk one-on-one. She was very specific about not involving you. She made me swear I wouldn't drag you into it. Her words." Tom glanced around quickly, as if my mother might be hiding on the staircase, ready to chastise him for breaking his promise. "We only talked for half an hour. Your mom said—essentially, she said there's something about Fiona the world doesn't know, and she wants to share it. Your mother was offering me the chance to break the story for her."

"Why *you*?" I asked it before I could stop myself, the accusation blunt.

Tom smiled, chagrined.

"Sorry," I said. "It just sounds like a big story. If my mother was going to take a risk like this, she'd have made sure everything was perfect. She'd have approached the biggest paper she could find." *Not the* Kansas City Telegraph hung there unsaid.

"I've written a lot about the Homestead over the years. It's not like I'm going to win a Pulitzer, but it caught your mother's eye." A spark of defiance when he said this.

"You never interviewed *me*," I pointed out.

"Not for lack of trying. I called your house when you were accepted to the University of Chicago and left my info, just in case. In fact," he said slowly, "maybe that's where your mother got my number. From your machine."

I watched him put the pieces together, his expression deflating. The possibility that my mother had reached out to him because of sheer coincidence, and not because she'd loved his work. My mother could do that to you. Pop the bubble of your ego. I could've warned him.

"So did you say you'd work with her?" I pressed.

"Of fucking course," Tom said. "Pardon my French. But after that first conversation, she never called back. I waited every day. I followed up a few times, but she never responded. It was like that call never even happened. Then I saw the fire on the news and . . . here we are."

The dark house. The damp rooms that still held a shadow of heat. "Here we are," I repeated. "Okay. Must've been a big disappointment. I mean, my mom says she'll work with you, then she vanishes on you? Did you ever come by the house? Maybe try a little too hard to get in touch?"

He blinked, his expression passing through wounded surprise and into a stony hurt. "No. Of course not. I wouldn't do that, I respected her privacy. I'm not a—I wouldn't do that."

"All right," I said, letting my doubt hang there. "If you say so."

"Hey, I'm only here to help you find your mom," Tom said. "That's it. If you don't want me here, just say so."

I hesitated. I was surprised by how reluctant I was to see him go; he was my only connection to my mother right now. "You really don't have any idea why my mother was interested in Fiona?"

"Not a clue. Your mother was careful. She wasn't going to give me anything until she was good and ready."

"She's always been skilled at withholding." I sighed and pushed my hair off my face. "Whatever it is, it must be big. Because I've had a lot of time to sit around this house waiting for you, and . . . I'm pretty sure this fire wasn't an accident."

He lifted his eyebrows, gave a low whistle. "Big claim. How do you figure?"

"My mom was terrified of fire. For obvious reasons, right? She unplugged the lamps and the coffee maker every night before she went to sleep. She never used a space heater or lit a candle. Ever. I know they'll try to pass this off as an accident, but it wasn't."

"I'm sure the police will take it seriously."

"You want to bet? The local chief of police hasn't taken anything seriously since we moved here. He's only equipped for the occasional domestic dispute or—or a cat stuck up a tree. This is way outside of his usual expertise."

He nodded slowly. "Do you have any enemies around town?"

I laughed, swift and bitter. "Yeah, you could say that." There'd been graffiti. Kids who'd follow me home yelling names at me. Freak, monster, devil baby, whatever. Someone once smashed a bunch of test tubes in front of our house on Halloween. "But I don't think this was vandalism," I said. "There's no V pattern. The geometry is all off. A fire will extend upwards from the point where it was set"—I sketched this out with my hands, broad sweeps—"but this fire doesn't have a pattern. It's like it started everywhere at once." Uneasy, I remembered that bird with its one singed wing.

"You know your fire patterns."

"A hobby of mine," I said, but the joke didn't have any energy behind it. Surrounded as we were by the pervasive smell of the smoke, the fire of 1977 felt too immediate. That fire had managed to take everything important from me, cutting short Dr. Bellanger's life, leaving his eight living creations abandoned and bereft. Not to mention snuffing out all the other sisters I could've had, hundreds or thousands who would've been born by now, instead burned along with Bellanger's irreplaceable mind.

I dropped onto the bottom step of the staircase and flipped through the notebook pages. Faces and headlines skimming by. Death and scandal, scandal and loss. And those notes that didn't make any sense. I spotted *birds* scribbled haphazardly in the margins, and my stomach lurched at the thought of that bird out on the lawn. Tom seemed distracted, shifting his weight from foot to foot. He stood there with his camera clenched in both hands.

"You're pretty much the only person she's talked to for the past year, and even you don't know anything," I said, but then I trailed off. Through the kitchen window, above the sink full of dirty dishes, I had a view of the street outside my house. Headlights. That car was back, the maroon sedan from earlier, driving by slowly.

"Hold on," Tom said. "I'm not the only person. Your mother was talking to other people about Fiona."

"Other journalists, you mean?" I asked, shifting my attention back to him.

He looked at me like he thought I might be kidding. "She was talking to the other Homesteaders."

I had to take a second, the sedan already half forgotten in the face of this bigger revelation. "No, she wasn't," I said automatically, even though it made sense. Why else would she have been compiling that list? "She never would've done that. Never."

"I got the impression that your mom wasn't exactly friendly with the others?" Tom asked.

"Yeah, you could say that. Not a visit, not a letter, not even a phone call."

"But you've gotten in touch with them yourself?"

I bristled. Most people assumed I'd had time to seek out the other Girls, that we were all good friends, sharing reminiscences of our bizarre babyhoods. "No," I admitted, terse. "I've been busy." The acceptance to the University of Chicago had triggered the busiest stage of my life. I'd hoped that the flurry of news pieces—"Josephine Morrow, First Human 'Virgin Birth,' Follows in Her Creator's Footsteps!"—would lead to calls or letters from the others, some congratulations. So far, only silence.

"Sure," Tom said, "I know how busy you've been. Totally understandable."

"I wasn't asking for approval, Tom," I said.

He shrugged, held up his hands, *Mea culpa.*

"I can't believe my mother got in touch with them, though, it's just—" I stopped myself. It was too bizarre to be sitting here talking to a reporter about my mother's personal habits. If I was going to track down my mother, I had to quit imagining the woman I'd left behind a year ago. I needed to track down this newer version, the one who'd apparently turned into a crazed sleuth before vanishing in a puff of smoke and flame. "Did she just call the others?" I asked instead, focusing. "Or did she actually visit?"

"She mentioned visiting some of them, yeah."

The newspapers had noted my mother's long absences from work. And I'd seen the disrepair of the house. The overgrown lawn, the piled-up mail. She hadn't been hiding inside. She'd been gone entirely. Out of town. Something nobody in Coeur du Lac would ever suspect of her.

"When I heard about the fire," Tom went on, "my first thought was that Margaret had gone to one of the others. It just makes sense."

The idea was exhilarating, but I had to think this through carefully. "The Chevy's still in the garage."

"Okay. Doesn't necessarily mean anything. How'd you get here? I didn't see a car out front. Maybe she left some other way."

My mother—not vanished, but rearranged. Optimism flared in me, hot and bright, and I didn't fight it. Maybe this didn't have to be so complicated. I could reconnect with a few of the other Homesteaders and find my mother at the same time. Figure out whatever she'd wanted to say about Fiona.

Tom watched me flip to the list. "Your mom mentioned Emily French by name," he offered. "She was considering visiting her when we talked."

"Emily," I repeated. I'd watched coverage of her mother's funeral from my apartment, textbooks open in front of me, too antsy to study. Emily, sitting alone in a sea of folding chairs. Behind her, protest signs that bobbed above Emily's head like cartoon thought bubbles. UNNAT- URAL! ONLY GOD CAN CREATE MIRACLES! My heart had been in my throat, imagining what it would be like to lose my mother. I'd nearly called home—just to say hello, to see how my mother was doing—but then I'd imagined how jittery and defensive she would make me feel about my work, even if she didn't say a word about it. All those old wounds reopening. I didn't call.

"Where does Emily live?" I asked.

"Kansas, actually. A town not far from Wichita. I drive through it now and then."

"Redbud?" My excitement sparked.

"Yeah. Why?"

I turned the notebook toward him as he sat on the step beside me, bringing his scent of unfamiliar laundry detergent with him. "Redbud. See? And five-twenty-four. That could be a street address."

"Emily's last known address," Tom said, unthinkingly pulling the notebook closer to him. I resisted, pulling it back, and he let go. "She's staying at five-twenty-four Twelfth Street in Redbud. I have contact information for all of these names." He ran his finger down the page.

I took a second look at him. He smiled back, suddenly shifting away. Maybe he'd realized how close we were, hips nearly touching. "You've been stalking the other Homesteaders?" I asked, trying to keep my voice casual. The pit of my stomach tightened. I was alone in this dark house with him.

Tom looked hurt, like I'd offended him purposefully. "I prefer the term *researching*. It's for work. I even helped your mom fill in a few blanks. Like the Grassis, Angela and Gina—you know how long it took to track down a reliable address for those two? It's my coup."

"How long did it take?" I asked.

He blinked. "A year."

I nodded, cautiously accepting this. He wasn't the first guy to research us. "And you're sure this is Emily's current address."

"Positive. So what now? Are you going to go to the police with this?"

I hesitated. Honestly, I didn't want to take it to the authorities. Not yet. I imagined being interviewed on the news, my classmates watching as I talked about my crazed mother running off into the night. No: I needed to find her myself. I'd given myself roughly three days before I returned to the dawn coming through the windows of my apartment, to the tranquility of the zebrafish tanks in the lab. Three days to return to my work, my promise to Bellanger that I'd finish what he'd started. A promise made public once I was accepted to the University of Chicago.

"Maybe I should just go," I said. "Kansas isn't so far." The keys were still heavy in my pocket, a comforting weight. But the Chevy was an ancient and erratic beast, only good for short commutes. Prone to grinding, squeaky brakes.

"I'm happy to give you a lift," Tom said casually, as if he'd read my uncertainty in my expression. "I've been meaning to go see Emily anyway."

I considered this. It would give me a chance to pick Tom's brain more. He was one of the last people to talk to my mother, as far as I knew. But he was a perfect stranger. All my mother's old cautions against trusting people too easily rose into my brain. "Thanks, but I can't ask you to do that."

Disappointment flashed through his eyes. "It's no problem, I'm happy to—"

"She's my mother, my problem. You don't have to worry about her." I stood up, slipped the notebook into my pocket.

Tom stood too, and a brief awkwardness settled between us. "Just so you know," he said, "I might pursue this myself. I mean, there could be a real story here."

"I can't exactly stop you," I said, restraining my irritation. "I'd just ask for a chance to find my mother safe first. She's not just a story to me."

Looking serious, he nodded once. "You have my number if you need it, right?" Without waiting for an answer, Tom turned around, waved to me as he moved toward the door. "Good to finally meet you, Girl One."

4

Time magazine — October 20, 1974

MIRACLE or MODERN SCIENCE?
Inside One Man's Attempt to Change Birth as We Know It

Daybury, Vermont, is a quiet hamlet, population barely reaching five hundred. *Bucolic* is the first word that comes to mind. There's a single general store across the street from the post office. Neighbors greet each other by name. But lately, sleepy Daybury has been disrupted by hordes of camera crews, candle-toting pilgrims, and sign-carrying picketers. All of these outsiders are drawn by a single cause. Here, on the outskirts of Daybury, a man who has long toiled over his scientific research in obscurity has achieved the impossible. More than the impossible, perhaps—the downright miraculous.

The Homestead is accessible only by a narrow, winding dirt road. A young woman greets us at the beginning of the property, silently opening the imposing metal gate to admit our vehicle. Her dress does a poor job hiding the telltale signs of a woman in the family way. Her ring finger is conspicuously naked.

The thick foliage breaks to reveal the rolling hills and verdant farmlands that border the commune. The compound includes a sizable farmhouse, a cherry-red barn, a disorganized vegetable garden where cucumbers sprout between the tomatoes, interspersed with weeds and wildflowers. The house borders on dereliction. Windows are hung with quilts to offer some respite from the creeping chill of autumn. Young women sleep three or four to a bed. It seems like no place for a child, but babies are the most prominent feature of this place.

A three-year-old child is the eldest, bright-eyed and sturdy. She takes after her mother, Margaret Morrow. Once you know that little girl is supposedly the product of only her mother's DNA, you find yourself looking too closely at her, hoping to detect some giveaway sign of a father's influence. A different nose shape, perhaps, or pale eyes in contrast to dark. But looking at Margaret and Josephine (Josie for short) is like staring at a time lapse—the same face looking at you as a toddler, as a mother.

Josie is first in line, proudly bearing the name of her creator, Joseph Bellanger. There are others. One-year-old Isabelle sleeps in a makeshift crib, a dresser drawer padded with blankets. Catherine wears a cloth diaper as her mother cradles her. One young woman is expecting her child to arrive any day, and still another informs us that she is newly pregnant. Nine young women form the core group of devoted volunteers, and Bellanger confidently claims that all the women will have given birth before long.

Dr. Joseph Bellanger is a charismatic figure. As he speaks about the women, one is reminded of an artist posing in front of his canvases. While the women keep their hair long and unbrushed, Bellanger retains a gentleman's composure in his bow tie and tidy white lab coat. His home is back in Maryland with his wife and two young sons, but he conducts his most essential work from an ersatz lab here on the compound.

According to the doctor, these miraculous infants are the result of work that began with his scientific experimentation on lab rabbits in the late 1960s, experimentation which produced parthenogenetic offspring, although the results were never replicated. Bellanger's time attending medical school at Maryland State University was marked by controversy. "I was too single-minded and ambitious even for fellow scientists," Bellanger notes with a merry laugh. "But I've learned not to foster grudges. That's all in the past now, and these Girls are my future."

By now, the nine women—unwed and romantically unattached volunteers—have become a vibrant group known as the Homestead. This wryly irreverent name was selected by Bellanger himself for its suggestion of traditional family ties—the very ties that Bellanger hopes to sever.

While some animal species can produce asexually, this is the first time in documented modern history that human beings have conceived without the presence of sperm. If Dr. Bellanger's claims hold any weight, he could be restructuring the very nature of mankind.

After departing medical school, Bellanger made the unorthodox decision to bypass further time in a laboratory setting and move immediately to working with human subjects. Bellanger explains: "You don't change history without taking a few risks."

5

The building at 524 Twelfth Street was sizable, three stories of Victorian grandeur, and for a second I was awed. Then I pulled the Chevy along the curb and all the problems came springing into view. Hanging drainpipe, missing shingles, Mickey Mouse bedsheets serving as ersatz curtains. Most unexpectedly: the concrete sign rising from the shrubbery. TWELFTH STREET HALFWAY HOUSE. EST. 1980.

I'd been driving since before dawn, too anxious to sit still and waste time, and as I stepped out of the car, I was alive with the shaky energy of sleeplessness. My mother could be here. Right inside. I remembered a time I'd stayed the night at a sort-of-friend's house, the kind of giddy slumber party my mother had always disapproved of. I'd woken in the night missing her so badly it was like a stomach cramp. Walking home alone at two in the morning, my neighborhood turned alien in the moonlight, I was shivering with nerves, trying to stay brave. A few blocks from my house there was an apparition down the street. Bathrobe-clad, Maglite in hand. My mother. Coming to find me.

How did you know? I'd asked, hand in hers, comfort falling over me like a blanket.

I always know when you need me, she'd said. *Same heart.*

It felt like early summer in Redbud, humid and drowsy. The afternoon air was heavy with the rattle of cicadas, the burn of sprinkler system chlorine, a dusty trace of charcoal from backyard grills. The front door displayed a small handwritten sign: NO SOLICITORS. I gave a stab at the doorbell, loose in its joint. After a few minutes, the door creaked open and a face appeared, partially concealed by the shadows.

"You read the sign?" A woman's voice, roughened at the edges.

My heart fell. It would have been so easy to find my mother right away. To have her waiting right behind Door #1, Monty Hall smiling at us.

"I'm hoping to speak to . . . Emily." I nearly asked for my mother outright, veering away at the last second.

"Emily." The woman sounded as if she'd never even heard the name before.

"Emily French? Is she here?"

"How d'you know her?" The woman had opened the door wide enough for me to make out only a few details. Sharply highlighted hair, a jutting chin.

"Family friend." Not exactly a lie.

The woman examined me before opening the door wider. She was all angles, knobs of elbows, cords in her neck. She squinted. "You're one of them, aren't you?"

I'd been asked questions like this a thousand times in my life, and I never knew what would follow. A request for my autograph—a request to buy my underwear—unending follow-up questions, plying me for memories I could barely scrape together. I always had to quickly decide between my options. Fight, flight, play along.

She snapped her fingers and waved her hand to physically coax the information out of me. "You're Margaret's girl." The easy intimacy of it made my breath catch. "I'm Wanda. I was a friend of Tami's before— well. Come in." She turned brusquely, and I just managed to slide through before the door swung shut.

Wanda marched ahead as if she expected I'd find my own way. The air in here was close, soupy. It had sounded as if Wanda already knew my mother. I looked around eagerly, like she might materialize from a hidden hallway or side room.

"She's gotten worse," Wanda said over her shoulder. "A lot damn worse." I nodded, a needle of panic working into my brain. *Worse? Worse how?*

"Emily's having a hard day," Wanda went on. So we weren't discussing my mother. I was relieved; I was disappointed. "I'm not sure you'll be able to get through to her."

Walking through the living room, past a Styrofoam cup abandoned on the deep-set windowsill of a stained-glass window, we reached an unassuming door. Wanda extracted a small key from her pocket. She fit it into the lock, turned the knob, and secreted the key in one practiced movement.

"What's that for?" I asked, uneasy.

"Just keeping Emily safe."

I peered around her at a long, thin stairwell, choked with shadows. From somewhere above us, a groaning creak. A woman's voice, too low to hear.

Wanda started up the stairs, then turned, like she'd known I'd be hesitating at the bottom. "Lock that door behind you, would you, sweetie?"

I felt my way up the stairs, following the confident staccato of Wanda's footsteps. When she opened the next door, light flooded the stairwell. I took the last few steps in a rush, stumbling into the attic. A large room with low-hanging eaves, illuminated by a single window at one end, the glass clouded with plastic sheeting.

A woman's voice, louder this time. "They're burning, burning. Just her dress is left now."

There was a cot in the corner with spindly metal legs and trailing sheets. A girl lay curled on the mattress, her bony back to me. Dark hair tangled on the pillow. A plate of food sat on the floor near her—untouched, spaghetti sauce congealed. Several cups of water at varying levels of fullness stood nearby, speckled with dust. The attic smelled intimately sour, like unwashed skin.

I hung back near the door, itchy with embarrassment. "Is it okay for me to be up here?"

Wanda leaned over the bed, and something maternal in her posture made my heart ache. "Emily? You have a visitor, baby. Get up and say hello." She was speaking in that falsely bright voice I'd heard parents use with stubborn children, more for my benefit than Emily's.

"The birds." Emily's voice slid between sleep-tinged and alert. "They're falling."

The birds. The bird outside my mother's house. The crunch of its bones.

Wanda turned and shot me a *told-you-so* look, as if she'd proved something we'd been arguing about for a long time. "Think you can do anything?"

"Don't go down into the basement again. Don't watch her magic. She's not you." The way Emily was talking reminded me of our radio back home when it would accidentally pick up truckers or nearby phone calls. Random voices springing into our lives, then vanishing into the static.

I took a step backward, away from Emily. That tangled clump of hair, the smells of a long convalescence, the clunky way her words fit together. Whenever I'd thought about meeting the other Homestead Girls as adults, I'd imagined a sense of finally coming home. We were the Miracle Babies, after all, only eight of us left. An endangered species. A rare breed. What I hadn't expected was the uneasiness I felt. For the first time in my life, I was the one who didn't know how to react, staring at her mumbling body the way other people had always looked at me.

Buck up, Josephine, I thought. My full name had always had a galvanizing effect on me. That name, his name. A reminder of where I'd come from.

"You're no use at all." Wanda nodded as if she'd summed up something unsurprising but disappointing about me. "Is Margaret coming soon?" She craned to look around me as if my mother might've secretly followed me in.

"My mother's missing," I said.

Wanda's expression was blank. "Missing? Like . . . gone?"

"Exactly that kind of missing. Yeah."

"But I just met her," Wanda said, and my heart jumped. "She came by. Real short visit. I was just glad somebody wanted to see Emily."

"My mother was here?" So Thomas Abbott had been telling the truth; I felt a brief gratitude toward him. "What did she want?"

"Oh, you'd have to ask Emily. Those two didn't have much use for me."

"Yeah, but when was this?" I didn't hide my urgency. "This week? A few days ago? If she was just here, then do you know where—"

"Lord, no, no, two weeks ago now," Wanda said. "I haven't seen her since."

I exhaled, shaky, my deflation keen as an organ collapsing. My mother was one step ahead of me. I had no idea where she'd gone next or where she was now, and I didn't have the time to stick around and figure it all out—

"Don't leave," Emily said.

Wanda exchanged glances with me, as surprised as I was.

"I've always wanted to meet you, Josie." Emily's eyes were open, startling and alive inside the chalkiness of her face. She sat up and pushed her hair back, tucking it neatly behind her ears. When she smiled, her chapped lips stretched painfully. "The birds, they're on the ground now," she said, half a whisper, as if to herself. "So many."

Emily didn't move from the nest of her mattress, so I perched at the end of the bed, legs crossed awkwardly at the knee like I was at a job interview. Wanda had promised to come back to check on us. I wasn't even sure which one of us was supposed to be reassured by that.

Emily's oversized Tweety Bird nightshirt kept slipping off one shoulder. She examined me frankly, her eyes roving over my face like she wanted to commit me to memory. "I don't know how long I'll be able to talk," she said. "It's been getting shorter and shorter, the time I'm awake."

I cleared my throat. "Yeah, sure, that's okay. You've been sick?"

"Sick," she said, like she was testing it out. "I guess so. I barely used to notice it. It's been a lot worse since my mother died." She didn't stumble over the word *died*, didn't even hesitate. I admired that.

"You've been sick for a while?" I tried to remember whether Tami had any kind of congenital illness, a hereditary condition that might've been replicated in her daughter's DNA.

"My mother says it's the testing that did it." And there it was, right on the heels of the easy way she'd admitted to her mother's death. She'd used the present tense just as instinctively. Like Tami was in Emily's past and present all at the same time.

The testing: back before Bellanger's death, we'd been subjected to rigorous tests, the whole world watching to see if our small bodies would betray the sordid truth of our origins. I'd revisited the experiments recently, and though their techniques were pretty primitive, the results were definitive. Proof of the impossible, right there in the serology results: all nine mother-daughter pairs with perfectly matching blood types. A taste test had us sipping tiny cups containing phenylthiourea, which tasted either like nothing or sharply bitter, depending on the genetic makeup of your palate. (My mother and I *could* taste it, a sting to the tongue.) In test after test, each pair was a matching set.

I still remembered Bellanger leaning over me, carefully explaining each experiment to me as if I could actually understand. Even at age five, I'd risen to the occasion, becoming a different girl than the one who ran outside, wild and barefoot, or fought my mother off at bath time. I became painstaking with him. Responsible. Hanging on his every word, eager for his smile of approval.

"But that was so long ago," I said now. "Bellanger was always careful with us."

"It wasn't a long time ago for me." Emily's hand shook on her blanket, a sudden convulsion, and she cupped her palm over it as if her hands belonged to two different people. "It was just a way to make money. The first doctor my mother saw, he gave us five hundred. That was enough for two months' rent. My mother didn't let me do it at first. She said she'd put me through enough already. So she did it first. But I saw what it did to her, Josie. I saw how she got sick from it. I had to help out too." Emily reached for me, and I didn't hesitate before reaching back. She folded my hands into hers, her skin cold and dry. "I couldn't make my mother go through it alone anymore. I was the one they wanted, anyway. We earned twice as much once I started. Didn't you do it too?"

So these hacks had been experimenting on her. Sticking her with needles, slicing her open, giving her who knew what kinds of pills or potions. When I was growing up, my mother had hated doctors, doggedly fended off my colds with herbal tea and Dimetapp. The one time I'd fractured my collarbone too badly for a first-aid kit, my mother accompanied me to the doctor's office and sat clutching my shoulder like I might fly away, or be removed from her care by a smiling social worker who'd decided that my life without a *stable male presence* was too dangerous.

"No," I said at last. "We never did."

Her face fell slightly. She nodded.

Dr. McCarter—my mentor at the University of Chicago, the principal investigator at my latest lab rotation—had been pressing me to take advantage of the genetic gold mine I carried around inside my body. *"Plenty of famous scientists have volunteered their own bodies in the name of their scientific research. Jonas Salk injected himself with the untested polio vaccine. John Paul Stapp subjected himself to g-forces before man ever set foot on the moon. At least think about it, Jo."*

But I'd put it off. I was there as the researcher, not the researched: I was purposefully moving *away* from being the test subject. Anyway, most of the tests McCarter was proposing would have required my mother's cooperation. Whatever impulse had led my twenty-three-year-old mother to agree to work with Bellanger, that curiosity had been bleached out by the intervening years, I assumed by the fires and the attacks and the prime-time preachers. But if I was going to truly restore Bellanger's lost work, it would involve human test subjects at some point. I only hoped I'd find volunteers as agreeable as our mothers had been.

"These men weren't very nice, Josephine," Emily said. "I thought maybe they'd be like Dr. Bellanger. But in the end it was always the same. They did whatever they wanted and then they sent us home."

Emily looking for Bellanger in these uncaring faces made a deep spasm of loss echo in my chest. "What did they want?" I whispered, curiosity and concern fighting inside me.

She let her hands slide out of mine, picking at the hem of her nightgown. "Different things. Some were trying to prove Dr. Bellanger was a fraud. Some were trying to do the same thing he'd done. And others . . ." She pressed her lips together.

"What?" I asked, feeling a sudden uncertain sickness. But Emily shook her head very slightly and I knew to back off.

My anger grew as I thought of these men. The lingering fascination that surrounded us could turn dark too easily. We were Bellanger's great unfinished works. He'd guarded his secrets, the nine of us, so carefully during his life, wary of the death threats—people who wanted to vanquish us like vampires, cut off our heads, burn us at the stake. Then there were the calmer and no less chilling threats from people who wanted to rehome us with *normal families*. All of us had been born under the shadow of those threats, but they loomed darkest over Bellanger himself. He was the one who'd started it, after all. If he were shot, stabbed, poisoned, burned, then his unholy work would go with him.

And that was the problem. He'd always brashly and optimistically assumed he'd have plenty of time to finish his work. For every person like Ricky Peters, claiming that if Bellanger flew in the face of God by spreading parthenogenesis beyond the nine of us he'd surely burn in hell, there was someone hounding him to reveal his hard-won secrets and share his glory. Bellanger had stayed silent; he'd burned anyway.

In the years directly following his loss, there'd been an arms race of scientists—a pharmaceutical company in the United States, the National Health Service in the United Kingdom, an eccentric multimillionaire in Switzerland, a university in Japan—all attempting to take up the controversial mantle he had left behind. A few even managed to produce pregnancies, usually to great fanfare, until they'd ended in early miscarriages, the embryos revealed to be nonviable. After a woman in Berlin nearly died from an early stillbirth, research stalled, fettered with ethical concerns and reignited protests.

Growing up, I grieved these lost opportunities. We were such a small population already, winnowed down to a mere eight before we'd even left childhood. But now there was a secret, guilty satisfaction at the bottom of that grief. I was going to do it myself. I was destined to follow in Bellanger's footsteps. Like father, like daughter.

"Look at this." Emily lifted the hem of her nightgown up her thigh. Her unshaved legs were downy in the sunlight. I blushed, throat warm, then realized what she meant to show me. A square of flesh, bubbled and shades lighter than the skin around it. A skin transplant. My shyness was swiftly replaced by curiosity. "Like yours," Emily said.

She gazed at me expectantly, and I rose, unbuttoned my jeans, and pulled them down just far enough to reveal my own small patch on my upper thigh, the size of a postage stamp, that had begun its life on my mother's body. I'd had it since I was five years old. Emily leaned in close. "These other men, these, uh, doctors and researchers—they were imitating Bellanger's skin graft?" I asked.

"Yes. One of them gave me the surgery a few years ago." She reached out one finger and traced the border of my scar, intent and delicate. I waited a second, my blush deepening, then hitched my jeans back up.

Emily's scar looked painful to me, clumsily transplanted. Back when we were little, my mother and I had received twin skin grafts under Bellanger's supervision. Proof to the world that I was genetically identical to my mother. No father's influence to react against her DNA. Under normal circumstances, my body would've rejected the foreign graft, but there was nothing foreign about my mother's skin. My body already knew hers. We were the sole guinea pigs for this method; the skin graft operation was too risky to repeat on the younger Girls. This had made me incredibly smug when I was little. I bragged about it to the younger Girls, showed the scar to any journalist or reporter who was willing to look, until my mother told me in no uncertain terms to stop.

But now, years and years later, another Girl had undergone a graft too. I wasn't the only one anymore. I imagined the matching scar that must be on Tami's thigh, underground in a coffin. I wondered where my own mother's matching scar was, right at that moment, and my stomach clenched.

"I saw you in the paper," Emily said. "You're becoming a doctor too?"

"Oh, I'm not like those men," I said quickly. I was used to explaining my ambitions to professors, to colleagues, to reporters. I'd cataloged the whole range of reactions. The people who congratulated me, both sincere and fake, who lectured me or condescended to me, who doubted me or laughed at me. Those last were my favorites, the ones I could defy. But Emily French just looked at me like she was disappointed in me. There'd only been one other person to react like that so far. My mother.

I had to get to the point. "Emily, I know you saw my mother recently." Pulling the notebook out of my back pocket, I flipped to the list of names. "I need some help here. What did she want from you? Do you know where she is?"

Emily didn't react for a few seconds. It was like the soundtrack of a movie falling out of sync with the visuals. "Your mother disappeared?" Her voice sounded dreamy, more like the voice I'd heard when I first entered the attic. "So did mine."

"I know, and I'm sorry. But look: My mother was interested in Fiona. Our Fiona." The possessive came easily. "Do you know what she meant by this? *Tell the world.*"

Emily leaned back on the bed, her knees tenting her nightshirt so that the fabric lit up, translucent with sunlight. "Your mother came and sat by my bed. Just like you."

I saw myself inside a perfect outline of my mother, the echo left behind.

A sludge of sleep worked its way in at the edges of Emily's voice. "She remembered things about the Homestead. The little red cup I liked to drink out of. And the cats that would come around, and how our mothers always fought about whether to feed them."

"So she wanted to reminisce." A funny sour feeling grew inside my chest: jealousy. I'd never really had to share my mother with anyone else. "Did she say anything about birds?" I asked.

Emily didn't seem to hear, her gaze blank.

"What about Fiona?"

This got a flicker of a reaction. "Oh. She said Fiona was strange."

Details floated to the surface of my brain. Fiona before she'd turned into a memorial photo. Her greasy penny-colored hair curling on the pillow next to me, how small she was. I'd been four when Fiona was born in April of 1975. My youngest sort-of sister. "Strange how?"

Emily ran a finger up and down her neck, reflective, her eyes drifting shut. "She could move things. Here and there. Wherever she wanted. Fingers everywhere." She lifted a hand and made lazy, delicate sweeps in the air.

Something crawled down my spine, even as I felt my curiosity click into a clean buzz at the back of my head.

Emily's eyelashes fluttered; her breathing was thick and even. Her eyeballs rolled beneath the paper-thin lids. "Emily." I was louder now. "Emily?"

Her lips parted, a shiny thread of drool webbed between her teeth.

She whispered something too low to catch, and I leaned in closer, and then she screamed. Her eyes opened too wide, those pinprick pupils pointed right up at the ceiling, and I looked up too, my heartbeat wild from the hard crack of adrenaline, my ears ringing. Nothing: just the yawn of the rafters. Nothing. I looked back at Emily. She was reaching for me, her hands at my throat, my shoulders, scrabbling. Her grip was too tight. Her fingernails, long, unclipped, pinched my skin.

"You're bleeding. Josephine, you're bleeding. They hurt you."

"No," I said. "No, no, no, I'm fine, it's a dream—" Wanda must've heard the scream: she must be coming. "Please. It's okay."

I backed away. Emily was half crawling out of bed now, knocking over the glasses, which rolled wildly, rattling. One shattered and Emily's foot came down on the scoop of broken glass, the edge sliding right into her heel. She didn't even stop—her footprints were stamped in red. "They hurt you," she said. "They hurt you. You're going to die—"

I looked down at myself, ran my hands over my body. My palms came away clean.

Emily wrapped her hands around my throat now, squeezing, squeezing. I reached up to pull her hands away and couldn't find any purchase, couldn't pry her fingers off. My breath was stuck somewhere in my breastbone and I thought, very distinctly and with a surprising calm: *What if I die right now?* Right behind that: *I'll never get to see my mother again.*

I looked into Emily's eyes. Greenish, stippled with a murky gold, darkening near the iris. Those dark pits of her pupils. How often did I look into someone else's eyes this closely or this intently? As I made eye contact with Emily, her pupils dilated, slightly but abruptly, a welling blackness. Dizziness swept over me, and I wondered if I was losing consciousness. Her pupils were the only thing I could see.

"Let go of me," I managed, a raw-edged whisper. "Let go now."

Emily's eyelid twitched slightly. She kept looking at me, unblinking, and then—then—a fucking miracle. She let go, and it felt like something many-fingered unraveling from around my throat, letting me breathe again. She swayed there, her arms at her side, like she didn't know what to do with herself.

I took a painful breath, coughing. The air rushed back, wild and sweet.

"Oh, Josephine, you're lost," Emily said. The attic shrank until it enclosed the two of us, holding us there. "She's lost too. Nobody can find her and you're scared, you're nothing without her." I couldn't speak. "But it's all right," Emily went on, and smiled. "It really is. He'll help you find your mother. He'll take you to her. He will."

"Who?" I asked, a hoarse whisper.

"Him," she said. "The one who looks out for you."

6

"She's sleeping now," Wanda said, returning from the attic, giving me a limp smile.

I was waiting downstairs. Emily had left a long pink scrape circling my throat like a necklace. The sweat had dried on my skin and I was chilly, pacing to keep warm.

"Emily scared you good, huh? You should count yourself lucky she talked at all."

"What's wrong with her?" *Sick* didn't explain what I'd seen in that attic. *Sick* was a simple term standing in for something bigger, the way I felt whenever someone described me as *fatherless*.

"Oh, you've seen what's wrong with her," Wanda said. "It's like she has trouble staying here." She tapped at the side of her head. "Or here." A vigorous thump on her breastbone. "When Tami died, Emily didn't have anybody else. I let her come stay with me here. She's just been sleeping more and more. Even when she's awake, she's not *here*. When your mother got in touch, I thought maybe she'd know how to help. I do my best, but—" She stopped.

"But?"

Wanda drew closer, even though we were alone. "One week, she was going on and on about the *people coming through the glass*. Jibber jabber. *They have glass in their hair*. But there was a bad storm that next weekend and a car ran the red light down near Cove Circle—" She gestured, as if I were familiar with the area. "Ugly pileup. Two people died. Went right through the windshield. I saw the photo in the paper, glass everywhere on the road."

I was on edge in a way that wasn't exactly unpleasant. It reminded me of the time my mother had taken me swimming in the lake and I'd ventured past the drop-off as I dog-paddled, my toes searching for land and finding only the deep, sudden cold. A thrill, a terror. "You—what? Think she was predicting the future?"

Wanda stiffened and stepped back, physically distancing herself from what she'd just said. "Emily, she says all sorts of things. You've heard her. Most of it is just noise. I've heard her talk about things that happened when she was a tiny girl. She talks about her mama all the time, and Lord knows that's all in the past now."

But it isn't, I wanted to say. It didn't matter if her mother was dead, vanished, estranged—she was there in Emily's past, her future, her present. Always.

"Well," Wanda said. "I should . . ." She gestured vaguely at the house around her, a signal that I understood meant, *Get the hell out already.*

"Right. Yeah. I'll get going," I said.

The Chevy was waiting for me against the curb. The alternator had been making an ominous, intermittent grinding noise for the last hundred miles; the air-conditioning had given out, so I'd been forced to roll down the only two windows that would still function. I thought about climbing back into the Chevy, heading out—to where? Back home to Chicago, already giving up on my mother, abandoning her to her fate?

At the door, I turned impulsively. "Do you know if my mom was on her way to see anybody else?"

"Let me see. She mentioned going to see . . . oh, you know. The famous ones. I don't know if she ever made it."

Back in the sun-warmed Chevy, I opened my mother's notebook and flipped, with shaking fingers, to the list of Mothers and Girls. Deb and Bonnie Clarkson, Mother and Girl Seven, were the only ones who fit the glossy term *famous.* Like sunflowers, the Clarksons always turned in the direction of the nearest flashbulb. I sometimes spotted them on afternoon TV with their identical teased bangs, feverish streaks of blush.

It felt like I'd been gone from Chicago for weeks already but it had barely been twenty-four hours. I had time left on the clock. Minnesota was a day of driving. It didn't sound unappealing. I wanted to keep moving. I wanted to go somewhere, talk to somebody else. I couldn't return to Chicago and pretend nothing was wrong. I had questions for my mother: I wanted answers. There was a tilted symmetry to it. Maybe my curiosity could bring us back together, since it was responsible for pushing us apart.

I yanked the key in the ignition, waiting impatiently for the Chevy to struggle back to life. *Him.* That kept rolling around at the back of my head. This male pronoun that was supposed to help me track down my mother. *The one who looks out for you.* Only one man had ever looked out for me, and he'd been dead for years.

It wasn't as if I had an overabundance of *hims* in my life right now, or ever. Growing up with the word *virgin* attached to me, I'd had an even rockier relationship with my hymen than most girls. I'd had sex for the first time at sixteen, a purposefully average age, selecting a boy from my class who was just unpopular enough not to brag. I'd only wanted to see how it would work. Was my vagina even functional, or was it really glued shut or lined with tiny razor-sharp fangs? My first time having sex turned out to be underwhelming, more a process of discovering that I could, in fact, have sex. Propped awkwardly on top of me, the boy had pulled back: "Do I even need to use—anything? You can't get pregnant *that* way, right?" A fierce blush on the word *pregnant.*

The truth was, I hadn't known. I still didn't. I knew I got a period roughly every four weeks, and since I'd moved away from home, I'd started testing myself for luteinizing hormone levels to catch ovulation. The joint privilege and annoyance of being the oldest Girl was that I didn't have anybody else like me to look up to. No other bodies to use as a guideline. Bellanger hadn't even lived to see me reach adolescence.

Since that routine deflowering, I'd had only short-lived relationships. Most men were less interested in me than in the story of me. The bragging rights involved in screwing the Amazing Unscrewable Girl. In eighth grade, a sweaty-faced man once cornered me in a dark parking lot, whispering that he was my *real father* while staring at my breasts under my Tears for Fears T-shirt. There were men out there who ranked the mothers of the Homestead from the ones they'd most like to fuck to the ones they'd least like to fuck. The daughters too, even before we'd reached puberty. It all made for a shallow dating pool.

The closest thing I'd come to a romantic prospect lately was Dr. McCarter. He was nearly twenty years my senior, but I responded to his keen intelligence, the way he could look at a woman and know the exact pattern of her internal organs, understand her abilities. At least I wasn't a surprise to him.

The Chevy finally sputtered to life, the lights on the dashboard muted and dim, and I took off into the late-afternoon light, Madonna on the radio, whispering seductively about sex and apologies and human nature.

7

Time magazine—May 13, 1973

In Praise of Patience

On Mother's Day, a day set aside to celebrate the too-often-unsung champions of home and hearth, it's difficult not to think about the woman who currently defines "motherhood" in an entirely new way. Dr. Joseph Bellanger took time out of his busy schedule to grant this exclusive interview, along with Margaret Morrow, the first woman to give birth at the Homestead.

Time: On this Mother's Day, Margaret, will you be sending your own mother any bouquets or cards? Will she get to meet her granddaughter?

Margaret: I'm not really in touch with my folks. The Homestead is my family now. Sometimes life doesn't give you the family you want and you have to make your own.

T: What was it that drew you to working with Dr. Bellanger, Margaret? Not many young ladies would agree to be part of such an unusual project.

Bellanger: Margaret was always wonderfully open to my ideas. All the young ladies have been such receptive listeners, and so patient with an old man like me. I'm quite grateful to them.

T: But surely you realized, Margaret, when you agreed to this project, that you might be shutting off other avenues in your life. You're only twenty-five. You still have time to meet someone and perhaps start a family with him. Do you worry that your unconventional daughter will prevent you from marrying?

B: You haven't given that much thought, have you, Margaret? Josephine is your whole world. Anyone can see that much.

T: But Margaret—if I may—do you think Josephine will one day want a father in her life? Do you worry about explaining where she came from, when she's older?

M: I would say that her fatherlessness is the most remarkable thing about her. It's what makes her special. Why would she resent the very thing that—

B: But then I certainly—I wouldn't say Josephine is without a father. On a practical level, I love that little girl as much as I love my own boys. Every milestone she reaches is a fresh delight to me. Not merely because I'm watching my creation take shape—monitoring her health, her development—but simply because Josephine is a wonderful child.

T: So even you, Dr. Bellanger, a man who's made it his life's mission to take fatherhood out of reproduction, admit that there's still value to fatherhood?

B: Scientific progress is one thing, and I'm certainly proud of what I've accomplished, but we can't forget the importance of familial ties.

T: What of motherhood? How do you think your work with parthenogenesis has changed our views of the maternal role?

B: Without the patience and faith of these young ladies, nothing would have been possible. Margaret, I hope you know that history and science owe a lot to you ladies for your willingness to listen to a man like me, before the rest of the world would put up with me. My hope is that your names will be listed every time I'm mentioned, as a reminder of the enduring virtues of faith and patience.

8

I'd been staring at the same giant, blank-eyed baby for nearly an hour. As the sun sank lower, the lights beneath the billboard popped on, illuminating the baby's round cheeks and startled O of a mouth. Aside from the arc of the overpass, this billboard for a pediatric hospital was the only thing out here. I was stuck on the side of the freeway, the Chevy swaying and rattling ominously whenever an eighteen-wheeler roared past. The tow truck wouldn't be here for another hour, at the earliest. The repair alone would cost four hundred dollars that I didn't have, and I'd have to figure out a place to spend the night in this waystation somewhere between Redbud and Topeka. It was as far as I'd gotten before the Chevy gave up the ghost.

I wished I had somebody I could call. Not for help. Just to talk. More than anything, I felt incredibly alone, not even the radio for company. It was weird—living with my mother for nearly twenty-two years of my life, I'd never felt alone, exactly, even though our lives looked lonely to other people. Even when I'd started undergrad courses and we barely saw each other, I knew my mother would have my back. Maybe that was part of the reason I lived at home.

It wasn't until I moved to Chicago and the first flurry of busyness faded that I woke up one morning to realize that I was on my own. Cut in half, almost. I hadn't noticed that constant, submerged sense of *someone-on-my-side* until it was fully gone.

Dutifully, I'd tried to get to know my classmates, but any potential friendships had been flattened into the pattern of an occasional study date or idle chitchat in the lab, where I spent most of my time trying to prove myself. My work at the lab involved exposing zebrafish sperm to the irradiating blast of UV rays, then using the sperm to fertilize eggs. The resulting haploid embryos were parthenogenetic, like me, carrying only genetic material from their mothers. They only lived a few days, at most, which offered us enough time to screen for any new mutations, but I was obsessed with each one. This was such a rudimentary version of what Bellanger had done. These fleeting, doomed little beings, dying off before they even started, stripped of half of their genetic material. The work gave me a tiny glimpse into what Bellanger must've felt. The electric brink of discovery.

Cars roared past in a steady stream. Eventually I got so sick of the stuffy air in the Chevy that I climbed out and leaned against the hood, ignoring the occasional honks and the trailing ribbons of shouts and jeers. Someone had thrown a plastic cup of pop at the car and neon-pink gore was streaked along the back windows. I toyed with the idea of trekking back to the closest gas station to call Dr. McCarter, but it would be hard to argue for more responsibility in lab rotations after he'd seen me stranded along a Kansas freeway.

Headlights bloomed on the grass in front of me, expanding for a second, hot against my back. A car had pulled off the road right behind me. I stiffened and turned, adrenaline kicking in as my brain scrambled to figure out what to do. For a second I remembered that maroon car that had been lurking outside my mother's house in Coeur du Lac, and I tensed, all too aware of how unprotected I was out here—I could vanish just as easily as my mother had—

The headlights blinked into darkness, the door thumped closed. A man's silhouette stepped out. In the purplish twilight, it was hard to make out any features.

"Josie?" he called. "Girl One? Is that you?"

"Tom," I said, and for a second I relaxed at the relief of seeing somebody I kind-of-sort-of knew, my arms unwinding. Until I realized how uncanny this was—running into Tom hours from where I'd last seen him. "Funny meeting you here," I said, hiding my suspicion behind a joke.

"God, I thought that was you," he said, stopping a few feet away. "Car trouble?"

Of fucking course, I thought. "It's the alternator. This old hunk of junk is only good for running errands. I should've known, but . . ." I shrugged. "Anyway. Why are you in the area?" I glanced around at the long strip of freeway, multiple lanes leading off into the horizon in either direction. "It's pretty wild that you were just passing by and happened to spot me," I said, letting an accusation creep in.

"Must be fate." When I narrowed my eyes, skeptical, he said: "Hey. I'm based in Kansas City. Remember? *Kansas City Telegraph*. This is my home turf." He gestured with a half-joking grandeur at the flat, scrubby landscape, the pinprick stars fizzling to life overhead. "I was passing through and I saw you and thought: *Hey, I know that girl.* Looked like you were in trouble. I had to turn around and come back. Like I said. Fate."

I'd forgotten for a second that he lived around here. "Well, fate is faster than the towing company, anyway."

"Towing? It's that bad? Shit. That's all you need, on top of everything with your mother." He hesitated, the two of us standing there with the Chevy's lifeless body slumped between us. "Not to pry, but does this mean you went to see Emily French?"

"Yeah. Yeah, I did go to see Emily."

"And your mother . . ."

There was so much hope in his voice. I saw the way he glanced in the Chevy's windows quickly, like I wouldn't notice. Like maybe I'd stashed my mother in there. How long would this go on: people looking past me for her? "Nope. Not there. But you were right," I went on, noticing the way his expression fell into disappointment. "She was there recently. She really was visiting the others. So. Thanks."

"That's great news," Tom said, and his pure excitement gave me a spark of hope myself as I stood by the side of the road, wearing jeans and a travel-grimy T-shirt. The air was getting cooler, and I hugged myself. "Now we know for sure that your mother's been visiting the others. So did Emily say anything else? What's the deal with Fiona?"

I hesitated for a moment. "Did my mother say anything to you about Fiona being strange?"

"Strange? Strange how?"

"Just—never mind. If she didn't say anything, then forget it."

"She didn't say anything. Strange, huh?" Tom gave it the same weight as I did, as if the word had changed its shape. "If she had reason to believe Emily was . . . strange . . . do you think that has something to do with her disappearance?"

"It's starting to look that way." I was buoyed by that mix of curiosity and fear, the hope that I might figure out what'd happened to my mother, the anxiety that I was already too late.

"What next?"

I gestured at the Chevy. "If I can't get this thing fixed, I'm—I'm going to lose a lot of time—"

"Let me help," Tom said immediately. "Anything you need. My offer to give you a ride still holds, just so you know. If you want it."

I started to protest—*It's not that simple*—but I stopped. Maybe it was exactly that simple. Emily's strange prediction came back to me, the way those words had steadied me as I'd stood there in the attic. *The one who looks out for you.* My mother had apparently trusted Thomas Abbott. Maybe she'd chosen him because his number was conveniently languishing on our answering machine, or maybe she'd seen something in his work. Either way. In the half hour they'd talked, my mother revealed a side of herself to Tom she'd never shown to me. He must know more than I'd first realized.

And there was the issue of money. I gazed at the Chevy, thinking of how much it would cost to repair the damn thing. It would clean out my savings. Tom's Volvo was sitting there, patient, available. Presumably with a functioning alternator.

"All right," I said, relenting. "Yeah. Sure. I could use a ride."

I could tell he was suppressing his happiness. "Right this way."

When I lugged my suitcase over to the Volvo, Tom was holding the passenger-side door open for me, and it was obvious he'd swept papers and books and boxes off in a hurry, the footwell messy. "Thanks," I said, sliding in. Other than the clutter, the car smelled clean, pepperminty, and when I made a quick sweep for any obvious red flags—guns, knives, *Playboys*—I didn't see anything. My eyes snagged on the closest magazine, a *Scientific American* I recognized. "A Brief History of the Homestead: Reproductive Science's Biggest Bust?" I used my toe to nudge it underneath the edge of a shoebox, not sure if it counted as a red flag or not.

Tom slid into the driver's seat. "What about the Chevy?"

"The tow company can deal with it. I'll come back for it once I've got my mom with me." A careless confidence that I hoped would translate into reality at some point.

"Sure. All right."

"You're a little bit past your destination," I said, calculating.

"What's that?"

"If you were driving to Kansas City, you've overshot it now, haven't you?"

"I was taking a different route. I know all the byways and back ways."

I nodded, checking that I still had my mother's notebook. I always had a nagging fear that I'd somehow lose it. As I flipped through the pages, I thought of the clock, the letter to my mother I'd found there a long time ago, signed with just an initial. *T.* Thomas. Tom. For a second, worry cinched my lungs. But I'd just been a kid when I'd found that letter. Tom wouldn't have been much older, in his teens. It didn't make sense. I exhaled slowly, letting the worry loosen.

Tom was making a show of looking around. "But while we're on the topic . . . unless I'm all turned around, you weren't heading toward Chicago."

I almost smiled. Maybe I deserved this. "Nope. You got me. I was actually going to see the Clarksons."

"Seriously?" His eyes lit up. "Deb and Bonnie?"

I was surprised by the familiarity. "Friends of yours?"

"In a way. I've done several interviews with them before. Did you call them?"

"Yeah, a while back. Nothing. Not even an answering machine."

"Deb won't speak to just anyone," Tom said, thoughtful. "Usually you'd have to jump through a few hoops. But you're Girl One. Once they realize it's you, they'll want to talk."

"No interviews," I said quickly. "Not right now." I was tired, I was bleary; just a few hours ago, a sleepwalking girl in an attic had tried to strangle me. My mother was gone. I couldn't imagine putting on my bright-shiny professional self to answer glossy questions.

"Fair," Tom said. "But you should know that if you agree to an interview, I could introduce you in person before you head home."

I mulled it over. Tempting. "You'd do that?" I asked. "All the way to Minnesota?"

"Listen, your mother reached out to me for help. I want to see this through." Tom tapped the steering wheel. "Because when I was watching coverage of your mom's disappearance, I saw Deb on *Good Morning America*. Joan asked her about your mother's disappearance. Of course Deb said she didn't know anything. *Such a misfortune, Joan.* Blah, blah. But I saw this look on Deb's face for a second. This panic."

"What do you think that means?" I asked, disquieted, intrigued.

"Deb's usually real chatty," Tom said. "This was different. It was a weird look, Josie. Like she was hiding something."

9

April 24, 1973

My beloved Josephine,

Two years old. You continue to be a remarkable Girl, in part because you are so unremarkable. You weigh twenty-one pounds. You have enough hair that your mother sometimes fashions it into small pigtails. You can jump, and stack blocks neatly in a tower, and count to five, and you know eighty-two words. Josephine, you even created your first sentence: you said, quite clearly, *That man go* when I departed for my weekend in Maryland. I can't tell you how difficult it was to leave you behind. More and more, I recognize that my truest life's work is being here with you. Your mother reports that you ask after me at every opportunity.

But I don't worry about it as much as I might, because your second birthday brings the most marvelous news. Another baby is on the way. Before too long, my Josephine, you will be joined by a sister. Many sisters, if I have my way. One day, not long from now, there might be hundreds of Miracle Babies. Nothing would make me prouder than to be the father of a generation of miraculous Girls, particularly if they are anywhere near as smart as my Girl One. May you soon be One of a thousand. A million. More!

Your loving father always,
Joseph Bellanger

The New York Times—June 24, 1977

Fire Destroys Vermont Commune, Claims Two Victims

On the morning of Wednesday, June 22, a small but notorious corner of rural Vermont was shrouded in smoke. Due to the Homestead's remote location, it took hours for the owners of a neighboring farm to notice the blaze. Firefighters were able to keep the flames contained, protecting the surrounding forest. By the time the blaze cleared, two bodies were found in the wreckage of what was once the site of scientific optimism.

One of the bodies has been identified as Fiona (no surname), the youngest subject of Bellanger's landmark experiment. The other victim was Joseph Bellanger, who has been a lightning rod for both criticism and admiration since inducing parthenogenesis in nine human women.

According to a statement from state medical examiner Leland Henley, "The extent of these injuries suggests a fire that was set intentionally and, furthermore, was meant to cause grave harm."

Local authorities have verified that dozens of people had been picketing outside the Homestead boundaries for weeks leading up to the fire. The group was led by Ricky Peters, who has made a name for himself as the most prominent critic of the Homestead and its occupants, having been quoted as saying Bellanger should "burn in hell." Authorities have not yet determined the cause of the blaze. No suspects have been identified.

10

"Why aren't you talking to your mother, anyway?" Tom asked.

We'd been driving since before dawn, the sky just turning gold and pink. The Iowa landscape raced by outside: fields, trees, scattered outposts of gas stations, everything both familiar and unfamiliar. Living in Chicago, I'd gotten used to the city, tightly packed and buzzing with energy. Here the country felt so big and open that anything might happen.

I'd been toying with the radio station, trying to coax something from the blur of static. Fuzzy music refused to get any louder or softer no matter how I adjusted the station. "Where do I even begin?" I asked, giving up and falling back against the seat.

As promised, Tom had procured an interview with the Clarksons as I anxiously hovered beside him. "Did you ask if my mom's there?" I'd asked, the moment he got off the phone. "It was just their manager," he'd said, "but no, he didn't mention Margaret." That didn't necessarily mean anything, I reminded myself. I had to talk to Deb directly. The two of us had stayed at a cheap motel (Tom volunteering to sleep in the car, an offer I'd accepted, grateful for a solid night's sleep on something resembling a real mattress) and started off as soon as possible.

In the morning light, I got a better look at Tom. He was probably ten years older than me, his hands on the steering wheel long-fingered, starred with ink stains. He had those grooves under his eyes that could've been from insomnia or could've been genetic, maybe both.

I took a stab at answering his question: "Ever since we left the Homestead, she's wanted to settle down and forget everything. That's not me. It might sound strange for a Girl without a father, but I take after Bellanger more than I'll ever take after my mother."

I'd said this exact thing on the phone to a reporter once, the line earning an appreciative laugh. I remembered turning around to see my mother in the doorway, hanging back, a stack of clean towels clutched to her chest like a shield. The look on her face: that betrayal, like she'd been slapped unexpectedly. I hurried past the memory. "Listen. If this conversation's going to end up all over newsstands, you need to give me warning. Especially with my mom missing like this."

I wasn't exactly allergic to journalists and reporters. After growing up in the carefully guarded silence of my home, I'd found it thrilling to dole out quotes and interviews over the past year since I'd left my mother's orbit. I had, admittedly, been surprised by the questions, which verged between fluffy and too nosy, sometimes both at once. Reporters interested in my body, my relationship with my mother, which lipstick shade Girl One preferred (orange-flavored ChapStick). It was a challenge to keep the focus on Bellanger's interrupted work and my attempts to restore his legacy, but I persevered. Usually with a smile. Flies, honey: all that.

"I'll be discreet," Tom said. "Of course. I honored your mom's request for privacy. I see no reason to stop now."

I considered this. I hadn't seen any evidence of the phone call between Tom and my mother splashed across the headlines. I let that thought comfort me.

"Besides, I've pulled back from my work at the paper lately. I'm working on my own thing. A book," he said, unable to keep the pride from his voice. "About you. Well, not *you*. About Bellanger's work at the Homestead. The greatest scientific breakthrough of our time."

The sky smoothed from pink to blue. A book. That explained why Tom had been hunting down the Homesteaders. "How's that been going for you?"

"Fine," he said, in a voice that suggested otherwise. I waited. Sure enough: "Hard to get interviews. A lot of you won't even answer the phone."

"Six," I said, staring out the window at a distant pump jack nodding at the edge of a field like a huge bird pecking at the ground. "There are *six* books about the Homestead and Dr. Bellanger. That's probably why they don't want to talk to you."

I'd been especially aware of my own presence in textbooks lately. Sitting in lecture halls, I'd gotten used to people turning and looking at me, some openly, some surreptitious. Because there I was, my baby picture, my little wailing face and wet, dark hair printed below headers like "Reproductive Anomalies: Parthenogenesis." Tamping down my pride, I'd always try to focus on the lesson like an outside observer, ignoring the fact that my mother appeared in the books too. Her face a perfect copy of my own, eyes boring into me from across the layers of time.

In a seminar on reproductive technologies, we'd devoted half a day to Bellanger and his legacy. I'd sat in the back row, and by the end I was vibrant, more certain than ever that I was in the right place, doing the right thing. Afterward, a classmate had looked at me as the other students filed out. I'd smiled at him. "You know you didn't inherit Joe Bellanger's genius, right?" he'd said. "That's the whole point of you. You don't even *have* a father. You're descended from the guinea pig, not the scientist."

I'd spent the next week seething, spinning out increasingly elaborate comebacks in my head. I waited until our next exam, lingering after class, waiting till I caught a glimpse of his grade: 56 percent. "Not bad for a guinea pig," I'd said, flashing my 85 percent. A grimy pleasure that sustained me for weeks.

The world won't greet us as friends, Josephine, but we must stay bold in our convictions. There were so many lines from Bellanger's letters that felt prescient, like he'd known exactly what I'd need as an adult.

Tom was talking: "I'm not reinventing the wheel. But Bellanger might be the single most important scientific figure that my generation sees. How many scientists have been murdered for their work? Galileo was jailed—Bellanger was killed." He'd gone somewhere else, his eyes intent behind his glasses. "Bellanger died before he ever got the chance to share his research. His legacy has been fading for years and I want to offer new insight into what he truly accomplished."

I shifted in my seat, feeling that familiar annoyance, a prickling territoriality that reared up inside me sometimes. Everyone wanted to sniff out some overlooked juicy detail from my past, find some sharp, shiny new angle that would reflect its light back on their careers. I felt like I was alone in wanting to build something new. To move Bellanger into the future. "Funny, that's what I'm doing too," I said. "I'm going to re-create Bellanger's original work. But I'm sure your *book* will be nice too, Tom."

The Clarkson home was a creamy mansion, lined with puffy shrubs. It suited the Clarksons so well it was almost comical, the way some people resembled their pets. The home was mostly hidden behind a high wall of honey-blond brick. Harmony Springs itself was less a neighborhood than an uneasy coalition of walled-off mansions and sprawling grounds, everyone maintaining a haughty distance from each other.

A young man with a clipboard opened the door to us. "Girl One," he said. "Come in, come in. We've been eagerly awaiting your presence."

The entryway was chilly white marble, larger than our entire house; through the doorways, more marble. The icy veins were like the arteries of the house itself, extending into every corner. An autographed portrait of Deb and Bonnie hung above the stairwell, cursive spidering across their collarbones. I was awed for a moment, and then I remembered why I was in Minnesota. "Is my mother here?"

"Here?" The young man glanced around, confused, concerned. "I was led to believe she's missing."

"But has she been here in the past few weeks? Has she talked to Deb?" I balanced my growing desperation to find my mother with the awareness that I needed to keep some things close to my chest. I didn't need the entire world to know that my mother had been visiting other Homesteaders.

"I really doubt it, Miss Morrow," the young man said. "Ms. Clarkson would've told me if your mother showed up at her doorstep—"

"It's fine," Tom said, interrupting. He gripped my elbow lightly for a second, a little signal. *Play it cool.* "We'd like this to be a private interview. Just the Clarksons, Miss Morrow, and me. Nobody else, thanks."

The young man made a quick calculation and shrugged, acquiescing. "The girls just got finished with Channel Five. Come with me."

The Clarksons' McMansion was even bigger on the inside, a trick of physics. Endless corridors, each one leading outward again. From what I could see through the open doorways we passed, all the rooms were alike—unused, some furniture still in plastic wrap or boxes, like a dollhouse designed by a child who'd wandered off bored. So this was what talking about the Homestead had given Deb and Bonnie. The opposite of my water-stained bedroom ceiling, of Emily French's attic, of the original compound where we'd been born.

Deb had always been an unlikely member of the Homestead, looking like she'd gotten lost on her way to a sorority mixer. She was both cautionary tale (*This could be your daughter, suburban parents!*) and inspiration (*This could be your daughter, suburban parents!*). I'd always had the distinct impression my mother didn't get along with her.

A door opened as we approached, and there she was. Deborah Clarkson, in the flesh. Up close, her TV makeup was expertly applied so that her cheekbones looked hollowed out. Her chignon was architectural and stiff with spray. Deb stared at me for a long moment, face unreadable, then took me by the shoulders, running her hands down my arms. "Looking at Bonnie, it's like looking in a mirror," she said. "But looking at you? It's like traveling back in time. It could be '71." She blinked, seeming to break herself out of a spell. "Margaret's with you?"

"I was hoping she was with you."

"With me?" Deb stepped back, a frown creasing only her forehead. In her eyes, a flutter of panic, though her voice stayed steady. "Why would she be here, sweetheart?" Before I could grasp her feelings, she was all professionalism again. Glossy and intractable. "Thomas! So lovely to see you again, my dear." Deb extended her hand to Tom as if it were a precious museum artifact she would loan him.

"We're excited to sit down with you and Bonnie." Tom shook her hand firmly.

"For Margaret's girl? Anything." We followed Deb into the room. Tom was all confidence, shoulders back. But when Deb's smile slipped away, she looked like a woman held hostage.

She knew something. She knew something about my mother.

The room was lined with windows, all of them gauzy with curtains that gave the room a womblike pastel hush. A chandelier shone like a flattering spotlight on a tufted love seat. The walls were lined with images of Deb and Bonnie, posing with a menagerie of people, celebrities and otherwise. Oprah. Johnny Carson. A local restaurant owner beaming over a pizza box.

Bonnie Clarkson wore a tight shift dress that matched the pink velvet love seat so closely she could vanish into it at the right angle. Her flossy hair was in a high ponytail. I couldn't help looking at the scar that snaked between her mouth and the top of her right cheekbone. Rubbery, shinier than the soft flesh around it, curved like a deflated letter J. When she saw me, her eyes widened, though she made no move to get up. "You're here." Bonnie darted a glance at her mother for clarification. "Josephine. The first one."

The way she said it gave me a rush of goose bumps. She was hung up on the sequence of the Miracle Babies, just like I was. Sisters squabbling over birth order. "Hello, Bonnie," I said. "The seventh one."

"We," Deb said, "are going to sit down with Josephine and Thomas and have a little chat." I caught something in her voice, a warning tapped in Morse code, hard for me to access. Bonnie scooted over and I approached, conscious of the rusty ketchup stain on my jeans, the careless bun at the base of my neck. It was the same style I wore in the lab, keeping my hair out of my face, but in here it felt too plain.

Deb was talking. "If you're here to discuss your mother, Josephine, you'll need to follow the same rules as any other guest. Don't dwell on anything too depressing."

"Too depressing?" I repeated. "Are you aware that my house was burned down and that my mother hasn't been seen in three days? Where's the positive spin on that?" I smiled, but the words were heated with sarcasm.

Deb maintained steady eye contact with me as she sat, smoothing her skirt over her thighs. "Well! To the point. Just like our Margaret. Little Miss Holier-Than-Thou. Let me clue you in about your mother: For all her brains, she never understood how to reach common ground. A little diplomacy goes a long way, but your mother couldn't be bothered. I see the apple doesn't fall far from *that* tree."

I was speechless for a second, hearing my mother described by someone who'd known her in a way I never could. *Holier-Than-Thou.* As a kid, I'd wanted to meet the other Homesteaders so I could piece together more about Bellanger, but this was unexpected. Seeing my mother as a brainy, self-righteous young woman, a pre–Mother One.

"We're so sorry, Deb," Tom said, smooth. "Josie is going through a lot right now."

"Sorry," I echoed, trying to calm down. Flies and honey: I knew this. I was usually pretty good at hiding my bluntness under a layer of politeness, something my mother had never taught me, something I'd had to learn from the world around me. "I didn't mean to snap."

Deb nodded, mildly appeased.

A framed photo of the 1982 reunion caught my eye, and I stepped closer. A significant chunk of us were missing from the image. My mother and me; the Grassis; the Kims. Only five Mother-Girl pairs had made an appearance. The women had changed drastically since the Homestead. Hair trimmed, breasts stiffened by bras, mouths lip-sticked for the camera. Bellanger was a glaring absence. He should have been there. Our organizing principle. The man who'd brought us all together, who'd made us.

Behind me, Deb clapped her hands briskly. "Let's get this over with."

"It's so amazing to have all of you in this room together. Three women with such a unique history."

Deb leapt out ahead of me, answering before Tom's last syllable had faded. "Unique as it may be, I always remind our fans that we're just like anybody else. You may be too young to remember the things people were saying when the Girls were first born—"

"I'm familiar with some of it," Tom said.

"Some predicted that these Girls would bring about the end of civilization. But here we are. I think Dr. Bellanger would be proud of the way these young women have managed to overcome their circum-stances . . ." They were words that had come through Deb's mouth so many times they were polished to sleekness, purely decorative.

Frustration grew under my breastbone. I was realizing that Deb's version of the Homestead was just as opaque as my mother's. She talked so much and so charmingly that she usually tricked me into ignoring all the silence underneath. Her role was to take our origin story, blood-soaked, flame-licked, and sanitize it. I was suddenly so tired of cowering, of simplifying our existence into something safe.

Tom was beginning another softball question, but I interrupted. "Why were you part of the Homestead if you wanted a normal child? There are easier ways to go about that, Deb. Or so I've heard."

Bonnie, in my peripheral vision, straightened. For a second I thought she was going to interject, but Deb was speaking: "All that talk of miracles seemed so silly once I had a baby in my arms. Bonnie shifted my priorities. Surely any mother can relate to that. All nine of us wanted the same thing for our Girls. An ordinary life."

I spoke without thinking. "But not all of us were ordinary children."

The silence felt prickling, stinging. Deb pressed her lips together briefly. "I'm sorry?" Every syllable a warning.

"I'm talking about Fiona." Just saying her name was a thrill now. "I know that my mother was in touch with you recently, asking about Fiona."

Deb stood and moved toward the door. "You're here under false pretenses. Time to go."

"Look, this is a misunderstanding, we can—" Tom said, placating.

I stood too, moving in front of her, instinctive. "This big beautiful house, your designer dresses. It's all because you give people fluffy quotes. I'm not looking for fluff. I want the truth."

A rough scoff of a laugh. "You won't like it any more than anybody else does." I was transfixed. In all her televised interviews—60 Minutes, Late Night—I'd never seen Deb like this. "The truth is that your mother loved to pull all the strings, then play innocent when it suited her. I always wondered how long Margaret could last in an ordinary life. There was something in her that wanted to destroy everything. I don't know if she could help herself."

I saw my mother sitting at home, lost in a book; I saw her keeping a slight distance from her coworkers clustered together, chatting, laughing, while she busied herself at the circulation desk with some solitary task. Blunt when necessary, but quiet. Focused. Not at all the woman Deb was describing.

Deb went on, her private anger turned visible. "Margaret loved it when I was just one of the background faces, doing what I was told. Now I finally get to tell the story, and I do a damn good job. Of course, Margaret resents me for taking over her pet project."

"Pet project?" I repeated. "What does that even mean? My mother was only one part of it—just because she was the first—"

"There's a reason your mother was the first," Deb said. "She was our ringleader. She drew us together, the nine of us, and then she tore us apart. She was the one who contacted Dr. Bellanger first, even when some of the girls begged her not to."

I exchanged looks with Tom, my head thrumming.

"Margaret didn't care what kind of damage she caused. I saw what she did to Patricia. She would've done the same to me if she'd cared enough to hurt me." Deb's gaze had shifted weight. She wasn't looking at me the way she'd look at a stranger. She was speaking directly to my mother.

"Margaret knew you before Dr. Bellanger?" Tom asked. I was grateful to him—I didn't trust myself to talk—but I was also irritated, suddenly aware of Tom absorbing all this information right alongside me. "Because my impression was that Dr. Bellanger put out a call for volunteers and you ladies only met each other through him," Tom continued. "Is that correct?"

Deb didn't even look at him, keeping her eyes locked on mine. "What I'm saying is that Dr. Bellanger takes the blame, but everything about that place can be traced right back to Margaret Morrow. She made Patricia set aside the land for the Homestead. She recruited the women to the commune. She wrote the letter to Dr. Bellanger. She brought us all together, and then she broke the whole thing apart. I hope she's down on her knees thanking God for my positivity every night, because there's a lot I could say that she wouldn't like. Not one fucking bit."

Bonnie was leaning forward, riveted, eyes shining, her pearly bra strap slipping down her upper arm.

"Patricia?" I repeated. "The Homestead was on her land?" I tried to picture Patricia Bishop, her small serious face, at least a head shorter than the other women in the group photos. I knew she still lived in Vermont, the only one of the surviving eight to do so, but I hadn't realized that she had any claim to the Homestead land itself.

"Margaret hurt everybody," Deb went on. "Not just Patricia. Not just us girls at the Homestead. Bellanger's real family—Marianne, poor little Junior and Bobby. They were abandoned when she lured Dr. Bellanger over to us. Margaret didn't give them a single thought. They were just collateral damage to her."

The chandelier's lighting looked soft and forgiving from a distance, but now that I was positioned beneath the glare, the lights burned against my skin. "My mother only learned about Bellanger when he called for test subjects." I clung to the story I knew. The one that had been repeated again and again and again, in everything from a sleazy made-for-TV movie to formal scholarly articles. "He recruited the nine of you. He created the Homestead. My mother didn't even—she couldn't have known about him, or about—she would have told me—"

"Are you sure?" Deb said. "Because lying is just what Margaret does. I'm sure she wouldn't want her own daughter to know about what she really did."

I breathed deeply, steadying myself, giddy with shock.

"Does this mean that Margaret Morrow was already interested in the idea of virgin birth?" Tom asked.

You're descended from the guinea pig, not the scientist. I squeezed my eyes shut.

"No, you don't," Deb said, voice suddenly tired. "No more from me. I've said too much. Get out of here. And don't even think about sharing any of this. Consider it off the record. Or I'll have my lawyers on you so fucking quickly that you won't know what's happening."

I opened my eyes, vision starred over for a second. "Did my mother contact you recently?" I asked, grasping for the original reason I'd come here. Nothing about my mother's past would matter until I could ask her about it directly.

"You're leaving, or I'm calling the cops—"

"Was she asking about Fiona?" I pressed.

Bonnie stood abruptly. "You need to tell her, Mommy." Deb and I turned, equally startled. Color rushed to Bonnie's cheeks, rough red splotches beneath the pastel blush. Wildflowers springing up inside a cultivated garden. "If you were missing and I came to somebody for help, wouldn't you want them to help me?"

"I wouldn't be in this situation at all," Deb said.

"Mommy, there are a lot of things that you don't say," Bonnie said. "But there are things that I don't say either. Things that we both want to stay quiet."

Deb's face tightened. She sucked an inhale through her nose.

"Tell her," Bonnie said.

Whatever passed between the two of them, Deb lost: she broke her gaze, turned back to me. "Margaret has been here," she said, each word cold and grudging.

"She has?" Instantly, I was focused. "When?"

"A month ago? I didn't keep track. It's not a cherished memory, let me say that much. She gave me a goddamn fright, banging on the gates until I let her in. That woman hid away for years, too stuck-up to agree to any media appearances, and then she came here making a scene? No. I wouldn't stand for it. I wouldn't be pulled back into her bullshit."

I tried to imagine this, electrified by the immediacy of it. My mother, right out there, rattling those big imposing gates, refusing to be turned away.

"I let her onto the grounds to keep her from alerting the whole neighborhood, but it was a short visit. She was rambling on and on about Fiona. Resurrecting dead dreams that nobody needs. Your mother is a very sick woman, Josie. When I heard that there'd been a fire? That she'd vanished into the night? I thought . . ."

"You thought what?" In a hard, ugly way, I wanted her to say it.

"I thought—no surprise there. The woman was unwell. It was bound to happen sometime." She looked me up and down. "And now you come here. All selfish demands and wild rants. No idea where your own mother is or what she's been doing."

I licked my lips, tasting the sting of perspiration. Deb stepped closer. Again, she touched me, gripping my chin, turning my face this way and that. I let her do it. It kept her talking.

"Do you know what it was like, waiting to get pregnant?" Deb asked softly. "Your mother was the first. Of course she was. We all had to wait our turn for our own daughters. She trapped us with that hope." Deb's touch turned unexpectedly gentle. "All Margaret ever wanted was a daughter. That was the point of everything she did. It was all just to get you. Here you are, her grand prize, and she can't even hold on to you."

11

April 24, 1974

My favorite Girl, my Josephine,

On your third birthday, my heart is unexpectedly heavy. I look at you, my Miracle Girl, and I think: How is she not enough? Well, it seems the world needs more than your mere existence to believe in my work. It's all an attempt to steal my ideas. That's an important lesson for you, Josephine. The world pretends it admires you only so it can take from you. The world won't greet us as friends, Josephine, but we must stay bold in our convictions!

Apparently the tabloids—and even respected members of the scientific community—have been saying that you, Girl One, are not enough. You are a disappointment. You were born in an unorthodox manner, so why are you no different from any other child? What merit does parthenogenesis hold if you are an ordinary girl in every respect?

But what the world has apparently forgotten is that remarkable children require remarkable parents. I have pictured you Girls being extraordinary, superior to other children. But if such qualities exist in you, they will take time to grow. The best I can do is show patience and guidance as we wait for you all to blossom into true Miracle Babies.

Your loving father always,
Joseph Bellanger

12

Excerpt from *Scientific Daily*—January 2, 1974

Sitting Down with the Man Behind the Real "Baby Boom"

Scientific Daily: Reproductive technology usually brings wide-spread change. It's estimated that up to 10,000 children a year are now being born via artificial insemination, though this method has only been used on humans successfully for less than a century. You, however, have introduced virgin birth as a parlor trick, if you will, given that other researchers in your field have expressed frustration that you so closely guard your methods. Do you think it's egotistical to hoard the secrets of parthenogenesis? Do you one day hope to see this method of reproduction more widespread?

B: [laughs] Well. A parlor trick. That's some parlor trick, wouldn't you say? I will not be bullied into sharing my own hard-won intellectual work. You may remember my predecessor, Gregory Pincus, who was stripped of tenure because of his parthenogenetic work with laboratory rabbits. Even thirty years later, are we ready for virgin birth among humans? My colleagues didn't think so. I didn't get here via cooperation and I don't intend to start playing nice now. Nonetheless, I do intend for my work to eventually become an accepted part of our reproductive landscape. On my own terms.

SD: I recall that when you first introduced your work to the world, you often spoke of these products of parthenogenesis—these so-called Miracle Babies—as if they may change the very course of humanity. There was a distinct attitude that these Girls would be different from, perhaps *superior to*, children born in the usual manner. But by all accounts, these little girls are like any others. Should they be considered special?

B: [silence]

SD: If you aren't willing to look into parthenogenesis as a widespread means of human reproduction—and if the children produced via this method are no different from any other children—is there truly a compelling reason for virgin birth to take precedence over any other method? We have to stop and think about what it may mean for fatherhood, for the very structure of the American family. These little girls will likely be growing up as pariahs, not miracles.

Do you truly believe, at this stage, that your experimentation has the potential to change the world?

B: Who's to say what may emerge, what may materialize, in these Girls, given time? And if not these Girls, then those that come from future experiments.

13

My mother writing to Bellanger first. It didn't make sense. Each stage of my origin—the beginnings, the births, the triumph, the downfall—was as clear in my head as the structure of a beloved fairy tale. Bellanger had gathered nine women from every corner of the country and together they'd transcended their lonely pasts and become the Homestead. Fertile wombs and bare ring fingers. The idea of my mother being a *ringleader*—contacting Bellanger, bringing the other women together—was a startling inconsistency.

I tossed and turned under the Laura Ashley comforter. Bonnie had convinced her mother to let us stay the night. I still didn't know whether to be grateful for the favor. The room was huge, empty, chilled by aggressive air-conditioning.

My mother obsessed with a dead girl, my mother visiting the other Homesteaders, scribbling, *Tell the world about Fiona*. Emily whispering about birds in the attic, the dead bird outside my house. Everything tangled together, and at the center of it was my mother's stubborn, terrifying absence. What the hell had happened to her?

The bedroom door opened with a thin creak. Someone slipped into my room. I sat up. It was one in the morning. The figure passed through a patch of moonlight. A ghost, a monster. Hair white in the moonlight, face flat and distorted and unnaturally pale. My chest tightened before I realized it was just Bonnie wearing a clay mask, mint green and cakey, the skin around her eyes and mouth revealed in circular patches. She ran as she approached the bed and jumped in, bare leg knocking against mine.

"Sorry about that," Bonnie said. Up close, she smelled both acrid and sweet. Self-tanner and the floral scent of the face mask. Boozy breath. Tipsy.

"Don't be. I couldn't sleep, anyway."

When she laughed, the clay around her mouth and eyes cracked into fine lines. "Sorry about Mommy, I mean. She gets so intense about this shit. It's all sunshine and daisies and God forbid anyone tell the truth."

"Yeah, well. She certainly seemed in the mood to tell the truth tonight."

Bonnie lolled against my pillow, fixed me with expectant eyes, like I'd called her in here. I tried to figure out what I'd ask her about first: Did she know anything about my mother's role at the Homestead? Could she tell me what Deb had meant about my mother hurting everyone? Before I could decide, she said, "Once you mentioned Fiona, I knew we *had* to talk alone." She spoke in a campfire whisper. "Mommy got sloshed one night when I was a kid and blurted out something about Fiona shutting doors with her brain powers." Bonnie put a hand on her forehead, waggling her fingers outward, a Rod Serling pitch. "Scandalous, right? Imagine if people knew Fiona was a freak." A cold finger traced up and down my spine, the blunt stridence of *freak* right in my ear.

Emily had known about Fiona; Bonnie knew. Everyone knew the Homestead's true history except me. "Your mother's never said anything about that to the press?"

"My mother won't even let me get a tattoo on my shoulder. Bad for our image. I'm drinking swag-bag champagne in the pantry with the lights off like I'm thirteen. She is *not* about to tell the whole world that one of the Miracle Babies was a mutant."

"More than one, maybe," I said. "Emily French too. She's . . . different."

"Emily? Seriously?" Bonnie blinked at me. Without her heavy TV makeup, her eyes looked small and bare, like the pistils of a flower sans petals. "I thought she was . . ." Bonnie whistled, *cuckoo*, whirled her finger around her temple.

"Maybe," I said, feeling defensive of Emily now that I'd met her face-to-face. "But my mother said Fiona was *strange*, and if Emily is too, then—"

"What about you? Have you ever felt anything strange, Girl One?" Bonnie asked, maybe-teasing.

This massive house was so quiet. All those rooms spread out around us, empty and still. It felt unnatural and exposed, nothing like the close quarters my mother and I had shared.

"When I was a kid, I fantasized about it," I said. "Do you remember all those editorials about how we must be witches or demons or—or monsters? Some people got all worked up over it." I hesitated, remembering. "Bellanger wrote me this letter when I was three."

"Oh right, your very special letters," Bonnie said, definitely teasing now.

"He was always so proud when he talked about us, like we were his masterpieces. But in this letter, Bellanger seemed disappointed that we weren't more special."

"Heavy. Guess I should be glad Bellanger didn't make me his little pen pal."

That letter had stuck in my head more than the others, haunting me. When I was in third grade, the kids were just starting to get mean. They figured out my lack of a dad wasn't due to a divorce or a car accident. I'd responded by fixating on uncovering some shimmering fingerprint that Bellanger had left inside my DNA. I'd grown moody, withdrawn, not eating, snapping at my mom. I'd jumped off the garage roof, trying to fly. Imagining it in my bones—that lightness and lift, the air cradling me—right up until I landed on the concrete and broke my collarbone. I'd just wanted to feel something special manifesting inside me.

"When I got older," I went on, "I figured I wouldn't sit around waiting for some magical power to show up. I'd look at the world the same way Bellanger did. He created his own magic."

"Brainiac." Bonnie poked teasingly at my arm. "Just like your mother." She stopped, peering at me, trying to gauge my interest. Her eyes were bleary from drinking. "Where do you think your mother is?"

"The million-dollar question."

"I saw the house on the news." She grimaced. "I'd be freaked out if that happened to my mother."

It occurred to me, with a catching spark of dread, that Bonnie Clarkson herself could hold the key to my mother's disappearance. Bonnie Clarkson: the one with the jagged scar to prove that people out there wanted us dead. The living testament to Ricky Peters's lingering wrath.

Here she was, scar and all, lying next to me, breathing hints of champagne onto my cheek.

"Well." I drew the syllable out. "I do have one theory." Bonnie murmured her interest, rolled closer, eyes bright. "The guy who attacked you. Do you think he might have come after my mother too?"

Against me, her muscles tensed, her breathing halted. When she spoke again, it was as if I'd managed to sober her up instantaneously. "Nah. That was years ago. It was an isolated attack."

An isolated attack. The words that had always comforted me as a child, back when a copycat attack felt inevitable. "But he was never caught," I pushed. "We still don't know who he even was."

Bonnie stared fixedly across the room, lost in thought, at the shag carpet and flowery wallpaper, all turned gray with moonlight. She reached up and touched her face. I imagined the skin opening at her touch—the pinkish muscles, the gleaming, carefully bleached teeth shining through. "You know why I wear these stupid face masks? When I look in the mirror, and my scar's hidden, I pretend he never hurt me."

I stayed quiet.

"I was only a kid. I was walking home from a friend's house. I can't even remember her name now. My first normal friend, not just somebody wanting an autograph. It was a reward for behaving nicely at the reunion. My mom let me walk there and back all by myself. I felt so grown-up. It was only four houses down. On the way back, I could see my living room window all lit up. I heard footsteps behind me. I turned around because I thought it was my friend, running up to tell me how much fun she'd had. I was so fucking stupid."

"You weren't," I said, but Bonnie didn't even pause, just brushed this off.

"I was smiling, and I was still smiling when I saw the knife because I didn't know what it was. There was this flash in his hand, like a match. He was wearing a hat or a hood or something, so I could see his nose, his jaw a little, but he just ran at me so fast, and I stepped out of the way, still smiling, too dumb to be scared . . . it didn't even hurt at first."

Something brushed my cheek and I yelped, heart hammering, fist-hard, inside my chest. Bonnie pulled her hand back. "Shit," I said.

"He only stopped for a second." Bonnie continued as if nothing had happened. "I started bleeding. My mother was screaming in the background—she'd come out onto the lawn, looking for me. That was when I understood that something was wrong. They say you can't remember pain, but I remember that. Like my whole face was just going to fall off. I'd worn this dress with stripes and buttons, because it was something Shelley Hack would've worn on *Charlie's Angels*, and it was just covered in blood."

I'd experienced this story at roughly the same time, only on an alternate plane, at home in Illinois. For me, it had been secondhand. My mother and I, nervous that we'd be targeted next, had left home for a few days, lying low in a motel in Carbondale. I remembered the shivery dread of waiting for a knife blade against my skin. Wishing I had Bellanger there to protect me.

"The police showed up pretty quick and they searched for the guy," Bonnie said. "Nothing, nada. No reports from the rest of the neighborhood. This is the only evidence he was ever there." She made a circling gesture around her face.

"So he could still be out there," I said. "He could have come after my mom."

Bonnie laughed. "You're such an asshole. That's your takeaway? Really?" She flounced back against the pillows. "I was a baby. An easy target. Like shooting little baby fish in a tiny barrel." She made a gun out of her fingers, *pew-pew*. "Setting fire to a house? Kidnapping a full-grown woman? That's different."

"There was a car," I said, remembering. "When I went to my mother's house. I saw a sedan hanging around. Maybe that was him. I should've written down the plates or something."

"You'll waste time if you get hung up on this."

"It's one of the only things I've got right now." It was disconcertingly easy to imagine my mother catching the wrong person's attention. A deranged loyalist of Ricky Peters spotting an easy excuse to hunt down Mother One.

"Seriously." Bonnie grabbed my arm. "It's not the same guy."

"How do you know?" I didn't hide my impatience.

Bonnie was on the verge of speaking. Then she smiled, an expression I couldn't read, and rose from the bed. Under her T-shirt, her body was outlined perfectly, and I was struck by her: by the fact that she was an entire human being who existed when she shouldn't have. Awareness of my own strangeness reverberated through my bones.

"You know, it gets old being the poster girl for shit situations." Bonnie moved toward the door, languidly unsteady. "Whenever anything bad happens to any of you, you're all coming to me like I'm the expert."

"Wait." I crawled to the end of the bed. "This has happened before? Who's come to you for help?" I tried to remember if I'd heard anything about the other Homesteaders getting into trouble recently.

Bonnie paused near the door. Her face mask was so cracked that she was like an ancient statue of herself. She balanced one foot in the crook of the opposite knee.

"Who?" I pressed.

"The Bowers." Bonnie unfolded her leg, stretched her body to one side in a broad arc. Her T-shirt rose over her hip. The Bowers: Tonya and Catherine. Mother Three. Girl Three. "It was a while back. They'd had some guy hanging around their house. Catherine called to ask me for details. Sort of the way you are now. I bet you and Catherine would like each other."

The air-conditioning left my arms stippled with goose bumps. "And?"

"And—it was nothing. The Bowers are fine, as far as I know." Bonnie sighed, softened. "I'll give you their phone number so you can check for yourself."

"Thank you, Bonnie. Seriously."

Bonnie faked a yawn. "Hey, anything for my sister," she said. Then she slipped back into her labyrinth of hallways, leaving only her scent on my pillow.

14

Jittery with impatience, I was out of the car before it came to a complete stop, hurrying to the pay phone that stood near the concrete picnic shelters. I slipped the quarters into the slot, punched in the number that I'd memorized by now. *Please pick up; please pick up.*

"No response?" Tom asked when I returned to the Volvo a few minutes later, defeated.

"Nope." I'd told Tom about the Bowers this morning. The decision to stop by Arkansas and seek them out in person was unanimous and obvious. As long as we were heading southeast, we could continue toward the Arkansas Ozarks to meet the Bowers and add no more than a day to our trip. A minor detour.

We pulled back onto the long gray ribbon of the freeway. I reached over to turn down the volume. I was sick of bad news, and all the radio stations were busy discussing Kurt Cobain's death, the upcoming anniversary of Waco, the hijacked cargo jet.

"I can't get over what Deb said." This was a particularly bland stretch of the Midwest. Trees and guardrails dotted with fast-food wrappers, billowing white grocery bags. "My mother reaching out to Bellanger. It doesn't make sense."

Tom glanced at me. "I'm going out on a limb and assuming you and your mother never discussed her decision to work with Bellanger?"

I had tried so many times to imagine my mother, a young woman, not pregnant yet, right on the cusp of a whole new future. The world before my conception. I'd wanted to know what it was like to be chosen by Bellanger. The idea of my mother choosing Bellanger instead left me fumbling in the dark.

"She said she volunteered because she wanted a baby. That's it." I sighed. "She never seemed interested in scientific progress or fame and fortune. Obviously. Look what our lives were like in Coeur de fucking Lac. My mother, she just—I always thought the only way a person like her would be involved in the Homestead was because Bellanger talked her into it. She didn't even understand what she was getting into. That's why this feels so weird. I might be Margaret's daughter, but I've never been her *idea*."

We were quiet for a minute. My mother—how she'd managed to unofficially take on new responsibilities at our small library despite not wanting to go to school for a library science degree ("I'm done with all that, Josie," though as far as I knew she'd never gone to school). I remembered her reading me books at bedtime and the subtle changes in her voice for each character, a lower octave there, a hoarseness here, until the whole cast of characters came alive. Watching her bent over crossword puzzles, tapping the pen against the edge of the table for a long time and then suddenly filling out the whole thing in a few minutes, looking at me with a shy pride, like she was checking whether or not I'd noticed.

"You don't know my mother," I said, not ready to accept a new vision of her.

"Maybe not," Tom said, "but I'm getting to know her daughter."

The motel that night squatted close to the freeway exit. I offered to take the car, leaving the room to Tom. I needed to make a call anyway. This was already the fourth night away from Chicago, the outermost limit I'd set for myself. I was expected back in classes by Tuesday at the latest. Tomorrow. Taking this much time off was unheard of. A girl in my class had been out for a week with the flu last fall and ended up dropping out. I had a decision to make.

The pay phone was tucked around a corner, hidden from the road and the parking lot. A small square of concrete beneath the phone was all that differentiated it from the weedy lot that bordered the motel. A dog barked somewhere in the distance, a raw and lonely sound. At the far end of the empty lot, a greenish streetlight illuminated a patchwork of metal fence.

I listened to the endless ringing that I now associated with the Bowers, my chest tight with the hope that one of them would pick up. That they were safe somewhere. Talking about Bonnie's attack had turned my fear more sticky and immediate, my head filled with blood, knife blades, heat. I just wanted to talk to the Bowers. Not only to hear that they were fine, but—selfishly—so they could tell me what had happened with the stalker, and maybe that, in turn, would lead me to my mother.

The truth was, I'd never imagined a world without my mother in it. I couldn't let myself start now.

When the Bowers didn't answer, I recycled another couple of quarters into the phone. It was late, and I wasn't supposed to use his home number except in emergencies. But there he was: "Hello?"

"Dr. McCarter? It's me, Josephine." I added: "Morrow."

"Jo," he said, brightening. "Our little scientific anomaly. Where have you been? Any word about your mother?"

"Not yet. I'm calling because I still need a day or two to make sure she's fine. Would it be all right if I came back on Wednesday—maybe Thursday—instead?" This was optimistic to the point of being unrealistic, but it felt good to say it, like maybe it would really happen.

Dr. McCarter was quiet for a moment. "Wednesday? We're going over the maternal immune system in class tomorrow. Have you arranged with a classmate to take notes?"

"It was all . . . so sudden . . . I just—"

"You have an exam in my class in one week," Dr. McCarter said. "I have your classmates covering for you at the lab, but they're busy too. It's not quite fair to them to force them to pick up your slack, is it, now?"

"Of course not. I'm sorry."

A sigh. "Jo, can I be honest with you? There's been some talk among my colleagues. Someone said we only accepted you as a publicity stunt." He didn't need to tell me: I'd felt this, reflected in classmates' gazes and fleeting comments. "You're bright, and usually you're a hard worker. I absolutely believe you can do what you've set out to do. This is just a distraction from your work."

"My mother's home was burned down," I said, "and she's missing, and—"

"Family matters are tricky, yes," he interrupted. "But couldn't you let someone else handle this for a while?"

"It's not like my mother has anybody else." And neither did I. No brusque father to pat me on the back, no aunts to rush in with casseroles and platitudes. It was just me now: my mother and I divided and sub-divided from our time at the Homestead. Eighteen women narrowed down to two, two down to one.

"I don't want you to lose your place in the program for something you can't help. I'll speak to the committee about the quality of your work and make sure they understand these are special circumstances. Let's prove those skeptics wrong, okay?"

"Thank you, Dr. McCarter."

After I hung up, there was a sudden rustle behind me, the unmistakable crunch of a footstep against the gravel. I turned, embarrassed and irritable, expecting that Tom had followed me out here to listen in on my conversation. It took a second to locate the source—the cherry of his cigarette came first, floating in midair, the rest of him resolving around that spark. He ambled toward me, not as tall as Tom but thicker and loosely muscled. Something about his gait, the easy stride, set off a primal thrum of warning at the base of my skull.

"Got a quarter I could borrow?" A hoarse voice, just on the edge of a cough.

I tallied my choices. I held out my last coin. The man extracted the cigarette from his mouth and dropped it, a plummeting comet that vanished into the gravel. He came closer to accept the quarter, our fingers touching. He flipped the coin, and in its arc it caught the streetlight, a dazzling, twisting beam above us, before snapping back into his palm. "Pretty late for you to be out here on your own," he said. "Just passing through?"

"I should be going. My husband's waiting." An easy lie, but I hated myself for it.

A scuff of a laugh. "No ring, huh?"

Another step back, smaller this time, half the length of my foot. A slow retreat, trying to disguise itself so he wouldn't notice. I was still smiling, one of those appeasing smiles that came automatically, the way an octopus releases a dark mist of ink. The way possums feign death. Possums didn't even do it on purpose, my mother once told me, whispering close in my ear. Their bodies did it for them, instinctively faking death to protect against the real thing. She'd told me this as we stared across the street at the soft throat of a possum that lay in the neighbor's yard. I never had found out if it was dead or just pretending.

"Nobody's waiting for you." The stranger sounded almost sad for me.

I knew where this could end up. I'd understood what people threatened to do to me or my mother, even before I knew the actual names of the body parts involved. I'd grown up with that fear, and it hadn't been until I'd overheard girls in the school restroom that I'd recognized that terror wasn't specific to the Homestead. That having a man's DNA wound through mine wasn't an antidote against other men.

I turned toward the front of the motel, moving as quickly as I could. Back here, we were hidden from the lonely service road that curved past. The nearest sign of life was the freeway overpass, distant headlights hushing overhead. Nobody would hear me.

The hand on my shoulder wasn't a surprise. Neither was the easy possessiveness of his grasp, a man reaching out to take what was due to him. He wasn't even holding on tight, not yet. This was just to stop me in my tracks. A precursor.

"I'm going back to my room," I said, soothing, conversational, like we were compromising together. Like I could gently place this idea inside his head. "I'm just going, okay? There doesn't have to be any trouble."

He didn't move. Just smiled.

When was the last time I'd been alone in a situation like this? I carried my car key between my knuckles when I walked home after late-night lab work. I didn't wear my hair in a ponytail when I was alone in case somebody grabbed it. But I'd gotten complacent. I'd been so distracted trying to find my mother that I'd been shaken loose from my usual routines of self-preservation.

"Please, let's not do this." I made it sound like we were in this together, both of us fighting against a power stronger than either of us.

But his grip only tightened, fingernails pinching. I remembered being with Emily in the attic. The way she'd wrapped her hands around my throat, the breath stuck inside my body. How I'd thought I might die up there. I'd almost given up until I'd looked into her eyes—until we'd spoken—

Turning, I attached my gaze to the stranger's, leaning toward him instead of stepping away. Until now I had avoided his eyes, and so we were both disoriented. His mouth twisted in subtle confusion, like I was accosting him. But I hung on—when he tried to twist his head away, I ducked to follow him, getting too close. What did I have to lose now? The whites of his eyes were bloodshot, veined in pink. Dizziness grew in my head until I felt balloon-light. I could only see those pupils, yawning wide.

I barely understood what I was doing. It was all instinct, guided roughly by the memory of being in the attic. The whole night around me turned dreamlike. Surreal but also sharply clarified.

"Let me go," I whispered, experimental.

The stranger stilled, his breath coming rabbit-quick. He loosened his grip. I took one step closer, my eyes stinging because I didn't even want to blink, my heart racing painfully. Part of me felt like it wasn't real. He was playing along. He was humoring me. But another part of me was completely awake. My body clicked into a more satisfying pattern, as if I'd been curled up tight my whole life and could suddenly stretch and yawn and flex.

"Let me go," I said, louder now.

He kept his eyes on me as he unclenched his fingers, pulled his hand away. It hung awkwardly next to him. He seemed to have forgotten his hand belonged to him. The stranger was scrawnier with all his bluster scraped away. The smell of his sweat reached me, stringent, bitter. I was slowly recognizing that he couldn't do anything to me. Not as long as I kept my gaze on him. It felt unnatural, dangerous, like I was standing outside in an electrical storm, daring the lightning not to strike.

"You're going to stand here," I said, and then made my words clearer, smoother. "Stand here while I go back to my room. And then go away. Go far away from this motel."

He gave no indication that he'd heard except for a muscle in his jaw denting inward. But he didn't move. I'd never experienced this before. Somebody held in place by my words alone. I laughed, the laugh cracking around the edges so it sounded closer to a sob.

Then I began to walk away. Cautiously. Slowly. There was no rush behind me. No hand on my shoulder.

I'd only gone a few feet when something occurred to me. I turned back around. The stranger watched me, warily blinking. I caught fear mixed in with the anger now—he'd thought he was free of me. "Tell me what you were going to do to me," I said impulsively.

His mouth moved for a few seconds, soundless.

"Tell me," I said, stepping closer, "what you were going to do to me."

I was right in front of him now. Our eyes locked again, and his big dark pupils had soured with rage. "I was going to have some fun," he said.

The euphemism was so stupid and insulting. I was ready to push him for more, when I realized that he'd already confessed: he was going to *have some fun*. Whatever that meant to him in the moment, I was meaningless. A means to his end.

I shut my eyes, opened them again. At the edge of the lot, the halogen glow flickered. I swore I could hear the underwater ebb of his heartbeat. "Have fun, then," I said. And I leaned in close, so close that my words stirred the hair at his temple, and I told him exactly what he'd do. Exactly how he'd get his fun. I wanted him to know what it had felt like when he'd grabbed my shoulder. What it felt like to be reminded that you were small and helpless.

He listened. He obeyed.

I'd never had the anxiety dream about losing my teeth, incisors and molars shedding out of my gums. In my dreams, I was already toothless, empty-gummed, my mouth loose and hollow. I knelt in ashes, stirring them with my fingertips, searching, searching, until I found all of the teeth. Fiona's teeth. So tiny, like seed pearls, and still blazing hot from the fire, searing the tender skin of my palm as I collected them one by one. I fit them into my adult mouth, sending electric waves curling right up into my brain.

15

"Tom," I said, impatient. "Let me try." The morning sunlight was warm on my skin, the air already humid. We'd been in Goulding for half an hour without tracking down the Bowers. Between my mother's notebook and Tom's careful research, we knew we had the right town, but nobody would share the Bowers' exact address with Tom.

Tom hesitated. "What if somebody recognizes you?"

He had a point. As her doppelgänger, I was a walking WANTED poster for my mother. Growing up, there'd been a reminder of our similarities pinned in the eyes of anyone who saw us together. The double-takes. The comments: *Why, you two could be twins!* Never with that twinkly friendliness they used with other mother-daughter pairs. With us, it was an accusation, a demand for explanation. It had only gotten worse since I'd sprouted into puberty.

"Just let me try," I said. What had happened last night was still buzzing around in my head. I wanted to feel it again.

Tom lifted his hands in mock surrender. "Yeah. Go ahead."

Goulding was a small town, accessible only via a long, twisting road, dropping off steeply on one side. Beyond the road, a vast ocean of Ozarks forest, trees for miles. The town proper was an unexpected tourist trap. Gift shops selling hillbilly souvenirs, hand-carved mallard ducks and walking sticks. Bins of mix-and-match healing crystals next to airbrushed T-shirts. I waited, watching the faces going past. A woman approached, her kind, sun-roughened face marking her as a likely local.

"Excuse me," I called, and she paused, patient in the way of someone who dealt with lost tourists on a regular basis.

At the back of my mind, I knew I could lock my eyes against hers and tug the information right out of her. I wanted it so badly. I let my eyes rest against her unassuming gaze. Her eyes a watery green, ringed in liner—but I realized that I'd be doing this in broad daylight, out in front of everybody, making it *real*, and I pulled back at the last moment. "Sorry, but do you know where I can find Tonya Bower?"

"You're in trouble, sweetie?" I nodded, bargaining with myself that it wasn't exactly a lie. "Don't you worry," the woman said. "Cate can help you out." The woman jerked her chin due north, downhill. "Use the back roads. There's a sign saying Mill Creek Lane, but it's hid by a tree branch, so look close. Go down Mill Creek, you'll come across a yellow house with lots of thingies on the porch." She made a cryptic fluttering gesture with her hands. "Cate's usually around this time of day." The woman leaned in. "Honey, take care of yourself. Whatever is going on, it doesn't have to be the end of the world." A pointed look at my stomach.

The Bowers' house was at the edges of Goulding, and it felt like we were in the middle of the forest, surrounded as we were by trees. The yellow house had a dozen wind chimes dangling from the porch, a glittering, clattering flock of them. The windows were shadowed by a deep-set porch. The lawn was profuse with wildflowers. I knocked on the Bowers' front door, tense with anticipation, praying someone would answer. The day was stifled with humidity, but here, the noise of the wind chimes was a texture in the air itself, a layer of coolness.

No response. I tried again, and again. "Are we sure they're home?" Tom asked.

I stepped off the porch, avoiding a flowerpot overrun with the tendrils of a climbing vine, and walked around the side of the house. Flowers and weeds brushed against my shins. A fence surrounded the backyard, wooden slats taller than me, some knocked crooked or slumped into each other. I stopped for a second, listening. A faint thread of noise, like a trapped insect.

"Can you wait here?" I asked Tom. The gate in the fence was locked. Grabbing the top of the slats, where the wood was sun-warmed and weather-softened, I hoisted myself up gracelessly, scrabbling over the top and dropping down to the ground below.

The backyard was beautiful. Just as abundantly overgrown as the front lawn, it was more organized, the chaos corralled into separate sections. Here, delicate pink hellebores, clustered close together; there, a smoke-purple cloud of rhododendron. The air was so perfumed that it nearly made me high. I followed that tinny, buzzing noise I'd heard. As I got closer, the sound resolved into music. A pulsing beat, the thin keen of a voice.

I nearly tripped over her. She knelt in the warm grass, wearing nothing but a pilled and faded bikini bottom, thick black hair parted and hanging down over her chest like a woman from a nineteenth century painting. Her naked back glimmered with sweat as she pulled weeds with a rigorous precision. She looked like she belonged at the Homestead. The only incongruity was the pair of headphones she wore, plastic arcing over her scalp, a big clunky bubble propped on either ear. She murmured along to the music, off-key.

I stood, not sure whether to approach now that I was in her backyard. I thought about touching her shoulder, but as I hesitated, she sat up straighter, the weeds falling from her hands. She reminded me of a deer, that alertness in her posture. Very slowly, she turned her head, saw my knees first—at eye-level with her—and then lifted her gaze, inch by inch, until she found my face. We stared at each other. Catherine, not Tonya. She was young, slightly younger than me.

"Shit." She rose, yanking the earphones off. They dangled around her neck, a clumsy necklace, before sliding free to the grass. I heard the music more clearly now. AC/DC. "What are you doing here?" Catherine asked. "How did you get back here?" She shoved past me, yanked at the locked gate. "You climbed in here? What's your problem, Morrow?"

"You know it's me," I said, oddly pleased.

Catherine grabbed a mismatched bikini top that had been hanging over a wheelbarrow handle, fastened it on. "You couldn't have let me know you were coming?" She snatched at a men's dress shirt in need of ironing, and slipped her arms through. As she buttoned quickly and carelessly, she left smudgy fingerprints on the white.

"I tried calling, Catherine. I couldn't get through."

"No, no, just call me Cate. What were you, raised at a cotillion?

Calling people by their full names. Jesus. Anyway, how'd you get my number?" She redirected her anger effortlessly.

"Bonnie Clarkson. She said that you and your mother had been harassed by someone a while ago. A stranger. Bonnie said that I should talk to you, because—well—maybe that man was the same one who attacked Bonnie?" I was rambling. There was so much to tell her, and I was racing against the timer of her limited interest. "My mother is missing, and if you've been stalked, you might know something about my mother too—or maybe she came to find you."

Catherine stepped forward now, quickly and gently touched my elbow. "Slow down, okay?" I relaxed. She wore a little pendant, a silvery lizard curved at the end of a leather cord. "That guy turned out to be just a standard asshole. Someone from around here who was pissed I'd helped his girlfriend behind his back. It had nothing to do with Bonnie."

I was disappointed, but I pressed on. "Have you seen my mother, though? Maybe she showed up recently, asking about—about Fiona, and—" I glanced around, as if my mother might be hiding in the bougainvillea. "You know what, can I just speak to Tonya? Your mom? She'll know what I'm talking about."

"No." Cate's irises were a brown so deep it nearly obscured her pupils. She was makeupless, her eyebrows unplucked, unruly: they were like punctuation marks, deepening the intensity of her gaze. "You can't talk to her. My mother's dead."

The Bowers' house was low-ceilinged. Shady, cool, private, like a cave. Plants hung from the ceiling, the walls textured with drippy abstract paintings. A box of Kleenex sat on a side table, alongside a cup of something that gave off a fetid smell when I passed. "I have a friend with me," I said, remembering.

Cate pulled aside one of the white curtains to gaze out, her eyes sharpening. "Is he bothering you? Is he dangerous?"

"No," I said, surprised by her urgency. "He's the one who gave me a ride here."

"I didn't ask if you owe him something. I asked if you feel safe with him."

"Yeah," I said. "I do. Mostly. It's—it's a long story. My mother reached out to him before she went missing. He's a reporter and she wanted his help. He got me out of a tough spot. I'm pretty sure Tom's on our side."

"Our side," Cate said. "What makes you think you and me are on the same side?" Then she caught my gaze and laughed, throwing her head back. I was pleasantly disoriented. Both annoyed and intrigued.

Cate let Tom in. He smiled as he entered and she returned it with a chill, a warning look, the traces of her laugh scrubbed out of existence.

"It was ovarian cancer," Cate said, sitting down on a sofa, tucking her long, bare feet beneath her. She patted the cushion next to her, commanding, and I sat. Tom, on his best behavior, chose a small armchair near the doorway, its upholstery dribbling loose. "My mother," Cate went on. "A few years ago. I was barely eighteen. She didn't want to live out her life surrounded by doctors and machines. So she died at home, and I managed to keep it quiet from the press. People around here, they can be protective of us when they need to be. We didn't have to deal with reporters and camera crews."

"I'm sorry for your loss," I said.

"She went out her own way," Cate said, graciously overlooking my awkwardness. "I took a while to recover afterwards. I'd never been without her before, really. I basically slept all day and night for a few months and then I woke up one day and I was back. It helps that people around here need me. Not much time for self-pity." She stretched. "Anyway. What's all this about? Your mother's missing?"

"Yeah. She is." I leaned forward. Through the windows, the filtered murmur and twinkle of the wind chimes made its way inside. "Did my mother get in touch with you at all?"

"She hasn't shown up in person. I don't answer the phone much. If someone needs me, she finds me." Cate gave a quick, sly smile, and I blushed without knowing why. "I would've answered if I'd known it was her, though. My mom always spoke highly of your mother. You were saying something about Fiona?" Before I could answer, Cate rose to her feet, lithe as a cat, firmly muscled. "Tea?"

"I'd love some, thank you," Tom said.

"Orange pekoe okay?" Cate asked, her disapproval cracking just slightly.

"My mother loved that." I remembered the distinctive grassy smell filling our home, trailing from the kitchen or the living room, wherever she'd brought her mug, the scent sweet and acerbic at once.

"All of our mothers did," Cate said softly. "They loved it at the Homestead." She moved into the kitchen, still visible through the narrow arch of a doorway. The clink and clatter of dishes, the hiss and rapid ticking of a gas burner. Through the doorway, a circlet of blue flames rose from the stovetop and I had to look away, my mind filling with the wreckage of my house, the ghostly veil of smoke clinging to our ruined belongings, my mother's stark absence—

"My mother has apparently been asking about Fiona," I called. "Both Emily and Bonnie seem to believe Fiona had powers. Telepathy?"

Cate came to the doorway, leaning against it, arms akimbo. She'd buttoned the shirt wrong, one tail sticking down too far. She widened her eyes, ricocheted a meaningful glance between me and Tom several times: "We're talking about this in front of him?"

I glanced at Tom. He gave me a benign smile back. But I could see how his gaze had turned sharper and brighter, and I realized that he hadn't known this particular detail yet. Only that Fiona was *strange*. I wondered how he'd take this. Would it just sound like nonsense, wild rumors?

"He knows more than you think," I said. "My mother was talking to him."

"I'm on your side," Tom said quickly. "Scout's honor."

"So I hear." Cate shrugged. "Well. It was telekinesis. Not telepathy."

"You've heard about it?" Beneath my eagerness to know more, there was that jealousy again. Everyone else's mother had been sharing secrets with their daughters.

"These kids at school? They used to say I was a witch because only witches don't have fathers," Cate said. "And no man wants to fuck a witch. So I asked my mother if I was a witch, and she said yes, yes I was. At bedtime she'd tell me stories about a girl who didn't have to use her hands the way people did, because her hands were in the air all around her." Cate held up her own hand, bent and flexed her fingers. "One night she let slip that the girl had hair like fire and I thought: *Oh. That girl must be Fiona.*"

"Did she give you any more details?" I asked.

"She said she was going to," Cate said. "On my twenty-fifth birthday. The age my mother was when she had me. But her death was so quick. Ovarian cancer is totally quiet until it's not. I forgot all about that promise. There were so many other things we needed to say."

I reached into my bag for the notebook, holding it open for Cate. "Okay, well, my mother never talked about the Homestead at all. That's why this is so weird. I found her notebook at the house after the fire. She'd apparently been tracking everyone down, all the Homesteaders, and she wrote this: *Tell the world about Fiona.*"

Cate took the notebook and ran a finger over the words. "Fiona," she said. "Wow. Do you know what your mother wanted to say?"

"Since she didn't tell *me* anything, it's tough to narrow it down," I said, hoping the wryness masked the bitterness. "It would have to be Fiona's powers, but why now? After so many years."

Cate looked thoughtful. "My mother held on to a lot of guilt when it came to Fiona. Because of the custody battle, mostly."

Tom piped up: "My understanding was that the custody battle was straightforward. Either Bellanger would take Fiona or she'd be adopted by a different family."

"Okay, let me guess." Cate squinted one eye at Tom. "You're writing a book? Big researcher?" She smiled at Tom's embarrassed nod. "Ah, such a treat for us ladies, another expert ready to explain us to ourselves. Can't wait."

I laughed before I could stop myself, and Tom smiled at his feet, acknowledging the barb.

"Anyway," Cate went on, turning the spotlight of her attention back to me, "there was another option that wasn't well publicized. Fiona could've stayed with one of our mothers."

It felt so obvious and natural now that Cate had said it. The women of the Homestead had been Fiona's ersatz mothers already. In the 1970s, there'd been a breathless tabloid piece about how the mothers took turns nursing all of the babies, not caring which infant latched on, as if we'd each been born to zero fathers and nine mothers.

"The world thought Fiona was better off with any random family as long as they had a golden retriever and a white picket fence and an emotionally distant daddy," Cate said. "Makes about as much sense as her staying with Bellanger's family. God. Stupid, isn't it? Bellanger wasn't even there for his own wife and kids, but he was supposed to make some perfect life for Fiona? Anyway. Poor little girl didn't go with anybody, in the end." Cate handed the notebook back. "It always weighed on my mother. She thought that if they'd just fought harder, maybe Fiona wouldn't have been at the Homestead during the fire."

"What went wrong?" I tried to imagine Fiona living with us. A third member of our family, someone to side with me against my mother during fights. Once, in first grade, inspired by my classmates' beamingly pregnant mothers, I'd asked my mother for a little sister, and she'd just laughed: *One miracle's enough for me, Josephine. I can't afford the grocery bills for two.*

"People already saw our mothers as monsters. How many unmarried women were adopting kids back in the 1970s, even the 'normal' ones? And . . ." Cate hesitated. "The Homestead was falling apart. Some mothers were leaving on their own. There was a big disagreement about which mother Fiona should've gone with. Your mom? My mom? Patricia? Barbara? My impression is that there was some tension between the women."

I thought of Deb's accusations and the pit of my belly tightened. "Cate, what do you know about our mothers *before*? Did any of them know each other before Bellanger started the Homestead?"

A low moan, rising to a sudden shriek. We all twitched with surprise. The teakettle. Cate turned and went back into the kitchen. Tom and I looked at each other in the silence. My own keen curiosity and impatience was reflected in him.

When Cate returned, she was carrying a misshapen handmade mug. She handed the mug to Tom, so abruptly that hot tea sloshed over the edge and nearly caught his thigh: he jerked his leg aside. "You." Cate turned to me, beckoning. "There's something I want to show you."

I trailed Cate down a narrow hallway and into a room at the end of the house. A bedroom, all windows, the bed untidy. An open cookie jar stuffed with a crunchy blend of what looked like old dandelion blossoms and oregano. A notebook was open, showing indecipherable recipes or poems: *espin. colorada? Floripon. Pen. Roy.*

Cate went to the bureau, squatted to yank open the bottom drawer. It was filled with a disarray of papers and old magazines. A few photographs fell out, and one caught my eye. Barbara Kim, Mother Eight, her rope-thick brown braid hanging over her shoulder. She sat next to Lily-Anne, who'd stripped herself of a surname as soon as she'd joined the Homestead—a detail that'd only stoked the growing fears of women casting off family names, family ties, becoming self-contained units. Lily-Anne's hair was a live flame even in the faded photograph. While Barbara sat on one of the many low, molting sofas that had populated the Homestead, Lily-Anne stood and faced the camera proudly. Her belly was round and swollen, and she clasped it like she was holding it aloft. A blurred halo at the edges of their bodies made me think of a self-timer.

"I've never seen this one," I said, like it was a rare collectible. After so many years of memorizing every available Homestead photo, finding a new one was a thrill. I recognized the room they were in, one of the many communal spaces, the wall wild with framed prints and photographs. There was the cut-off edge of a *Time* magazine cover, a patchwork of women's portraits. It tugged at a memory. The year American women had been collectively recognized as Person of the Year.

Next to the *Time* cover, a framed copy of the tawdry, glaring headline that had announced my birth to the world ("MAD SCIENTIST CLAIMS BACHELORETTE'S BABY HAS NO HUMAN FATHER!"). I'd learned to read when I was four, taught by the Mothers, and I remembered sounding out those syllables, not realizing that I knew the people in the headline. That I was the fatherless baby, Bellanger the mad scientist.

"Where'd you get this?" I asked.

"My mother was forward-thinking." Cate winked. "A nicer word for 'paranoid.' People were always trying to buy shit from them back in the seventies. The clothes off their backs. So my mother went through and took photos, letters, whatever, to save them from museums or some weirdo's sock drawer. But that's not what I wanted you to see." Cate plucked something loose, scanned it, and handed it to me. "Maybe it's your mother's?"

It was plain notebook paper, yellowy and brittle. I clutched it delicately, afraid the paper might crumble into dust. The writing was loose, with traces of grade school cursive—the lopsided curlicues of *a*'s and *d*'s—but it was definitely my mother's, the same writing I'd seen on receipts, to-do lists, overdue checks. The same writing that came from my own hands.

The date was listed primly at the top right, like a reflex from an etiquette guide. November 10, 1969. A relic of my mother's life before me. My mother in an undocumented state, the lost years before I'd taken residence in her womb as a lone, moony egg.

Dear Doctor Bellanger:
We are reaching out because we're huge fans of your wild and wonderful brain! We have some questions for you that are of utmost importance and would love a reply if you are amenable to answering them. You may contact us, if you would like, at the below P.O. Box address. We are not scientists or doctors or anything of that sort but we would really appreciate a response. We promise it will be worth your time.

I could see ghostly eraser lines that hinted at a diligent writing process, going through multiple revisions. Dr. Bellanger; November of 1969. Eight months before my infamous conception in July of 1970. "We," I said, touching the words on the page like they could transmit this hidden history through my fingertips. We. Us. Plural pronouns, scattered all over the page, a collective voice rising out of the past. Before this, I'd only seen our mothers as given context by Bellanger. "Deb was right. Our mothers knew each other already."

"Yup. Bellanger was the last to join the Homestead, not the first." Cate sat on the edge of the bed, stretching her legs, pointing her toes. Flecks of grass still striped one shin.

"But I barely ever saw a photo of our mothers together without Bellanger there too. And after his death, we all just scattered. He was our— our nucleus."

"Nucleus," Cate repeated. "Pretty fancy."

I ignored this. Heat rose into my face. "If our mothers knew each other already, if they were friends, or colleagues, or whatever was going on, wouldn't they stay close?" But even as I said it, I remembered Deb's words: *She drew us together, the nine of us, and then she tore us apart.* Cate watched me as I worked it out, feeling more and more flustered, my voice rushing ahead of me. "Yeah, I don't get it. Bellanger wasn't famous until he created us. How did they know about his—" I consulted the letter. "His 'wild and wonderful brain'? Jesus. My mother never showed any interest in science. I would've known. This is crazy."

This had been the topic of plenty of think pieces written about the Homestead. Much was made of the fact that women who'd never even completed a college-level biology course would now grace the covers of *Scientific American.*

"You seem pretty upset by this, Morrow."

"Maybe it's old news to you. But it's— Look. I've met Emily now, and Bonnie, and you. Every one of your mothers told you about the Homestead. My mother shut me out of it. She just didn't trust me. And it's okay. We weren't close, that's all." I was stumbling along, trying to make it sound casual, hide my hurt. "I had to learn everything from Bellanger's letters—"

"Oh right," Cate said. "Your letters. My mom mentioned those." She shifted. "Can I be blunt, Morrow?" That little lizard gleamed at Cate's throat as she idly twisted it, back and forth. "You say you aren't close to your mother, but here you are, hundreds of miles from home, in a stranger's house, trying to find her."

I brushed this away, impatient. "Anyone would do that."

"Nah. No way. A lot of people would let the authorities deal with it. This little road trip of yours isn't exactly standard procedure." Cate gestured at the notebook. "Where'd you find it?"

"Oh. Uh, inside the clock."

"The clock? Funny place to keep something. How did you know to look for it?"

"My mother always hid things inside there, it was like her secret spot when I was little."

"Hid them from—"

"From me. Until I got wise to it." I looked at the notebook, realization dawning, warm and heady. I flipped to the page with the message, dog-eared by now. Maybe the instruction to tell the world about Fiona was a purposeful message. A directive my mother had left, not to herself, but to somebody else.

To me.

"I was thinking," Tom said. "It's obvious something was going on with Fiona. Margaret clearly thought so too. If we figure out what was happening with Fiona, we'll figure out where your mother went. Two birds, one stone. So. Who did Fiona spend the most time with? Who were the two women who stayed at the Homestead till the very end? Margaret Morrow"—a nod at me—"and Patricia Bishop. Patricia must have a full picture of what went on with Fiona, right up until the moment Fiona—" He stopped.

"Died," Cate supplied calmly. "You can say that here. We're grown-ups."

"Patricia's still right there in Daybury," Tom went on. "If anyone can shed some light on your mother's life at the Homestead, it would be her. She can explain this letter too. And what Deb said about how she owned the Homestead's land."

I took a sip of tea to stall for time. "Arkansas to Vermont. That's two days of driving if we make good time. Two days back. If I'm not in Chicago by the weekend, I could lose my place in the program. If I haven't already," I sighed, restless. "This is the worst possible time for this to happen."

"We'll call the Bishops first, then," Tom said. "Just see what they know. If it's a dead end, we'll just get you back to Chicago. Deal?"

"Deal," I agreed.

During dinner that night, I kept my mother's letter right next to my plate, picking at the fresh salad Cate had prepared to complement an assortment of whatever she'd had on hand. Sugary cereal, crackers, half-eaten blocks of cheese, canned ravioli. "I'm not much of a cook," she'd explained. "But I can at least force you to eat your vegetables. I doubt you've been eating well on the road." The salad was shockingly fresh compared to the bagged lettuce I'd always eaten, the big, crisp leaves garnished with a sheen of olive oil and delicate edible flowers.

Cate had allowed the two of us to spend the night, an invitation she'd extended with what I was recognizing as her usual mix of sarcasm and warmth. "Better than wasting your money on some cheap Goulding motel that'll either be full of tourists or drug deals or both," she'd said. But now our meal was tense with an awkward silence. I couldn't calm my mind, my thoughts swirling, bumping up against each other.

"Do you think I'm crazy?" I asked at last. "For going after my mother like this?"

They both looked at me, startled. Tom frowned. "What? Of course not."

"She's your mother," Cate said, as if that alone explained it.

"I'm so worried about her," I said, my eyes stinging with sudden tears. "I don't know what happened. I don't know why she has this note-book, or why she was reaching out to the others. I'm worried that the man who attacked Bonnie came back for her, or maybe another one of Peters's followers. I want to know she's safe, and I want to know what she's looking for, and then I also . . ."

"Also what?" Cate asked gently, when I paused for too long. She twirled her fork, which impaled the bright yellow of a dandelion.

"My mother never wanted me to do this. Any of this. She didn't approve of the letters Bellanger left me. I used to beg her to read them aloud to me when I was too young, and she wouldn't. I had to wait till I was older. If she caught me reading the letters, she gave me the silent treatment. She thought it was all a phase. When I told her I wanted to pursue experimental embryology, she barely spoke to me for a week. So the fact that my mother has disappeared right at the worst possible time for me? Right at the end of the first year?" I hesitated, not sure if I could put it into words. "What if it's all on purpose?"

Cate examined me, still twirling the fork. The watercolors in here were deeper tones, reds and purples, stormier and richer than the greenery in the living room. I looked down, flicking away my half-angry tears. Tom waited, then grabbed one of Cate's mismatched cloth napkins and handed it to me. I accepted, a little embarrassed.

"It feels like I have to choose," I said. "My mother, or Bellanger. I never wanted to make that choice. *She's* the one who turned it into a competition."

"I can only imagine how weird this all is for you, Josie," Tom said.

Cate bit her lip, then clattered down her fork decisively. "That seems pretty ungenerous to your mom, Morrow," she said. "The woman's clearly in trouble, I don't think she was doing this to mess up your exams."

I prickled. "It just seems strange, that's all. And my work is important. It's not only about the exams, you know, it's—it's restoring a legacy that'd been lost, it's trying to change the world for—for other women—"

Under Cate's intent gaze, I found myself tongue-tied and defensive, but also, weirdly, excited at the prospect of proving myself to her. "Oh yeah?" she asked. "How so?"

Steadying myself, I leaned back. "How much do you know about my work?"

"As much as you've shared with the press, plus my own research," Tom said, jumping in. "I can follow along with the basics. You're attempting to finish what Bellanger started."

"I don't know jackshit," Cate said. "I haven't been following along. We aren't all fanboys." But a little glimmer in her eyes, a challenge tucked there, made me wonder if she was telling the truth. "So why don't you explain it to the rest of us?"

I fidgeted with the tear-damp napkin. "Bellanger wanted to make his research accessible, turn it into something reproducible and tangible. A medication women could take, like clomifene. I'm retracing his steps so I can do that. Or . . . well. Trying to."

Cate leaned forward, knees wide, folding her hands underneath her chin. I liked that: someone who listened with her whole body.

"What he did basically comes down to genomic imprinting," I said. "That's the way DNA is marked with important genetic data, including paternal or maternal origins."

"Which is the interesting part," Tom cut in. "Bellanger was messing with the very ways that certain genes are expressed or silenced during conception. It was revolutionary, what he managed to do—"

Cate held up a hand. "Please. Thomas. Let the lady finish."

"I guess the easiest way of thinking about it," I said, "is that whenever a mammal reproduces, the mother is a lock, and the father is the key. Mammals need both the lock and the key to create a functioning, fully formed infant, whether it's a—a lab mouse or a human being. But you have to realize that the lock isn't necessary. Other animals—oh, like reptiles, amphibians, fish, insects—they don't need a key because they don't have this lock. But somewhere in our evolutionary history, mammals locked the door."

"So Bellanger invented a key that unlocked parthenogenesis?" Cate asked.

Tom started to answer, fell silent at a look from Cate, pressed his lips together, and twisted his fingers in a *my-lips-are-sealed* gesture.

"Not exactly," I said. "Bellanger's trick wasn't to make a new key. Because, think about it. If you take away the lock, you don't need the key at all, right? You can just walk through the door. No key necessary. That's all Bellanger did. He removed the locks from our mothers, and so a father's key was no longer needed. But," I added, deflating a little, "we aren't sure exactly how he did it, and long story short, that's why I'm at the University of Chicago."

I felt that old buzz of focus—a mix of excitement and control. Taking a question and examining it from all angles. Dr. McCarter's research project was bolstered by the kind of plummy funding I hoped to secure for myself one day. The more I delved into Bellanger's world, the more impossible it seemed that I actually existed. I hadn't ended as an arrested blastocyst, noted down in a scientific abstract and then forgotten by the world, but had become a woman, standing in a lab in a scratchy white coat, peering through the microscope to watch the natural world creep closer to what had already been accomplished inside my body.

Inside my mother's body.

"Well," Tom said. "If anyone's going to do it, it's going to be you, Josie."

I nodded a quick thanks, but I found myself looking across the table at Cate, who gave me a small smile, a sliver of approval, that ignited in my chest as if a fire had been lit there.

16

Little hands were in the air. All over the air. Little hands, the thumbs interlocking, flapping like wings, like big moths, like pale birds. They pressed into the room so tightly, fluttering so thickly, that the air turned hot. Stifling. The hands were slipping over my mouth. Over my nose. *Ssh, ssh.* I was sweltering, sweat-sticky, couldn't draw a breath. Hands over my mouth. Hands on my chest, pressing down, pressing down, and I tried to gasp but couldn't—

"Morrow." I opened my eyes, slowly. No hands over my eyes, but the room was dark, dark. My eyes were stinging and gritty. The voice floated above me, urgent. "Come on. We have to get out of here."

I sat up. The ghostly hands were gone, but I still couldn't see. Everything was hazy, a strange fuzz across the air even in the dark, and I kept having the impulse to open my eyes again. Like there was a second layer to my eyelids.

Cate grabbed my hand, dragging me out of bed. I stumbled behind her, too surprised to fight back. Smoke, hanging greasy in the air. A primal memory kicked in, my mother's hand in mine, the two of us running, running. The trees transformed, all that tender summer greenery replaced with red, yellow, the choking blackness of the smoke.

She was there, for a minute. My mother. Hair to her waist. Feet bare, soles flashing. Her long arm reaching back, tethering me to her, and then she turned around and she smiled at me, a bright, hard smile, though the world around us was burning.

"Morrow," Cate said, voice muffled. "You have to go faster."

My mother vanished. We passed through Cate's living room, the front door hanging open, the night visible outside, clean and silver-blue and moonlit. The living room was illuminated with a harsh, unnatural glare, everything weirdly shadowed. The heat was so intense it itched.

I looked back at the kitchen as Cate dragged me toward the door, the flames licking their way up the cabinets.

The night was clear and cool. It was like stepping into cold water at first. I gasped. Cate let go of my hand and I nearly fell into her. The wind chimes cast long-fingered shadows onto the road. I was trying to understand, to shake off the last of sleep. Another fire. Cate's house was on fire.

"Your friend's still in there." Cate had something—a dishrag, damp—clamped over her mouth and nose, but her exposed eyes were raw and red, watering. Before I could say anything, she'd vanished back into that hot and airless space.

I stood in my T-shirt and underwear, legs exposed, the ache in my eyes and throat ebbing slowly. The moon was a fat crescent. In patches, the clouds broke to reveal brilliant clusters of stars. I patted myself down, panicky. The letter and notebook must still be where I'd left them when I fell asleep, tucked under the pillow in Cate's spare room. Shit. My mother's handwriting was going to be lost in the blaze. I'd gotten her back, even in such a tiny form, and now she was being tugged down into the same fate.

A light prickle across my shoulder blades, like I was being watched. The houses on this shady street were spaced far apart, no lights on in any windows. I turned. There, down the street—in a little dip, where the shadows collected more thickly under an outcropping of tree branches. A silhouette. Someone tall stood, motionless, watching me. For a minute I was sure it was my sleep-soaked mind playing tricks. A tree trunk or a pole, transfigured into a person by darkness and paranoia.

He began walking toward me, a few steps.

I moved toward him too, unhesitating. He stopped.

Behind me, a flurry of movement as Tom and Cate lurched through the open doorway, Tom bent over as he wheezed, Cate awkwardly angled beneath his body to keep him upright. I noticed that Tom was holding something—the notebook, my mother's notebook, thank god—and then returned my attention to the shadowed figure.

I took another step forward, and adrenaline hit me in a woozy rush. The man took a step backward now. Too quickly, he turned and

launched himself into the shadows, racing up the steep curve of the hill.
I took off after him. The man was up ahead not fifteen yards.

I heard nothing but the pavement slapping beneath my feet, the
scattered rhythm of my heartbeat. I was out of shape, my lungs turning
tight, and I couldn't go too fast without shoes—already my soles were
burning. I tried to memorize all the details I could. He wore a dark suit.
The jacket flapped open when he passed one of the bright pools cast by
a rare streetlight. I tried to make out his features, but he was focused,
never once looking behind him. I couldn't close that gap that hovered
between us.

Most of all, I wanted to look into his eyes. To feel that dizziness that
I now associated with reaching into the world and getting what I wanted
from it. "Stop," I called, but it came out thinned and unconvincing, and
the stranger's footsteps didn't falter.

At the top of the hill, he intersected with the trees and the shadows
in a way that hid him for a second too long, and I stopped, scanning desperately. There was a flicker of movement. Just a squirrel racing across
the road. I limped to the top of the hill, seeing only trees and road, pavement lacy with the shadows of the branches. Nobody else. Nothing else.

Down the street, a sudden slam. Lights blazed on, twin circles. A car
separated from the deep darkness at the side of the road, hiccupping as
it went over the curb, too fast for the narrow road. The license plate in
the front, shiny white, caught the moonlight and I tried to memorize ·
the plates, but it was too dark, I only caught the bright red logo near the
top, the chipper cursive loop of a state name. A V or a U—

The headlights engulfed me completely, a chemical glare of white,
like a surgery light bearing down. In my wildness, I considered standing
there until he either stopped or ran me over. But at the last second my
instincts took over and yanked me back, and the car was gone before I'd
blinked the starbursts from my eyes. The maroon sedan I'd seen outside
my mother's house the night after the fire.

At sunrise, the three of us were in the backyard. Cate couldn't keep still.
She wore a loose tie-dyed T-shirt that reached her knees, a faded stir of

blues and greens. With her half-tangled hair clouding out around her, rage burning in her eyes, she paced the perimeter of the yard. Tom and I both sat stunned on the dew-damp grass. Back here, in the garden, things felt safer. The flowers were a protective shield all around us. The air was filled with birdsong, the sky lavender and then hot orange and then a cleansing yellow.

"The work I do here," Cate said abruptly. "The work I do here is with women who need safety. And protection. I can't ask them to come here. Not when someone is trying to kill me. Not when he knows where I fucking *live*."

The fire had been mostly contained within the kitchen, which was destroyed now. The official diagnosis was that a dish towel had caught on fire, spreading to the clutter on the counter nearby, the tea boxes and oven mitts. The firefighters had efficiently lectured us, believing it was one of us who'd left the burner on and then drifted to sleep. An unfortunate but unremarkable household incident. I hadn't brought up the sedan until the firefighters had left.

"Maybe he was a rubbernecker." Cate was bargaining, turning a gaze toward me that was equal parts accusation and pleading. "Just the typical gawker."

"I don't think so, Cate." I didn't see any point in comforting lies right now: not with her house behind us, a deep hole puncturing the roof above the kitchen. "Why would his car have been hidden way up the road? Why would he have run away instead of calling for help? And . . ." I had to tell them. "I've seen his car before. He may've been following us for a while." I quickly explained, noting Tom's honed interest.

"Did you get the plate numbers?" Tom asked.

"No, but I saw a V or a U."

"Not from around here, then. That's a long way to come just to rubberneck," Tom said.

"Think about it. He's like Bonnie's attacker in two ways. He ran away immediately, and he acted after dark, when nobody could identify him." I ticked these off on my fingers.

"Then why not attack us in our beds?" Cate asked. "He could've just—" She made a quick slicing gesture across her throat, the blade of one finger pressing into her skin. I flinched.

"This attack might not be exactly like Bonnie's," I said, "but it's exactly the same as my mother's."

"But your mother vanished," Tom said. "We're still here."

I was still here. I was sitting with the sun moving hot across my skin, with the wet grass piercing my thighs.

"My home is ruined. My business is gone. Nothing is safe," Cate said, a dull litany. "And, what?" Cate turned on us. "You two come into my life, you raise hell, and now you're just going to fuck off into the horizon." She flung her hand upward, a sweeping gesture that didn't conceal the surprising ache in her voice. She was hurt. I hadn't expected this; I'd thought she'd be relieved to see us go.

"I don't know where we're even fucking off *to*." Tom sounded tired. The Bishops hadn't answered our calls. We'd spent all evening calling and reached only their brisk, chilly answering machine. *This is Patricia Bishop, please leave a message.* It was Wednesday morning and I didn't feel much closer to figuring out where my mother had gone. I could be home by tonight, back in the lab by morning.

Cate dropped to the ground in a low crouch, kneeling with her head bent. She groaned.

"If I go back to Chicago," I said suddenly, "what will you do, Tom?"

He blinked, lifted his glasses to scrub at one pink-rimmed eye. "I'll go to Vermont. I still want to talk to the Bishops for my book, if nothing else. I'm not ready to walk away from this."

Tightness clamped around my heart; I felt territorial, jealous. Tom going on without me, hunting through my history. Now I was torn. I did truly want to return to Chicago. I wasn't at the school as a publicity stunt. I was there because I belonged, using the brain that Bellanger had created to make him proud.

But I looked down at the notebook that Tom had managed to retrieve from Cate's house last night. What if Cate was right? What if finding my mother's notebook inside her cheap broken clock hadn't been an accident but a message? *Come find me, Josephine.* It was the first time

I'd felt my mother actively pulling me into our past. Inviting me in. How long had I waited for this?

"Okay," I said. "Maybe I have time to go to Vermont. I mean, who knows—what if my mother is there? With Patricia. She visited Emily, she visited Deb—"

Tom looked at me like he didn't quite believe me, though already a smile was building at the corners of his mouth. "Yeah?"

"Do you think there's any hope of returning to Chicago by the weekend if we do this?"

"We'll drive all night if we have to."

"One last stop," I said. "What's one more?"

Cate straightened. She stood, swaying, looking down at us. Her face was calm and unyielding now. "If you're going, then I'm going with you," she said.

My heart jumped.

"You're welcome to come," Tom said. "Of course—but it's also a big decision, and—"

Cate held out a palm, stanching his words. "I know how to make a big decision. I don't need your permission here." She looked at me. "Josie? This is a search for your mother. I don't want to intrude."

"You'd just leave everything?" The idea of Cate coming along with us was unexpectedly happy, a brightness that nearly made me forget the smoke leaking into the morning sky.

"Goulding can wait. It'll be here when I get back." She was different now, that anger turned, through some private alchemy, into resolve. "This may be my best chance to find out what my mother was going to tell me after all these years. Maybe my mom would've wanted this."

"This is the second attack on a Homesteader in the past week," I said. "It all has to lead back to Ricky Peters. That's the cleanest explanation, isn't it? Occam's razor and all that. The three attacks must be connected. Bonnie's, my mother's, this one."

Cate was inside packing while Tom and I were loading our suitcases into the trunk. Everything reeked of smoke now. We'd carry it away with us. Tom was quiet, focusing on the task at hand. Usually he was totally forthcoming with his own theories. His silence grated.

"What?" I was sizzling with nerves. I gave his suitcase an unnecessarily hard shove with my elbow. "Why aren't you saying anything?"

Still, he held fire for a second. "Josie," he said, not looking at me, resting his hands on the lip of the trunk. "Listen. You want to know what my book is about? What's going to make it stand out?" He took a deep breath. "I'm not convinced that Ricky Peters had anything to do with Bellanger's death."

I stepped back, startled and then annoyed. The fact that Ricky Peters had murdered Bellanger—and in so doing had robbed me of my chance to know my sort-of father, had cut off the bright future I'd meant to herald into existence—that was a given. In every account about the final days of the Homestead, historians and journalists and fans and critics largely agreed that Ricky Peters murdered Dr. Joseph Bellanger. "Be serious," I snapped.

"I didn't want to say anything."

"Peters killed Bellanger. He was convicted, he pled guilty, for fuck's sake—"

"The evidence was circumstantial." Tom looked at me, impatience starting to edge into his voice too. "Peters still claims that he was set up, forced into a plea deal. You've never had doubts?"

"Ricky himself said that Bellanger would burn in hell, the week of the fire. It was caught on camera." I clenched and unclenched my fists. "Even in prison, he's been convincing half the country to hate us for the past two decades."

Tom rubbed his neck, looking unconvinced. "Look, what I think is that . . . uh . . . Bellanger was a complicated man. A man who challenged everything we know about reproduction. But Ricky Peters as a villain is simple. Too simple. He's a stock character from a morality play. Science versus religion. What if we convicted him because it was the simplest answer?"

"Yeah, well. From where I stand, a lot of good things in this world are destroyed by simple men."

Tom gazed at me for a second, then took a deep breath. "I don't want to fight about it right now," he said. "That's why I didn't want to say anything. Forget it. I'm going to get my bags—"

Cate passed him as he walked back to the house, did a little double-take at his expression. "Lovers' quarrel?" she asked me, raising her eyebrows.

"It's nothing. I'm just on edge. We're all on edge."

She gave me a searching look.

"What if I'm just making things worse for everyone?" I asked impulsively. "If we hadn't come to see you, you'd be fine now. We brought that man here. He's been following us all this time." If I'd confronted the driver way back, the first night I arrived in Coeur du Lac—if I'd trusted my instincts instead of reaching for fear and caution, I could've pulled what I needed from him instead of turning myself into a target, oblivious, not sure who was chasing me or why.

Cate shoved a box aside to make room for her things. The box was filled with books about the Homestead. *Experimental Embryology: A Manual and History. The Virgin Farce: The True Story of Joseph Bellanger.* Deb's memoir, her face gleaming a Crest-ad grin up at me.

"Hey, don't let that weigh on you," Cate said. "You know what I think? With everything going on? That man wasn't here just because of you. He would've been here anyway. That's why we need to find the others." She slammed the trunk shut. "To warn them."

17

"So, Tom. Thomas Abbott." Cate ate a fry, neatly, in three deliberate bites. "What's your story, young man?" She hung over the edge of my seat as we drove, breath warm on my neck.

The Volvo smelled like the fire, a constant reminder of last night. I checked the rearview mirror compulsively, scanning for a car following us. Nothing so far.

"Kind of a waste to talk about my story when I'm with the two of you." After our argument, Tom was a little stiff around the edges, but I saw him soften under her attention.

"Start with that, then." The bag rustled as Cate fished for another fry, though the food had gone cold an hour ago. "What's so interesting about the Homestead? Are you a weirdo? One of those guys who say our mothers wouldn't be virgins anymore if you could just get your hands on them?" She waggled her eyebrows.

Virgin birth had always been a colloquialism, fitting our mothers uncomfortably. It was the births that were virginal, not necessarily the mothers. Late-night hosts, politicians, medical researchers: they loved to speculate about our mothers' sexual histories, with Bellanger himself being the most obvious Lothario. Of all the mothers, mine had been paired with Bellanger the most often. I'd assumed it was because she came first in line. Now, knowing what I did about my mother's earnest letter, I wondered if it was something deeper. A compellingly odd couple: Bellanger's easy confidence, my mother's tentative smile. I'd seen the editorial cartoon of my mother crowned with a Virgin Mary halo as a leering Bellanger threw her on a bed and undid his belt.

"Nah, it's not like that at all." A blush reddened the back of Tom's neck. "There hasn't been a book published about the Homestead for nearly ten years now. The eight of you have grown up and the world is moving on, people care more about—I don't know, IVF and sperm banks than what Bellanger did. I just wanted to revisit Bellanger's legacy and shed some more light on what he actually accomplished. I know it's a long shot. I'd almost given up on it when Margaret called me out of the blue."

Cate leaned back. "Hmm. You know what I'd like to see? A book that discusses the way the Homestead affected *women's* lives. You writer types love to obsess over the lost science, or Bellanger's grandstanding, or the dead bodies. But what about the way it impacted women? Like, maybe it wasn't strange for a single woman to raise a baby alone. Maybe it was a miracle instead." In the rearview mirror, I caught the intensity of her gaze. "I hope whoever follows in Bellanger's footsteps pays more attention to that."

This felt pointed. Before I could defend myself, Tom was talking.

"Oh, I agree," he said. "One hundred percent. Personally, I've always wondered if Bellanger's work has been less kosher because it involved women's lives. That is, women's independence." He glanced back at her, hopeful, looking for praise. "My mom raised me singlehandedly."

"Oh yeah?" Cate asked. "Shit dad?"

"Never even met the guy. Total deadbeat. As far as I'm concerned, there are a lot of kids out there without a father, you know? One way or another."

Cate's voice relaxed just slightly. "Your mother must've gone through a lot."

Tom nodded and shrugged at the same time, apparently embarrassed that he'd said too much. "I'm trying to be thoughtful," he said. "With this book. Respectful. Just so you know."

I couldn't resist a little barb: "How does figuring out Bellanger's *real* murderer factor into your plans for the book?"

"All part of figuring out who Bellanger really was," Tom said, unfazed.

Cate piped up: "Just don't forget that we're human beings with actual lives. I have people to protect."

"What exactly do you do?" Tom asked. "You're some kind of doctor?"

"I help women. Whatever that means to them."

"Just like Josie's in med school," Tom said.

"Well, I'm a little less interested in the publicity side of things," Cate said. "You were appearing on every damn talk show for a while there, Morrow." I wanted to say that it had been a reasonable number—just three programs—but I bit my tongue. "So you're following in Bellanger's footsteps, huh? Experimental embryologist. Just like him."

"Just like him," I echoed, defiant. Cate cultivated a nonchalance about Bellanger that verged on hostility. It rankled me, a nagging defensiveness. It wasn't the first time I'd considered that this devotion hadn't been passed down to all nine of us. I knew my role as Girl One, the oldest, the favorite, put me in a unique position.

"Watch out," Cate said. "I've seen med school turn people into real assholes."

"Exactly the kind of thing an asshole would say," I shot back.

Cate waited a second, then threw her head back, her big, full laugh bouncing around inside the car. "Okay. You got me, Morrow. But I've seen what can happen. People in Goulding don't always have the money for doctors. Or they've been hurt by them. After the Homestead, my mother started helping. She knew which herbs could soothe a sore throat or ease postpartum depression or kill a flu. People need an alternative."

"I never realized your mother had any medical training," Tom said. "That's fascinating." I noticed a shift in his voice now, switching into the glossy interview tone he'd used with Deb, like he was stepping closer with a magnifying glass. "Did she train with Bellanger at all?"

"Not that she told me."

"So did she—do you—ever work with pregnant women?"

"Why do you ask?" Cate was cool, cautious. She caught the prying note too.

"Because of where you come from. Because of who your mother is. Was."

"Yes, Thomas," Cate said. "My mother helped pregnant women. She taught me how to deliver a baby when I was sixteen. I help however I can now that she's gone. Sometimes it's delivering a baby for a woman whose last doctor tried to convince her she was too weak to do it on her own. I've seen women who'd been traumatized by forceps or so drugged they couldn't remember anything." I thought of the look the woman had given my belly before giving me directions to Cate's home. "And sometimes it means ending pregnancies, if that's how I'm needed. At its best, what Bellanger accomplished was supposed to be giving women choice and control. That's what I'm doing too." She gave me a quick look. "And I hope it's what you're planning on doing, Morrow."

When we stopped that night, Tom slept in the car, volunteering his duties as a sentinel, leaving the single bed to me and Cate. I lay on my side, watching the thin curtains, imagining a silhouette rising. A struck match: a knife blade.

"Are you planning to fuck that guy?" Cate asked, like she'd been having this conversation in her head for a while and had finally decided to let me in. She rolled over. Even in bed, she wore that necklace, the curves catching the light. "Is that what's happening here?"

"No. Come on. Tom's a—a colleague."

"You have a boyfriend, though? You seem that type."

I considered telling her about Dr. McCarter, the closest thing to a boyfriend I'd had for a while. "Well, I'm not a virgin," I said instead. "I'm not my mother."

Cate barked with appreciative laughter. "Let me guess. The boyfriend: Mike or Joe or Jason. He's an understanding guy. He *forgives* you for your past. Or maybe he gets off on it."

"Just because men are like that with you—"

"Men aren't any way with me. And I'm not any way with them." My heartbeat settled in my throat. Cate shifted, turning over onto her back, and I glanced sidelong at the shape of her, stretched long under the covers. "I knew I was gay from when I was a little girl. The idea of being with a man never even occurred to me. My mother didn't have too much time for dating, but she only ever brought women home. All of us should be lesbians, scientifically speaking. We were made without men. What do we want with them now?"

The room felt smaller, more intimate, the air suddenly charged. I was intently aware of Cate next to me, long hair spread across the pillow and nearly touching me. She smelled like sweat—briny and sweet at once—overlaid with the peppermint sting of her castile soap. Stubbornly, I wanted to point out that Cate wasn't entirely right; Bellanger had been involved every step of the way. But I was distracted, thinking about the thin space between our two bodies, my pulse quickening.

"A girl at my high school was a lesbian," I offered instead.

"Was? It's not a temporary state."

"Yeah, sorry. Is. I just don't know her anymore."

Lacey. That was her name. She'd dyed her shiny, shoulder-length hair with Kool-Aid sometimes, neon colors against her otherwise plain outfits. Like me, she'd stayed on the fringes of things, biding her time, keeping her head down. One time—in line in the cafeteria—she'd told me how much she liked my backpack, and a square-jawed kid a few spots down had started stage-whispering, "Man-haters club," until Lacey and I had wordlessly gone to opposite sides of the cafeteria.

"Yes, we're all over the place, I hear. Dozens of us," Cate deadpanned, and I started to apologize, not sure why this memory of Lacey had only made me more flustered, but she went on. "I'd almost respect you more if you just wanted to sleep with Thomas. Better than thinking he's a savior who's going to find your mom. 'Cause, from my perspective? You seem to be doing most of the legwork."

I hesitated, remembering Emily in the attic, the predictions that had stuck with me. "If I tell you something, will you think I'm crazy?"

"I won't," Cate said, matter-of-fact, like that wasn't an option.

It was easier to tell her while lying in the dark, listening to her soft breathing, not having to watch her face. Emily French, Girl Five. The people coming through the glass. The birds falling. Those words that could have been future-touched, brought to us by a different time. Me, lost, alone; Tom leading me to my mother. "What if there's something strange about each of us?" I asked when I was done telling her. "Something special . . ." I trailed off.

We lay there together, silent for a while. "Hey." Cate propped herself up on one elbow, resting her head in her hand. "I'm a healer. You know that much." I waited, sensing by the intimate shift in her voice that this was important. "My mother helped people with herbs. She'd give women comfrey-leaf baths to heal their tearing or a red clover infusion to regulate their cycles. It was all in knowing when to administer the right medicine. She taught me to do that too. I was proud of the work I did. But for me, ever since I changed, it's something else too."

"What do you mean by *changed*?"

"Things became real," Cate said simply. "One day a woman brought her daughter to me. The kid had broken her wrist. Her arm was bulging. Curved, like she was wearing gloves that were too big for her. I kept telling this woman to take her daughter to the emergency room, but she was paranoid as hell. Living off the grid and convinced doctors and the FBI were all in it together. I could see what would happen. She'd let her daughter's wrist heal without a cast and it would always give her problems. It was up to me. So I . . ." Cate sat up, leaned forward, took my wrist very gently. She held it, cradled it, and the warmth grew, a faint and pleasurable pins-and-needles sensation, beneath her touch.

"I had to hold her wrist for half an hour, maybe. I had to tell them to be patient, because I knew it was working. I couldn't let myself doubt myself. Then that girl walked out of there as if nothing had even happened. She shook my hand when she left, nice strong little grip." Cate let go of my wrist, fell back into bed. "My mother did her best, and she was good. I thought following in her footsteps was enough for me. But now I know I'm real. Like everything else was just practice for who I am now."

"That's why you weren't surprised," I said softly. "About Fiona's . . . abilities."

I felt Cate's smile in the dark beside me. "It crossed my mind that it has something to do with the way we were born. But it's also just who I am, you know?" She paused for a minute, impatient, then brightened. "Like when you're first having sex, right? You go through the motions, and it's good, it feels fine, and you think you're doing it. But then the first time you're with someone that you *really-really* like—and she knows what she's doing—and it actually works for you and you realize—*this* is sex. And it makes you look back at all the other times and think, yes it was fine, but was it *this*? Was it real?"

It was unfamiliar to me, the way Cate described her abilities. *Real.* Not strange. A return to what she'd already been, not a departure to unexplored lands. "I could feel it," I said. "When you touched me just then? Like a tingling."

Cate was quiet for a long moment.

"What?" I asked, nervous I'd said the wrong thing.

Her voice was gentle, verging on laughter. "I wasn't actually doing anything. I don't know what you felt, but I wasn't healing you. Hard to heal you when there's no wound."

"Sorry. Forget it." That warmth spread at my pulse points. Cate could turn me clumsy and awkward so quickly; I tried to find it annoying.

"So what about you, Josephine Morrow? Girl One? You have anything special about you?"

"Maybe." Even that one word, coy and hesitant, felt dangerous in my mouth, like the time I'd licked a nine-volt battery on a dare as a kid. That hot spark against my tongue.

Her eyes glimmered in the dark. "Do tell."

"I can't talk about it. Not yet. It's not the same as with you. Just— look, please don't tell Tom yet? I want to figure out what's happening first."

"Yeah. Um. Of course I'm not going to tell *Thomas*," Cate said, affronted that I'd even ask. "But if you want to talk about it, I'm here."

We lasted another few minutes in silence before I broke. "You're so casual about it. Like it's part of your life already. But I'm out there in the public eye. I'm trying to finish what Bellanger started, restore everything we lost when he died. How do I—how does this even fit into my life?"

"What did we lose when he died?" Cate asked.

I hesitated, surprised by the question: first because the answer seemed so obvious, and then because I struggled to articulate it. "The chance for there to be more of us."

"Hmm. Yeah." Cate sounded thoughtful. "So you're worried about your credibility if you yammer to your scientist friends about superpowers?"

"Sort of," I said. "Scientists are supposed to be cold and rational, but I think we have to be more curious than other people. *More* open to impossible questions. Why else would Bellanger have taken a chance as big as the one he did? But if we have . . . powers . . ."—that word felt less corny every time I said it, taking on a weight and energy—"then I'm treading new ground here, and maybe I'm not ready yet." I pressed the heels of my palms into my eyes until I saw starbursts. "I wish Bellanger could've known about it. That's all. What if he'd known what he'd actually achieved?"

Cate was quiet for long enough that I assumed she'd fallen asleep. Her hand found mine in the darkness, threading her fingers through mine, squeezing my hand swiftly. "I know you were close to him. For what it's worth? I bet he'd be fucking proud of you if he could see you now. He'd be an idiot otherwise." She let go of my hand. "You're not alone as you think. There is somebody who'll answer your questions. We've just got to find her."

Catching her meaning, I smiled into the dark room, rueful. "Mother One," I whispered, and my mother felt at once very close, closer than she'd been in years, and impossibly far away.

18

We arrived in Vermont in the late afternoon. I'd watched the landscape change outside the windows, a topography hillier and greener than I was used to, the billboards less insistent about meeting God. Even the run-down areas were quaint instead of dilapidated. Sometimes we'd drive past nothing but trees for close to half an hour, then suddenly the trees would break to reveal white houses nestled along the side of the road, barns overgrown with ivy.

I was a native Vermonter. When I thought about my past, the weirdness of my birth usually obscured the more commonplace facts, like my star sign (Taurus), my birth weight (seven pounds even). But this part of the country was my birthplace, and I looked around, wondering if it had shaped my DNA. When I said as much to Cate, she laughed. "You know we barely ever left that compound?" she asked. "Only about ten acres of the great state of Vermont can claim any effect on us."

"Do you have any memories of that time?" Tom asked, glancing back at Cate.

"Why? In the market for some good footnotes?" When he winced, she went on: "Nothing personal, but I know how writers can get. A while ago, one of the Homesteaders had this big-shot interview in *Rolling Stone*. I heard she made a real fool of herself. Good reminder to always watch what I say when there's a tape recorder nearby."

"I'm not recording anything," Tom said, wounded. I was quiet. "Come As You Are" wailed from the radio. An endless refrain of Kurt Cobain lately. *Memoria, memoria.*

"That was me," I said at last. "I was the one interviewed in *Rolling Stone.*"

"Shit," Cate said. "That was you?" She leaned forward so that she was between us, elbows poking out like wings. "Morrow. I wouldn't have said anything if—"

"Oh, I think you knew," I interrupted, and Cate bit down a sly smile, eyes shining with suppressed laughter. We passed a covered bridge, candy-apple red, nestled among the trees. "Look, I wanted to do it. I never got to talk about the Homestead, growing up."

"What'd your mother think about it?" Tom asked.

"We weren't speaking by then." Pines rose in peaks on either side of the road, casting spiky shadows over half the freeway. The sky beyond was a blue so clean and bright that I wanted to dip my fingers into it. "I actually tried to call her. I was proud of that interview. *Rolling Stone!* But she never picked up."

"What could even *make* you ignore each other for a year?" Cate asked. "I'd give anything to talk to my mom again."

"We're stubborn." That stubbornness, replicated perfectly, not leavened by the genetic influence of a father. "She always wanted me to go along with her and pretend our lives together in Coeur du Lac were all we'd ever known. Coeur du Lac, god. Mom went out of her way to pick the most ordinary town she could. Like I was ordinary too instead of—instead of what I am. What we are." I gestured at Cate, and she nodded, soberer now, listening. We telegraphed a quiet understanding over Tom's head.

"Maybe the normal routine would've worked if I'd been younger," I said. "Maybe Barbara Kim could convince her daughter that Bellanger never existed. Helen was only two years old when the fire happened. I was *six* when Bellanger died. I couldn't forget him if I tried. You know he used to let me help him in his lab? When we ran from the Homestead, I didn't even believe he was dead. I would wake up screaming for him."

"Of course you never had a chance to be close to your mom," Cate said softly. "You were too busy missing him."

"My mom and I were close," I said, defensive. "When I was little, she'd stay up all night if I had a nightmare, or sing lullabies to distract me. I woke up crying for him, but she was there instead." I stared out the window. Nirvana on the radio again: *Distill the life that's inside of me.* "She'd always helped me with my school projects. We'd work together

to make posters of nineteenth century novelists, or a tornado in a pop
bottle. She always knew these random facts about whatever we were
working on. Nathaniel Hawthorne and Louisa May Alcott lived next
door to each other, or the F scale for tornadoes is named after Ted Fu-
jita. I looked forward to homework because of her. But in seventh grade
I wanted to make a presentation on the Homestead. Bring in Bellanger's
letters for show-and-tell. Mom just shut down. She wouldn't help me
with anything. After that I was so mad, I didn't ask for her help with any
of my other projects. And she stopped offering."

Cate nodded as if to herself, gazing out the window. I wondered if
she understood.

"I always wanted the Homestead to bring us closer," I said. "But she
always made it so the Homestead stood between us. Every choice I made,
it felt like I was moving farther from being identical to my mother. She
wanted to hide, I wanted to be . . ."

"Famous?" Cate asked.

I shrugged, nodded. "Something like that. Anyway. It was easier to
just fight."

Cate stretched her arms over her head, clasped hands bumping the
ceiling. "Well, now you know your mother had a different role. Maybe
she had her reasons to hide that from you."

"Why hide the truth? I deserved to know. She was just protecting
herself."

"Maybe," Cate said, "she wasn't protecting herself. Maybe she was
protecting you."

19

Excerpt from *Rolling Stone* magazine—September 17, 1993

A Miracle Baby, All Grown Up

On the topic of Dr. Joseph Bellanger, the late genius who masterminded the experiment that led to her birth, Josephine Morrow lights up as if someone mentioned a rock star. "You know how people say we're his 'brainchildren'? Then that makes him my brainfather," she says as we sit in a small Illinois diner. It's just the kind of delightful neologism you'd expect from a girl who's an evolutionary neologism herself.

I get a chance to ask the big question that's on everybody's mind. When you're forever connected to the word "virgin," what is it like to do the deed, bump uglies, knock boots? "I have all the parts, if that's what you're asking," Josephine says. "Yes, sex is physically possible for me. And yes, I've done it."

This is interesting news from a girl who's studying how to take the sex right out of reproduction. Josephine insists that she's not trying to create a world without men, contrary to popular belief. "I don't want to scare anyone away," she says. "Bellanger is a man, after all, and he's my biggest inspiration. This is about science, not feminism."

So if Josephine had the chance to go back in time and work with Dr. Joseph Bellanger—if she was in the same position as her mother, many years before—would she do it? Would she agree to be part of the experiments that made her own mother famous?

Josephine thinks about this for a while. "I'm not sure I'm ready to be a mother," she says, flipping her long, dark hair over one shoulder. "But I'd love a chance to work with Bellanger as an adult, more than anything. So yes. I'd say yes."

20

The NO TRESPASSING signs started out small. A modest sign on a tree trunk, discreet, almost quaint. By the time we reached the driveway proper, the signs were cluttered so thickly they felt like a physical barricade. They hung from the low, rustic wooden gate; they were stapled to the trees. NO TRESPASSING. Urgent against what otherwise looked like a scene copied from a rustic promotional brochure. A two-story clapboard farmhouse, weathered white. The Bishops didn't live on the Homestead grounds. They were on the other side of town, miles away. But its presence seemed to hang in the very air. Leaning out the open window, I recognized a certain quality to the light, a distinct pattern to the birdsong. I remembered.

We parked at the base of a tree, near a broken beer bottle half buried in a tangle of ivy. Brown shards and a torn silvery label. The back of my neck prickled with unease. "The house is still standing, at least," I said.

Cate glanced backward, and I checked too, half expecting to see the sedan trailing us. But there was nothing, just birdsong, breeze ruffling the trees.

At first I thought no one would come to the door. I was about to return to the car and wait when the door opened. Patricia was small, only five feet, but the imperiousness of her posture made it feel like she loomed over me. Two long fawn-colored braids hung down her back. Her black turtleneck and ankle-length denim skirt covered most of her body. In the background, a dense layer of classical music.

When Patricia's gaze touched me, she flinched and looked away too fast. She spoke, addressing some nonspecific point beyond the three of us: "You can't be here."

I stepped forward, handed her the letter like it was a ticket, *admit one*. Patricia took it, still without looking at me. I watched her as she

read, seeing the message again in my mind: *Dear Doctor Bellanger.*
When Patricia looked up, her face was completely blank. "You need
to go," she said to Tom, then turned to Cate: "You two. Come inside."

"Well, wait a second," Tom said. "It's important for us all to be here."
Patricia blinked at him, stony. "It's not important to me."
I was torn. "We've all come a long way—"
"Morrow," Cate said. "He can sit this one out."
"Okay," Tom said. "Of course. Yeah." He leaned in close, breath stir-
ring the hair at my temple. "Tell me everything, all right? Good luck."

We followed Patricia into the house. The exterior reminded me
fleetingly of the Homestead, but this was where it diverged. The Homestead had been all chaos inside, a disorderly stretch of discarded clothing, soiled cloth diapers, unwashed dishes. This place was obsessively
tidy. Dark, staid furniture. Blinds closed tight. The cool, cutting scent
of citrus.

Patricia didn't invite us to sit. She was wandering the edges of the
room, reading the letter again and again. I looked around for Isabelle,
Girl Two. No sign of her. I wasn't sure Patricia could hear anything over
the heavy throb of music. Cate finally went to the record player, which
was tucked inside a bookshelf, and switched it off, the silence ringing.

Patricia couldn't take her eyes off the letter. "There's no name," she
said softly, tracing the bottom of the page with one thumb. "That was
clever. As if all of us wrote the letter together. But it was one girl's choice
to reach out to Joseph Bellanger. The rest of us never agreed."

"You didn't approve of Bellanger joining you?" I asked, my mind
racing. This was verification of what Deb had said. Patricia spoke as if
she'd assumed I already knew. Then I came back to myself, my actual
purpose here. "Patricia, my mother's missing. Is she here? Has she been
in touch?"

"Of course she's not here." Patricia's grip on the letter tightened. "I've
always hated the way he hijacked the Homestead. He wasn't content
with you Girls, he had to own the nine of us too. Our whole histories.
Our very relationships with each other."

This was the first time I'd heard somebody close to Bellanger
speak about him with that much disdain. I'd heard the bullhorn-loud

criticisms, the sanitized slights published in scholarly journals, but not something like this. Up-close, raw hostility.

Patricia went to the somber Persian rug, kneeling to pull it back. The floor beneath was the same glossiness as the rest of the floor. No undercoat of dust. She deftly pulled up a floorboard, revealing a dark cavity, and reached inside, retrieving a small shoebox. Then she sat next to me, settling the box on her lap, and pulled out a crumpled pack of Virginia Slims. She plucked loose the cigarette, reached into the box for a lighter. Her hands were trembling. She exhaled a fog of smoke.

"The year you were born," she said, "there was an ad for these cigarettes that your mother and I loved. It showed a woman. A superhero. Tall red boots, red cape flowing all around her shoulders. Standing with her chest back and her legs wide. The copy claimed that Virginia Slims were designed for women because women were 'biologically superior.'" Patricia opened her eyes halfway, examined her own cigarette as if she'd forgotten she'd lit one. "Mere pandering. But that woman was beautiful. She looked exactly like Margaret."

Patricia stirred the contents of the shoebox with her fingers. I wondered why she'd kept it. The hiding space felt like a soft spot in an otherwise impenetrable suit of armor. I thought of my mother's hiding place inside the clock.

"Did your mother ever tell you about me, Josephine?" Patricia asked quietly.

"She told me you would steal her cigarettes," I said, irritable. Her hostility toward Bellanger had set me on edge. "I see you have your own now, at least."

Patricia laughed, her expression not lightening.

"I'm confused," I said. "How did you all know each other, if it wasn't through him?"

I was starting to feel like she couldn't see me at all. Patricia addressed the room instead: "I met your mother in New York City, both of us arriving there without knowing a soul. We were roommates in a little walk-up. Margaret could barely scrape enough together to pay rent on that place, even with three other girls sharing the space. I had some money—my parents were generous enough with their money, if not with anything else—so I had a bedroom to myself. It was hardly a glamorous place. We had to pass two peep shows every time we went down the block." But Patricia was smiling as she spoke, the smile of a woman handling precious memories. "New York was a fresh start for both of us. She was waiting tables, and I had a position at the public library."

"You were a librarian too?" I asked. "My mother—she's also—" But something in Patricia's expression stopped me. Cate put a quick hand on my shoulder: *Be patient.*

"Your mother seemed so sure of herself, she intimidated me," Patricia said. "Even though she worked long shifts at a diner, I saw her studying in her free time. She'd come to my branch and check out these dense, incomprehensible science books. I began to realize Margaret and I had a lot in common. As beautiful as she was, she didn't go out with the other girls when they invited us. She had no interest in boys and parties. Eventually, I invited her to split my bedroom with me. She'd been sleeping in a curtained-off nook, but I had room for another bed in there. She started to spend a lot of time in our room. To me, that room soon felt like the safest place in the city. Our little refuge."

I felt my fluttering heartbeat tucked in my throat.

"One day, I was getting off the subway, heading home from work, when I noticed your mother heading in a different direction. I followed her. I admit, I was curious. Imagine my surprise when she walked right onto a college campus. Back then, some of the most prestigious schools still wouldn't even admit women. But your mother walked with her head high and vanished into a building. A while later, I finally worked up the courage to confess I'd seen her. Margaret seemed happy I mentioned it. I think she needed a friend as much as I needed one. She told me she'd worked out a way to sit in on biology lectures."

Patricia paused, took a long drag on her cigarette. My mother had been interested in biology. Why had she never told me? Why hadn't I asked? I'd always treated her story as if it started at the same time as mine did, when I came squalling into the world. The details she'd offered me—that she didn't have much family, that she'd been adrift before she decided to heed Bellanger's call for volunteers—were the same blandly mechanical ones offered up by textbooks or tell-alls.

"Your mother was particularly intrigued by Gregory Pincus," Patricia said. "Pincus co-invented the birth control pill, but before that he was interested in the opposite. Not sex without birth, but birth without sex. That's what caught her imagination."

I knew all about Pincus. His white rabbits, quivering and pink-eyed; those fatherless fetuses that had plagued Pincus's reputation until he'd been forced to give up on them. I just hadn't learned about him from my mother.

"Pincus passed away in '67." Patricia held her cigarette in one hand, clutching her opposite wrist with the other. "But Margaret was taken with his work. She envisioned a world where women could have children without becoming beholden to men. There were a lot of unhappy women in your mother's life, growing up. She told me she'd once seen a neighbor crying because she'd learned she was pregnant again. This woman wanted the child. But it would mean she had to stay with the man who was hurting her when nobody was looking. Your mother was looking. She always saw those bruises."

"She told you all this?" I asked, astonished at the intimacy.

"Margaret told me everything," Patricia said. "Everything. The two of us, we'd formed a close friendship. Very close. I would've followed her anywhere."

With a strange rush, I remembered the letter I'd once found inside the clock in my mother's bedroom. That agonized mix of love and hate. Signed only T: Trish. My mother had torn up that letter before my eyes, and now I was sitting with the woman who'd written it. *You can't ignore me forever.*

Patricia reached into the shoebox. She handed a photograph to me, and I almost didn't want to accept, but then I did. Patricia and my mother, so young, sitting together, smiling into each other's faces. Patricia's long, pale brown hair was tied back into a ponytail with a piece of yarn that made her painfully young. Just a kid. The two of them sat with a sliver of space between them, and when I looked closely I could see their hands resting there, my mother's fingers looped with Patricia's. My mother had never been with anybody as long as I'd known her. Not men, not women. She was solitary and self-contained, immaculately lonesome as any saint. In this photo, the openness in her face transformed my mother into somebody else. Into a girl named Margaret, dreaming of creating a new world with the woman she loved.

When I glanced up from the photo, Patricia was examining me. That flash of pain came again, contracting the fine muscles of her face. When it cleared, what was left was a tenderness that made me uncomfortable, like I was accepting something that wasn't mine to take.

"I understand, Patricia," Cate said softly. Her thigh was lightly touching mine, warmth radiating against my skin.

"Once I knew that your mother was interested in virgin birth," Patricia went on, "the idea took over my brain too. I wanted to help, however I could. During my spare moments at the library, I looked into other books for her, dipping my toes into the vast mythology of virgin birth. So many stories throughout history. It had to have come from somewhere, didn't it? Soon your mother and I were a real team. I brought home books and I listened to her theories and tried to understand as best I could. She'd bring us leftover pastries from her work and we'd eat those stale Danish and Margaret would pace and pace, describing her wild theories to me. I'm sure our roommates thought we were huge bores, hiding away all the time. They had no idea what worlds we were building in there. There was a sense that we were handling something very sacred, very dangerous. Your mother filled entire notebooks with notes and quotes and articles—"

I thought of my mother's notebook, the manic, chaotic energy of it. Maybe not as strange as I'd first thought. Maybe a return to who she truly was.

"Margaret's scientific theories expanded to include more metaphysical notions. She'd encountered an old concept: Aristotle, or some other old dead blowhard, had claimed that men provided the soul and the humanity of each child. Women were mere incubators. No more important than nests for eggs. But if a woman was too wild, too independent, she'd give birth by herself. Only she'd give birth to a monster. Your mother heard *monster* and she thought *miracle*. She thought if we could go back to a time before memory when women reproduced freely and without obligation to men, we could be powerful again. Better than the trapped and ordinary humans we've become."

Monster, miracle. The night outside the motel, what I'd felt as I held that man inside my gaze. A bottomless, ferocious fearlessness that changed the world around me as much as it changed me.

"She decided we needed to band together and rid ourselves of men so that our abilities to self-conceive would reawaken. Men had come in and made us reliant on them, and we began to believe that it was just the way of things. But maybe, within the right environment, our bodies could remember again. There are animals that reproduce parthenogenetically when they're in captivity without proximity to males. In our case, Margaret said, it would be a similar mechanism, but a freeing from captivity." She smiled. "Such a bold mind on her. Listening to her talk was like nothing else."

I'd never seen the Homestead from this angle before. The women existing without the influence of men. Bellanger had always been such a prominent figure, standing there in that blazing white lab coat. "That's how you started the Homestead?" I asked.

"Back then, everyone knew someone who was part of the back-to-the-land movement. I had a little stretch of land in Vermont that my parents left me, and so I proposed to Margaret that we move there. The least I could do was support her with whatever resources I had. Margaret had the vision, I had the means. A classic pairing, don't you think?"

"How did you find the others to join you?" Cate asked.

"Oh, they found us and we found them. Girls from other communes, mostly, and girls on the run from abusive men. I was the one who organized these things, but I wasn't charismatic. I know that about myself. I'm always getting in my own way." She touched her hair with her free hand, suddenly self-conscious. "I tried to keep quiet. It was your mother who wooed the others. She made it seem so possible. She was our North Star."

The secret boldness of my mother's curiosity overwhelmed me for a second. If I hadn't grown up poring over Bellanger's letters, if I hadn't seen my own body as proof in the mirror every morning, would I have known it was possible?

"At first it was the start of something new and wonderful. We were on our way to bringing this impossible plan to fruition. We lasted about six months like that. Six beautiful months. Six painful months. No men—oh, we saw to that. But no babies. All that hope with nowhere to go. We weren't taking care of ourselves. Some girls were fasting or using drugs. Taking herbal concoctions that nearly killed us. Angela had to go to the emergency room. They assumed she was just some poor hippie, strung out. We were all getting discouraged. We'd known it wouldn't be easy, but this was too much."

Outside the windows, the ruffling breeze scraped through the trees, a low-hanging branch tapping against the glass.

"Margaret was more and more insistent that we had to rely on solid research if we wanted to get our babies. She could be so stubborn. I loved her for it, and hated her for it too sometimes. She believed that we needed to reach out to scientists and ask for professional advice. Some of us strongly disagreed, particularly since many of these scientists were men. I said, 'A little strange, isn't it, asking men to help a group of women rid the world of the male persuasion?'"

Cate gave a little huff of agreement. I felt myself gently disconnect from the two of them; I'd never fully envisioned a world without men. There was this huge thing they shared that I didn't, setting me apart. I pulled my thigh away, crossing my legs, and Cate gave me a quick glance I couldn't decipher.

"But when your mother had an idea, she wouldn't let it go, and I trusted her. So Margaret wrote to Joseph Bellanger. A former up-and-comer kicked out of medical school. Maybe that made him more open to us, as crazy as we sounded. I think he reminded Margaret of Pincus, because of his controversial experimentation with rats and sheep. When Bellanger's colleagues heard that he was aspiring to move on to human experimentation, he was ejected from his school and blacklisted from the official ranks of the scientific community. It unsettled me. Margaret just took it as proof that he had ambition. He could be exactly what we needed him to be: a scientist who didn't follow convention. He had nothing to lose by working with us."

I'd always loved the vision of Bellanger as a maverick, an outcast bold enough to defy the meek rules of society and alter history itself. Apparently my mother had felt the same way about him. For a moment, my mother felt so close. Like she was right there in the room with us, hanging back in the corners. I could turn and ask her: *What were you doing? Why did you never tell me?* I nearly did turn my head, the back of my neck going cold.

Rising abruptly, Patricia went to the kitchen and deposited the cigarette into the pit of the garbage disposal. A harsh, mechanical grinding as the sink ate the evidence. She reached for a small can of air freshener, spritzed the stinging smell of artificial pine throughout the room.

"Do you know what he did to those poor creatures?" Patricia asked conversationally, still intent on her task, erasing the nicotine like a teenager hiding vices from her mother. "The truth is that the offspring produced by those sheep and rats weren't right. They were virgin births, but they were barely alive. Just sickly collections of tissue and skin and teeth. Poor beings. So you see why Bellanger's colleagues warned him against trying his methods on human women."

"Teratomas. Maybe more advanced than that, but not by much." I looked at Cate, queasy at the idea of these lost animals, the rats and sheep, their genetic code stirred and warped by Bellanger's influence into something that couldn't exist. After having seen the slides of ovarian teratomas firsthand, clumps of tissue with teeth and hair, I understood exactly how unlikely the nine of us were. Fully formed women.

Cate, sitting next to me. Hair bundled over one shoulder. Her feet, planted on the floor, rising onto tiptoe, like she was about to launch away. She was perfect. But maybe that weirdness, pushing against the boundaries of possibility, had slipped into her in some other way. An internal strangeness, disarranged where people couldn't see it. Something beautiful and terrifying alike, caught in her fingertips as she stitched people back together.

"Margaret was delighted when Bellanger wrote back," Patricia said, returning to the couch. She replaced the lighter and the cigarettes into the shoebox; I noticed that she added the letter, but kept quiet. Let her have this lost piece of my mother. "I was stunned. I hadn't expected him to take us seriously. But it was hard to be angry with her, looking at all that joy and hope. The two of them wrote back and forth for several months. He helped us as much as he could through letters. I thought it might end there, after all. He recommended some supplements. It was starting to work. Our menstruation was syncing up. Even the girls who hadn't been taking care of themselves started to feel healthier. I remember my breasts were swollen all the time. I had little pangs in my hip bones, these twitches, like something was settling there.

"Finally, Margaret said it was easier to just let Bellanger come and see us. We had to wait weeks to hear back from him each time. You can imagine what it was like when we decided to have that man actually come to the Homestead. By that point we'd almost forgotten what a man looked like. Then, after he . . . worked on us, the first of us fell pregnant."

"My mother," I said.

"Your mother," Patricia acknowledged, inclining her head toward me. "Do you know how they used to test for pregnancy? They had to kill a rabbit. You injected that rabbit with urine from the mother and you checked to see if the rabbit's ovaries had swollen up. That's how Bellanger discovered that you would be coming into the world, Josephine. Our very first."

The dead rabbit, Bellanger's gloved hand glossed red with its blood, its insides exposed, the vulnerable swell of its ovaries mimicking the changes in my mother's own body. So my life had begun with a small and overlooked death.

"I almost left then," Patricia said. "I couldn't bear to watch Margaret bring our vision to life with that man instead of me. The way he named you after himself—but when she gave birth, I couldn't leave. You were so perfect. A duplicate of your mother. Nobody was going to send Bellanger home after that. It took years for the next baby, and while we waited and waited, it began to feel almost like your mother had fallen pregnant because she was so accommodating. Maybe we all needed to be more welcoming to Bellanger. He'd helped us, after all. And then I had my Isabelle."

Isabelle had been the next baby after me. Girl Two. I'd mistaken this for random chance and not a conscious connection, Patricia following in my mother's footsteps.

Cate shifted, impatient. "Sorry, but once the rest of you were pregnant, couldn't you have shown Bellanger the door?"

Patricia's face slipped into true vulnerability, collapsing before she recovered. "Do you think he would've just walked away? You were his precious creations too. You were his tickets into this realm of scientific acclaim. A world that he both scorned and desperately wanted to be part of. He wasn't ever going to leave. Not once we'd let him into our midst, and given him full access to our bodies and our hearts and—and our hopes and ambitions. We should've known. It was such a powerful thing to want you Girls. But once Bellanger was in our lives, we signed ourselves away."

"Yes, but it was your idea, and Margaret's," Cate pressed. "It was—"

"What do you think they would have done, a group of girls living on their own with babies?" Patricia asked, a sudden bright flare of anger that woke up her face. "Bellanger gave the world something to focus on. He made it scientific progress instead of witchcraft. If it had been just us women there, death would've come for us much sooner."

This new story fit jaggedly over the one I'd already known, rubbing raw at the edges. I remembered Bellanger smiling down at me, my hand in his, the sense of safety and belonging. Patricia and maybe my mother hadn't wanted any of that—they'd wanted him to arrive and then vanish, unknown to me forever—

"So you see why your mother would never come here. I've followed her disappearance on the news, but as far as I'm concerned, she vanished years ago." Grief moved across Patricia's face, wince-quick. "I've told you everything I know about the letter. The whole ugly story. If there's nothing else—"

After a silent consultation with Cate, I rose and showed Patricia my mother's line in the notebook. "It's not just the letter, Patricia. We were hoping you could tell us more about Fiona. My mother was interested in her, and we think it's because of what Fiona could do. Her powers." I spoke steadily. Patricia knew more about the Homestead than anybody else I'd encountered so far; no need to play coy.

As she read, a muscle near Patricia's eyebrow twitched.

"You were there with Fiona at the Homestead until the very end. You and my mom. If you know what she was talking about—"

"You want to know about Fiona?" Patricia stood, suddenly resolute, and I stepped back. Her small figure was swamped by all that fabric, only her white face and hands exposed. "Come with me," she said. "I can do better than tell you, Josephine. I can show you."

21

April 24, 1975

My darling Josephine,

Here we are at your fourth birthday already. I remember looking down at you when you arrived and marveling at you, my little one, but also worrying for you. You were so very alone when you were born. The only one of your kind. A true first, the rarest being on the whole planet. At the time, I didn't know if there'd ever be more of you. I didn't know if you would thrive at all. Your mother has always done her best to look out for you, but I worried that she couldn't fully understand how special you are. You're her dear, sweet little girl, and she doesn't always see the specialness that lies underneath. That's my job.

The grandest news is that just last week, your Aunt Lily-Anne gave birth to our perfect ninth baby. She has completed the puzzle you have started: Girl Nine to your Girl One. With her arrival, I've proven the critics wrong and accomplished everything I set out to do. There are nine of you where before there were none. Take good care of your littlest sister. I have a suspicion that she will need a big sister in her life, for she seems to be quite the special Girl. Show her the sisterly love you've shown the others: Isabelle, Catherine, Gina, Emily, Delilah, Bonnie, and Helen.

Your loving father always,
Joseph Bellanger

22

The basement held a subterranean chill, and the hairs on my arms rose as we descended a long stairwell. I remembered climbing into the attic to see Emily French a few days ago. This space was all gray concrete, slick and smooth. A secret tunnel under the house. I could barely connect it with the farmhouse above. A large white projector screen stood against one wall. In front of it, a simple black couch. No windows. No doors other than the one we'd come through. I looked at Cate, anxious, excited, lower belly pinched with nerves.

In one corner, a table held a clunky projector, all wheels and gears. Patricia gestured at the couch. "Have a seat, girls."

We sat next to each other. In front of us, that looming blank screen. Cate smiled at me sidelong, encouraging. I was deeply and fiercely grateful for her presence here. If she'd stayed back home in Arkansas, I'd be doing this alone right now.

Patricia clicked the lights off. Startling blackness for a moment. The rising whir of the projector. The screen came to life, striped and dotted with interference, transforming into a tilted view of a room, large and gloomy. It was the Homestead. I recognized the kitchen table, long and low and rough-hewn, covered with dishes. The simple freestanding sink. I remembered this place. For a moment it was so clear, as if I'd never left.

The camera took a moment to adjust, swooping in a seasick curve, wobbling over to the table, and narrowed in on a little girl. She sat there, almost too small to see over the edge, her face drawn and sullen, her hair glowing red even in colors muted by time. She stared off into space. A two-year-old. She seemed younger, bird-boned.

"Fiona." Patricia's voice was singsong. "Fiona, look over here."

A slow, imperious swivel of her head, an owlish blink. Fiona had been crying. Her rounded cheeks were glossy and sticky-looking. I felt a gasp stuck in my chest, my amazement lodging there. Fiona, resurrected, right here.

"Can you do that again?"

"I want Mama." Fiona used both hands to push her hair off her face, her scowl deepening. "Mama. Where is she?"

"The trick again. Like earlier."

Fiona stared, baleful. She shook her head, burying her face in her hands. "Mama," she said, muffled, and I imagined Fiona trying to comprehend the loss of her mother, trying to understand that the person she loved most wouldn't be coming back.

I swallowed, dizzy for a second. The camera zoomed in. It must've been a Super 8, faded and flickering, everything washed into nostalgic watercolors. The video had the dreamy, harmless quality of a home video. Fiona breathed heavily, on the verge of tears.

A rattling noise. A fine, quick shudder. The camera moved away from Fiona to focus on a candle, sitting inside a lumpy clay holder, perched at the edge of the table. There was something strange about the flame, the way it seemed to flicker to life just as the camera panned to it. An unnaturalness at the edges. At the sight of the flame, I felt a familiar jolt of fear.

An agonizingly long moment, and then the candleholder shuddered. It quivered against the table like it was caught in an isolated earthquake, even as the rest of the kitchen stood still, not even a curtain twitching. I heard a whisper—"*My god*"—and wasn't sure whether it was the Patricia holding the camera or the current version of her, standing behind me.

The holder rose just barely, not even an inch. It hovered, or maybe it was a trick of the light, my brain trying to turn it into an illusion even as I watched it. The flame hovered in the center of the screen, so bright it felt like it could reach through into the present and eat away the entire basement. Then the candleholder came down hard, shattering into jagged puzzle pieces. Beside me, Cate flinched. The candle fell onto the table, and Patricia's hand reached into the frame to press the flame out before it could spread.

From the projector, a high-pitched wail rose, sludgy with tears. The thump of little footsteps, growing distant, as Fiona ran.

We stayed on the shattered pieces a moment longer, as if this would convince us that it was real. That what we'd seen—cause, effect, object rises, object breaks—had truly happened. I imagined that the version of Patricia stuck forever in 1977 couldn't make herself look away. So different from the woman who'd refused to look me in the face.

"Fiona. Come back." The camera tracked her down the hallway, quavering, trembling with the movement of Patricia's body as she chased after the girl. Fiona was visible in snatches: tangled hair, little feet. She veered off into another room, one I recognized. The room with the big saggy couch, the same one in that photo of pregnant Lily-Anne I'd rescued from Cate's house. The view panned across the wall, catching the edges of the pictures and artwork, and I spotted the same framed *Time* cover on the wall. I thought of Lily-Anne standing there heavily pregnant in that Polaroid. Now here was the product of that pregnancy, in that same room years later, trembling and feral.

Fiona stood in the corner, hugging herself. She looked so small. The camera crept closer, and I imagined Patricia approaching this girl the way she'd approach a cornered animal. A hard dread grew in my chest.

Patricia said, "I know you're hurting, little one. I'm so sorry it's all so heavy right now. I'm here for you." A pause. "Remember the candle? Can you do it again? Just show me. One more time." Fiona's hair hid her face. Those damp, angry eyes, shining out from behind her matted curls. Which—in the shadowed room—looked as dark a red as dried blood. "Please," Patricia said. "Show us all what you can do. Our little miracle."

Fiona was shaking her head again. "Where's my mama?"

Cate tensed beside me. I felt it too. This desire to reach through that flimsy projector screen, all the way back through the layers of time, and defend this little girl. It was the first maternal instinct I'd ever felt. I was

Girl One. The iconic daughter. The one famous for having been mothered. Right now, all I wanted was to help Fiona.

"Mama will come?" Fiona asked. She had gone very still. "I do trick?"

Cate's hand slipped into mine. Reassuring.

I missed what was happening until it was right there. Fiona was rising—shifting one hip upward, unnaturally high, canting it until it seemed impossible, until her dangling toes were barely touching the floor, even as her other foot was planted firmly. It was like an invisible rope had been attached to Fiona's left hip, yanking her higher, higher, until her small body was distorted, unnatural. Impossible. Her other foot began to follow until she was hanging there, suspended.

A churning ache of wonder grew in my stomach, trying to reconcile this with what I knew. Of Fiona, of the world around me, of the laws of physics. This was no rumor. It was an observable phenomenon, right here in front of me, and while I felt that hard, clean curiosity—the desire to examine it, understand *why*—there was also a simple gut reaction. Fear and amazement. An early human seeing fire for the first time.

This was what it looked like when we altered the course of human history. A little girl alone in a room, a camera aimed at her, her body defying everything we knew.

A sharp hiss of electricity, a droning noise, and the camera angled upward, revealing a bare bulb suspended from the ceiling. The hot orange lightning bolt of its filament glowed in the dimness of the room. The hiss came again, and then the bulb exploded, and in its brief dying flash of light I could see the glitter of broken glass. Dark. A textured darkness, the faint pant of breathing. I thought Fiona would reappear. I thought she'd leap out of the darkness, bared teeth, shining eyes, like an animal emerging from the back of a cave. I was tense all over, waiting. But there was just a soft laugh. The picture vanished, showing scribbles of interference, and then the whirring of the projector stopped.

The sudden silence was so loud it echoed.

Behind me, the sounds of Patricia walking over and flicking on the lights. The fluorescent bars lit up section by section, bright strips coming to life across the ceiling. We were here, in 1994, in this cold, artificial light, and I could almost forget everything I'd seen. Already it was turning murky.

"You filmed Fiona?" Cate asked. Her palm against mine was sweat-slick, but when she moved her hand, I missed her touch. "It's an invasion of her privacy."

Patricia blinked, like *privacy* was a meaningless word in this context. "I didn't know how long Fiona would behave that way. I needed proof. That footage ended up being priceless. You understand, Josephine. Or you would, if you're anything like your mother."

"When my mother died," Cate said, "I wanted time alone, not a camera shoved in my face."

Cate and Patricia stared at each other, a hot challenge passing back and forth. I was torn. There was something terrible in the way Fiona was trapped at the other end of the camera, unable to escape our eyes and our wonder and our fear, even seventeen years after her death. But I was also grateful that Patricia had the footage. I was glad there was evidence.

"Why would you have kept this a secret, Patricia?" I asked. "This is huge. It could change everything."

"This is our history," Patricia said. "Our past. We still live in a world dominated by men. Who knows what they'd do to us if they saw this?"

"But did Bellanger know?"

"Of course he did," Patricia said, and I exhaled, shaky. "After Bellanger saw who she was, he was very attentive to Fiona. Why do you think he wanted to adopt her after Lily-Anne died? I sometimes think that if Bellanger hadn't known about Fiona, he wouldn't have insisted on keeping her so close to him. Maybe she would've been with one of us, when the fire started, instead of with him. Maybe—" Patricia cut herself off with a crisp shrug.

Bellanger had died before he could fully examine and understand what he'd done. But now I knew. We knew. *Tell the world.* What had seemed so simple and cryptic at first was now shining with significance.

"Once a week, I have my Izzy watch this film," Patricia said. "I've reminded her that it's possible. This power could lie within her too."

Izzy. I realized she was referring to Isabelle, Girl Two. I'd totally forgotten about her. I wondered where she'd been all this time, while I was having my whole history twisted and warped.

"Once a week?" Cate repeated.

"She needs to remember where she comes from," Patricia said. "I may've lost Margaret, but I've held on to her vision. I've let it grow and grow in my heart since that fire took the Homestead. It's just the two of us now, Izzy and I. Well. That's all it ever took, according to Margaret. A woman and her daughter. If there's some specialness inside Isabelle, we're going to find it."

A private theater where a single memory from the past played over and over and over again to an audience of two. I wondered if it would be better or worse for Isabelle than growing up with the spell of silence my mother had cast over our home.

"Some days, it seems obvious that we didn't produce nine miracles at the Homestead," Patricia said. "We created one miracle and eight ordinary Girls." She spoke without malice. "Isabelle is a young woman now. Perhaps I should accept that our one true miracle is long gone."

"But I'm still here," Cate said. No apology, no attempt to hide who she was.

I wanted to erase the words. I felt protective of Cate, and I didn't know how Patricia would react. Patricia absorbed her meaning immediately. She stared at Cate, her expression so reverent that I wanted to look away. At the same time, I understood. I knew exactly what it was like to look at Cate and feel that rush of amazement.

"Catherine," Patricia said, stepping forward. "You too?" Cate nodded, and Patricia turned her intensity toward me, a question hanging there. I hesitated. What had happened that night at the motel still felt sticky and impossible. Something private. I was torn between standing beside Cate, marking us both the same, and keeping my secret under my control.

Patricia seemed to take my silence as an answer. "What did you do to make this happen?" she asked Cate instead, brisk and intent.

"Nothing." Cate was startled by her forcefulness. "It happened on its own."

"There must've been some reason," Patricia insisted, like she was going to turn this into an equation. She reminded me of myself, suddenly, an uncanny mirror. "Something you did. You must've encouraged it or—or figured it out. Somehow."

The blank white of the projector screen hovered in my peripheral vision, a reminder of Fiona.

"Where is Isabelle?" Cate asked gently. "I'd like to meet her."

23

Everything out here was wild, pure, and green. Even the sunlight was brighter and softer. I'd watched Patricia trying to find Isabelle in the house, her agitation growing, shutting Cate and me out. I'd escaped, mumbling some excuse about checking on Tom. The Volvo was gone, which nagged at me, but I stayed out here, trying to clear my head. I needed space. I needed fresh air.

Walking in the sunlight, I grasped for my own memories of Fiona. Something I could piece together for myself, beyond the video footage, tabloid portraits, secondhand stories. She was only two years old when she died. I was six. I'd treated her with an older-sister mix of jealousy, affection, pompous authority. If I focused, I could remember Fiona being different after her mother died. A haunted quality that made her seem set apart from me, a member of a different world. I'd thought it was just because she was a motherless girl. Now I knew.

It wasn't until I'd wandered beyond the bounds of the makeshift backyard, lost in my thoughts, that I saw her. The girl in the water. My heart jolted.

A creek ran through the narrow dip of the valley, down at the bottom of the property. There was hair caught in the current, thin and brown, trickling over the rocks. A stark white face in the water, bluish lips. There was one moment when I stood, staring, shocked, before the adrenaline kicked in and I scrambled down the hill, my dress snagging on rocks and outcropping branches as I rushed toward the girl in the creek.

I waded into the water, slipping and clambering, the cold water compressing my breath into a sharp gasp. The water wasn't so deep, only halfway to my knees, but the girl was floating, so small and still she resembled a sleeping child. The water ran in rivulets over her lips. Abruptly, she opened her eyes halfway, as if my clumsy splashing had bothered her. She had to be gripped with hypothermia already.

I slid my arms underneath the girl, pulled her up out of the water. She didn't fight. I was pulling her back toward the shore, stumbling against the slick rocks and pebbles at the bottom of the creek, when Isabelle wrenched free of my grasp, her sudden strength surprising me.

She stood and faced me as if we were meeting under normal circumstances. The vein at her temple was a pronounced pulse.

"Are you all right?" I asked, steadying myself in the mild tug of the current. "God, are you okay? Let's go back to the house, get you warmed up."

She was a perfect copy of young Patricia in the photographs. Annoyed more than embarrassed, she pressed her lips together. "I'm fine." She began splashing toward the bank, arms crossed. "What are you doing out here, anyway?"

Confused, a little irritated, I followed her. "I—I saw you, and I thought you needed help, you looked dead. Did you slip?"

"You shouldn't be sticking your nose in other people's business."

"Yeah, well, you shouldn't be drowning yourself." Isabelle must've been twenty years old already, but she looked younger. Unformed and delicate, a plant grown in the dark. Her baggy denim jumper had a plain T-shirt beneath it: first-day-of-junior-high clothes, chosen by a too-strict mother. Everything was clinging to her body now, revealing the curve of her back.

Back on land, the air felt twice as cold as before I'd entered the creek, my sneakers damp and heavy. Isabelle marched ahead of me, back toward the house. "You're Josephine."

"You got me."

She turned, examining me quickly. "You look just like her photograph. The one that always makes my mother cry."

Before I could react to this, there were footsteps, a shout, and Isabelle stopped. She adjusted her posture, back straight, expression wiped clean. Patricia and Cate came hurrying down the hill toward us, Patricia frantic, Cate trailing behind, her concern turning into be-musement when she saw me standing there half-soaked. I shrugged, mouthing, *Don't ask.*

"Izzy," Patricia said. "Where have you been? What have you been doing?"

"Nothing much." She gave me a quick, furtive look, like she was worried I'd tattle. Like we were little again, hiding in the dark corners of the forest just to cause mischief, shushing each other as our mothers drew close. I gave what I hoped was a convincing smile.

Patricia looked back and forth between us, and I realized she was seeing her younger self and my mother. Roommates, lying on their narrow beds, absorbed in their reading, inventing a future together. Two girls with nothing, no loving families, no certainty, who dared to design a world for themselves. I smiled, and Patricia softened, briefly, before turning away.

"Catherine, surely you have some advice for our Izzy? Something that will illuminate her own powers."

We'd been invited to stay for dinner. I'd recognized right away that this invitation was less an act of hospitality and more an attempt to wring some useful knowledge out of Cate. I didn't even care; Patricia was a good cook, and I craved anything that didn't come in a greasy wrapper. Isabelle stared at her plate, rearranging bites of her steak, barely eating. There was a little color to her lips and cheeks, her hair drying slowly. Frizzy on the top layer, darkly damp beneath. I tried to make eye contact to telegraph comfort or solidarity. Isabelle had come to terms with her own perceived failure. Known its boundaries. Now, I could tell, her awareness of herself had changed—her lack brought into contrast by Cate's powers. The sting was fresh again.

I remembered being that little girl on the garage roof, genuinely believing I'd rise into the air and soar when I dropped my body toward the oil-stained stretch of driveway.

"Advice?" Cate repeated, doubtful, pausing with a forkful of salad halfway to her mouth. "What kinds of things have you been doing so far?"

Cate addressed Isabelle, but it was Patricia who spoke up again: "Part of Izzy's process has been reminding herself of Fiona's abilities, certainly. As she's grown older, Izzy has become only more devoted to bringing any nascent abilities to the surface. We've also been careful not to let her become too corrupted with outside ideas. Not to see herself as 'ordinary.' Izzy has been educated right here at home with me." Patricia severed a bite of steak, bringing a surgical grace to the knife cut. "Same with relationships. Izzy doesn't have time for all that groping and fumbling."

"Eh, groping and fumbling can be fun with the right person," Cate said.

A bare flicker of a smile over Isabelle's face. I caught Cate's eye, and she winked, joking and conspiratorial. Heat flushed along my spine and I coughed, cleared my throat.

Patricia ignored all this. "Izzy has done some studies that lead her to believe they may arise from pushing oneself. Finding a certain level of perseverance and endurance."

"What do you mean?" Cate had stopped eating, her lips shiny with oil, and I realized that I had stopped chewing too. We both looked at Isabelle, who wouldn't look at us.

"Well, abstaining from meals," Patricia said, matter-of-fact. "Abstaining from sleep. Very hot or very cold showers. Methods like that."

At this, Isabelle lifted her eyes to mine, defiant. Her body in the cold water, half-drowned, half-dead, and the way she'd been surprised—angry—that I'd interrupted her private ritual. I got it. That leaden desire to manipulate your body and brain into extraordinariness. I felt a sudden ache for my mother. Patricia and Izzy were so aloof, like they'd grown up on a remote island, isolation closing over them. Patricia talking so casually about their methods, violence transformed into an ordinary litany. My mother's crustless sandwiches and late-night reruns, her suburban normalcy, were generous in comparison.

Cate set her fork down with a clatter. "Fuck. In that case, no. I never starved myself or scalded myself, if that's what you're asking. It doesn't sound worth it to me."

Patricia settled back. "How do we know that you have abilities?"

"You're free to believe me or not," Cate said, unruffled. "It doesn't change anything."

"Then show us." Patricia spoke casually, but I saw the intensity behind her eyes. She'd been planning to ask this already.

I felt a tug of curiosity mixed with discomfort. I'd never even thought to ask Cate to exhibit her abilities to me. It would've been asking her to perform, lift her skirts in a peep-show tent. But I was guiltily curious. After seeing Fiona in the basement—after that night in the parking lot, my own body changing—I craved more. I wanted to see that same impossibility manifesting inside a different body, a grown body, still alive, still here, proving it wasn't just a fluke—something I could watch as an observer. Not just the little silvery zebrafish, but a human being.

"It's hard to heal someone when nobody's hurt," Cate demurred.

"Oh," Isabelle said. She grabbed her steak knife from beside her plate and slashed it quickly against the underside of her forearm. It was such an exact yet careless cut, like she was slicing a vegetable for dinner, that I barely registered it until the blood started welling. First just a thin red outline, as neat as if made by a marker tip, and then, suddenly, too suddenly, the blood was pooling. I was frozen.

Patricia half rose from her chair as her daughter's blood dripped onto the fine white fabric of the tablecloth, each spot spreading rapidly, rootlike fingers shooting out as the blood followed the grain of the fabric. Her expression torn between fascination and horror, mirroring my own.

Cate, on the other hand, was calm and focused. Standing, she grabbed a napkin and pressed it to Isabelle's arm. Isabelle was as unresisting as a doll, watching Cate with those big eyes. Cate pulled the napkin away and examined the amount of blood. After moving her fingers over Isabelle's flesh delicately, pressing down, she wrapped both hands around the wounded part of her arm and shut her eyes, her face slackening. Cate's eyelids fluttered shut, the globes of her eyeballs moving side to side underneath the thin skin, like she was trying to take in the whole room with her eyes still shut tight.

How deep had Isabelle managed to get with that one swipe of the knife? It was so practiced. Isabelle was used to treating her own body with a functional recklessness.

Patricia's expression had settled into a keen wonder. Cate's skin was draining of color. A ribbon of a vein pulsed at her throat. A fine layer of sweat stippled her forehead. She was gripping Isabelle's arm so hard that my own stomach sucked in sympathetically, but Isabelle wasn't reacting. Just waiting. Waiting.

Cate opened her eyes and let go. She held on to the back of her chair, supporting herself. Isabelle grabbed a napkin and scrubbed too roughly at the skin surrounding the cut. Patricia came closer then, reaching down to trace one fingernail over the skin. The deep slit in Isabelle's arm—it must've been two inches across—was gone, even as the evidence still stained the tablecloth and spattered the floorboards. Where the cut had been, a pinkish line lay against her skin. It faded even more as I watched, barely there.

Cate sat, nearly slipping off the chair. She wiped a hand across her forehead and left behind a rusty streak, blood mingling with the sweat over her eyebrows.

"Are you all right, Cate?" I asked.

She nodded, managed a smile. "It's usually not that fast," she said, a whisper so low only I could catch it. She looked down at her hands, almost marveling.

"Can you do it again?" Isabelle asked, hard and eager.

"No. God." There were shadows of fatigue beneath Cate's eyes that hadn't been there a few minutes ago. "Please don't hurt yourself, Isabelle." But I could hear the echo under it. It hurt Cate too: she hadn't mentioned that part.

Patricia moved back to her own seat. She clasped her hands beneath her chin, looking at each of us in turn. I kept staring at Isabelle's arm. It reminded me of my own scar, the skin that surgeons had painstakingly grafted onto me: the scientific breakthrough of that versus the raw, simple magic of what Cate had just done. Maybe they weren't so far apart. Maybe the skin graft had been a little moment of witchcraft and Cate's ability to stitch Isabelle's nerve endings back together was a physiological response, no more inexplicable than a cut healing on her own skin or a heartbeat pushing blood through a body.

"For all Bellanger's precision," Patricia said, "he only managed to create miracles in a few of you. I don't understand *why*. Look—look at Fiona. Look at you, Cate." Patricia was reverential but also hostile. "Why not Isabelle?"

"What happened to all those books you and Margaret had? About the lost art of self-conception," Cate asked. "Those could help you understand some of this."

"They burned. They were at the Homestead during the fire. I couldn't save them."

Another loss, one I hadn't even known about. Not just Bellanger's work, his research, his notes. But this other part of our genesis. All of it gone in the fire that Ricky Peters had set. Devouring more of my history than I'd even realized.

"Perhaps it's something about us," Patricia said, the bitterness deepening. "About Margaret and me. Maybe as your mothers, we should hold ourselves responsible for your lack. There's no bond like the one between a mother and child."

"Maybe so," I said, suddenly impatient, and Patricia snapped to attention. "You both went about this the wrong way. You and my mother. Where did all that ambition go? All those dreams? My mother just let it vanish. She's spent years trying to pretend we're normal. And I've resented her for it. But now I look at you and Isabelle, and . . . maybe my mother was right to just forget the past. That ambition's only hurt Isabelle. Would your past self be proud of that?"

The room felt too still after my outburst. Through her hair, Isabelle stared at me with her diluted blue eyes, uncertain, looking like she didn't know whether to be scared of me or grateful.

Then she put her hand out, palm up, laying it on the table like an offering. Her fingers blossomed open, waiting. Patricia gave her daughter a small smile, the two of them communicating privately, as if Cate and I had vanished. She placed her own small hand in her daughter's and they locked fingers, staring at each other, and I didn't know whether what was happening was forgiveness or apology, accusation or challenge.

Patricia broke the gaze first. "If you'll excuse me, Girls." She rose, leaving the dining room without another glance, her posture very straight. Isabelle waited a few seconds, sitting there surrounded by the drying bloodstains, all the leftover proof of a wound that didn't exist anymore. She stood and followed her mother out of the room, leaving Cate and me alone.

24

Tom still wasn't back. I had no idea where he'd gone. Maybe he'd abandoned us to the Bishops, driving off as easily as he'd appeared on that Kansas freeway. It was late, shadows overtaking the inside of the house. Cate and I sat on the sofa in a single pool of lamplight. The isolation drew a tighter and tighter noose around us. The closest outpost, a forlorn convenience store, was miles back. I imagined the crunch of gravel as the maroon sedan crawled up to this defenseless house. Patricia hadn't shed any light on who was following us. He was still a mystery, a ghost who could pop up any second.

Sensing my uneasiness, Cate took my hand. I thought of her hand on Isabelle's arm, all her power concentrated in one spot. My skin warmed in response. A quick fluttering deep in my belly. The lizard necklace nestled between her collarbones. "What is that necklace, anyway?" I asked, as much to distract myself as anything else.

"Oh, this? A whiptail lizard. They can reproduce without male lizards. A whole community of lady lizards. My mother had this made for me." She tapped the necklace softly with her free hand. "A reminder of what we could be, someday. Not just the eight of us scattered around the country, god knows where, but a community. Kind of like your mother's theory." She smiled, half to herself. "I wish my mother had been alive when you went off to school, Morrow. It hurt her that the Homestead never went anywhere after '77—that we just stayed stuck. She would've loved to see one of us grow up to put everything back together."

"Well, I'm no Bellanger."

"No Bellanger?" Cate's grip loosened. "You're still comparing yourself to him? We just learned that we weren't even his idea."

I hesitated for a moment. "Look, I'm not going to discount Bellanger's work over what we've learned. That seems like an overreaction."

"Shit, seems like a perfectly reasonable reaction to me. We just found out that the test subjects were the masterminds. If that doesn't change anything for you, then you're . . ."

"What?"

"I don't know. Brainwashed."

Brainwashed. I pulled my hand out of hers, folded my hands on my lap. "If our mothers had been able to do it, they wouldn't have needed to call on Bellanger," I said, not hiding my anger. "They were there for a long time and nothing happened. Patricia admitted it herself. They needed Bellanger. He's the one who created us. Without him, eventually they would've given up and we never would've existed."

Cate stared straight ahead, her profile rigid, her jaw working.

"They needed someone with a scientific background," I said. "I admire my mother for reaching out to him. I admire the fact that she took initiative like that. But I'm not going to give up on Bellanger entirely. He's still the one who made me."

"If your mother's involvement wasn't important, why did Bellanger hide it?"

A light creak came from the shadows that collected at the foot of the staircase. We both turned. Patricia stood, a muddy outline before she turned on the lights and we were all blinking in the glare. I looked for Isabelle and didn't see her.

Patricia moved across the room, standing opposite from us, posture very straight. "You have to understand," she said, as if we were picking up a conversation we'd just finished. "Isabelle is my life. I've poured every moment into making sure she's reaching her potential. You two come into our life. and within a few hours Isabelle is blaming me."

"Oh, Isabelle is an adult," I said, tired. "She's twenty-one. Stop treating her like a kid."

"Don't talk to me like that. You have no idea what I've been through."

"You need to let her go."

"Like you let your mother go?" Patricia asked.

"Okay! Okay, we should leave." Cate began to rise. "It obviously won't do any good for us to stick around—"

"You don't understand," Patricia said. "You should know the truth, because I doubt Margaret has ever told you." The tension in the room was so thick it felt like something would explode if I moved the wrong way, my hip or elbow rupturing the membrane separating us from chaos. Patricia lifted the hem of that thick black turtleneck, revealing her torso, stopping at the lower edge of her breasts. Her skin was shiny and marbled, sections raised like ropy vines. The scar tissue covered her belly, her ribs, wrapping around until it reached the other side. I stared at the burned skin, like hieroglyphics tattooed on her lower torso. "I was able to spare Izzy injuries, but a tree branch fell in my path. My nightgown caught fire. I pulled the gown off—I was nearly naked when they found me." She rested a hand on her side. "I carry that night with me, always."

"I'm sorry." I was quiet, sobered. "I didn't know at all."

"Your mother is with me all the time. Every time I see this scar, I'm reminded of Margaret. Because . . ." Patricia hesitated. "Because your mother is the one who set the fire that night, Josephine. She's the one who burned the Homestead to the ground."

Cate touched my shoulder. I registered the warmth of the gesture, but I also wasn't in the room anymore. My mother setting the fire. The fire that had disintegrated the last bonds between the women of the Homestead, that had taken Bellanger away before he had a chance to share the mysteries of our origins with the world. If my mother was behind it, then she'd been the one to take everything from me.

"No," I said. "It was Peters, we know that. She wouldn't have done that to Bellanger. Or to any of you. She wouldn't have done that to—"

Fiona. To Fiona. I thought of that little girl on the film, crying for her mother. My mother hadn't killed that child. The same woman who'd competently brushed my hair every night, who'd reminded me to wear a coat on cold days, who left me the last cookie in the box every single time, even when I didn't ask? It couldn't have been her. No. No.

"She never intended to kill Fiona. I imagine that guilt has been harder on Margaret than anything," Patricia said. "But it doesn't change what she did."

"Ricky Peters confessed." I stated the fact, solid and immovable. Of course my mother hadn't started the fire. The man who had set it was behind bars. Even as I said it, I remembered Tom's pet theory: that Ricky Peters's indictment was too pat, too simple. That Bellanger was a complicated man with complicated enemies. Well, my mother was complicated too. A headache started at the base of my skull. "My mother testified at his trial," I said. "So did you."

Patricia's smile was small and twisted, like it hurt her. "Yes. I did."

"Patricia." Cate spoke steadily. "First you tell us that Margaret is the one who brought Bellanger to the Homestead. Now she killed him?"

I shot her a grateful look, some of our earlier tension wordlessly forgiven.

"We planned it together," Patricia said. "After Lily-Anne's death, when Fiona started behaving strangely, everything changed again." Patricia's voice shook, and she rested a hand against her neck, steadying herself. "Bellanger pushed us out. He stole the spotlight. He even offered to buy the Homestead from me, my own land, and add it to his investments in Arizona or Nevada or wherever. He'd stop at nothing—he was a cancer."

Her rage built as a sour heat in my own breastbone. I couldn't tell if I was angry at her for talking about Bellanger this way, or strangely ashamed, as if she were criticizing me too. I'd inherited his mind, after all. I saw the world through his eyes.

"I didn't think Margaret understood," Patricia said. "She thought I was jealous. But one day, she came to me and said she'd discovered certain things. Bellanger was trying to get legal custody of all of you. Not just Fiona, all of you. He'd had us sign contracts back when we were loopy on drugs. We had no lawyers, no real counsel. There were no legal protections for children born to only one biological parent. Children who shouldn't have existed at all. If anything happened to any of us, Bellanger could have taken you. Your mother hadn't known until Lily-Anne died and the custody battle came to the forefront."

Becoming Bellanger's daughter. Living with his two sons. Bellanger himself reading me bedtime stories by the soft radiance of a night-light. This was a well-worn fantasy, embarrassingly soothing as an outgrown toy. I'd never felt guilty over it before—it was a secret dream, not my mother's business—but now the memory was mixed with a sharp humiliation, and the tight beginnings of anger. I hadn't even known what I'd been wishing for.

"Margaret had a plan to end everything so that we didn't have to worry about Bellanger. She wanted to burn the whole place down. Make it look like it was the protesters. They were the perfect foils, out there every day and yelling about hellfire. I was pulled right back into her orbit. The two of us against the world again. So I stayed with her on the Homestead, even as the other women ran off into their own lives. They could see the writing on the wall. They knew that place wasn't long for the world, they wanted to find safety and normalcy for their girls while they still could. Then one day, out of nowhere, Margaret told me it was over. She told me to take Isabelle and leave the Homestead."

"Why didn't you?" I demanded.

"I had no chance. That very night—the fire."

My mother had killed Fiona so that she could keep me, and then I'd turned around and abandoned her, and now she'd vanished, a whole chain of loss and want and grasping that had led to this night.

"I testified that Ricky had started the fire," Patricia said. "I lied to protect us. After the trial, Margaret promised me that we'd be together again. Just as soon as the dust settled, she said. I waited and waited. A year went by. More. She stopped answering my calls. Wouldn't answer my letters. So I gave up on Margaret Morrow."

The headache was building now, pounding. Patricia began to say something else, but the twin halos of car headlights entered the room through the crack in the curtains, refracted against the wall, hovering above the mantel before flicking into darkness. Tom. Or the stranger: while we'd been lost in the past, we'd left our present selves open and vulnerable.

Patricia moved over to the window and twitched aside the curtain. "Your friend is back."

Before we left, I turned to her. Our gazes met; for the first time, she looked bereft. She was watching my mother leave her all over again. "I'm worried about you and Isabelle," I said to her, a sudden impulse. "I think we're being targeted by somebody. All of us. Be careful, okay?"

Stepping closer, Patricia grabbed my hand like she'd dared herself to do it. "Take care of her," she whispered, fierce, her eyes slipping past me and landing on Cate. "Don't you dare hurt her just because you're afraid. Either love her fully or not at all."

"What are you talking about?" I asked, glancing back, worried that Cate had heard. Heat stirred in my stomach, and guilt, and something like excitement—

Patricia shook her head, let go of my hand. "Goodbye, Girl One."

25

The farther we got from the Bishops' solitary farmhouse, the more I realized how far-flung we were, barely a lit window in sight. I was floating—my body unable to withstand the weight of what I'd just learned. The Volvo's gas gauge hovered precariously near empty, the road illuminated by cold stripes of moonlight. Cate was asleep in the backseat, her breathing soft.

I told Tom everything, brusque and objective. Like I was a stranger to the story. Tom didn't speak for a long time. I watched his face closely, and even in the dimness of the car interior I could tell that he wasn't shocked. A muscle jumped along his jaw, and he nodded as he listened, but if anything, he seemed angry. Like I was only verifying something he'd known.

"Well?" I asked at last. Daylight was impossibly far away. "Aren't you going to say something? Do you think my mother killed Bellanger?"

"I don't know why you're asking me." Tom was speaking too carefully.

"Because you were the one who suggested that Peters didn't kill Bellanger."

A heavy exhale. "Yeah. Okay? Yeah, I knew," Tom said. "At least, I knew it had to be one of the women at the Homestead. Something went wrong way before the fire. Lily-Anne's death should've pulled everyone closer together instead of chasing them away."

My head was tight with the pain, palms clammy. I wasn't sure whether to be grateful or resentful that he'd kept this hidden from me for the past few days, giving me the gift of assuming my mother was the innocent party.

"I wanted to be proven wrong," Tom added, more softly now, some of that anger dissipating. "I know this is hard on you."

If he felt sorry for me right now, I was going to break down. Any tiny sign of kindness would push me over an edge. "Please don't," I said. Crying would sap the last dregs of my energy.

We drove in silence for a while. "Where to?" Tom asked finally. "We need to crash for the night soon. I spotted a motel about ten miles back—"

"The Homestead," I interrupted, surprising myself. "I need to see it."

"Josie, that's not such a good idea," Tom said, speaking gingerly. "I went there already. It's . . . not what you'd expect. It hasn't been well maintained."

"I want to go."

Tom didn't press the issue any further. This late, the radios mostly produced static or lovelorn songs dedicated to people who weren't listening. I almost drifted down into sleep, again and again, but each time I began slipping into those pockets of darkness my mother waited for me, the flicker of flame reflected bright in each pupil, and I'd jerk awake.

"We're here," Tom said at last, and I sat up straighter, looked around. For a second I thought Tom was joking. Then, in the moonlight, I spotted a pentagram spray-painted onto a tree trunk, neon-orange against the muted silvers and grays. We were at the right place.

I emerged into the stirring chill of the night air. Insects chirped and sang. The woods had grown back, reclaiming their spot. In my head all these years, I'd imagined that the Homestead would still be a smoldering ruin, perpetually leaking smoke into the sky. But it had healed, of course; the trees, younger than me, were small and upright. The clearing was overgrown with calf-high grass. This spot where the course of human history had been irrevocably shifted. If Bellanger had lived, this place would've become a museum or a research institute. As it was, the only glimmers of its former glory lay in how heavily it had been vandalized.

Graffiti ribboned around tree trunks. I spotted glinting nests of old food wrappers, beer bottles, trash. A few memorial wreaths, now limp and weather-damaged. Near my feet, a yellowish tangle lay in the grass, a deflated balloon of a condom. I stepped back quickly, trying to imagine the people who came here. Curious tourists passing through, having noticed the Homestead in some guide to off-the-beaten-path attractions. The remaining zealots, both those who loved us and those who hated us. Teenagers, late at night, escaping their parents' attention. The idea of teens making out at the very spot where sexless birth had enjoyed its heyday had a skewed romance to it.

I shut my eyes, breathed deeply. Had Bellanger died knowing what my mother had done to him? Did her guilt extend to me too? His letters had held almost nothing but love and pride, a constant push for me to do better. To never forget my role as Girl One. If he'd somehow been able to write a letter to me after 1977—a letter on my seventh birthday— what would he have said? Knowing that my mother had taken him away from me. Knowing that I'd grow up to look just like his murderer.

"Do you know," Tom said, "when a forest grows back after a fire, sometimes it's not even the same forest? Different trees grow faster because the soil's been changed by the fire. So really, you might be looking at a whole new forest now."

A breeze tugged at the hair around my temples, sending wisps into my eyes. I'd interpreted my mother's silence as a sign that she wanted to move from the past. I hadn't considered that she'd been hiding and protecting another woman—one who was daring, defiant, an impossible dreamer, and a ruthless killer. A Margaret Morrow who was a fugitive from both herself and her own daughter.

"I need to ask my mother about this," I said, a flare of grief. "She's the only one who can tell me the truth. And I might never find her now."

"There are still other Homesteaders out there," Tom said. "Don't give up just yet. The Kims, the Grassis. The Strouds. Your mother could be visiting them. She has that whole list, and we know for a fact that she visited both Emily and Deb."

I was so tired. I thought of my apartment, the predictability of the cool, pale lecture halls, the zebrafish darting and sparkling. Chicago was a place where everything about my past was confined inside the pages of textbooks. Where I knew who I was and where I was going. For a while the future had felt auspicious, welcoming, and now it was cluttered and overshadowed by a past I hadn't ever understood.

"The others might know more about who really set the fire," I said. "I'm not sure I trust Patricia." But then I realized something. We were right here in Vermont. Why waste time with secondary sources? "Tom. I should talk to Ricky Peters in person. If he's spending his life in prison for a crime he didn't commit, he'll jump at the chance to tell me what happened."

Tom hesitated.

"What?"

"You can't just walk into a prison like it's a hotel lobby. You need to be on an approved list, pass all kinds of background checks. It could take weeks for you to get in to see him, and that's if Ricky even allows it—"

"Even so," I said, determined now. "I'm going to try."

A sharp knock.

I woke up. My neck held a complicated ache from sleeping in the Volvo. My eyes were sticky and bleary. I let it all come back to me: my mother, the custody battle, fighting with Bellanger, lighting the match. This was the last morning I'd wake up and have to reconstruct this. From this point on, it would be a simple reality. My mother the murderer.

In the driver's seat, Tom was asleep, long legs pulled up uncomfortably, chin to chest; in the backseat, Cate curled into a fetal position, her face relaxed in sleep.

Another hard tap against the glass, right near my temple. I jumped more fully awake, heart hammering, muscles gripping suddenly. The stranger had followed us here. The man in the maroon sedan. He'd hunted us, tracked us, and now we were sitting ducks. Unguarded and asleep in this little car, no weapons, nothing. Hidden from the main road.

Slowly, I turned my head. Someone was leaning down to stare inside the car, face too close for comfort, backlit and shadowed by the rising sun, whites of the eyes glinting. I was going to scream: I could feel the sound in my throat, constricting, rising—

"Isabelle?"

She smiled and pulled back, gesturing for me to open the door.

I glanced around. Tom and Cate had stayed asleep, though Cate mumbled to herself and turned over. I stepped outside, shutting the door as softly as I could. The morning air was cool and fresh after the muggy interior of the Volvo.

"I knew I'd find you here," Isabelle said. Her long hair was tucked back in a high ponytail, and she wore a starched white blouse and puffy floral skirt, too old for her. She was flanked by two suitcases. Childish ones, with embroidered rainbows arcing across the sides. A purse, nice brown leather, old-ladyish, was resting on her hip, the strap cutting into her shoulder. She was channeling three different age ranges at once, all of them wrong for her.

"Where did you even come from?" The clearing behind her was empty. We were miles and miles from the Bishops' house.

"I took a taxi," she said. "This was the only place I could think of that you might be."

I gestured at the suitcases. "What's this all about?"

Isabelle was radiating something different: she was sharper, energy thrumming off her in neat waves. Her deferent slouch was gone, straightened out as if somebody had taken her and tugged all her bones in the right direction. "Guess what," she said. "I'm coming with you."

26

I filled out the paperwork carefully, extracting each detail from my memory before I put pen to paper. I was wearing the plainest outfit I had, black dress pants that pinched at the waist and left my ankles exposed, a white T-shirt. I kept my head down, willing myself into invisibility, hoping the guard wouldn't notice how little I resembled the person I was supposed to be. The heavy lights buzzed overhead. I felt the electricity building behind my eyes, the light tug of temptation: I could just convince the bleary-eyed man in front of me to let me through, no questions asked. I had the ID and the forms. I looked reasonable enough to a casual observer. It would only take a few seconds of eye contact to get what I wanted.

But the guard merely took my paperwork with a single weary sigh, flicked the barest glance at the top, and said, "Thank you, Miss Bishop."

Quickly adjusting to this unexpected luck, I moved over to the door. Everything here was gray, greasy, stuck behind layers and layers of windows and doors, a sturdy labyrinth of defenses. As I waited to be admitted into the next circle of this strange afterlife, I shook my shoulders back, swallowed the taste of sour anxiety that was drying out my mouth, and prepared to meet Ricky Peters.

It had been Isabelle's idea. She was already proving useful: she'd brought along a wallet stuffed with money, replenishing our dwindling funds. Even more valuable, she'd suggested that I pose as her to gain access to the prison. Patricia had apparently visited Ricky over the years, and she'd included Isabelle on the approved visitors list just in case her daughter ever wanted to meet the man. ("I didn't," she'd said, "he has creepy eyes.")

I had to know. The question of whether Ricky had killed Bellanger was the center around which my biggest questions rotated. Who was following us; where my mother had gone; what, exactly, my mother had done. Who she really was.

The plastic chair was punitively uncomfortable. A thick plastic window in front of me was framed by small lips of brick on either side, a comical illusion of privacy. To my left, a woman in a red raincoat, even though the day was sunny: to my right, an older man who looked like he'd been pulled from the dryer still damp. They were probably wife-of, father-of.

The prisoners began shuffling in, wearing baggy jumpsuits. A disturbingly peppy shade of orange. I kept scanning each face. I'd only seen Ricky in photographs. I tried to age him mentally. Gray the hair, add crow's-feet. I was so busy searching that it was a surprise when somebody was sitting down on the other side of the glass, picking up the black phone receiver, clearing his throat. The push of his Adam's apple: he was speaking. I couldn't hear anything.

Fascinated by him, struck by the weirdness of the moment, I couldn't even make myself pick up the phone on my side of the partition. A clutter of laughter, tears, low voices had risen around us. Ricky Peters was nobody special. I could've passed him on the street without looking twice. He was that bland. He must've blended right into the stream of prisoners' faces passing me by. Once I examined him closely through the fingerprint-smudged window, I could see traces of the man from the photos. Weak chin, the wide-set eyes. The mole on one side of his neck. Above all else: the look of contempt on his face, the way it radiated outward, crawled over me.

Snapping out of it, I reached for the phone. The plastic was gritty and slippery at once. His voice was waiting for me. "It's been quite a while since I've had a visitor," he said. A clipped voice, almost mannerly, but with something sticky lurking underneath.

"I'm Isabelle Bishop," I said. "Patricia's girl."

"Isabelle," he repeated. His eyes drifted freely up and down the length of my body, assessing, and I resisted the urge to cover myself up, as if my clothes had suddenly melted away. "Your mother used to come and see me sometimes. A nice enough lady. She mostly wanted to reminisce about Margaret Morrow."

"I'm here about Margaret too. She's missing."

"Is that right, Josephine?" Ricky asked, and winked. "I don't know anything about your mother."

I swallowed hard, embarrassed by the weariness in his voice, like he was bored of humoring a young child. Of course he knew who I was. This man who'd devoted himself to our undoing. Such a powerful force that even after Bellanger was dead and Ricky was behind bars, their rivalry—the push between good and evil, God and science—had shaped my whole life and my place in the world.

"The peculiar thing about seeing you girls," Ricky said, "is how much you resemble your mothers at the same age. I could swear you were Margaret, coming to deliver me that look she always gave me." He pointed, his face breaking open with a brief delight that turned him younger. "Exactly that one."

My mother had been resurrected on my face just a second ago and I hadn't even known.

"It does a man good, as a matter of fact, seeing the same faces reappearing like this. It makes me feel twenty years younger to look at you." His eyes moved to my breasts.

This time, I did grab for the front of my T-shirt, instinctively trying to cover myself. "You've aged more than twenty years, yourself," I snapped back.

Ricky gave a small nod, amused.

"Did you send somebody after my mother?" I asked, knowing I was losing my cool, not fighting it. "Did you tell somebody to set that fire? Do you know where she is?"

"Such a chatterbox. Any other questions, while you're at it? The meaning of the universe, perhaps?"

"Just those three."

"The answer to all three is the same thing: no."

I leaned forward until the damp man and the raincoated woman on either side of me were hidden from view. Ricky leaned in too; without the glass we might've looked like we were about to kiss. "Patricia Bishop told me that you shouldn't be in here," I said, so low that nobody could overhear. "She said that you weren't the one to start the fire."

He didn't seem surprised. "So she came around."

"You were found guilty."

"That I was," he agreed. "I'm sure it's been easier on you all, knowing that I'm locked up in here. Everyone's happy. Of course, sometimes I worry for you girls."

"We're fine," I said brusquely. "Don't waste time worrying about us."

"But I do. Because I'm not a bad man, Josephine. And the real killer is still out there."

As a child, I'd known Ricky less as a person and more as a disembodied threat: a distant voice leading rhythmic chants at the edge of the compound, the anger flattened out by repetition until it was no more remarkable than birdsong. I'd only seen him in person a few times, on the rare occasions when we left the grounds. Those faces clustered at the edges of our property, all those grown-ups turning to stare at me, jostling for a better view. Most of them were angry—gazes so hard and cold I had to look down at my own arm, sun-freckled, to remind myself I was there. That I hadn't actually turned into a monster. But there were other faces, curious or kind.

Later on, I'd been baffled when I'd first identified Ricky Peters as the ringleader, the one who'd murdered Bellanger. I remembered him as one of the friendlier faces, a man who'd sometimes smiled at me. Now those smiles took on a slippery quality in my memory, more threatening than the scowls.

"If you're not guilty, why did you accept the plea deal?" I demanded. "Why let yourself rot away in here for something you didn't do?"

"You have no idea," Ricky said softly. "I was proud, back then, and idealistic. I wasn't going to waste my best years in prison when I was an innocent man. You better believe I was full of fire. They'd slapped me with so many trumped-up charges. Trespassing, aggravated assault, arson, two first-degree murders. I'm not from Vermont, you realize. I traveled here all the way from Alabama. I had to come here once I saw that doctor on the news. After the fire, though, they painted me as an outsider who'd brought scandal and death to this nice little state. They were out for my blood. My lawyer counseled me to take the plea bargain. One charge of second-degree murder, one charge of manslaughter for the little girl. I refused. I wanted to bring the real killer to justice, you see. So I brought it to trial. I trusted that the world would be on my side. I'd shown the world what you were. I told the world what it meant for women to have babies on their own—what it meant for us men, if it kept on. And what good did it do? Nothing." He leaned back. "People get too distracted by the shiny and the new, and you girls were shiny and new. There were baby dolls of you girls in the stores, for little Suzy to get under the Christmas tree. Like it was something little girls would want for themselves one day."

I'd seen my baby doll in old ads. A generic doll, bubble-headed, tufty-haired, with a ONE on her bib. It had been discontinued, but apparently the dolls sold for a lot on underground markets now as novelty items.

"The world *was* on your side," I said, my heartbeat gathered in the spot where my cheek pressed into the receiver. "They did hate us."

"As it turns out, they were not on my side," Ricky said, his voice holding long-ago bitterness. "You should've seen that trial. Those young women weren't the enemies anymore. They'd turned into victims. As sweet as could be. The world looked at me and saw a man who'd murdered a little girl. They forgot who that girl was, and they forgot what she stood for. They just imagined one of their own little girls burning in a blaze set by a monster like me and they wanted justice."

The world on our side. I was a little sorry I'd missed that.

"I had my evidence and I was going to remind the world what Dr. Bellanger had actually done. I was just biding my time. But then your mother took the stand—oh, your mother took the stand! You should've seen her. A girl you'd take home to your mother. Pretty dress. Nice hair, la-di-da. She sat up there and she talked about how I'd threatened all of you. She talked about how scared she was. Everyone in that room was in love with her. It was after her testimony that I went to my lawyer and said we should take the plea bargain. 'I can't do it,' I said. 'Nobody will believe my evidence, coming on the heels of that.' "

"What was your evidence?" I asked, riveted in spite of myself.

"The evening of the fire," Ricky said, "your mother came to talk to me. Usually the ladies steered clear of me, and I steered clear of them, but here she came, out of the shadows. She was jumpy, like she had bugs under her skin. She got real close, whispering. 'You're right about Bellanger,' she said. 'You're the only one who saw it all along. He's a bad man.' It felt like a miracle. I'd been waiting for those girls to recognize how much they'd debased themselves by aligning themselves with the doctor. All my hard work was finally paying off."

"That's it?" I asked, ignoring the chill down my spine. "My mother telling you that she hated Bellanger? That's nothing."

He held up a hand, a simple command: *Wait*. His skin was surprisingly smooth, almost poreless, protected from direct sunlight for years "She showed me a gun. She was carrying it with her. A handgun. She said, 'Let's you and me do this, Ricky, end it all now. Don't let him get away with it. He has my girl under his spell, and he'll never let her go.'" He locked eyes with me and he didn't look away.

End it all now.

"Bullshit," I said. "There was no gun found in the wreckage. No gunshot wounds." But there was a slick of betrayal in my belly, this image of my mother wielding a gun, wild-eyed, willing to ally herself with a man who'd dedicated his life to destroying us. And it had been because of me. Her jealousy over Bellanger's role in my life.

"Exactly. I've had a lot of time to think about it, and I figure she changed her mind. Do you know why she set the fire instead of using the gun? So it would be easier to pin it on me. She'd heard me yelling at Bellanger about hellfire. The whole world had heard it. With a fire, you don't have to worry about fingerprints or who bought the gun. I never gave her an answer, but she found a way to pin the whole thing on me."

"I don't believe you," I said, trying to make it sound true.

Ricky Peters opened his palm flat, as if showing me he had nothing, even as his eyes glittered dully against me, mocking. I knew he was enjoying this.

"Why do you think I ended up here? All the evidence points to me. I threatened to take that man's life, and I truly did want him gone. I've never denied that. I was on the compound the night of the fire. I left behind evidence. There was gasoline found at my apartment. I was forced to take a new plea deal. Fifty years behind bars, and I waived the right to appeal. It was the best I could do. If I went against your mother without physical proof, and that courtroom looked at me the way you're looking at me, I'd have been facing the chair. So I did what I could."

I breathed in, breathed out. My mother with a gun. My mother with a match. The wild look in her eyes as we ran, that freedom, that thrill.

"Do you want to know what gets me through the lonely nights? Maybe I didn't convince the whole world that Dr. Bellanger was an evil man," Ricky said. "But I convinced your mother. And now look: His work was lost. Nobody else managed to step into his shoes. For a while, life was restored to the way it should be, just men and women creating families together. Or I thought so, until you showed up in the news." I felt that deep-seated hatred beneath the surface, cold and unyielding, always there.

"You're upset that I'm trying to restore what Bellanger achieved at the Homestead," I said. "Is that why you had my mother attacked?"

He didn't even blink. "We just covered this. I'm not the bad guy here."

By now some of the other visitors were trickling away, the guards' stares drawing a tighter lasso around the room. "Bonnie Clarkson," I said, and his expression shifted. "That attack was in your name. A little girl left scarred."

Ricky's face stayed closed off.

There was the sudden pull at the back of my skull, an almost overwhelming desire to draw the information out of him. To reach inside him and extract it by force, have that control over this man who still saw me as a threat to his own power. But we were surrounded by strangers and witnesses. "Somebody's been following me and the other Homestead survivors," I said instead. "A man in a maroon sedan. Friend of yours?"

"You can't use me as a scapegoat for the rest of your life," Ricky said.

Fine. Enough. Leaning forward, I sought out his gaze and locked eyes with him, feeling his sudden stillness. The dizziness swelled and crested more quickly this time, like it was a muscle I'd been training. "Tell me if you had anything to do with my mother's disappearance," I said into the receiver, and imagined the words traveling that brief distance, striking his eardrum, sending the fine vibrations and electric signals crawling up the auditory nerve and landing in his brain. "Tell me," I repeated, "if you did anything to my mother."

His face twitched with a quick muscle flinch, like he was trying to shake away a bad memory and couldn't. His mouth dropped open. "No," he said, like a sleepwalker. "I didn't do it. I know nothing about it."

"Tell me if you set the fire that killed Bellanger," I said. The dizziness made me clutch the edge of the chair.

"I didn't set the fire."

I absorbed the shock quietly. So everything I'd known about my origin story was a lie. It felt like my DNA was untwisting in response, taking me apart. I hesitated for just a moment. "Tell me," I said slowly, "tell me if my mother threatened Bellanger the evening of the fire."

"She did," Ricky said. "She spoke to me just like I told you. I'll always remember the look in her eyes. That long, dark hair." He lifted a finger, sketched a line up and down, up and down, as if he were stroking my hair through the plastic.

The visiting time was almost over. To an outside observer, Ricky and I were doing nothing wrong—just two people talking, like any other pair in this room. But I felt conspicuous, wild, reckless.

"Do you know who's after my mother now?" I asked, and realized too late that I'd phrased it all wrong, a question and not a command. The dizziness fell away, and Ricky began turning his head, responding to the guard's announcement. Our connection wavered and I was scrambling, ordinary again.

The prisoners were rising. People were hanging up phones, gathering their things, preparing to walk away. I tried to catch Ricky's eye, but he kept his head lowered. "Sixteen years, Josephine," he whispered into the phone. "The first plea deal. The deal I turned down. Do you know what my idealism cost me? I could be a free man today. When your mother set that fire, she hurt a lot of people. A lot of people. More than you know."

"What does that even mean?"

Still, he wouldn't look at me. "Think it through slowly, Girl One." Then he was walking away, absorbed back into the bloodstream of jumpsuits as if he'd never been here at all.

27

"Well, if it isn't the woman of the hour," Dr. McCarter said. "I walked into the lab today expecting to see you in your usual spot, and yet—"

"I'm sorry," I interrupted, leaning against the sun-hot brick of the gas station. "I'm on my way home right now."

I said it aloud partially to remind myself that this was the right decision. That it was the *only* decision. I'd felt it in my gut as soon as I'd walked out of the prison: I couldn't help my mother. I didn't know who she was anymore. I'd been on the bright verge of abandoning everything—all I'd worked for, all Bellanger had worked for—to rescue a woman who'd never wanted rescuing. I was going home. Within a few days, I'd be back in the lab, goggles humid against my cheekbones, my mother forgotten. Relegated to the past she'd hidden from me.

"I've been keeping up with the story about your mother," Dr. McCarter said. "It sounds to me like you've done your best and now you can rest easy."

"Wait. What are you talking about?" With one fingernail, I traced the clumsy geometric initials carved into the side of the phone booth. Dr. McCarter couldn't possibly know about my conversation with Ricky, but everything was so scrambled right now that I couldn't be sure who knew what, all the edges of my life turned soft and pliable.

Dr. McCarter hesitated before he answered, like he thought I might be joking. "Well. It's been revealed that there were no accelerants. No signs of foul play. The fire had multiple points of origin. The authorities are thinking it could've been insurance fraud. Apparently it's not uncommon—especially with no deaths or injuries—"

"They're saying she did it herself?" I paused with my fingernail lodged in the crook of an *M*, trying to identify whether it was relief or unease growing under my skin.

"Listen, Jo," Dr. McCarter said. "You should be thinking critically about how to address this to the press. We've had quite a few requests for interviews, and that's not the kind of publicity anybody wants. I'll offer you my support, of course, the whole department will. You don't need more distractions. But we do need to get out ahead of things."

I shut my eyes for a second, hit with the blunt end of the realization. It was happening again. My mother had ended Bellanger's work the first time, reducing his brilliant brain down to ashes, and now, seventeen years later, she'd used the same tactic to disrupt my own work, disappearing before she could even be held accountable.

"Really, Jo, it's a testament to how exceptional you are. Raised by a single mother in poverty. We don't fully understand the far-reaching consequences of how parthenogenesis affected the mothers. A mother who was undereducated, with mental health issues—"

"What are you talking about?" I asked. "She doesn't have mental health issues."

A silence. "I'm just basing this on what you've told me," he said too carefully. "The isolation of your upbringing, her reluctance to confront her own past. You've said yourself it's not normal behavior."

"I never said that," I said, surprised by my own defensiveness, even as I thought of the disappearance and the notebook and the abandoned house, my wild-eyed mother knocking on doors, ranting about dead girls. Lighting a match. I swallowed, my throat dry, my tongue heavy.

"I'm not trying to insult you," Dr. McCarter said. "You should be quite proud to have come so far on your own."

"Yeah, well," I said. "Maybe you should explore the far-reaching consequences of parthenogenesis on the daughters too. You could've saved me a lot of time if you'd addressed that sooner. Anyway, I'll be home soon," I said, before he could respond, and hung up.

When I turned around, Tom was waiting for me, and I knew from his expression—jaw set, eyebrows tugged together—that we were about to have a serious talk. I groaned. "God, not now, Tom. Please. I don't need an after-school special."

I began walking back to the Volvo at a brisk pace, arms crossed. Tom fell into step beside me. "You're doing this, huh? Giving up. That's it.

What about the notebook? Your mother's notebook? You aren't even curious about why she—"

I stopped, facing him. "Is this about *your* book? Because we need to talk about that. I'm not sure it's a good idea. I don't know if you should be sharing these things with the world."

"I was under the impression that you cared as much as I do about bringing Bellanger's work back to the forefront."

"That was before I knew—look, Tom, I'm worried that if you run off and publish a book about this, my work will get derailed. I'll be dragged down into the scandal." *Even deeper into the scandal,* I amended mentally. "I need to be running damage control right now, not making things worse by yelling to the world about murder or Fiona's powers. If you care about my career, you'll keep it between us."

I hadn't told Tom about the footage in the basement or about Cate. These felt like things I needed to keep private. I'd liked bouncing ideas off him, hearing his theories, but this was too personal, a part of my very skin and bones. And now I was glad I'd let Tom stay in a world where Fiona's abilities were still rumors. The less he knew, the better.

"What about Margaret?" Tom demanded. "She could be in serious danger, and you're running home to Chicago to hide away in a lab?"

"She can take care of herself," I snapped. "She's been making sure of that for years."

Tom looked as if he were preparing to go on, but then exhaled, controlling himself with an effort. "It's your choice, of course."

"Don't lecture me," I said. "I can't go chasing after my mom. She never wanted me to be part of her life. Never. Whatever is going on here, she shut me out for a reason. She even told you to keep me out of it, didn't she?" Tom nodded, quieted in the face of my anger. "My mom didn't want me to know who she really was. I started to think she planned this on purpose to drag me away from my studies. But maybe even that's too much effort on her part. Maybe this whole—this quest— this whatever-it-is—it has nothing to do with me. She didn't expect me to come after her, and she didn't want me to." My hands couldn't stop shaking. "So I'm going to focus on my future," I said, "and let my mom do whatever she needs to do. Without me."

Across the empty lot, a fluttering V formation of birds took off from the telephone wires, darted one way and then another before vanishing up into the sky. It nearly knocked me over, the depth of this anger. Why hadn't my mother told me? Why hadn't she let me in? I wanted to understand why she'd done . . . everything. Why she'd wanted me so deeply, this impossible daughter; why she'd killed Bellanger. How she could have let Fiona die. How she'd felt standing in that courtroom, willingly putting an innocent man behind bars. It was the first time that I'd felt the same ache of loss over my mother that I'd always felt toward Bellanger. I'd lost her, and unlike Bellanger, she'd vanished on purpose.

I didn't have the space in my heart to mourn both of them. If my mother hadn't wanted me to carry on Bellanger's work—if she'd had something to tell me—she should have spoken up.

"Josie," Cate said abruptly. "Can I have my mother's things back? The letter and the photo you took. It's not like you're going to be using them."

I was hunkered low in the passenger seat, gazing out the window. For the past few hours, I'd given in to the grubby luxury of sulking. I'd assumed it would feel good to head back to Chicago, but instead there was an empty space in my gut. I tried to fit myself back into my lecture halls and polite TV appearances, knowing what I did about myself and about my mother. It wasn't as easy as just turning around and heading the opposite direction on the freeway. I had to figure out how to return to my old life as if my whole understanding of myself hadn't been ripped apart and put back together. I wasn't sure I was up to the task.

I unfurled, glancing back at Cate. "Yeah. Of course. Patricia kept the letter, but you can have whatever else—" I reached down for the little marble-bound notebook that had started it all. What if I'd never looked inside the clock? Never found Tom's number? Never set off to find Emily. Never met Cate. My mother would still be missing, but it wouldn't be my problem. That should've felt comforting, but the emptiness only expanded.

"Just take this whole thing," I said to Cate. "You're right. I won't be using it."

As I reached back to pass the notebook to her, a photo slipped loose from the inside and dropped onto my lap. Lily-Anne's bright, knowing smile. Her heavily pregnant belly. The framed images behind her. This time the photo felt more intimate, like it had just been taken a day or two ago. Maybe because I'd seen it during the footage of Fiona. I lifted it up to take a closer look. There was the headline about my birth. There was the framed *Time* cover. Rows of faces, too tiny to make out clearly. Bold white letters read "OF THE YEAR."

Cate held her hand out, gently impatient, but I didn't let go of the photo. "Hey. Does anybody know when the *Time* Women of the Year cover ran? It was the early seventies, right?"

"I can't recall—" Tom began, but Isabelle was talking over him.

"It was 1976," she said confidently.

"How do you know?"

"There was a photo of that cover hanging on the wall," Isabelle said casually. "I've watched that movie every week since I was ten years old. I've seen the camera go past that wall hundreds of times. I know that frame. You can see it clear as day. The *Time* cover is from January of 1976."

"This cover?" I handed the photo back to Isabelle, who gave me an odd look but accepted it. "Because that can't be right," I said. "Fiona was born in April 1975. She was nine months old by the time that cover came out."

I knew the dates. Lily-Anne had become pregnant in July of 1974. She'd given birth in April 1975, almost exactly four years after my birth. It was the last pregnancy on the Homestead, the last human virgin birth ever recorded, although nobody had known it at the time.

Cate leaned over to take a look. My excitement grew. I was getting too used to this, I realized: having other people around to share my curiosity. I hadn't experienced this at the University of Chicago yet, where I so often felt hemmed in, uncertain, defensive.

"Maybe you got the date wrong," Tom said.

"No," Cate said slowly. "Because 1975 was International Women's Year. I remember my mom talking about this *Time* thing. She hated it, thought it was all for show. The article said something about how women's lib was like 'discovering a new continent.' Oh okay, we've only been around for two hundred thousand years, but burn a few bras and suddenly you notice us?"

"So let's say this photo *was* taken in 1976," I said. "Lily-Anne couldn't possibly have been pregnant with Fiona. How is she pregnant in this photo, then?"

Nobody answered.

"Did your mothers ever tell you about a tenth pregnancy?" I asked.

"No," Isabelle said, and Cate shook her head.

Tom spoke up: "We would've heard about this. A tenth pregnancy from a mother who'd already given birth? This should've been front-page news."

"We could go back and ask Patricia if she knows anything," Cate said, looking at Isabelle, who instantly and vigorously shook her head.

"No," Isabelle said. "I'm not going home."

"Then we should be talking to Barbara," Cate said. "She's right here in the photo." Her expression was tight, like she wasn't sure what to think.

"The Kims are in North Carolina," Tom said. "More than a day of driving, and it would take us seriously out of our way if we're heading to Chicago." His gaze flicked to me, gauging whether or not I'd yield. I kept my face neutral. "But there's another possibility if we're all okay with a shorter detour. Another Homesteader lives nearby and might know something about this. Vera Stroud."

Mother Six.

"She and Delilah live in upstate New York," Tom said. "A town called Kithira."

28

Stately colonial houses, red brick and crisp white shutters; the fresh green of the leaves and lawns making everything look newly washed. We were heading to 1512 Skylark Lane, the Strouds' last known address. It was one of those towns where every building had a complex family history. A great-grandmother who'd planted a particular oak; a distant uncle who'd named a sawmill. Completely unfamiliar to me, this idea of long-reaching and tangled family ties. My mother and I were it.

As we drove, the houses changed, slumping and shrinking. Skylark was just a trickle of a road. It might've been the optimistic beginnings of a subdivision, but had given up at just one or two homes. A wide swath of undeveloped forest lay a few yards away. It was late in the afternoon, the sky heavy and golden.

The Stroud house had dingy white siding, a steep staircase leading to a cramped front porch. There were no lights in the windows. Standing on the porch stairs, I worried the four of us looked less like visitors than trespassers. I noticed all the signs of long absence. A stack of mail flaking onto the porch, leaking out of the overstuffed mailbox. Pine needles clogging the gutters.

Cate gave up on the doorbell and was shading her eyes to peer into the window, craning over the edge of the porch railing. "Hello?" she called, and knocked. The door creaked open at her touch. There wasn't anybody on the other side. Just darkness, shadows, the humped silhouettes of furniture. "What the hell?" she murmured.

We exchanged quick glances, all of us equally alarmed.

Inside, the Strouds' home smelled both musty and ripe. The rooms were gloomy with the blinds shut. The sour smell only grew more potent as I moved through the living room—the TV was playing but muted, an anchor laughing at her cohost with her lipsticked mouth wide open.

While the other three branched off, I hung back, trying to ignore how much this reminded me of entering my mother's flame-ravaged house. The same impression of a life abruptly interrupted. My skin crawled.

I passed through the kitchen, looking for Cate. The source of the smell was a plate of food in the kitchen. A sandwich, blackened and haloed by flies. I had to cover my face with my shirt, my eyes watering. A photo was stuck to the fridge, Vera Stroud and her daughter, their arms draped around each other's shoulders. The refrigerator door was ajar. The coffee maker was plugged in, light glowing red. A purse yawned open on the counter.

"Morrow." Cate's voice was bright with urgency, coming from deeper inside the house. "You have to hear this."

I traced her voice to a small nook off the kitchen. She stood next to a clunky gray answering machine resting on a side table, surrounded by cast-offs of a normal life. Bobby pins, a bright green scrunchie, a gum wrapper. Cate hit a button, and there was a whir, then a mechanical voice—*First saved message*—and the date, back at the end of March. A young man's voice, nervously clearing his throat. *Hey, Del, it's me, uh, call me back—*

Cate pushed the button. *Next saved message.* This one from only a few weeks ago. I was aware of Cate looking at me, watching me closely and gently. My mother's voice was filling the room. *Vera. I know it's been a long time. I was hoping to discuss . . . well. I was hoping to discuss Fiona. There. I said it.*

It had been so long since I'd heard my mother's voice that for a second it shifted in and out of focus, sounding both like her and not like her at all. She was what I heard inside my head. Older, maybe, and throatier, but my own voice. I closed my eyes so that she was all around me, and if I peeled away the Strouds' house I could be back in our own home. Bent over my homework as my mother talked on the phone to a coworker, or talked to herself in the kitchen as she prepared a frozen meal.

My mother. How could I have ever thought we were done with each other when her voice was the one I heard in my own head? A thought darted through my brain. Maybe my mother had had her reasons to set the fire. Maybe if I just asked her, I'd understand why she'd done it. The thought was a betrayal at first. Traitorous to Bellanger. Discomfort twisted in my belly.

Then I breathed deep, let the thought stay. What if?

"Play the message again?" I asked Cate, opening my eyes and blinking the tears away. This time I listened more closely.

It's—it's difficult to explain over the phone. I would rather speak in person if you'd let me. I understand if that's—well, if you don't want to see me. But I have to try, Vera. We let Fiona down. We let Lily-Anne down. I—look, maybe I'll talk to you soon. She recited our home number, the familiarity of it making my heart throb. *All right. Goodbye.*

"So we know for sure she was in contact with the Strouds," I said into the silence.

Cate nodded. "It'd be great if we could ask the Strouds about it."

From the other room, Isabelle called out a wordless exclamation. Cate and I exchanged quick glances before hurrying to her. We found Tom coming from the other end of the house, his face tight with worry. In the kitchen, Isabelle had pulled the dusty tartan curtains aside, letting the brilliant early evening sunlight into the kitchen. She crouched near the back door. "Look," she said simply. I knelt beside her. A rusty smear stretched along the wall, and in the slanted light, it was hard to tell whether it was a deep brown or closer to red. The stain resolved into a familiar pattern. It was a dark brownish blotch, rounded and cleft, and then two longer, thinner stains extending from the top. An interrupted handprint, stamped in blood.

A spiky dread climbed up my spine. Cate's face changed: it dropped into shock and then, just as quickly, hardened into determination.

Isabelle rose, brushing her hand against her skirt, and opened the back door. There was another small porch out there, a rickety set of stairs leading down into a threadbare backyard, the forest looming a few yards beyond the edge. Isabelle stepped outside, the sunlight catching bronze in her mousy hair. She turned in a slow circle.

"There's more," she called. "On the porch railing."

I didn't know how Isabelle could speak so calmly. My pulse was a hard rhythm now. "The stranger in the maroon car," I breathed. He'd found the Strouds before we had. We'd come here too late to warn them, too late to do any good except to be the witnesses to what he'd left behind. This impossible ghost, always one step ahead of us.

It was dazzling with sunset outside, unfairly beautiful, steeped in peacefulness. Isabelle knelt in the grass, pressing her palm flat. She straightened and pointed, her pale arm highlighted by the sun, her outstretched finger aiming right into the heart of the forest. "It goes that way."

The forest was weedy and dark, as if the shadows were generated from an unseen source, fleshing out the spaces between the thin and tangled branches. Even in the spring, dead leaves choked the ground. We'd entered another part of the world. "Should we be yelling for them?" Tom asked, hushed.

Now that we were in the woods, we'd all gone quiet, sticking close together. The underbrush was dense and wild, an untended pocket in the middle of Kithira's carefully arranged domesticity. My arms had broken into thick goose bumps.

"Let's keep a low profile," Cate said.

I wondered how far from civilization we'd gone in just a few minutes. It was more and more silent, noise swallowed up in here. A few bursts of birdsong; the low hum of insects. But overall, the whole forest seemed to hold its breath.

"Up ahead," Cate said, gesturing.

A break in the trees, a loosening in the closed ranks. I caught a flutter of movement. A flash of white. I was instantly, urgently optimistic, picking up my pace, hurrying through the underbrush and over the rocky terrain until I nearly lost my footing.

"Hold on," said Tom, "Josie, wait—" He reached toward my elbow, but I wasn't listening. I locked my eyes on that shimmer of white that moved between the trees, like a woman dancing, or fleeing from me. Without thinking, I began to run. I broke through the trees and stopped short, my brain not catching up with what I was seeing.

A dress hung from the lowest branches of a tree, twisting and quivering in the breeze. It was strung up by its sleeves so that the empty fabric created the silhouette of a woman, headless and handless and limbless, shivering. The earth here was blackened and charred. There were no trees in this clearing, just the dark bones and stumps of burned trees. The smell of fire and ruin had reached me before I had a chance to guard myself. I didn't even realize I was leaning over, heaving and coughing, until I felt Cate's hand on my back and looked up, eyes watering, to see her high above me.

Tom was staying back, not venturing farther into the clearing, like he was afraid of contamination. Isabelle went to the dress and tore it down from the branches in one swift movement. One sleeve ripped slightly, leaving behind a trailing clump of threads. Isabelle held up the dress to her own body like she was trying it on. When she turned the dress around, there was a bloodstain near the waist, layers of maroon and brown, overlapping continents.

"We don't know what happened here," Tom said suddenly. His eyes were glassy, a strange cast to them. "We don't know if this has anything to do with the Strouds. We just came to town."

"What do you think happened?" Cate spat. "Somebody killed them. Someone hurt Vera and Delilah and then dragged them here. Maybe to burn them alive, or burn the evidence after the fact."

"Just like there was a fire that killed Bellanger and Fiona," I said. Bile collected at the back of my throat. "Just like the one at Cate's house. Just like there was a fire that—" But I couldn't complete the thought. My body folded in half, and I threw up again, grateful for the way the sensation took over my body. When I looked up again, the back of my throat as raw as a wound, Cate was staring into the trees.

Tom swallowed, scrubbed at his lower face with the back of his hand. "We need to tell somebody." His voice cracked a little, but he was firm now. "We'll go to the police. Whoever did this came to Kithira. Maybe people around here saw him. Maybe they met him. It's a small place. We need to ask around, figure out who did this—"

"Coeur du Lac is also small," I said. "Nobody saw who set the fire there."

"This is different," Tom said. "He's left evidence behind."

What if somewhere on the outskirts of Coeur du Lac, on the bank of some lonely reservoir or in the middle of an overgrown vacant lot, there was a spot like this? The remains of my mother.

"We aren't going to the cops," Cate said, low and vicious.

"But something's wrong," Tom said.

"This has been here awhile," Cate said. "Why didn't somebody see the smoke and investigate? Why didn't anybody check on Vera and Delilah? I don't see how something like this could've happened and then gone unnoticed for months."

"What are you trying to say?" Tom had lost some of that stunned quality, his initial panic shape-shifting into denial.

Isabelle was still clinging to the white dress, running a hand over it now, the idle, soothing way she might touch a newborn baby or a small animal.

"I'm saying that it might not be that simple," Cate said. "You think we're about to catch the bad guy, but we can't get reckless. We don't know anything about Kithira or the people who live here."

"This is our best chance to figure out who's been targeting all of you," Tom said. "This person is sick. He's dangerous. We need all the help we can get."

Cate's expression didn't change. She shook her head, mute. I could tell that Tom hadn't convinced her, and my own disquiet was mounting. All the violence in my past had happened when I wasn't looking, locked in a place beyond the reach of memory. This—the ashes, the blood—I couldn't think straight.

It had dipped into evening now, the sun hot and golden all around us, the kind of brilliance that came on the very cusp of darkness. Tom spoke up again, and this time he was gentler: "I get your hesitation, Cate, I do. So I'll take the lead. This is bigger than I realized. We need outside help." He paused. "This could be the only way we find out what happened to Josie's mother. I don't want to get in the way of that. Do you?"

Cate inhaled as if he'd struck her. All three of them were looking at me now. "I don't know," I said, miserable with the choice. "I want to find whoever did this to the Strouds. Of course I do. And my mother—" I couldn't even finish the sentence. I remembered Emily in the attic, the way she'd said that Tom would lead me to my mother. The simple comfort of that moment. "Tom's right," I said. "We can't handle this by ourselves anymore. It's too much."

"We'll go back to the Strouds' house," Tom said, relieved. "We'll call the police."

He turned to go. Cate didn't look at me as she moved, her face flinty. After a second, Isabelle followed, still holding the dress against her chest. I thought about telling her to leave it behind, but I couldn't stand to think of that dress hanging alone, in the trees, abandoned.

Following the others, I stopped at the edge of the clearing. There was something odd about the trees near the charred circle. Their bark looked strangely textured. Tattooed. I went closer, squinting. There were words carved into the skin of the trees, so linear they looked like hieroglyphics.

The markings appeared fresh, exposed skin still raw and pale. I reached out to touch them with my fingertips, like this extra information would help me interpret what was happening. I saw what looked like two Vs right next to each other, and my mind kept thinking V-V, V-V, or maybe five-five, until the two symbols consolidated into one letter. W. Then all at once: *Witches.* Hewn into the wood with those sharp angles, the S just a harsh series of connected lines. Three slashes. There, below it, another word, not quite identical, but similar. *Witches.* Another one, another one. A dozen. Some angled. Some written in huge letters, as long as my palm, others so small I could barely read them. The word was always the same, and it spread from trunk to trunk like an infection.

WITCHES WITCHES WITCHES WITCHES

29

I waited outside, listening dully to Tom and Cate argue next to me. Being inside the Strouds' house felt wrong. Morbid. The TV set flashed bright against the opposite wall, visible through the windows. All those laughing faces playing to an empty room. Those trees screaming WITCH into the silence.

"It's the right choice," Tom was insisting. "We can't go home without knowing what happened to Josie's mother. If this sheds any light on what happened to her—if this helps us catch the guy—"

"Is this about Margaret? Really?" Cate demanded. "Because I think this is a power play. You just want to show that you know what's best. And who *are* you, Thomas Abbott? I understand why Josie's looking for her mom, and why Isabelle's here, but I can't get my head around you—you talked to Margaret one time? That gives you some authority here?"

Isabelle was inside the house, watching from the window. The fighting crashed over me in waves. I kept thinking of my mother. Her voice on the answering machine.

"Josie trusts me," Tom said, tight. "I've been doing everything I can to get Margaret home safely. Everything. I'm helping you find the Homesteaders."

"You give us addresses? Big deal. You know, the yellow pages can do that too," Cate snapped. "Last I checked, the yellow pages didn't rat people out, so they're starting to seem like a better deal compared to you."

"This was a mutual decision," Tom said. "A careful decision. Talk to Josie. She trusts me."

A scoff. "Don't flatter yourself. Morrow only trusts you because—"

"Cate," I said, reminding her not to reveal Emily's secret, but she'd stopped anyway. Down the street, the low rumble of an engine. Cate turned, eyes burning.

"Don't tell them I'm here," she said. "I'm going to wait this shit-show out."

A police car was approaching, and right behind it a truck, their lights catching me in a glare so blinding that I turned away. The vehicles pulled into the driveway. I stood in the spotlight for a second too long, unable to see anything, the world gone white.

The engines fell silent, the headlights fading, winking out. As I blinked to clear the hectic spots of color from my vision, there came the heavy slam of a car door, echoed by two more. Multiple silhouettes were moving toward us in a slow pack. More men than I'd expected. In this tiny town, I'd pictured one politely beleaguered officer.

"Hello, there." A voice issuing from the shadows. "You the folks who called about something suspicious going on at the Stroud residence?"

"That's me. Thanks for coming, gentlemen." Tom hurried down the steps. Watching him reach out to shake hands with one of the men, I recognized that Tom had an automatic confidence with these strangers, perfectly at ease among them. It gave me a funny envy for a minute: how quickly he took control, seemingly without needing to prove anything to them.

Tom consulted with the others in voices too low for me to catch. Before I knew what was happening, two men had left the group, heading with Tom toward the back of the house. The beam of a flashlight bounced and swayed through the darkness before they vanished.

Two other men stayed behind. One stepped forward into the pool of light. He wore black shoes, so shiny I could almost see myself in them, an elongated and ghostly reflection. The man nodded at me in greeting. "Evening, miss."

"Where are they going?"

"Your friend is taking some of the boys to show them what you found in the forest," the man said. "In the meantime, we're going to need to get your statements. How many of you are in there?"

Isabelle was watching us, her face a pale thumbprint against the glass. "Just the two of us," I said. "Me and my friend."

The man started up the stairs toward the Strouds' small porch, the steps creaking under his weight. His voice was gentle, kind enough that

I relaxed. "I hope you don't mind if we step inside. If there's somebody out here causing trouble," he said, "then we don't want to leave you young ladies all alone."

Both men were dressed like they'd just arrived home from office jobs, crisp khaki pants, button-ups. I wondered about that, the lack of uniforms. The younger man, wearing an orange shirt, looked at Isabelle, his gaze catching on the white dress. It was folded over her arm, the bloodstain hidden from view. I caught his flinch of discomfort.

"First things first," Black Shoes said. "Why are you ladies in the Strouds' home? Are you friends with the girls who live here?"

That present tense gave me a brief flicker of hope, summoning the Strouds back into the world for a second. "We're just acquaintances."

"Acquaintances," Black Shoes said. "The Stroud girls have lived here for nearly twenty years now. I can't say they've ever had visitors before. Now, your friend out there said that you ladies have been stalked. Is that right? Somebody's after you?"

Orange Shirt had wandered into the kitchen now, moving toward the fridge. He leaned in close to examine the photograph hanging on the fridge. Vera and Delilah smiling together.

"There's a man," I said. "He's been following us for the past week. We're worried that he might have gotten to the Strouds first."

"Why would the same person be after the Stroud girls and after you?" Black Shoes went over to the couch and sat next to Isabelle. The glow of the TV screen flashed hot blue against his throat and chest.

"We come from the Homestead," Isabelle said. "The same as Vera and Delilah."

Orange Shirt twisted around at this. Black Shoes nodded, slowly, thoughtfully. "Both of you?" Black Shoes asked, gesturing toward me and Isabelle.

"You've heard of the Homestead, sir?" I asked.

"Of course I have," he said. "You think I'm out of touch just because I'm an old man, is that it?" He laughed, and a cautious warmth spread through me. Something about him reminded me of Dr. McCarter. He had that same good-natured self-assurance, like he could fix everything. "With Vera and Delilah living right here in town, we all tried to learn more about that place. Now what's that you've got there, sweetheart?"

Isabelle let him take the dress from her. He shook it open, fabric hanging in the light of the TV screen. The bloodstain was unmistakable, blossoming dark against the soft, brittle white fabric. "Is this Vera's dress?" he asked, his voice tightening. "Delilah's? Good lord."

"Like I said," I went on, "we're concerned that somebody who's been chasing us found the Strouds and—and hurt them."

"Can you give us a name? Anything?"

"No," I said, hating how flimsy it sounded. "We don't know exactly who's after us."

The men exchanged worried looks. "Can you give us a physical description?" Black Shoes pressed. "That'd be a big help."

"He's tall," I said, hearing how inadequate this was. "He has brown hair, I think. He drives a maroon sedan." And I hadn't seen him in three days now. I was miles and miles away from the last place I'd spotted him. The stranger wavered, flickered like a phantom.

"People around here know their neighbors pretty well," Black Shoes said. "We're a close-knit place. Anybody from out of town would've stood out to us right away."

"They sure would have," Orange Shirt agreed. He was even younger than I'd first assumed, closer to my own age.

"When's the last time anybody talked to the Strouds?" I asked. "Maybe that could help narrow it down."

"That," Black Shoes said, "is some smart thinking, young lady. We'll have to get on that, ask around. Not sure it'll do much good, though."

"You said you were a close-knit town," I said, biting down my frustration.

"Those two kept to themselves," Black Shoes said. "It's too bad. Maybe if they'd been friendlier, we would've noticed sooner. There's a lesson there for you girls," he said, like it'd just occurred to him. "You can't help that you were grown in a test tube. But you can always try to be civil. You don't have to be like Vera and Delilah." He made eye contact with me now, steady. "You don't have to hide away like witches in a storybook."

Those trees, the word repeating and repeating, hewn again and again. Precise and urgent at once. A litany, an excuse, a justification. A curse and a prayer. W I T C H E S. The work of multiple people, I realized now. Dozens. There'd been too many words spread across the trees for all the writing to have come from one person. I should have recognized that the moment I saw those words ringing the clearing. It hadn't been the work of just one man, arriving in the shelter of night. It had been a whole town.

And now Black Shoes had brought that word into the room, placed it between us like a dare.

He was watching me. It was a test. Would I swallow the word, pretend it was nothing? Would I smile and agree with him that we could be nicer, *sure, of course*, recognize the threat, let this go? Leave the Strouds' fate unexamined, unmourned, and unavenged? If I said something—if I spoke up now—I wouldn't be able to go back to my old life. I understood that, cleanly and clearly. Choosing between saying something now and letting it go would break my life in half. The freedom to leave and return to my old life, or violence.

I made my choice. "You killed them," I said, not breaking our eye contact. "It wasn't a stranger from out of town at all, was it? It was you."

Saying the words aloud changed me. It reached down into me and altered the shape of who I was. The men were unsurprised; they'd understood the inevitable conclusion of this evening as soon as they had walked in. I'd been the only one in the dark, trying to play along with them.

Ignoring me, Black Shoes held out an arm to Isabelle. "You look uncomfortable over there, sweetheart. Why don't you come closer?"

Isabelle gave me a searching look, like I was taking on the role of Patricia now, the person who could tell her what to do. But I was frozen. She moved closer, just an inch. Black Shoes shifted closer until he was next to her. His thigh nearly touched hers.

"Has it been you all along?" I asked tightly. "Have you been following us?"

"I haven't been *following* anybody," he said, a contemptuous laugh wrapped around the word. "All of us here in Kithira mind our own business. We never went looking for trouble."

The dizziness began at the back of my skull, washing forward. Without even thinking about it, I leaned forward, stared directly into his eyes. Those small, dark pupils, little holes in the fabric of his being. I could slip a hook in there and just pull the truth out.

But the night at the motel, I'd been alone. It was a private, impulsive act, an opportunity seen and seized in the dark of night. Even the prison had offered a certain anonymity. Now I was surrounded. Two men in here, two with Tom. I wasn't sure what the other men would do if they realized what I was, what I could do. And they were watching my every move.

Black Shoes seemed to view my silence as an invitation to explain: "I remember sitting there watching TV, back in the seventies. *The Homestead*. Every time one of you was born, there were photos and interviews. Front-page headlines at the breakfast table. That doctor fellow went on TV and told the world that this was only the beginning of a bold new future." He held his hands up, a clownish mockery of wonder. "I looked at him and I thought, does he know what this means? Does he know what this means for him and his wife? For his own father, for his own *sons*? This man was teaching women how to take over the world, and nobody else seemed to notice. Nobody ever stopped to think exactly what we were progressing *to*. Thank God for Ricky Peters. That man restored a certain level of moral clarity to the whole conversation."

"By murdering innocent people?" I asked, a reflex.

"He's a hero. When Ricky Peters set that fire, he killed one man, sure, but he also short-circuited the wholesale destruction of mankind. That should have been the end of it all. But you girls couldn't leave well enough alone. You're from that place, aren't you?" He directed this question downward at Isabelle. "Then maybe you can explain why you girls couldn't just take your disease somewhere else. Make another little freak show for yourselves. Why you had to force yourselves on the rest of the world, come and live in good God-fearing towns."

My rage was a low hum, slowly building.

"Vera, now, she was quiet," Black Shoes said. "She mostly kept to herself. But that girl of hers was nothing but trouble. A knockout from the time she was little, and she knew it, too. She walked around town like she owned the place. Delilah. You have to wonder why her mother chose a name like that for her. A father would've known better."

That photo on the fridge. Delilah's long curly hair, heart-shaped face, big dark eyes. Heartbreaking.

"She got tangled up with a young man," Black Shoes said. "A few months back. A young man who could've had any girl in town. Delilah always thought she was better than the rest of us, but going after him like that? I've thought about it a lot. Why she'd do that. Delilah wasn't born of the love between a man and a woman. Love doesn't mean the same thing to her. Seeing her with that young man, it devastated us all. We should've drawn the line sooner. But a woman who's not part of the normal order doesn't respect the ties that bind. She takes what she wants. That kind of woman will chew men up, spit us right out. We used to call girls like that *sluts*. Now they're supposed to be miracles." He laughed.

I stood there, the word *sluts*—the blunt, slick hurt of it—dripping down me, staining me.

"This is a town where we still believe in consequences." Black Shoes raised his eyes to mine, and I could feel the air leaching away. "I don't know if you're aware of this, Madame Scientist, but on the inside, you girls work a lot like God intended you to. You can make a baby the old-fashioned way just fine. No hocus-pocus required."

"Are you trying to say we can get pregnant by men?" And then the realization formed fully: "Delilah was pregnant." I tried to wrap my head around it. That was the realm of our mothers—we were too young. We were still the daughters, eternally the Girls. We shouldn't be pregnant ourselves.

Black Shoes ran a hand over his lower face. "The young man came to his senses and broke things off. But Delilah, she went crazy. She wasn't anybody's miracle anymore, just another sob story with a baby and no man. Not long after, that boy got sick. He started throwing up all day long. He lost weight. They thought it was the stress at first. Then they thought it was a stomach bug. Something in the water. A flu. Cancer, maybe, a tumor on the brain. But the doctors couldn't find anything wrong. You don't know what it does to you to see a healthy young man wasting away in his bed, and nobody can tell you why. Then it started spreading to all his friends. Then to all the young men. A quarter of the population of Kithira, vomiting, sick, unable to eat a thing. Nice young wives handling things alone. Businesses shut down. Classrooms empty. We were watching our future waste away right in front of us. That was a hard time for all of us. A hard time."

Goose bumps rose along my arms. "What does this have to do with Delilah?" I asked, even as the awe spread inside my blood. Delilah, retching from her unexpected pregnancy, all alone: Delilah, reaching into the men's throats and guts, returning the sickness tenfold and then spreading it.

"It was her," Black Shoes said simply. "I don't know how, but it was her. I want you to understand that we warned Vera. We went to speak to her, me and some of the other boys from the station. We let her know what was going on with her daughter and with our sons, and asked her if she'd be willing to leave Kithira. This was a chance for her and Delilah to just walk away. But they didn't. They made a choice. And you know something?" He leaned back. "After what happened to the Strouds, those boys got better and better. The very next morning, my nephew was sitting up in bed, eating a huge breakfast. Bacon and eggs. The greatest thing I ever saw in my life."

His nephew. The rooms felt suddenly cooler. I thought of Delilah and Vera, alone, no relatives here, the mutated branches that had twisted away from the family tree.

His voice was so reverent and joyful that it seemed like he expected me to join in. "It's been three weeks now and every young man is back on his feet."

The Strouds had made their choice. Now I'd make mine.

30

A knock on the door. Orange Shirt moved to answer. *Please be Tom*, I thought, my heart knotted up with a mix of fear and hope. Afraid that he'd walk into danger and not be able to help any of us, not even himself; hopeful that he'd make them understand the situation. Maybe they'd treat him differently. I couldn't get Black Shoes' words out of my mind. *After what happened*. The Strouds had bled; they'd burned. The way Black Shoes glided over it, a minor detail on the way to his nephew's stupid fucking breakfast.

But it was a stranger at the door, one who sized me up with a quick up-down sweep. He consulted with Orange Shirt for a minute, a low mutter, and then the third man was entering the house. The proportion of these men to the two of us, Isabelle and me, had shifted again. I had to act. I had to act. But I didn't know what to do—there were so many of them—and I still didn't understand the limits of my power.

"We didn't think anybody would come looking for them," Black Shoes said. "Nobody ever had before. This was between us and the Strouds, that's all. I'm sorry that you young ladies had to come here. I'm sorry you've become part of this now."

"There are more of them," Orange Shirt said. "One more, hiding somewhere. That's what he said."

Tom. Tom had told them about Cate. The betrayal was sharp enough to cut through the panic, a stinging ache.

I watched the stranger vanish down the hallway, adrenaline surging through me. Cate's hands on Isabelle's arm, the way the wound had vanished, absorbed back into Isabelle's body. What would the people of Kithira do to Cate if they found out that she had the same weirdness inside her as Delilah?

"You still have time to let us walk away," I said, all desperate bravado.

"People will come looking for us. Just the way we looked for the Strouds. I'm all over the news right now. There's no way people won't notice—someone will come looking—" But whether I was famous, or infamous, I knew that nobody in my life was close enough to come searching.

Black Shoes stood and approached me. "Don't feel sorry for yourself. This is on you."

"How so?" I asked, a whisper.

"After Dr. Bellanger died, the world went back to normal. Every day, hundreds of thousands of babies are born, each one with a mommy and a daddy. In the face of that, what's nine girls? But suddenly you're all over the TV screen. Josephine Morrow. Girl One, in the papers, claiming that you're going to finish what Bellanger started. I know it's a publicity stunt: a pretty girl, trying her hand at being Dr. Franken-stein instead of the monster." Anger overcame me, hot and acidic. "But it's got people thinking again. Soon enough, it'll have them wondering whether women even *need* men. Whether men have a place in the so-ciety that we built ourselves." His eyes on me had turned flat and heavy. There were fine whitish marks around his eyes, crevices the sun hadn't reached. "Nature rewards the brave. If you're going to make men irrel-evant, we'll take back our place in the gene pool by whatever means is necessary."

Whatever means is necessary. Something about the way he looked at me, up and down—something about the story, Delilah's pregnancy—

"He raped her," I said, my rage compressing the words, turning them clear and precise. "Your nephew raped Delilah. To prove that you mat-ter. But it wasn't enough, was it? She was still so powerful that you had to kill her—"

A scuffle of movement. Orange Shirt came back, Cate with him. Her arms twisted behind her back so that she had to walk in an awkward crouch, fighting against him. Blood ran from her nose to her mouth, thick stripes. My own mouth filled with the taste of rust.

"You're going to kill us the same way you killed the Strouds," I said.

"No," Black Shoes said gently. "It will be quicker than that. I can do that much for you."

"You're cowards," Cate spat.

They barely reacted. "Deal with these two," Black Shoes said, like we were something to tick off a checklist. The people of Kithira had worked a miracle of their own, banishing the Strouds. They would dispatch us just as effortlessly. The third man grabbed me. His arm, slung across my chest, pinched hard against my breasts. In the scramble and confusion, I'd lost my chance. Black Shoes was turning away from me. I couldn't reach his eyes.

Black Shoes went to Isabelle, holding out his hand. I tried to telegraph some of my own urgency to her: *Wake up, dammit.* But, unmoved by Cate's bleeding, she accepted Black Shoes's hand. He lifted her off the couch and led her out of the living room, toward the back of the house. He was gentle with her, almost mannerly. I thought of Delilah, alone, pregnant against her will, furious and scared. That bloodstained dress, a pale banner in the trees.

My rage arrived as purely and completely as a breath drawn after I'd been held underwater. Every nerve ending flickered, alive with heat. The world slowed down to accommodate me. I was what had been hiding inside all along.

Cate stared at me. Her lips moved, a whisper: a prayer, an encouragement, the syllables of my name.

"You'll have your turn," Orange Shirt said in her ear, voice humid with a leer.

Orange Shirt was looking at me. Openly, brazenly. His gaze flickered, up and down my body, but when I caught his eyes again I held them, snagged them, thinking *Don't look away, don't look away.* Burrowing deep. "Let her go," I said.

His facial muscles slackened instantly, his arm around Cate faltering and then dropping, distracted. She didn't move, face tense, like she didn't trust that she was safe to go. Still clutching me close, the third man watched, and I sensed his surprise, the way he was more bemused than scared.

"I know your voice," I said to Orange Shirt. "You raped Delilah. You killed her." I recognized his voice from the answering machine message. It was hard to connect those stumbling, earnest words with this cold-eyed young man.

He didn't answer. I spoke directly to his mind, the deepest, primal parts. "Tell me if you've been following us all this time," I said.

"No," he said. "I haven't followed you. I don't know what you mean."

"Step away from her," I said.

He didn't even hesitate. He took a step, creating half a foot of space between his body and Cate's, and I saw her muscles visibly unfurl in relief.

"What the hell?" the other man said in my ear, looking for the joke. "Get it together, man." His arm around me was still pinching.

I had to think carefully, quickly. Choose each word to hold as much power as possible. "Shoot him," I said to Orange Shirt. Clear and calm. "Shoot him in the leg."

It was a gamble. I wasn't even sure Orange Shirt had a gun. But he was reaching into his waistband, pulling out a revolver. Pressed against me, the third man stiffened. His breath against me, that tangy smell of his sudden fear. He began a syllable in his throat, a protest. In that second, he let go of me, stepping toward Orange Shirt, reaching out—

Orange Shirt, his gaze emotionless, like a dreamer's, angled the gun downward and fired. The sound was so loud, in that still and quiet room, that for a moment I was sure he'd hit me instead.

But I was still standing. I was free. The man who'd held me crumpled to the floor, his body strangely graceful in that split second. He screamed in pain. "Goddammit," he said through gritted teeth. "Are you fucking her too? Why are you listening to this—"

I spoke over him, addressing Orange Shirt. "Put the gun to your head," I said.

Orange Shirt convulsed once, his hand holding the gun trembling. I watched him, fascinated in a cool corner of my mind. The way he tried to fight against it. The trapped look in his washed-out blue eyes. The man who'd been shot in the leg was clutching his thigh, his fingers slicked with blood, his jeans stained with a rapidly spreading blackness. When I looked into Orange Shirt's eyes, I saw that same disbelief that I'd seen with the man at the motel. He didn't think this was really happening: a girl was forcing his body and brain to bend to her own. I was inside a childhood dream, bounding unharmed off a cliff, wondering what I'd ever been afraid of.

Cate moved across the room, carefully, finding her way to my side.

Orange Shirt held the gun against his temple. "Are you going to kill me?" he asked, his face greasy with sweat.

"Am I going to do what you'd do if you were in my place, you mean? That's what you're all afraid of." He blinked rapidly. "Keep your eyes on me," I said, and he stopped blinking, eyes collecting a glossy scrim of unshed tears.

In the paralysis I'd created, Cate whispered in my ear: "We need to find Isabelle. We have to get out of here, Morrow. Please."

I didn't move. I didn't want to step outside of this current of power I'd created. I had no idea how long it would hold. If I told Orange Shirt to press the trigger, his finger, obeying my words instead of his own brain, would make the one tiny movement that would end him.

For a moment I wanted to. I wanted to so totally and completely that I couldn't even imagine feeling guilt afterward. Was this what my mother had felt, holding the match? When I'd seen that joy in her face, was it because she'd just murdered a man who'd deserved it? Maybe it had been the purest thrill of her life, blazing so brightly that the rest of her life could only ever be pale and ordinary in contrast. Maybe she'd played it safe, my whole childhood, just to save us both from that hot, dark impulse always tugging at the back of her brain.

"I have a daughter," the man with the gunshot wound said. He was saying it in a whisper, resentful, like he didn't want to admit it. "A little girl. Please."

"Morrow—" Cate said, urgent.

"You," I said to Orange Shirt. "Kneel down." He was shaking as he obeyed, lowering himself onto his knees; I crouched next to him. Gently, I pulled the gun from his hand, laid it on the ground. I took his belt off and wound it around both his wrists in a sloppy figure eight, then strapped the belt tightly to the leg of the couch until he was held in place. "Don't move," I said. Then I took his gun, which was heavier than I expected, metal warm to the touch. I examined it, uncertain. The gun almost felt like a movie prop to me, unreal.

"The safety," Cate said, urgent, and when I hesitated, she took the revolver from me, quickly clicked a lever into place. She tried to hand it back.

"You keep it," I said.

I fixed my eyes on the men until we turned the corner; they watched me back, baleful. I didn't know how long my hold over them would last. I didn't know how long it would continue after I snapped that wire that stretched between our eyes. Would it linger for five minutes, an hour, more?

Cate and I hurried down the hallway. The walls were scuffed and bare, all the doors closed. I caught a noise, a weak mewl, a sound of distress, and I opened the nearest door.

It was a bedroom, floral wallpaper, untidy piles of clothes clotted around the baseboards. Black Shoes was with Isabelle. They were together on the bed, Isabelle on his lap, skirt hiked up to expose those tender, skinny thighs. I took in their bodies together, the way Isabelle lifted her head up to look at me in surprise through tangled hair, Black Shoes's stare that met my own without wavering or apology as he sat against the headboard, surrounded by the frilly bedding of Delilah. The girl he'd murdered.

It took me a moment to realize that Black Shoes was dead.

Isabelle adjusted her dress on her shoulder, smiling at us. Black Shoes's skin was already lifeless and slack. Looking at him, drained empty, I felt my own hard pulse drumming through me. Alive, alive.

Isabelle rose off his lap and came toward us, smoothing down her dress. "Are you okay?" she asked, and reached up to tuck a strand of my hair behind my ear. "You look upset."

I couldn't stop staring at Black Shoes. The first corpse I'd ever seen outside of a medical setting; the heavy slump of his body. Those dark, gleaming shoes, shining more brightly now that he was fading. A deep and savage relief passed through me. As I watched, a thread of blood drooled down his chin.

"How did you do that?" I asked Isabelle quietly.

She shrugged like she didn't know what I meant. Turning, she wandered toward the dresser, Delilah's dresser. She ran her hands over the balled-up socks, lip-gloss tubes rimmed with glittery crust, library books, crumpled receipts. She picked up a book with a bright pink cover, flipped through it. Her eyes widened.

"Isabelle, don't touch Delilah's stuff," I said, queasy. "Don't touch anything."

"This could be important," Isabelle said. "It's her diary."

Cate had gone to the window and pushed aside the blinds, hands shaking as she scrabbled with the lock. She managed to hoist the window open. She stood for a second, head cocked, listening, then slid the screen free of its frame. The night air that came in was chilly, throbbing with the sounds of insects. Cate slid her way through, dropping to the grass below. I followed. As I reached up to help Isabelle, taking her small hand, I marveled at the flexible lightness of her body. Such a tiny thing, to have left behind a death. She'd kept the book with her: I didn't press it. All I wanted was to get out safely.

Moving together, close enough to hear each other's breathing, we crept around the side of the house. The Volvo was still sitting where we'd left it hours ago, as if nothing had changed between that moment and this one.

The front yard was empty.

Cate whispered: "Does Tom have the keys?"

I cursed under my breath. "He does." For a moment escape had been so close that I could feel freedom on the back of my tongue, light and cool. "Maybe there's a spare set."

But I wondered what they'd done to Tom in the woods. Would he be as easy to discard as the three of us? Or was he on their side now? I wasn't even sure what I wanted for him after he'd betrayed Cate. My anger and fear roiled in my gut.

After a silent consultation, we ran across the grass toward the Volvo. I heard shouting from inside the house, only a few windows illuminated. Isabelle tried the car doors—locked, all four of them. Cate slumped against the side of the Volvo, exhausted. We were stuck here, in this strange town, at night, bloodied. How far would we get with no vehicle?

"I'll have to go back for Tom."

"Forget him," Cate said. "Please, Morrow. You've seen what those men are like—" She reached for my hand, held on so tightly it almost hurt, and I understood that she was transmitting something to me that went beyond just our survival. But I had to focus on getting us out of here.

"We can take them on. We just have to find the Tom and get the keys—"

"If he's even alive," Isabelle said calmly.

"Morrow—please. We have to look out for ourselves. We told him not to call anyone, but he did what he wanted, and now look—"

Before I could answer, the crunch of footsteps approached from the side of the house. Two forms emerged from the shadows, one loping casually, the other hunched and bent. Tom. As they stepped into the light from the windows, I saw that Tom's face was bruised and swollen, a starburst of blood against one eye. His hands were tied behind his back with thin yellow ropes. The man behind him held a gun to the back of his neck. Tom's role as a betrayer flickered. So they'd hurt him too. I softened.

His captor was tall, his lower face obscured with a heavy beard. The stranger stopped, said something too low to hear, and Tom fell to his knees. I realized, with a strange shock, that Tom was the most defenseless of the four of us right now. While the stranger was distracted, I gestured to Cate, frantic, holding out my hand at hip-height: she understood, passing me the gun, the soft *click* letting me know she'd undone the safety again. I stepped into the light. I held out the gun, taking my certainty, letting the confidence I felt in my own power extend into this weapon.

It took Tom a moment to catch on to my presence and look up. His face tightened with panic—I watched him begin to frantically mouth, *Get away, run*, but I ignored him. Instead I looked directly into the stranger's eyes, catching his gaze as he looked up. I pushed myself through into his skull, settled in there. As easily as winding my fingers through strands of hair and tugging. "Drop the gun," I said. "Untie him."

The bearded man's face loosened into blankness. He dropped the gun; maintaining eye contact, I stooped to retrieve it, kicking it backward toward Cate and Isabelle. The man began to fumble with the knots that were holding Tom's hands behind his back. "Go faster," I said sharply, and the man hurried, fingers slipping.

"Let me drive," Isabelle called behind me.

"I don't understand this," Tom said. "Why is he listening to you, Josie? What is this? Is it—" His ropes slid loose, slithering to the gravel. Still training the gun on the stranger, I started backing away. Tom looked at his hands like he wasn't sure they were his anymore. His wrists were embedded with ligature marks, thick and red. "What are you doing?" Tom asked.

I didn't have time to explain. I looked Tom in the eyes, and for just a second before his face went blank, I saw a twitch of betrayal. Hurt. Like he could sense what was happening to him, could sense my influence behind it, and he hated it. "Give the keys to Isabelle," I said. "Get inside the car."

He stared at me before he broke away, obeying.

As Tom moved toward the Volvo, the man glared at me, furious now. "What'd you do to me, you creepy bitch?" he asked, low.

Inside the house, shadows and movement. Fuck. Orange Shirt must've gotten loose, my power over him waning, my makeshift handcuffs not strong enough. Or maybe it was the stranger who'd been shot in the leg—and they were going to find Black Shoes soon—

I backed away from Tom's captor, the gun aimed at his chest. "Stay there," I said. "Stay there and don't move. We're getting out of here."

But it wouldn't help. That was what I knew at the back of my mind. Delilah. What they'd done to her body. Forcing men back into the gene pool, violently, cruelly. I'd recognized the frank anger in Black Shoes's eyes when he'd said that, but there'd been something else beneath it, thin and bitter. Fear. This wasn't a lone incident—it was the beginning of something bigger. Ricky Peters, innocent or not, had known this would happen. That when he'd landed in prison he would still be connected to a hatred that he'd only briefly dipped his fingers into. We weren't safe. Even after we left Kithira, we wouldn't be safe.

The Volvo's headlights punched on, catching me in the illumination. The engine rattled to life. When I glanced back, I saw that the others were in the car already. Cate pounded the windows, shouting something at me, her face unrecognizable in its urgency. I heard shouts—noise—coming from inside the house, a sudden turmoil. I ran for the car. The noise didn't matter. Just dispatches from a different world. We were free now. Free.

I reached for the door handle. A single crack rang through the night. The noise was so loud that I felt it inside me, condensed down into a hard knot, slamming into me.

I collapsed into the backseat and then Tom was yelling, "Drive! Drive!" Isabelle, at the wheel, lurched us out of the driveway, tires spinning, the worn-out brakes screeching with the sudden movement, and we were off, going too fast for Kithira's narrow roads. It didn't matter, nobody was going to stop us now, we were okay, unhurt—I looked at Tom and grinned, loopy with triumph, but he didn't grin back. His eyes were wide.

"Morrow." Cate craned around from the front seat. "Jesus Christ, you're—" Then she turned around. "Isabelle. Stop. Stop. You have to fucking pull over."

"Not yet," Isabelle said, reasonable and resolute. "They'll get us if we stop now."

The pain burned, deep and hot, but it was more than that. The wrongness of something foreign and unfamiliar stuck in there with all my organs. I brought my hand away from my stomach; it was blackened and slick.

"How did this happen?" I whispered. I'd let them off too easy, and now—now—

"What are we going to do? We can't let her—" Tom was saying, frantic.

I was trying to hold on, trying to stay present, to cling to their voices, but I was slipping now, going too quickly backward, into the darkness that waited, ready to suck me up, ready to take me under.

31

It was quiet, the air close and stifling. Swollen with the fake florals of cleaning solution. I was flat on my back, stretched out. I shifted against a cheap nylon coverlet that was already slippery with blood. Somebody loomed above me. My mother. No, Bellanger. No. My eyes adjusted and I understood that it was Cate.

"Where are—are we—" I was trying to articulate a question that hovered beyond the reach of my clotted mouth. "Are they—the others—"

"Morrow, listen. Do you think you can relax for me?"

I could only lie there, my body heavy and drugged, and watch as Cate closed her eyes, then opened them again to reveal a different face than before. She held her hands above me, hovering just over the flesh. Energy built between her palms and my body. The tug of a magnet against its opposite. It made the pain flare hotter for a minute.

I couldn't bear it.

Then Cate's hands were on my stomach, her skin soft against mine. My heartbeat thumped up into her palm, so steady that after a moment it felt as if she were transferring the pulse into me directly from her own body. She'd taken over, she was giving life back to me, that shivery beat spreading across every inch of my skin, slipping across the surface, settling into my corners and edges and crevices. Through the murkiness of my pain and confusion came a stirring of life, hard and stinging and good, like the blood in my veins waking back up.

Kneeling over me, she was backlit, dark hair glowing and wiry. A saint: she looked like a saint. Or maybe a witch, face obscured. "Josephine. Lie still, okay? Don't push yourself."

"I don't want you to hurt yourself," I said. The room was unfamiliar. Wood paneling, punctuated by a print of a red barn in autumn. The light was muffled by a heavy lampshade. My voice was the voice of somebody imitating me, thickened and hoarse. "Not for my sake—"

"You're going to die," Cate said, harsh. "Do you understand that? If I don't help you now—you don't make it. You're losing too much blood. I'm not sure I can do this, but I have to fucking try."

The tarnished scent of it, pungent in my nostrils. A warmth that felt wrong, inside-out. I should've been panicking, but I felt numb. She was right. And yet.

"I deserve it," I said. "Don't you get it? To make up for—"

"For what? For saving everyone's life?" Cate asked. She looked into my eyes. "You saved my life back there, Morrow. Let me save yours."

"But I didn't save Fiona."

"You were just a kid."

"I should have known," I whispered. "I'm the oldest. I should've seen more."

"Josephine Morrow, I'm not going to let you go." Her hands were on me again, the electricity so sharp that I was sure I was going to dissolve from the sheer power of it. But I'd let go already, anyway. I'd let go, let go. I felt myself sinking into blackness, quickly, quickly, and then gently, like a feather drifting. It was the sensation of falling asleep when I was very tired—

32

Warm breath brushed against my neck and then receded, over and over, gentle and even, like the tide withdrawing.

My mother. So many nights she'd come into my bed and curled around me to protect me, or sometimes to shield herself from some private nightmare that she'd never share in the morning. Now I turned enough to see Cate's dark curls spread across the pillow, her skin waxy and brittle. I had an impulse to press against her forever.

But I was also restless, my whole body lit up. If I returned to that moment of standing on my garage roof as a child, I really could take off and fly. Anywhere I wanted. Anywhere at all.

I sat and looked around the motel room, careful not to wake Cate. The slant of sunlight that came through the crack in the floor-length drapes suggested late morning. The tacky striped coverlet was imprinted with splotches, pale pink to deepest black. Somewhere, a faucet tapped steadily. Across the room, Isabelle slept on the floor, her narrow white back to me, spattered with freckles like a trout's markings. She had a pillow under her head, no blanket.

I didn't see Tom. Rising, I pressed a hand to my abdomen. The gunshot: Had I imagined it? I felt good. Amazing. Like I'd slept for a very long time. I walked to the bathroom mirror and lifted the edge of my dress. Blood trailed across my hip bones. I pressed at the lightly pooched skin above my navel—soft and firm, giving at my touch with a light buoyancy. No pain.

I went higher, sure that at any second I'd accidentally slide my fingers inside a gaping wound or touch an exposed organ. Nothing. My skin felt wrinkled, soft and moist and too smooth, like that bluish skin that I'd find beneath a Band-Aid when I was a kid. I couldn't detect that foreign sensation, the stuck feeling that had burned between my rib cage.

Behind me, the door opened and sunlight fell in a brilliant triangle inside the mirror. I turned. In the bed, Cate stirred slightly.

"Josie." Tom wore a pair of dark sunglasses. His gaze drifted downward until he abruptly looked away, neck going pink. I remembered that I'd lifted my dress, exposing my hips and thighs. To me, my body had become a novelty, nothing to be embarrassed about. For his sake, I dropped the hem of my dress.

Tom nudged the door closed with one heel. His arms were loaded down with filmy plastic bags, peppered with the logo of some drugstore chain. He dropped the bags onto the bed. He started toward me, then stopped. His hair was damp and smelled like shampoo from across the room. Tom seemed to want to say everything at once: instead, he said nothing.

"Are you okay?" I asked at last.

"Am I okay?" he repeated. "Josie, you were—you were dead."

I laughed. "I wasn't dead."

"For a few minutes, yeah. It felt like forever." He was struggling to stay calm.

"Come on," I said. "Dead? Truly dead. Heart stopped—no brain waves—"

"I know what death looks like."

The way Tom was staying back from me, like I was a ghost, told me all I needed to know. Inside Cate's half-open palm, a glimmer of something dull and metallic. Moving to the bed, I gently pried her fingers open. A bullet, varnished metal, tapering to a blunted tip, slightly misshapen. I touched the bullet with the pad of one finger; it was warmed from Cate's body. This little thing felt so utilitarian, so unremarkable, like dozens of things I'd come across during my daily life: frying pans, door handles.

"I'm confused, Josie," Tom said. I could tell he'd rehearsed this in his head. "I don't understand what happened last night. I don't understand how Cate saved you. You were dead, now you're—" He took a deep breath. "And you. God. You did something to me. It was like I couldn't—like I was in a dream, watching myself. I've never felt that before. It was you doing something to me, wasn't it? Something weird."

"It was me." It was a relief to admit it.

"How?"

"How do you think?"

A long silence. "The rumors about Fiona aren't just rumors," Tom said. "It's all of you, not just Fiona."

"That would about sum it up." I spoke casually, but my heart was beating too quickly. I was half worried about how he'd respond. He wasn't one of us. I felt that so keenly right now. What would happen when more people knew? Not people who were actively trying to hurt us, but people like Tom. Observers. Recorders. How he responded, I realized, would show me how others would—maybe—at some point in the future.

Tom stared at his feet, and I saw the emotions playing out over his face: the shock, and then the wonder, the awe as he considered all that this would mean for Bellanger, for the Homestead. Standing here covered in my own blood, I felt powerful, my shape in the world changing in Tom's eyes. Tom felt small to me, like everyone else had diminished in response to my own potential.

"Why didn't you tell me?" he asked. "You don't trust me?"

"You've been a huge help." Emily's prophecy darted through my head. "But I don't understand all of this myself yet. I wanted to know more before I shared it with everyone—"

"I'm not just anyone. I thought I was your friend."

"It means more to me and to Cate and Isabelle than it does to you," I said, an edge of impatience.

"Sure." Tom rubbed at the back of his neck. "But that doesn't mean you had to do it to me." There was a wounded, frayed quality to his voice. "You—you used your . . . powers against that fucking monster who had me tied up, and you used them against me."

Like they were the same. "I did what I had to do to save us," I said carefully. "It wasn't personal."

"I would've helped you, Josie. Willingly. Don't you know that?"

"Yeah, but Tom—you told them that Cate was in the house. You told those men that there were three of us. I wasn't sure whose side you were on."

"Yours," Tom said at once. "Yours. You didn't give me the chance to prove it. You know I'm not like them, right? You have to know that."

"I'm sorry. I was just trying to keep us all safe."

Tom sighed, nodded. "Yeah. Yeah."

"Truce?"

He softened, looking exhausted. "Sure."

From inside the drugstore bag, a woman smiled at me. Kneeling, I dug through the supplies: boxes of dye, different colors and brands, identical-looking models showing off icy blond curls, a vampiric black bob. Several pairs of cheap sunglasses. Scissors. "What is all this?" I asked. "Disguises?"

Tom was watching me, creases between his eyebrows. "About Chicago—we can't go back the way we planned. A man is dead. None of us will be able to go back to our normal lives, not until—"

"I know." He was so earnest, as if he were having to do his duty and break my heart. "You don't think I realized that already? Look, honestly, it was stupid to even pretend I was going back to Chicago. I was so angry at my mother, but . . . I understand now. She might've been backed into a corner. I need to hear her side."

Tom didn't answer for a second. "You think she might've been justified in killing two people and putting an innocent man behind bars?"

My temper flared. "Short truce, huh?"

"Sorry. I know it's hard to see your mother in that light, but we're supposed to be looking for the truth here. For her sake and for Bellanger's."

My view of Bellanger had shifted in painful, disorienting ways. Like looking into a funhouse mirror and seeing just enough familiar features that the warped parts—the taffy-pull neck and distorted mouth—were even more grotesque. I loved the parts of Bellanger I still recognized. I hated the parts I didn't know. And those two extremes existed too close to each other. It made me wonder what version of Bellanger my mother had suddenly seen in 1977, after working with him for years, trusting him with her body and her life and her dream.

"Bellanger is still important to me," I said, "but I want to know more about my mom and Patricia starting the Homestead. The custody battle. If my mother was grappling with all that too, then maybe . . . I don't know. What I felt last night . . ." What I'd felt was a rage that'd made even the unthinkable options seem, for a moment, like the only way forward. "We'll know more when we talk to her in person."

"I'm still committed to finding Margaret," Tom said. "I hope you know that. No need to—I don't know, enchant me or hypnotize me or whatever you call that."

"Is that why you're wearing the sunglasses? So I can't do anything to you?" I reached for the shades, half teasing, and Tom flinched back. I stopped, seeing myself in the dark lenses of his sunglasses as he must see me now, my unwavering eyes.

"Not really," Tom said, and pulled his glasses off to reveal the mottled bruise surrounding his eye. "No need to draw unwanted attention."

"Right," I said, and looked around the dingy little room, feeling in my bones the actual smallness of it. I wondered exactly how long we would be stuck here.

We'd come unstitched from time. The room was a couple of hundred square feet, with one big bed that had been ruined by bloodstains, a bureau that held a small TV set. A mirror made the space look bigger, as though tucked inside a too-small birdcage. The four of us began an uneasy dance, trying to share space without complaining.

Cate was sick after she woke up—drowsy, glassy-skinned, shivering. Tom bought her Gatorade, and she drank down the lukewarm neon-yellow without comment as I propped her head in my lap, her hair tickling my skin. Slowly, over the next day, she perked up more, gaining some color, her eyes losing their dullness. I was relieved; the glow of wild vitality I'd felt after she saved me had started to seem stolen, like I'd drained her energy for myself.

We ended up in the bathroom together one evening, as I stood brushing my teeth.

I leaned over to delicately spit out the toothpaste, very aware of Cate's reflection behind me as she pulled her hair into a bun, fingers working deftly. "Thank you," I said impulsively, mouth stinging with mint. In the mirror, Cate stiffened. "I know that's not enough, I mean, it feels so stupid to even say it like that. But thanks for saving my life and everything."

"You're welcome and everything," Cate said.

We smiled, and I felt shy, everything zinging inside me. Cate brushed past me to get her own toothbrush, and my heartbeat quickened. "I didn't know you could even do that," I said. "Bring somebody back to life."

"I didn't know either." She was trying to sound casual.

"Really?" I watched her squeeze a curl of green toothpaste onto the bristles. "You'd never—that was your—"

"My first time. Yeah." Cate was looking at the toothbrush as if she'd forgotten what she was doing with it. "Yeah. I didn't think it was possible. I've never done anything harder than a broken femur before. I didn't think it was going to work until it did."

"Holy shit." If I hadn't known how to thank her before, I never would now. The awareness of her sheer power filled this tiny space—the cracked tiles, the shell-pink shower curtain, the perpetually dripping tap—and I felt alive with it, like something integral had been split apart in Cate and placed inside me too, an unbreakable thread between us

"Holy shit," Cate repeated. "Being around you, it's making me think about who I am. I guess your whole scientist thing is rubbing off on me. I have a theory."

"All right."

"Maybe it's trauma connected to our mothers that triggers our abilities," Cate said. "Loss, I guess. Grief. Fear. Think about it. I didn't get mine until my mother died. Same for Emily, based on what Wanda told you. And Isabelle. You didn't understand yours until your mother vanished, did you?"

"That's true," I said, thinking it over.

"Maybe we don't have our powers when we're with our mothers because our mothers *are* our powers. This is just a substitute." She was silent for a moment. "Too romantic for you?"

"No," I said. "No, I like it." Something occurred to me, the shape of an idea rising at the back of my brain—I felt focused, like I was back in the lab, absorbing and recording the world around me. "One of the risks of parthenogenesis is that it makes communities more susceptible to threats, while sexual reproduction at least gives you some diversity. If there's a—a sickness, or a common predator, offspring that are identical to their moms can't always evolve past that threat. Maybe in our case, these powers are a correction. There's something in human DNA that's only triggered when women self-conceive. These abilities give us an edge—keep us from being too alike, because we each have our own strengths."

Cate leaned against the cracked basin of the sink. "But it doesn't really explain why we're changing now."

"Being around each other," I said impulsively.

"Yeah?" She considered this. Her T-shirt was thin and worn, and I tried not to stare too openly at the slope of her collarbones, the swell of her breasts. "The same way our cycles are supposed to sync up? Pheromones?"

"Maybe it's another way we stay strong as a group. We'll always evolve as long as we're together."

Cate smiled at me for a minute, and I thought she was going to say something else, and my pulse beat flutter-hard at my temples and deep in my stomach. Then she swiveled back toward the mirror and began brushing her teeth, and I quietly left the room, turning everything over in my head.

Tom had bought food, greasy chips, sugary cereal, and we ate with our hands straight from the packages, crowded in front of the TV. Isabelle still had the book from Delilah Stroud's bedroom. Every time I saw her reading it, it broke my heart—the pages covered in a looping, bubbly cursive, all innocence and playfulness, different colors of ink. It also gave me a sense of grim satisfaction over what we'd done in Kithira. We'd avenged Delilah, at least.

"How did you do it?" I asked Isabelle one evening, my curiosity getting the better of me. "Kill that man."

Isabelle looked at me as if she didn't know what I was talking about.

"You can tell me." I thought of Patricia's hunger to uncover anything remarkable in her daughter's body. Now here it was, manifesting miles and miles outside of Patricia's reach.

"I don't want to talk about it," Isabelle said, and I was about to push her until I remembered how long it'd taken me to admit what had happened at the motel, even to myself.

The days dragged by, surreal, each one a day that I technically shouldn't have even experienced. Commercials blared and jangled from the TV set. With the blinds drawn, it was hard to tell the time of day. I kept remembering the period after Bonnie's attack, hiding out with my mother in a motel on the edge of town, fearful of copycat attacks.

Bonnie. Every time I thought about her, there was a scratch at the back of my head. I remembered that scar running across her face.

We were in a small town in Pennsylvania. When I ventured outside, I understood why the others had chosen this motel. It was isolated, forests huddled in close. Something about the dreary midday light reminded me of wintertime. Only one other car besides Tom's Volvo sat in the lot. This was a place where people came to be alone. Nobody would bother us here.

I hesitated, then went over to the graffiti-scrawled pay phone, fishing in my pocket for a quarter. I punched the zero button. When the operator answered, I asked to be connected with Bonnie Clarkson in Minnesota. I didn't even think she'd answer, but then suddenly her voice arrived in my ear, bored and casual: "Yeah? Who's this?"

"It's Josephine," I said, picturing her in her vast, marble-cool house. "Morrow."

"Girl One," Bonnie repeated, some of the boredom falling away. "I didn't expect to hear from you again."

"Remember when you asked me if I'd ever acted strange? My answer has changed." Bonnie didn't speak, but I could hear her breathing shift, the catch of interest. I told her about the man at the motel in Iowa or Missouri or wherever we'd been after we left the Clarksons, what felt like decades ago. The way he'd cornered me. Grabbed me. "I hurt him. I told him to pick up a piece of broken glass and hold it against his throat. I just wanted him to feel what it was to be helpless, the way he'd made me helpless. And I enjoyed it."

She was silent on the other end for a moment. "You made him do it? How?"

"He did anything I said."

"Wow," Bonnie said. Her lack of surprise was exactly what I'd expected. "Crazy."

"Listen," I said, "I need to know what happened to your attacker, because I need to know who's following us. If you know something that you didn't share with me, then—"

"That's why I tried to *tell* you it would be a waste of time, Josie," Bonnie interrupted, frustrated now. "My attacker wasn't the one who burned your mother's house down. He's already dead. I took care of it a long time ago. I would've told you that night, but my mother never wants me talking about it. It's the one promise I try to keep."

I inhaled. Of course. "What did you do?"

"How much detail do you want? For years, I obsessed over him. I pretended to my mother I was okay. I pretended that all the therapy worked. But every night I just lay there remembering the attack, so he would be fresh in my mind when he came back. Because I knew he would, and he did. I was thirteen and I'd just been in some god-awful Christmas special." I remembered watching this special on TV while my mom was in the other room, volume muted so she wouldn't catch me in the act, enraptured by Bonnie wearing a Santa-red, fur-trimmed minidress and singing along with a host of C-listers. "I guess the guy had a thing for carols because he got in touch. I wrote him back and he finally included a picture. There he was. That same crooked grin. I told him to come to my house on a night when I knew my mother would be out late. When he got there, I was waiting in a little slinky dress and Cherries in the Snow lipstick.

"He said he was obsessed with me because I was the prettiest of all of us. He told me this like I'd be fucking flattered. His excuse for hurting me was that if I was less pretty, all scarred up, he wouldn't be tempted. You know, I don't give a shit that people think that scar is ugly. What bothers me is that it means I don't look like my mother anymore. He took that from me."

I leaned against the cool brick, sick to my stomach, imagining this man summing us up with our gap-toothed smiles and choosing Bonnie, marking her with something she'd never asked for and couldn't escape.

"So I'm sitting there across from him. The guy's getting ready to make his big move. He has flowers and wine. I'm *thirteen*, remember. He asked me to get on his lap. I didn't. He—he started coming toward me, and then he stopped. He was looking around, wild-eyed, calling my name. I looked down and I couldn't see myself anymore. I was right there, but I also wasn't there. I saw the marble floor. I saw my mother's big ugly floral arrangement on the sideboard. I went to the mirror and I couldn't see myself at all, just the room, and that creep running around yelling for me. It was like a dream. Meanwhile, he was getting angrier and angrier, thinking I'd tricked him on purpose.

"I just went with it. Once I realized what was happening, I moved as fast as I could. I knew where my mother kept the gun. I knew what to do. He was still looking for me, hunting all over the house. I followed him. I watched him. And then I—I did it."

That scar, sloping along Bonnie's face. Maybe every girl hid a different version of herself buried under the surface, waiting to become necessary.

"My mother and I got rid of him. She went into this mode I've never seen before. Dumped him in the trunk. Drove him out to nowhere. Bleached the blood out of the carpet and tiles. We never mentioned it again. Never. Either of us. Not once."

So he hadn't been chasing us. I'd been afraid of a specter. Of a man buried somewhere in Minnesota's wildlands, already rotting down to his bones, just a collection of hair and teeth in the dirt. Nothing. I squeezed my eyes shut. It hadn't been Ricky Peters; it hadn't been Bonnie's attacker; I was left with nobody.

"I wish you'd listened to me," Bonnie said.

"Yeah, I don't know what I'm doing," I said, and laughed, exhausted, everything pressing in. "Apparently Ricky Peters didn't even kill Bellanger, did you know that? It was my mother."

Bonnie was quiet for a minute. "No, I didn't know that. Damn."

"I'm surprised your mom didn't say anything. She never liked my mother much." Although now I felt an unexpected sympathy for Deb Clarkson. Her contempt for my mother seemed less petty, more substantial. A spite with a true grief hidden at the center. The Homestead must've meant more to her than I realized, and my mother had taken it all. Maybe I should have listened to Deb more closely instead of assuming she was bitter and frivolous.

"Mommy always said Margaret Morrow ruined everything," Bonnie continued. "She felt so bad for Bellanger's family. I didn't get it at first. But if your mother took their dad away, and then she was the one to kill him too—I can't imagine what they would feel."

I didn't answer for a second. It hit me: Of course. Ricky's hints made sense now, everything reassembling into a pattern I should've noticed already. Bellanger's family. I'd spent so long benignly ignoring them that they'd slipped past my attention when it mattered the most.

"Oh my god," I said slowly. "That's it. That's who's after us." When I'd started this journey, it had felt like there was no good reason to come after my mother. But I understood the lure of revenge. The lit match; Bellanger, his remains charred beyond recognition. A family left in pieces, ignored and unseen. "Bellanger's boys," I said. "His sons have been after us all along."

33

April 24, 1976

My lovely Josephine,

There's an old song that you may, by chance, hear one day:
Come Josephine, in my flying machine. I find it stuck in my head
quite often lately. You are my little flying machine. We're going big
places together, you and me, my first and favorite daughter. You're
such a good little helper, curious and patient with an old man. I
watch you with the other Girls and see how they look up to you. I
couldn't have asked for a better Girl One, a true big sister in every
way. Happy Five Years to you!

I'm sorry I haven't been around as much. Trust me when I say
that I'd rather be at the Homestead. Can you imagine Galileo
being called away from his telescope to handle a memo? Edison
interrupting that first phone call so that he could tell his wife
whether he wanted the pot roast or the Salisbury steak? One day,
when you are a famous scientist yourself, you may understand these
frustrations! Of all the Girls, you're the most like me, Josephine.
You have that same spark in you. That same curiosity. You see the
world through my eyes.

But daily life continues with its usual demands. My son has
been struggling with an unfortunate medical issue, and so I must
attend to my duties at home. But my heart—my heart is with you.

Your loving father always,
Joseph Bellanger

34

"Junior's trying to kill us?" Isabelle asked. "Or the other one? What was his name? Billy?" She lolled back on the bed, arms straight out, knees in the air.

"Bobby," I said. "Junior was the younger one."

During the space of that conversation with Bonnie, the Bellangers had gone from bit players to the people who might have set everything into motion. The ones who'd set the fire at my house, taken my mother, lured me out of my old life and into this.

Marianne, Junior, Bobby. Bellanger's family. His other family. Even as an adult, I'd never thought that much about them. Their precedence in Bellanger's life had been mostly symbolic, proof of his wholesomeness as a family man. Proof that he couldn't want to get rid of the nuclear family because he had one himself.

"How do we know it's not both of them coming after us? *If* it's even one of them," Cate added, a caveat. I was trying to be cautious too. Still, it made more sense than anything we'd considered so far: The symmetry of it. Eye for an eye, tooth for a tooth. Fire for a fire.

Mother for a father.

"Do we remember anything about his sons?" Cate asked. "Josie, you must remember."

I shrugged, helpless, frustrated by my failed memory. "Bellanger barely ever brought them to the Homestead. I do remember—okay, maybe—there was a time when they were visiting us. It was weird to have these boys running around. I was upset about something, and one of them—I don't know which one—he helped me. He was actually pretty nice."

Cate's eyes narrowed for a second, a flinch of skepticism. "We need more to go on than that if we're going to take this seriously."

"We weren't invited to the funeral," Isabelle piped up. "None of us."

Cate and I looked at her, surprised. My mother and I hadn't attended the funeral. We'd already been in Illinois, and I'd been lost in the haze of grief and confusion. Our absence hadn't struck me as strange before now. I'd just assumed my mother didn't want anything to do with the Homestead.

"Maybe they were worried about more attacks," Cate said.

"But Bellanger wanted us at the funeral." Isabelle said. "There were empty chairs up front, just waiting for us. The eulogy was about Bellanger's accomplishments. That's us. We should have been there, but Mrs. Bellanger barred us."

It was difficult to picture Mrs. Bellanger at all, that face I'd only ever seen adjacent to Bellanger's own. She only made sense in a particular context. I tried to take her usual expression, sweet and limp as cake batter, and stir it up into rage, despair, grief. I recalled only an impression of her hair. She'd once dyed it from mousy blond to a darker brown that matched Angela Grassi's—or my mother's.

We'd all changed recently. Cate had chopped my hair to my chin, giving me bangs that made my eyes look shadowy, my cheekbones higher. She dyed it an inconspicuous blond, muting the similarity to my mother in a way I'd never quite had the courage to do. I looked in the mirror and saw neither Mother One nor Girl One. Not the original, not the copy. Somebody new. Cate had shorn her own hair to ear-length, leaving it the same color. The shorter length made her curls spring wildly, a thick halo. Isabelle dyed her hair a lusterless black: she was arresting, the mousy girl I'd first met almost entirely erased.

"My mother said Mrs. Bellanger blamed us for taking away her husband. She wanted the funeral to just be hers and the boys'." Isabelle repeated this in a way both careless and exact, like it was something she'd heard her mother say a thousand times.

We were quiet, imagining it. The dry rage that had been growing, the brittle layer of loneliness, resentment, spread out over the Bellangers' entire childhood.

A soft knock and then Tom entered, carrying more supplies, wearing his usual hangdog expression. He'd been sleeping in the car lately, keeping an eye out for trouble, but also, I thought, paying his penance for what had happened in Kithira. I caught a new wariness to his attitude now. He understood who we truly were.

"I bring sustenance," he announced.

"Thomas," Cate said, running her hands through her hair till her curls bristled like a lion's mane. "Your time to shine. What do you know about the Bellangers? Where they are now?"

"The Bellangers?" he repeated. "You mean . . . the other ones?"

"His wife. His kids." Cate was impatient.

"Why are you asking me?"

"You're the one writing a book." Every syllable slowed down pointedly.

I jumped in: "You know everyone else's address. We're trying to figure out if one of the Bellangers is after us now."

He inhaled at this. "Wow. Like, the follower? One of his sons. Shit. I never—"

"Do you know anything about them?" I asked.

"To be honest . . ." Tom set the bags down on the bed, then rubbed hard at the back of his neck, not exactly looking at any of us. "They've been pretty hard to track down. I know they stayed in Maryland for a while, probably to let the boys finish school. Marianne was savvy about protecting her own family from the press—she'd use fake names, hide from paparazzi. Once the youngest boy graduated, they went their own ways. The money from Bellanger could've tided them over for a while. Her last known address was in California—"

"You don't know where they are," Cate said, cutting him off. "Long story short."

"I'm not entirely sure, no."

"You're writing a big tell-all about Joseph Bellanger and you're not talking to his sons or his wife?" Cate demanded.

"Look, I was getting around to it," Tom said, defensive, crossing his arms.

"Could you maybe get around to it now?"

That subtle redness, rash-like, drifted up Tom's neck. "Yeah, I'd love to talk to the Bellangers. Of course I would. But I have to be respectful. They didn't ask to be part of this."

Irritation shot through me, and I saw it mirrored in Cate's face.

"Did they not?" Cate asked. "Bless their hearts. Shall we just leave them alone, then, poor dears?" Her voice was tight with sarcasm, exploding into sudden anger. "Why are you even here, then, Thomas? What do you want with us?"

He stuck his hands in his pockets, wouldn't look at anyone directly. "I thought we were just talking about our next move. I don't want a fight."

"*Our* next move. Who invited you, anyway?"

"Cate," I said. "Okay. It's not his fault. Tom's been in this from the start."

She bit at one fist, then let go, sighed. "Yeah? Well, maybe if he'd put any effort into finding the Bellangers and talking to them, instead of hunting *us* down, we wouldn't be in this situation at all."

"Christ, I could use a cigarette." Tom tipped his head back against the brick wall, staring up at the grayish night sky. Even the sky around this motel was grimier, greasier, the stars dulled. I'd followed him out there, hoping to smooth things over.

"Me too." I didn't know what it would mean if my mother had attracted the attention of the Bellangers, those strangers whose lineage was knotted through ours. Had they attacked her and threatened her? Had they kidnapped her, or had she escaped? The questions beat frantically inside my head.

We sat together on the gravel, the little rocks piercing my thighs. Tom leaned forward, sought out my eyes, and held my gaze. After a second, I understood that he was looking into my eyes as an act of trust right now, purposeful and intent. "Hey," he said. "I'm sorry. I'm sorry for calling the cops. I really thought we needed help, but I almost got you—"

I touched his knee quickly. "It's okay. I'm fine now. Better than ever."

"But you could've—"

"But I didn't," I said firmly. "We both thought it was the right move."

He smiled a little, relief softening his face. "I wasn't expecting any of this." He rubbed his forehead too roughly, eyes looking tired in the scratchy dusk. "When I set out to research this book, I just wanted to find out what had really gone on at the Homestead. I wasn't expecting to be in a motel with three fugitives, hiding from someone who wants you dead."

"You're one of us now." I punched his shoulder, both teasing and not. "An honorary Homesteader."

He gave a strange, quick smile, and I wondered if I'd hurt his feelings. But then—"Oh. Hey. I have something for you." Tom reached into his back pocket, rising a little, and placed something gently into my palm. A photograph.

"What is this?" I asked, laughing, confused. Then I saw that it was a Polaroid. Not a professional shot. It was intimate and unstaged. My mother. Her hair was darkened with sweat, damp curls around her ears and temples, her head tilted back. An expression I'd never seen before: she looked exhausted and too full at the same time, emotions brimming on her tired face, everything close to the surface. Her robe was slipping to nearly expose one nipple, and she held me to her chest, my body small and naked, tiny limbs sprawled open, starfish-like. The loose spiral of an umbilical cord stretched to the bottom of the frame.

"Where'd you get this?" I asked, quieted. "How?"

"I found it as part of my research. Never published before, I guess. Took up most of my savings to get ahold of it. I thought it was worth it."

I gave a laugh that was closer to a sob. "I've never seen her like this."

"Happy birthday." Tom sounded shyer than usual.

Stunned, I calculated quickly. He was right. In the middle of everything, my birthday had gotten lost entirely. It had passed unnoticed. I remembered my birthdays back home, those homemade birthday cakes. My mother's soft voice singing alone. *Happy birthday, dear Josephine, happy birthday to you.*

I gave Tom a quick hug and felt him tense, his breathing coming quicker.

"I, uh, may be trying to butter you up," he admitted.

"Oh yeah?"

"I keep thinking about what you said," Tom said. "About the book.

You asked me to stop working on it. I'm not sure if you were just angry, or—"

I loosened the embrace. "Right. So were you going to put this photo in your book?"

He gave a small, sheepish smile, staring at the ground. "I considered it. I—I think it belongs with its true owner. It's yours. It's your mom, your story. But the more we learn, the more I feel like this story needs to be told, somehow, some way. I was hoping you felt the same."

"This story needs to be told," I said slowly. "But I still need you to wait." I kept thinking of what it would look like, our history spread open to the world. My mother, no longer the guinea pig. My mother, no longer innocent. My origin not a neat trajectory of progress and downfall but a confused and wavering line. "I'm not saying you should give it up entirely. I just need to understand this story before the whole world knows it too."

"All right," Tom said after a minute, words tinged with disappointment. "I can do that."

"Look, maybe when this is all over and I have my mom again, I can even give you an interview," I said, impulsively generous. "Formal and official and very much on the record."

"Josie." Tom was staring beyond me, whispering. "The car."

I made myself move slowly, casually. I edged backward from Tom, pretended to play with my hair, lifting it off my neck, as I turned. A car idled on the thin service road. The maroon sedan. The driver was indistinguishable, just a blurred shadow. The headlights were milky against the dusk.

"He followed us," Tom murmured.

My palms were damp, my heartbeat pounding, every nerve taut. Before I could decide what to do next, the sedan pulled away. Driving too fast, it sped around the curve of the road, hidden by an outcropping of trees. I got up at the last second and ran after it, ignoring Tom calling out to me. I stared at the plates: Utah, in red lettering. With an exclamation point. *Ski Utah!*

I just had time to register the ridiculous peppiness of this before the car vanished and Tom and I were alone again.

"If that cre_p's been following us, who knows what he's seen?" Cate asked, pacing in wild circles. "Maybe he saw what happened at Kithira. Maybe this was a message. He wanted us to see him this time."

"We can't stay here," I said. "It's not safe. He could burn this whole place."

"Yeah, no, we leave tonight," Tom said. "That's not even a question. The question is—where to? Do we find another motel, bunker down, or do we keep going?"

The idea of moving again made my pulse pick up. We were all eager to get out of this purgatory. I felt it even more strongly than the others—the time we were losing, and what might be happening to my mother while we stayed still, treading water—

"Is it safe?" Cate asked. "If this guy is following us, are we just leading him to people's doorsteps? We shouldn't drag the others into it."

"Apparently the Clarksons are still fine," Tom argued. "This guy, whoever he is, seems to be following his own logic."

"But maybe not. And if he's hunting us down, that's a big gamble to take with people's lives, Thomas," Cate said. "Though we already know you like to take big risks if it'll scratch your ego."

Tom swallowed, gave a tight shrug.

"Maybe we stay here and set a trap for him," Isabelle said, her voice brightening.

"A trap?" Cate repeated, trying to understand. "Like . . . let him catch us here?"

Isabelle started to nod, but I wasn't in the mood for her wide-eyed eccentricity, my nerves sharpened to points. "Whatever you've learned from your homeschooling, Isabelle, it's not going to work that way in the real world," I said. Seeing her expression, I softened a little: "Sorry. Sorry, but we need to take real action. There are only two women left that we haven't visited. Angela Grassi and Barbara Kim."

"Barbara would know about the photograph of Lily-Anne," Isabelle said quietly. She shut her eyes. Her eyelashes were still pale, giving her a ghostly look, framed by the severity of that black dye. "She's the only one who knows for sure. She's right there."

The photograph. I'd nearly forgotten. Lily-Anne pregnant, a second time, not part of Bellanger's original and documented experiment. I was at once curious and nervous: The idea that something this big and this integral could've been concealed. What it might mean for everything.

"I guess we could try." Cate dropped her hand from her hair. An energy moved into the motel room, clear as a beam of light, disrupting the fog of our fear and uncertainty.

"Barbara Kim's in North Carolina," Tom said. "A town called Sweet-land. I don't have her home address, but she runs a business there. A flower shop. She runs it with her family."

35

"Isabelle?" I asked. "What's wrong?"

A blocky TV set hung precariously in the corner of the gas station. Isabelle was standing right in front of it, head tilted upward. The lines of her body were so compact and unmoving that I had the uncanny sensation of seeing a paused movie.

We'd left the motel that night and entered North Carolina in the dreamy gray of the predawn hours, stopping at a gas station to refuel. Isabelle and I had come inside the convenience store to stock up on our diet of chips, Twinkies, watery coffee. The place was nearly deserted this early, just one employee.

The drive between Pennsylvania and North Carolina—nine hours—had been tense and jumpy, all of us feeling stripped-down. I couldn't shake the sensation of being chased. By the Bellangers; by the men of Kithira. Who knew who else? I'd set out to find my mother and had instead picked up a trail of strangers in my wake, none of them the person I wanted.

"Izzy," I said, still at the counter, wallet out. I didn't want to draw undue attention to ourselves right now. "Are you okay?"

"Don't call me Izzy," she snapped. "Only my mother called me that."

Isabelle's face was on the screen, staring back down at the actual Isabelle. Staring right at me. But of course it wasn't Girl Two. It was an old photo of Patricia, muted brown hair swept over one shoulder. The photo vanished, replaced by a carefully somber newscaster.

"She's dead." Isabelle was poker-faced, voice not shifting register. "They killed her." Behind the counter, the woman froze, eyes darting toward us. "The men from Kithira. They were going after me but they got to her first."

My whole body went numb. Patricia: gone. The woman who'd

brought the Homestead to life along with my mother, the one who'd been a secret part of my origin story, a signed initial at the bottom of secret love letters. Gone. They'd hunted her down. How much worse would they do to us? I'd thought I'd avenged the Strouds, but maybe I'd only introduced more harm to the world, opened the door to more violence against the Homesteaders.

I tried to speak in a gentle voice. "Let's get back to the car. We can talk about this when we're alone."

Isabelle turned and came to the counter, moving too quickly. She grabbed the woman's wrist, and the cashier yelped, trying to pull away. "They shot her in the back while she was trying to get away," Isabelle said, still with that eerie calm. "My mother's dead."

The cashier began to say something, but nothing came out of her mouth, her face drooping. Blood threaded from the corner of her mouth, slipping, bright and hot, down her chin. Just like Black Shoes.

I shouted Isabelle's name. The blood dripped onto the cashier's polyester blouse, staining the yellow with little blossoms. I grabbed Isabelle's hand and tried to pry her fingers open, but she was too strong, gripped with some wiry strength I hadn't known she possessed.

I was frozen, conflicted. I didn't want to turn my powers against the others. It felt wrong, much worse than when I'd unthinkingly used them on Tom. Before I had to make a choice, Isabelle let go and abruptly stepped away. The woman gasped, fell back, looking from one of us to the other, Her chest heaved

"You need to get control of yourself," I said, careful not to frame it as a directive. "We need to focus. Are you sure it wasn't the Bellangers who came after your mom?"

"No. The news showed the security footage. I recognized the truck. It wasn't the red car that's been following us." I should have known that Patricia Bishop would have outfitted her home with cameras to complement the barricade of NO TRESPASSING signs. "They know what I did to that man and they came after me. But they only found her."

Patricia, her serious eyes. I'd walked into her life wearing my mother's face and I'd taken everything from her all over again.

Isabelle turned her head back toward the TV screen. "I wanted to be special," she said. "I wanted it more than I wanted her. You don't even know what I did to my mother before I left." Her voice was growing in urgency. "Did you think she'd just let me leave?"

Outside, the sky was rosy with sunrise. On the TV, a woman in a bathrobe smiled at her daughter over a cup of coffee, the two of them pressing their foreheads together. The cashier ran her hand under her mouth, stared at her blood-dipped fingers. We couldn't stay here.

Looking at the woman, I groped for the words that would fix this. "I'm sorry," I said. "She's not well right now. Please just—just forget this happened."

She didn't answer.

I wrapped an arm around Isabelle's shoulder, and together we walked away from the counter. I guided her. Slowly. Slowly. Past the obnoxiously cheerful candy, cheap penknives, pastries inside humidity-dewed wrappers. When I opened the door, the cool morning air landed on my skin and I could breathe again.

"It's my fault." Isabelle's voice had softened, like she was just waking up. I pushed her into the Volvo and climbed in myself, both of us crushed into the backseat with Cate. I patted the back of the driver's seat like I'd thump on a horse's flank, urging Tom to go.

My breathing didn't settle until our car had vanished into the flow of vehicles heading toward North Carolina. Morning commuters. Truck drivers. We fit in, anonymous, harmless.

"My mother was going to lock me in my room," Isabelle said. Cate started to speak, but I hushed her with a lifted hand. "She forbade me from going," Isabelle said. "I didn't even want to go *with* you. I just wanted to see you one more time. But my mother wouldn't listen. She talked over me. She was going to lock me in my room until I got my head on straight. I grabbed her and begged her to stop," Isabelle said. "Suddenly she was coughing, and there was blood."

Outside the car windows, towering trees grew wild. A little beige brick church squatted in the dip of a valley, only the cross jutting above the guardrails.

"It felt so natural," Isabelle said. "Like I'd been doing it my whole life. I could make her stop yelling. Just by touching her. After all those years, I'd finally become special, and what had I done with it? I'd hurt my mother."

I thought of Black Shoes in Kithira, glassy-eyed on the bed. "Isabelle," I said gently.

"When I touch people," Isabelle said, and held up her hands, "I can feel their insides. The veins and the bones. I can just"—she demonstrated, a delicate pinching gesture—"twist them. I can make the blood come right to the surface. I can pull it right out of people."

I squeezed her hand, trying to soothe her. Her pulse was wild against my palm.

"When I saw my mother on the TV, I thought I'd killed her myself." Isabelle turned an agonized gaze to me, like she knew I'd understand. I did. Of course I did. The two of us had passed our daughterly guilt between us like witches fumbling over their shared eyeball.

"It's not your fault," I said.

"It is," Isabelle said. "Those men came after her because they were trying to get to me. I hurt my mother. I broke her heart and I left her alone. Then I led those men right to her."

I wrapped my arms around Isabelle. After a moment, her small, stiff body relaxed into mine. She accepted the embrace the way a child would, leaning into me, eyes drifting half-shut. "The basement," she murmured. "They showed the basement on the news. They got to it."

"The basement?" I repeated. Cate and I shared a tense, thrumming glance. I understood at once what it meant. Fiona. The proof of who she was, now in hostile hands. I felt sick.

"They must have the film," Isabelle said softly. When I looked down at her, I saw Patricia, for just a moment, her face empty, lost to me. Gone. My heart swelled with grief.

36

Yoon Flowers & More was an unassuming storefront that opened to a space filled with light and fragrance. As we entered to the fading chime of the bell, I saw Cate had tears in her eyes and realized she was thinking of her garden back home. Isabelle ran a fingertip along an orchid's frosty petals, saying nothing. She'd been disturbingly quiet ever since the gas station, brushing me off anytime I said anything comforting.

Tom had waited in the car at our request. I kept thinking about the fact that Barbara Kim was married. It was almost more disorienting to me than finding Isabelle drowning herself or Emily in the attic. A new family. A new life. All the rest of us had stuck to our two-person bubbles, for better or for worse.

A voice floated from the back of the store: "Coming!" A second later, Barbara Kim came hurrying to the front counter, smiling, her face a bright question mark. Her dark brown hair was tucked behind her ears, and she wore a belted dress, looking as crisp as the flowers surrounding us. She was trailed by a girl, maybe twelve or eleven, with a high ponytail and a striped T-shirt, intent on her Gameboy.

"Can I help you?" the woman asked.

She looked so much like Barbara, but the timing was off. She was closer to my age. I'd slipped backward in time, into the 1980s, and I tried to get my balance. "Helen?" I asked.

The young woman laughed, and the girl looked up from her video game system, contemptuous. "Helen? She's Soo-jin."

Helen—Soo-jin—whoever Barbara's doppelgänger was, she kept smiling at us. "Are you here about the Smith-Roberts wedding? I have some lovely cascades ready for you."

It seemed impossible that she wouldn't recognize us. Surely Soo-jin had seen our mothers' faces frequently enough that some familiarity would sneak through. Maybe the dyed and chopped hair was enough to throw her off. Or maybe—maybe—

"We're looking for your mother," Cate said, taking over. "Is she here?"

"Oh, she's busy." Soo-jin sounded genuinely regretful, like this was her loss as well as ours. "But I can help you. I've been helping my parents with this place since I can remember."

"We'd really love to speak to Barbara," I said. "We're—"

"Old family friends." A warning note in Cate's voice. She didn't want me to say too much.

"I'm sure my mom would love to talk to you, but—"

"She's downstairs," the younger girl broke in. "She's getting flowers ready for a baptism. Just go down." She jerked her head in the general direction of the back of the store.

Soo-jin smirked gently, a *what-can-you-do?* expression. There was something so different about the Yoons: every other Homesteader pair had been solitary, I realized now, tucked inside that isolated mother-daughter pairing, no room for anybody else. These two girls seemed happy together in a way that made my heart squeeze.

Light came in through thin rectangular windows that were interspersed at ground-level, revealing the grass and flowers growing right outside. Barbara was standing in front of a long, thin table covered in daisies, wielding a small pair of scissors in one hand, ribbon in the other. She turned when she heard us, smiling, clearly expecting one of the girls.

I felt the three of us become predators, walking into this woman's ordinary day with our impossible questions. One of us was a murderer; one of us had brought a dead woman back to life; one of us had been dead days ago. Being around the Yoons made me feel how far we'd fallen from normal life, its small, familiar pleasures.

Barbara's smile faltered for a moment, a razor's edge of grim shock, and I could almost see her deciding what to do next. Then she pinned the smile back in place. "Can I help you ladies? This space isn't for customers." She was softer now than when she'd been on the Homestead;

she wore slacks, feet seamed with pantyhose. Glasses subtly changed the angles of her face.

"Barbara," I said. "We're here about my mother."

"Your mother? How do I know her?" Barbara asked, a warning underneath the politeness. "Is she—are you friends of—"

"My mother was Tonya Bowers," Cate said. "She died last year. Josephine is Margaret's daughter, and Isabelle is Patricia's daughter."

Barbara's expression wavered, then turned stony. "What are you doing here?" she asked, voice tight with suppressed anger. "Don't you know better than to come by here? This is my family business. Our livelihood. Anybody could see you marching in here." She glanced up at the ceiling. "My girls," she breathed. "Did you talk to them? What did you say?"

"Don't worry," Cate soothed. "We barely spoke. They have no idea who we are."

"Didn't your mother tell you to leave me alone, Josephine?" Barbara said. "I told her I didn't want anything to do with her or you."

"You heard from my mother?" I asked, that old optimism springing up again.

"You aren't listening to me, young lady," Barbara said. "I don't want you here."

"Please," I said. "I'm sure you've seen on TV that my mother might be in trouble—if you know anything about her—"

For one cold moment, I thought: *I could make her tell me.* I was tired of playing nice, always trying to ease information out of people who didn't want to talk to me. These women who'd been involved in my very creation and wouldn't tell me the things I needed to know, cloaking my history from me, keeping me from my mother. I just wanted to know, and I had the power to find out. What was I doing standing here, limp and compliant? It would take almost nothing to drag it out of Barbara. No harm done. Not really.

But before I could say anything, Isabelle was speaking: "That's your other daughter? The girl with the video game?" she asked.

Barbara's face tightened. "Yes," she said. "It's not what you think. I had Min-ji with my husband. She's his daughter, in every way."

"You never told your daughters about us at all," Isabelle said to Barbara. "Soo-jin didn't recognize us and she grew up with us. She has no idea who she is, does she? She's so special, but she thinks she's just like anybody else."

"She knows she's special," Barbara said. "She has a loving family. She has a good home. She's brilliant, kindhearted. What else does she need to make her special?" The rest of us didn't answer. Cate and I were both wedged in a fraught silence.

Isabelle shrugged. "Maybe she deserves to know."

Barbara's mouth twitched into a sudden, contemptuous smile. "Are you blackmailing me? You're just a kid. I remember changing your diaper." She was amused, giving us a glimpse of the past Barbara. Fierce, outspoken Mother Eight. Always more willing to joke or roughhouse than the other mothers. Always up to be *it* during a game of tag or hide-and-seek.

Barbara stepped forward, took Isabelle's chin in her hand. She gently turned Isabelle's face to the side, examining her. "Your mother," Barbara said at last, "was always stealing my things. I couldn't leave anything out or she'd assume it was hers too." Barbara let go of Isabelle's chin. She moved across the basement toward the stairwell, locked the door. "You have ten minutes." She pointed at the clock. "After that, you leave town and you never come back and bother us again, or there will be consequences."

"Yes," I said at once. "Of course." The other two nodded.

Barbara sat on the one folding chair in the workroom. We stayed standing, close together, the wet, green scent of the flower stems all around us. Now that the moment had passed, I was relieved that I hadn't given in to the grubby temptation to force her to talk. Still. Ten minutes. My lungs tightened at the idea of fitting everything into such a short time. I pulled the photograph of Lily-Anne out of my pocket and handed it to Barbara.

She cradled it behind the other hand as if sheltering a guttering flame. "Where did you find this? I was sure it was destroyed in the fire."

"My mother held on to it," Cate said. I craned my neck to take in the photo again, Barbara and Lily-Anne. Now I noticed a deeper texture to Lily-Anne's smile. It reminded me of Bellanger. The kind of smile he wore whenever he was photographed on the heels of a breakthrough. Triumph.

"We thought she was pregnant with Fiona," Cate said. "But this is from at least January 1976." She tapped the edge of the framed image. "Fiona was already a nine-month-old baby at that point. Lily-Anne couldn't have been pregnant with her."

Barbara held the photograph up at different angles, as if the light might alter the image. "This photograph was taken even later than that. New Year's Day in 1977. I knew it was a mistake to frame that silly *Time* cover, but Tami thought it belonged in the timeline of the Homestead. She thought we'd helped to inspire this shift."

I exchanged a glance with the others. The same year as the fire. There was a pressure growing around the edges of my skull. "Why is Lily-Anne pregnant in this photo?" I made myself ask.

"It's too much. I can't catch you up, I don't want to revisit all that." She squeezed her eyes shut briefly, reopened them. "You girls aren't ready."

"We know more than you think," I said. "We know about Fiona's abilities. We know that my mother was behind most of what happened on the Homestead."

Barbara processed this quietly.

"It's our story too," I said. "We need to know."

I could see her relent. "You're right that this wasn't Fiona," she said, touching Lily-Anne's pregnant belly. "It was her little sister."

A tenth baby. Another miracle, one the world hadn't dissected and documented. Bellanger's lost creation.

"At first I was the only one who knew about it," Barbara said. "Lily-Anne was my dearest friend, and she barely even trusted me with this secret. She was so quiet, staying in one room and sleeping a lot. We thought it was the stress. The rest of us had to look after little Fiona." She peered at me. "You don't remember any of this, Josie?"

"I remember that . . . that Fiona was always around," I said slowly. "I was jealous of her. For a while, my mom watched Fiona more than she spent time with me."

Barbara nodded. "We all stepped in and helped when Lily-Anne couldn't handle things anymore. One day, I was checking on

Lily-Anne and she showed me that she was pregnant. Five months along by then. I couldn't believe it. That's when she asked me to take the photo. How could I say no? She was glowing. She begged me to keep it quiet from the others, and I did. Dr. Bellanger had been home in Maryland for months at that point. One of his sons needed his attention. He'd just had an operation for his scoliosis and it had finally convinced Bellanger to spend more time with the poor boy."

Judging by Cate's small inhalation, this detail stood out to her too. A week ago I would barely have thought about Junior.

"It was the longest Bellanger had ever been away," Barbara said. "Lily-Anne was so excited for him to come back. She wanted it to be a big surprise for him. She really thought it would be his greatest triumph, the miracle without the medicine. A new stage." I thought of that triumphant smile in the photograph. "But when Bellanger found out, he was furious. He insisted that she was endangering the baby by carrying it to term without his assistance." Barbara took a shuddering breath. "Bellanger instantly moved her to his lab, away from the main house, so she was even more isolated. He started her on medications every day, trying to make up for lost time. He wanted that pregnancy under his control, I suppose."

"Why didn't Bellanger announce that he was starting a second phase?" I asked. That would have been breaking news, the perfect complement to his plans to share his research, his proposed idea of releasing a medication to induce parthenogenesis. I couldn't understand why this pregnancy had been hidden away all these years.

"There was no *second phase*," Barbara said, impatient now. "Josephine, if I'm going to talk, then you need to listen. Bellanger didn't have anything to do with that pregnancy."

"It was a normal pregnancy," I said. "By a man." Another layer of reality spread out beneath the known one. A past in which there were men, fathers, hairy and anonymous, who'd brought us to life, provided us with the other half of our DNA, and then vanished.

Cate squeezed my arm, quieting me. "Lily-Anne did it without Bellanger?" she asked. The anonymous men dissolved as easily as they'd stirred to life.

Nobody spoke or moved. It felt like we were held inside this moment, forced to slow down, absorb the meaning, and let ourselves change in response.

"Her own virgin birth," I said.

Barbara nodded, barely a movement at all. "Yes," she said at last, a whisper, like she could scarcely bring herself to say it. "Her very own."

Lily-Anne's second pregnancy, one that was truly hers, no male influence at all, no test tubes, no hormones, no drugs. Stripped down: just a woman alone, creating life, spinning it to existence in the deepest pit of her being.

The impossible.

"How do you know Lily-Anne's pregnancy wasn't caused by Bellanger?" I asked, trying to stay rational about this. It had been one thing to know that my mother was interested in parthenogenesis before ever meeting Bellanger, or to understand the nine women as a sisterhood that preexisted outside of Bellanger's reach. But the nine of us had still been the result of Bellanger's work; we'd had a father, even if he hadn't shown up in our DNA. This—this was different. Behind my skepticism, I felt a steadily building thrill. Pure amazement.

"Like I said, Bellanger had been out of town around the time Lily-Anne would've conceived," Barbara said. "By that point, he was so busy granting interviews and being photographed that he didn't have time to work with us. But he hoped to present this tenth pregnancy as something he'd planned himself."

The small, triumphant smile on Lily-Anne's face in that photograph made sense now. That baby would've been different from the rest of us. I could see it perfectly. That baby would've been Lily-Anne's alone. No contracts, no custody, no obligation binding her daughter to Bellanger. A true virgin birth.

I took a steadying breath. What had happened in our mothers' bodies had been miraculous in terms of the mechanics of conception, the old dance of sperm meeting the egg interrupted, but it had always been presided over by Bellanger. If Lily-Anne could've revealed that pregnancy to the world, then her baby would have eclipsed us completely— the ability to self-conceive restored. I remembered my mother and

Patricia, bent over their shared books. The women had spent months and months attempting to use that knowledge before my mother had convinced them to contact Bellanger. Maybe that knowledge had just needed to grow in Lily-Anne's mind, take root, and here it was, a final result Patricia and my mother had never known about. A result that now Patricia would never know about, I remembered with a queasy jolt.

"And this photo was taken in January of 1977?" I asked. Just one month before Lily-Anne's death. I tried to reconcile these two things. Lily-Anne's death of heart failure and this pregnancy. They had met in the middle somewhere: secret life and familiar death.

Isabelle leaned forward, her eyes burning. "Where's the baby now?"

Barbara didn't answer.

"What happened to the baby?" Cate echoed. "She didn't just disappear."

Barbara was stroking her finger down Lily-Anne's face like she could somehow bring comfort to the woman in the photograph. "It was a hard birth," she said at last. "Lily-Anne started having contractions three months early, much earlier than we expected. So far, we'd had good births, healthy and safe. I didn't realize just how precious that was until I saw Lily-Anne in labor the second time. She was sweating and crying, talking to herself. Saying, 'Save her, please save her.' It all happened so fast. Lily-Anne was still in Bellanger's laboratory, hidden away from everybody else. I was the only one allowed in." Barbara took a deep, shuddering breath. "I kept catching glimpses of Lily-Anne when the door would swing open. She was more and more wild-eyed. And then she was gone. No life in her eyes. I'd never understood, before then, just how obvious it is when somebody dies. There's just no mistaking it."

Cate was concentrating on Barbara. Isabelle was fidgeting, restless, bouncing on the balls of her feet. I couldn't draw a full breath.

"Bellanger delivered the baby," Barbara went on, now with a resolve that seemed practiced, like she'd learned how to suppress the emotions that accompanied this memory. "I went in to see her. I didn't hear a cry. She was just a little doll. Not even wet or bloody, just this tiny perfect baby. I could see she had red hair too. Like Lily-Anne.

Like Fiona, her big sister." Barbara paused. "Lily-Anne had never even told me her name."

"What happened to her?" Cate asked softly. I imagined this little infant, this slippery scrap of a miracle, so small that maybe she'd have just vanished, dissolved into nothingness.

"Bellanger brought in a friend," Barbara said. "An old colleague from medical school. Dr. Henley. I forget his first name. He'd come by the Homestead a few times. Maybe you remember him. He took them both, mother and baby. I was left to clean up—the lab and the secret. I'd watched my best friend die, and her baby too." Barbara reached up and pressed both hands to her cheeks, like she was trying to remind herself she was really here.

"The day after Lily-Anne's death," Barbara said, "Vera came into the kitchen and tossed down a newspaper. The headline said that Lily-Anne had died of a heart attack. A naked lie. I just wanted the bodies back, to hold a proper funeral for them. Bellanger said he needed to understand what had happened. He needed to run tests. They were just cut open and examined and burned in some anonymous lab."

"Why did you never share this?" Cate asked.

"Dr. Bellanger said that if I ever told the world about Lily-Anne, or even told any of the other women, he'd have me committed and Soo-jin would go to him, as his own little girl. I left that place as soon as I could. I fled. Fiona distracted everyone. I was able to slip away without too much trouble."

I had to close my eyes for a second. The first time Patricia had suggested that Bellanger sought custody of the nine of us, it had held a stubborn nostalgia. The way Barbara described the situation now stripped that nostalgia to the bone. It was a threat, naked and uncompromising. Bellanger had been flawed—I'd known that. Nobody succeeded without making a few enemies. But the man she was describing—I didn't know him. He was a monster.

"I met Bill Yoon at the first job I took," Barbara said. "Such a kind-hearted man. I changed Helen's name. Bill adopted her and made it legal. People sometimes even say she looks like her father, although—" A quick, unhappy smile. "Maybe white people are going to say that to us no matter what." She shifted. "You girls think it was hard on your mothers? People claiming they'd bring about the end of the world? They were white girls. What do you think people did when they saw me? The kinds of things they said about me. The fear that I'd overrun the country. An invasion of little fatherless foreigners. That's the type of thing I had to deal with."

There was a sudden rift between us. The awareness that even though we'd shared a heritage so particular, so singular, that only a few people on the planet had known what it was like, Barbara's experience had still been happening on a different plane from my mother's.

"I could finally give Soo-jin a normal life. I changed her name. When I decided to have a baby with Bill, I wasn't sure it would even work. Maybe whatever Bellanger had done to me could never be undone. I was so happy when I missed my period, but I didn't fully heal until I held that little girl in my arms and saw Bill's eyes looking out at me. I just put everything else behind me. Having a baby with someone you love can be miraculous too, you know."

I glanced at the clock. Time was up, but nobody seemed to notice. "You mentioned that my mother called you," I said. "What was it about?"

"Just a short phone call. Margaret wasn't . . . she wasn't well, Josephine. I'm sorry. She was rambling, words spilling out, not making any sense."

Deborah Clarkson had said something similar, days ago. I latched on to this: the same interpretation from Barbara now. "What did she say exactly? I can handle it."

Barbara sighed, relented, not looking at me. "She thought she'd seen Fiona alive."

Somebody walked by outside, shoes disembodied, cut off at the ankle. Whoever it was walked by three windows in a row, shadow flitting into the basement at intervals, before vanishing around the corner. We all exhaled at once. The atmosphere in the room felt so precious and fraught that being reminded of the outside world was jarring.

"It was some news segment from Texas," Barbara said. "Your mother said that she'd seen a redheaded girl in the background, and at some point the girl turned to the camera long enough for Margaret to recognize her as Lily-Anne's double."

"What was the news segment about?" I asked.

Barbara blinked, startled by the intensity of the question. "Birds," she said slowly. "Something about a flock of birds dropping out of the sky. Your mother was having a hard time explaining it to me. Margaret said she tried to call the station, but of course they hadn't paid any attention to a girl in the background. So your mother called all of us. She kept asking me if I thought Fiona might somehow be alive. Usually I wouldn't have even stayed on the phone, but Margaret seemed so desperate, Josephine."

This was the closest I'd come to piecing together the time just before my mother's disappearance, that broad gap between the time I left her and the night she vanished. My mother, alone, day after day, month after month, in a town where she'd never quite belonged. What would it have been like to see a familiar face appear in the middle of a crowd? Was she afraid, seeing this dead Girl resurface from the past, or was it a pure relief to see someone she knew? Somebody to look for when she couldn't bring herself to come looking for me.

I remembered what Deborah Clarkson had said to me back at the start of this journey, my mother *resurrecting dead dreams that nobody needs*. My mother must've also told Deborah about the girl.

"I've imagined Fiona too," Barbara said. "I've seen Lily-Anne in a crowd before I realized it was just a stranger. I've had dreams about that baby. I understand what it's like to be haunted by the past. I pray for Margaret to find some peace." And then Barbara rose, movements definitive and efficient as she picked her scissors up again. "My time's up. I've told you all I can. Good luck, Josephine. I do hope you find your mother. Margaret always did adore you. You were the light of her life."

We walked back up the stairs and out into the sunlight. My head was spinning, too full. Another pregnancy. No intervention. Nothing to do with Bellanger. I'd dedicated my life to unlocking his secrets and restoring his research to its rightful place in the scientific community, and Lily-Anne had done it all by herself.

I wanted, desperately, viciously, to talk to Lily-Anne. She'd torn apart my history. Her death had always been blanched of tragedy by time and repetition. Now I wanted to knock on a door and find Lily-Anne waiting behind it. I wanted to question her, yell at her, poke around inside her brain.

The sunlight was deep and bright and dazzling, like we'd walked out into a new world. The Volvo sat across the street. I stood for a moment, digging my hands into my hair, which felt stiff and weird from the dye, too short, not my own. I heard Cate exhale sharply. I opened my eyes, instantly alert to any sign she was in trouble.

Someone hung back in the shadows of the alleyway next to the storefront, beckoning to us. Soo-jin. The three of us looked at each other, a wordless consultation, before we went to her.

Soo-jin glanced around, walking backward, making sure we were following, until we were just hidden from view. "I wanted to give you this." Soo-jin reached for my hand. She pressed something into my palm. A newspaper clipping. "It might help you find your mom. I've been keeping up with that story. If it were my mother missing, I'd do anything."

I examined the paper: the *Dallas Morning News*. From March 15, 1994, just over six weeks ago. "Shower of Dead Birds Leaves County Officials Scratching Heads." It was such a silly headline that I wouldn't have paid attention under other circumstances. Now it felt like a bomb going off.

The birds. Emily talking about the birds. The little dead bird with its singed wing outside my house, a lifetime ago.

Soo-jin went on: "I heard my mother on the phone to Margaret. I tried to remember the details and I found this in a newspaper at the library. Do you think it has something to do with Fiona? Do you think it's the same thing your mother saw on the news?"

I was too busy reading to answer her. It was a brief piece, skeptical, almost wry. Overnight, a thousand starlings had fallen out of the sky, scattered across lawns and parks and fields, stuck in tree branches, rooftops, rain gutters. A single grainy photo showed the feathery bodies splayed like ink drops on the side of the road, a child's bicycle in the background. Most confusingly, some of the birds had been burned. Just charred skeletons. The phenomenon had occurred in a small town not far from Amarillo. Freshwater, Texas.

"Soo-jin," Cate said. "Your mother thinks that you don't know about the Homestead at all. You acted like you didn't know us earlier. Is that—"

"I couldn't say anything in front of my sister," Soo-jin said, as if it should be obvious. "She'd tattle." Then, more seriously: "My mother doesn't realize how much I know about my past. I'm not going to hurt her. It's important to her that I don't know."

"But the Homestead's where you come from," I said.

Soo-jin looked at me evenly. "My mother is where I come from."

Isabelle hugged herself, looked down. I took a deep breath, defensive and galvanized at once. My mother. My mother, who'd changed the world just to get to me.

"Tell me something," Soo-jin said, talking quickly now. "Are any of you—different? Because there's something wrong with me."

Cate and I exchanged quick glances. "Wrong with you?" I repeated. "No. I doubt it."

"When I was a teenager," Soo-jin went on, "I used to sneak out to parties. My mother didn't know about it. She thought I was studying or staying with friends. Most of the time I was, but sometimes I just wanted to be the 'bad kid' and see what it felt like. There was this one time I went to a party out in the middle of this field. A big bonfire and everybody drinking too much. One by one, my friends trickled off, and suddenly I looked around and I didn't know anyone. This guy—he was too old to be there. He was looking for trouble. He kept chatting me up, getting me these hard lemonades and, like, cherry vodka." She swallowed like she could still taste the sickly sweetness. "This guy's asking me about my life, about school, whatever. Getting me to share all my favorite books. Before I know it, I looked back and the fire was so distant, and we were alone in the woods. I started walking, mumbling some excuse, and he got in my way."

Everything she'd felt back then was inside her voice. All the fear of that disorienting moment, still alive.

"It was my mom who taught me to scream if I ever got in trouble. She said, bad people will think you'll be too nice and quiet to do anything. They *hope* you're quiet. So you have to scream. Be as loud as you can. I always said, okay, whatever, Mom. She was always on my case about this stuff when our life was so safe and quiet. Back then, I didn't know about the Homestead. I didn't think my mom knew what she was talking about. But there I was with this guy and I just knew in my gut that this was it. This was the time. So I did, and at first my voice was normal, sort of soft. I felt like I was acting. Then it got louder, and just kept going. It was like I was inside my own voice. Like I *was* my voice, big and powerful and wild. I lost track of time. When I came back, the guy was on the ground—dead, I thought, and I started running. I ran past the bonfire and everyone was lying still. I figured I'd killed everyone. I ran home and curled up in bed waiting for the police to show up. Next day at school, though, they're all okay. Talking about what a great party it was. Everyone drank till they blacked out, including that jerk who'd tried to get me alone. I caught him giving me funny looks sometimes, but . . . he never said anything, and he kept away after that. They had no idea it was all me, but it was. I know that."

It didn't matter how many times it happened. When one of us brought our impossibility to the surface, it made my heart still inside my chest, a sense of wonder so buoyant I could rise into the air.

Soo-jin's face was glowing with secrecy. "I haven't done it again, really. But sometimes I just go way out into the woods and I scream—I just scream. To hear myself."

"All of us are like this," I said. "Not in the same way, maybe, but every one of us."

She nodded, taking this in.

"Soo-jin, come with us," I said impulsively. "You should know where you came from."

She looked at each one of us and I wondered what she saw: these three fatherless Girls, motherless Girls, our bodies scarred and bruised, our hair flat, artificial colors that didn't look quite right. There was a flash of longing in her eyes, clear as daylight. But she shook her head.

"No. My mother needs me. My sister, my father. My friends." She laughed a little, opening and closing her arms. "I can't leave them. Not right now."

"We understand," Cate said.

"Maybe one day," I said, "you'll come find us."

Soo-jin smiled, a little proud, a little wicked, and she looked more like her mother than ever. "Maybe one day, you'll come find me."

"What do you know about Freshwater, Texas?" I asked, sliding into the car, clutching Soo-jin's newspaper scrap close.

"Besides the fact that the Grassis live there?" Tom asked.

Around me, the world expanded and contracted. The Grassis: Mother Four; Girl Four. The last of the Homesteaders on my mother's list, the only ones we hadn't contacted. The dead birds, scorched; the red-haired girl; the Grassis.

"They live in Freshwater? You're sure?" I asked.

I opened the notebook, flipped through to what had seemed like a nonsense word in my mother's sloppy handwriting. *Birds.* I showed it to Cate, who inhaled softly.

"As far as I know, the Grassis are still there," Tom said. "But they were difficult to track down. They've never answered a single phone call or letter, not even to tell me to back off." He paused. "Wait, why do you ask?"

Isabelle and Cate were both turned toward me, and I could tell at a glance that they were on my side, my eagerness and resolve reflected in their faces.

"We're going to Freshwater," I said. "My mother is there."

37

April 24, 1977

My lovely Josephine,

Your sixth birthday. I look at you and I no longer see a little child. You reach my waist now. You are playful and serious in equal measure. You show flashes of a stubborn pride that delights me. A reporter was quite taken aback when you corrected him: "I do have a father, and he's right there." What a happy papa I was that day!

But there are blessed few reasons to be happy these days, I am afraid. The loss of our beloved Lily-Anne has been a terrible shock, and the unkindness of the world only makes things all the more painful. I know you miss your aunt Lily-Anne, and I hope you will continue to show kindness to poor Fiona, who now misses her mommy very much.

So many of the bright faces that once made this place feel like home have now vanished. Women who owe everything to me insisting on breaking ties. I fear that one day these sweet girls will no longer know me. Miracles stolen from the miracle-worker. I can only hope that your own mother will not follow suit, for I couldn't bear to say goodbye to my precious Girl One.

I pray you hold this letter one day and laugh at me. Laugh at my silly pessimism. Laugh at my despair. I hope you bring me this letter and we can smile together, seeing how dark those days were, celebrating the lightness that has thrived instead. We move onward into the future.

Your loving father,
Joseph Bellanger

38

Bats fluttered around each underpass, the streetlights a yellow fuzz against the bruise-dark dusk. Tom snoozed next to me. I was glad to drive. I couldn't sleep anyway. My curiosity was a hard engine pushing me forward, forward, forward.

"Josie." A whisper. The familiarity of it, close to me in the darkness, sent warmth down my spine. "You awake?"

"Ha." I focused on the neat hyphens of the road markers slipping past my wheels.

"The birds," she said. "Falling from the sky. And some of them burning. That must've been Gina Grassi, right? Her abilities. Something to do with her powers."

"Well, we have proof that eight of the nine of us aren't exactly normal. Why wouldn't Gina be the same?"

"Making birds fall out of the sky like that," Cate said. "It feels wrong to me. There's something creepy about it."

"And there's not something creepy about what Isabelle can do? Or me? Or Bonnie, or Delilah, or Soo-jin—" I stopped, swelling with both pride and trepidation. "Anyway. Maybe when we talk to Gina, we'll know why she did that. There's always a reason."

A silence. "But I've been thinking a lot about Lily-Anne too," Cate said. "Knowing that she had another baby changes so much. God, so much." We passed a mile marker. Half an hour until Memphis. On the radio, turned low, a mournful country singer whose voice hummed and sighed beneath our conversation.

"We used to imagine there'd be more of us one day, but it was always reliant on Bellanger," Cate said. "He could share his research. He could help women reproduce with a medication or a procedure. But it would always be *his*. It would always be him controlling it, or another doctor like him. What was the difference between reproducing with a man you slept with or a—a man in a white coat injecting you? Bellanger was such a prick about it too. He acted like he'd invented childbirth. Like he'd improved upon it singlehandedly. People like—like Ricky, or like those assholes in Kithira—they thought he'd unleash this world without men. But wasn't his world always going to include men? Didn't it put men at the very center of childbirth? Still. Always."

I was quiet, focusing on the road. She was right. Nothing we'd found out so far had threatened the image of Bellanger I held in my mind as much as Barbara had when she told us about Lily-Anne's second pregnancy. The other revelations had shifted the pieces of the story, showing an uglier side of him, but this was different. Hiding Lily-Anne's death. Lying about that lost baby. If it was all true, then Bellanger was a terrible man. Selfish, cruel, a liar. Irrelevant.

All that love I'd poured toward Bellanger—my father, my creator, my guide—had gone in the wrong direction. I didn't know what to do with it now. It was like an empty spot at my core where all that adoration used to fit. Whenever I thought about him too closely, there was a hollow ache of loss and anger.

"Knowing what we do about the way we are," Cate said, softer now. *The way we are.* A quick throb under my rib cage, muscle memory of when she'd eased that bullet from inside me. "Doesn't it make you wonder how many more of us have been scattered throughout history?"

There weren't many cars on this stretch of freeway. We were alone.

"All the stories about vampires. Witches. Werewolves, monsters. They had to come from somewhere," Cate said. "Maybe it was from women like our mothers. Women who didn't have men in their lives. Women who wanted children more than they wanted men. All those fairy tales about the couple desperate for a child and they magically get one, but the kid is a freak."

My mother had told me stories like this when I was little. Rapunzel born of cabbages, with her too-long hair. Isis procuring a son, Horus, from her husband's dead body. Princess Kaguya inside a bamboo stalk. I'd memorized other myths on my own as a kid, desperately intrigued by any story that reminded me of my own. My classmates could make construction paper family trees for Father's Day, tracing themselves back for generations. I had to rely on heroes, legends, myths, and rumors.

"It must've happened before, if Lily-Anne was able to do it back in the seventies," Cate said. "There must be women throughout history who got pregnant all by themselves, maybe on purpose, maybe accidentally, and they had children like us. And those children ended up dark secrets, but they managed to show up in rumors and fairy tales anyway. The nine of us might not be groundbreaking at all, Morrow. We might just be the first ones to appear in textbooks instead of as bedtime stories."

"Cate," I said. "Catherine." I was tired; it was late. But when she'd talked, just then, I'd seen my own small story expand and expand until it took up everything, until it was everywhere, and I was just a tiny part of something enormous and all-encompassing. I felt wild and full. How many more of us were out there?

"You think it's stupid," she said.

"No," I said. "Never. You're the smartest person I've ever met."

The very air around me turned warmer with her laugh.

She leaned over the headrest and kissed my cheek. It was so intimate and gentle that I almost shied away; everything about it made me skittish, thrilled and nervous at the same time. Cate, sensing this maybe, pulled back. I turned my head from the road, quickly, just enough to smile at her. Cate murmured my name with an intonation I didn't quite understand. She kissed my cheek again. She moved down to my neck, pressing her lips against the soft, downy part of my neck just beneath my ear. Right where a vein throbbed. My body came to life, as purely as that night in the motel.

Next to us, Tom shifted, blinking, and sat up. Quietly, Cate retreated into the backseat again. When I glanced in the rearview mirror a few minutes later, she glanced at me, our eyes meeting quickly, charged, before I was forced to look back at the road. My heartbeat was a wild rush.

"You should get your own room tonight," I said to Tom, watching Cate and Isabelle carry our suitcases into the motel room. "For a change." It was two in the morning, and this little town we'd stopped in—the edges of Tennessee—was dark and drowsy, our secret. "It's too dangerous to stay in the car if the Bellangers are on our tail. Or the Kithira men. Or god knows who else."

"I *could* use some actual lumbar support," Tom said. "But honestly? I'm not even tired."

"Neither am I." Half a lie.

"You've been driving for the past ten hours. Get some sleep."

I hesitated, spotting the dive bar that stood across the street, the type of all-night seedy place that you could retreat to with no questions asked. Muffled music floated across the street. The only outpost left open in all of Tennessee and here we were, right next to it. I didn't want to be alone. I was bristling, restless, and being in the motel room with Cate felt like being too close to a live wire.

"Tom," I said impulsively. "You know what? Maybe this is it. Maybe this is the right time for our big interview."

"Now?" His eyes brightened, but he was surprised, almost suspicious. "I thought you said it would be when this is all over."

"We're getting so close," I said. "Why not? Now or never. To be honest," I added, "I could just really use a fucking drink."

39

"So? When's the interview start?" I leaned closer, confidential. "Something tells me you're not very good at this, Thomas Abbott."

One drink. Vodka, the cheap kind that blazed through me swiftly, leaving me pleasantly hollow. This place was perfect. Accidental mood lighting from busted bulbs, the low whine and melancholy wailing of country music, a few obvious regulars at the bar. Tom and I sat hidden in a booth near the back. He had a beer in front of him, dewy with condensation.

He laughed. "Be fair. I'm not usually interviewing my subjects at three in the morning in a shitty bar in—Alabama? Where are we again?"

"Close enough. Come *on*," I said. "Ask me something. Anything."

"Fine. Uh. What are you thinking about?"

"God. I've had truth-or-dare questions more hard-hitting than that. But okay . . . I'm thinking about my mother. I'm thinking about her imagining a dead girl coming back to life. What if that's what she meant by, *Tell the world about Fiona*? Not Fiona's abilities, but whoever she saw on the screen. She wants to tell the world Fiona's alive." I hesitated. "Tom, what if Fiona is really alive? What if my mother wasn't imagining things?"

"There were bodies. Found and identified. That's pretty hard to argue with."

"Yeah, I know, but—" I held off.

"But?"

"I've been wrong about so much else. I don't want to go right back to assuming my mom is crazy."

"I'm not saying she's crazy," Tom said carefully, turning his beer bottle around and around. Each time the bottle landed with a scuff. "But the guilt must've weighed on her. Especially over Fiona. Maybe she was seeing what she wanted to see, letting herself off the hook."

I took a long slug of my drink, the ice clicking against my teeth. "It's all my fault, anyway." At his look, I went on: "Leaving my mother behind like I did. I was always so hard on her for not acknowledging the Homestead. Okay, so now she's looked into the past and all of a sudden she's running off chasing ghosts." I sighed heavily, the gust fluttering the edge of a napkin. "I hope she's in Freshwater. This is our last stop. No more Homesteaders after this."

Tom tapped his finger on the tabletop. "What happened to your house, if your mother just ran off? Where'd the fire come from?"

I hesitated. "On the record? I have no idea."

"And off the record?"

"Off the record . . . maybe she did set it herself," I said. "You think she was broken by guilt." My mother, alone, standing there in the middle of that impossible heat just to feel what she'd done to Fiona and to Bellanger. Punishing herself for that long-ago crime. But it didn't fully fit. It didn't explain the maroon sedan, or the fire at Cate's house. I let some of my frustration bubble up: "God, Tom, why didn't you track down Bellanger's sons? If we knew where to find them, we'd be able to get answers."

Tom took a sip of beer, tilting the bottle back. "The Bellanger boys always seemed beside the point. I was more interested in the Miracle Babies. You're Bellanger's actual inventions. Edison's light bulbs. Bell's telephone."

"Edison's light bulb, huh? Nice line. I bet you say that to all the girls."

A strange smile. "Hmm. Just you, actually."

We held the smile, the music pulsing around us. "Well," I said. "They'll probably catch up with us anyway. Let them come to us, right? Cut out the middleman."

"Gallows humor." Tom lifted the bottle in a salute. "I like it, Morrow."

The way he said that, *Morrow*, tugged at me for a second, but I picked up my glass. "To light bulbs who like it dark," I said, and we clinked, laughing.

Two drinks. The edges of everything fuzzed and glowing.

"I appreciate that you're letting me be part of this." Tom kept nudging the puddle of condensation with his finger, making the water change shapes. "One day, if you're comfortable with it, I'd love to be your official biographer." The heavy reddish light over the bar caught in his hair, which had grown longer on the road, unruly. "I wish Bellanger had gotten the chance to see what he really did. The full extent of it. Not just Fiona. All of you."

At hearing Bellanger's name, I went still for a moment, my pleasantly loopy state bottoming out. Every time I remembered Bellanger I felt this particular disorientation, a dread and anger I didn't know what to do with. Lily-Anne. The tenth Girl, lost to us. The way he'd interrupted my mother's plans to reawaken that lost ability of self-conception. I wondered if it had been worth it, in my mother's eyes. Worth it to invite him. Worth it to get the nine of us out of the bargain.

"Did I say the wrong thing?" Tom asked.

"It's fine." I automatically produced a smile. So maybe Bellanger had kept secrets: my mother had kept secrets too. I truly was an orphan now. I didn't recognize either of my parents anymore. "Another drink."

Three drinks. Four. Maybe more than that because I would steal some of Tom's beer, no longer cold because of how long he'd been nursing it, the warmth bringing out the bitterness. The world was a quicksilver spin, everything tilted.

The music throbbed, swift and erratic. I had to come over to the other side of the booth to be heard: I was yelling right into Tom's ear. I half considered flirting with him. I'd never been a good flirt, too blunt and too impatient. And even when I'd gotten it right, flirting had been a negotiable power. A masquerade. Now that I'd felt what it was like to reach into a man's brain and rearrange it into exactly what I wanted, there was something sad about trying to recapture this smaller manifestation of control. Like crawling after I'd learned how to fly.

"What do you think your mother would say, if she knew about your—your powers?" Tom asked.

"She'd probably be disappointed," I said, my thoughts sliding and shimmering now. "She never wanted me to be different. You don't raise your kid in Coeur du Lac if you want her to be special."

"Nah," Tom said, shaking his head. "You'll never be a disappointment. Never."

I leaned my head against Tom's shoulder, and he tensed. "I'm disappointing you," I said. "Not letting you write your book."

His voice vibrated and hummed against my cheekbone. "It's not about the book anymore. It was never—look, if you think this is all still for the story, I don't even know what to—" He stopped, frustrated. "Josie," he said, trying to start over. "Josephine Morrow. Girl One."

There was something in his voice. We were so close, our mouths nearly touching, and I could see the calculations happening behind Tom's eyes, how easy it would be to close the space between us. He was wondering what I'd say, what I'd do, and for a second I wondered too. I almost leaned in. His stubble had grown in lately, thicker and darker than the sun-kissed hair on his head, and I imagined pressing my mouth to his, our lips stinging with alcohol, beneath the funhouse glow of this bar lighting. I'd come to like Tom—I was friendlier with him, anyway, than any of the handful of men or boys I'd slept with before.

It would have been easy to give him what he wanted and wake up the next morning convincing myself I wanted it too. That tongue-tied, damp-eyed longing turned him vulnerable, transferring the power to me. I could've gone along with it the way I'd gone along with other sexual experiences. A *why not?* that wavered between clinical and carefree.

Cate. The way she'd described the difference in sleeping with someone *real*. Real. A heat settled low in my stomach, and I pulled away from Tom, worried he'd sense my sudden undertow of desire and mistake it as belonging to him.

"One last drink?" I asked, covering the sudden coolness I'd created.

———

I sat up. It was six in the morning. I recalled the previous night as a patchwork, isolated scenes badly merging. Too many gaps. I'd stumbled into this motel room with Tom, not wanting to wake up Cate and Isabelle. No—that wasn't why. The real reason I was nervous to be around Cate was still there, refusing to dissolve.

Now I lay in the same bed as Tom. For a second I was gripped with a queasy curiosity, wondering what my body had done while I was away. But we were both fully clothed. Tom and I had turned from each other in our sleep, pushed far on opposite sides of the bed. All the times I'd woken next to Cate, the way she was always pressed against the crook of my shoulder or nestled into the small of my back like she belonged right there.

Tom murmured in his sleep, shifted. His shirt rode up on his back. I looked again, curious in spite of myself. The section of back revealed by his shirt showed a deep shadow following the shape of his spine. I hesitated, then reached over and tugged the sheets off his back, carefully lifted the edge of his shirt. The shadow continued. Almost without realizing it, I'd tugged the shirt high enough to expose his entire back. I tried to make sense of what I was seeing.

A scar. Puckered, darker than the surrounding skin. It almost looked like a zipper in how neatly it followed the curve of his spine, right in the center of his back. The longer I looked at that neat, serrated scar, the more surreal the whole thing was. I was hungover enough that understanding felt just out of my grasp. Tom had always known so much about me, interior and exterior, my history, my baby photos, and he'd been keeping a secret from me. It was a surgery scar. Something in him had been corrected and then re-stitched.

Something like—

I stood up from the bed, heart slamming.

Tom was awake. He realized that the sheets were pooled low on his body. He turned all the way around and sat up. I couldn't even look at him: it was like I was in the room with a stranger. Or . . . not a stranger, never a stranger. We'd known each other all along.

"Which one are you?" I asked.

A tremor of recognition. He reached a hand around his body with a practiced gesture. I knew he must've touched his scar sometimes, angled himself in the foggy bathroom mirror to look at it. I did the same thing with my skin-graft scar.

"Josie—" he began, and I couldn't tell whether he was defensive or bargaining, his voice shifting between the two. "This isn't—it's not—"

"Which one?" I pressed, angrier now.

We stared at each other, the possibility of fury and shame and violence tightening the space between us, not decided yet. "Tell me the truth," I said. "I want to hear you say it. Tell me who you are."

I didn't think it would work. I didn't feel the dizziness this time, just a clean snap of electricity, unthinking as a clenched fist. But he reacted at once, flinching back, and I was gratified to detect the fear in him. His face was touched with both reverence and terror.

"I'm Junior," he said. He pronounced it like a joke. Not even a real name. "It was supposed to be an honor, getting named after my father, but nobody ever used Joseph or Joe for me. Just Junior. Even after my father died."

"I don't know where to start, Junior."

"You can keep calling me Tom."

"I'll call you whatever I want." I ignored his quick hurt. "Why have you been lying?" When he hesitated, I locked eyes with him and began to form a command.

"Please," Junior said, half rising. "Don't. I'll tell you the truth, I promise. Just—just let me do it myself."

I held his gaze, not sure whether to grant this one small request or give in to the anger that was thrumming through me. "Don't lie to me again."

Junior nodded, took a deep breath. "The thing is, I never meant to lie to you."

"You've been with me for over two weeks, learning about my past. *Our* past. And you never said a word. You're a liar. That's the definition of a liar." Something occurred to me. "The book. Is it even real, or was it just some stupid excuse?"

"It's real," Junior said quickly. "Of course it is. I've wanted to write it for a long time. There's been some interest from publishers. A book about the Homestead by Bellanger's own son could be big. But they all want it to be a cheesy exposé. I don't want that. If I'm going to write about my father's work, I'm going to bring a new perspective."

"You've got one now," I said, stomach dropping as I remembered everything he'd found out.

Junior smiled, quick and miserable.

"You could've told us who you really are. We would've talked to you." I began pacing in front of the bed, making the circuit of the same lineup of standard cheap-motel-room supplies. Table, upholstered chair, defunct coffee maker, *TV Guide*, Gideon Bible.

"You wouldn't have," Junior said. "The way you're looking at me right now, Josie—Jesus. It would've been even worse with some of the others. Knowing that I was connected would've changed everything."

I stopped in my tracks. "My mother knew that you were Bellanger's son, didn't she? That's exactly why she got in touch with you. You were never just some random journalist." I half laughed, buried my face in my hands. "God, I'm an idiot. Why didn't I see it?"

I hadn't seen it because I wasn't used to giving my mother that much credit.

"She knew who I was, yeah," Junior said. "She always was closer to my dad than the others. She knew my mother's maiden name is Abbott and that I preferred any name other than Junior. The phone call was weird. Your mom was threatening me, almost. She said she wanted me to break this story about—about my father. So that I could learn who he really was. But then we started reminiscing and she got friendlier. Like she felt bad for calling me up. And then she never got back in touch with me. Until . . ."

Until I found his fake name and number in my mother's things.

"Then you called me up out of nowhere, Girl One," he said. "I didn't expect to meet you. I thought you were in Chicago, miles away. And we met, and you trusted me, and you were so curious and adventurous. I saw all these doors just opening and opening, finally."

"Finally," I echoed, a bitter mockery.

Junior rubbed the back of his neck. "I was afraid if I told you, it would all end. Just when I was learning about my father and what his work really meant."

"What was all that bullshit about your family? Your deadbeat dad that you never met?"

"A white lie. Barely a lie. My father was never around. He was always at the Homestead or on conferences and trips. Sometimes months would go by and the only way I'd see my father was in a newspaper with one of you. I was only thirteen when he died. I barely have any real memories of Dad. So, yes, my mother was a single mother. Same as yours."

"But you still had his money," I said. "You still had that."

"There was no money," Junior said, impatient. "My dad had sold everything to pay off debts we knew nothing about. My mother was traumatized. Her husband had just been murdered. She always waited for him to have time for us, always next year, next year. Then he was gone for good. Your mothers *wanted* to be part of the Homestead; they were willing participants. My mother didn't ask to be part of anything. When Mom first married Dad"—he stumbled a little over *Dad*, the plain tenderness of it—"he couldn't get a job cleaning pipettes. He was an outcast. She stuck by his side through everything, and once he got famous, the Homestead took over his whole life." His face turned older and younger at once. "Bobby was always distant, so it fell on my shoulders to help Mom. I spent a lot of time with her as a kid. I favor her. I guess that's why none of you recognized me. I kept waiting for somebody to say, it's him, it's that boy. Bellanger's son. But I looked too much like her, and neither of us ever mattered much."

I looked at him more closely. I realized I couldn't even remember Mrs. Bellanger's face enough to recognize hers in Junior's.

"Emily," I said. The betrayal was so sudden, so intense, that I could feel it rising inside me like a sickness. "Emily French. She said you'd lead me to my mother. Junior," I said. "If you know where my mother is—if you hurt her in any way—"

I would kill him. Right here in this motel room. Nothing that had passed between us, no kindness or familiarity, would save him.

"What are you talking about?" Junior asked, sounding genuinely confused. I was gratified to detect the fear in Junior's voice, the way his face was touched with both reverence and terror.

I explained about Emily's prophecy in the attic, what felt like a thousand years ago.

Junior was silent. "I think I know what she meant," he said slowly. "I promise, I haven't seen your mother since I was a child. That phone call is the only contact I've had with her. Listen. Emily was . . . I think she was remembering the past. I helped you find your mother once. Don't you remember?" He looked into my eyes, seeking forgiveness: I didn't have any to give. "It was your birthday. It was a big day, visiting dignitaries. My suit was stuffy and hot and they had you in some stupid dress. You looked so miserable and scared. I felt bad for you. It wasn't a kids' party at all. Your mother was in some other room, stuck with the reporters. I noticed you crying. Nobody else saw it. So I went over and I took your hand and I brought you away from everybody, and I helped you find your mother again."

A hand in mine, leading me away from the crowd, bringing me back to the one person who mattered. Emily's prediction had kept me going for weeks and it had never been a prediction at all, just a fragmented memory. For a second my anger cooled into sadness, but then I focused again. "Is it your brother, then? Is he the one who's been following us?"

"I haven't been in touch with Bobby in a long time," Junior said. "I don't think he cares about any of you enough to even look you up, much less come after you. He has a wife and kids now. They don't know anything about his past. So, no. I don't know who's after us."

We stood there in the drowsy morning light that came through the thick motel curtains. Making a decision, I moved for the door.

"Where are you going?" Junior asked, sounding like he didn't know whether to be scared for me or scared of me.

"I need to talk to Cate and Isabelle. They deserve to know about this too." I opened the door and stepped outside. "Either you tell them or I do."

In the motel parking lot, Cate was leaning against the Volvo, her expression unrecognizable. Over her shoulder, I could see the bar where Tom and I had been laughing just a handful of hours ago, now a deserted shell of itself, parking lot empty. Cate was reading something. A stack of papers. When she looked up, she wasn't even surprised. She'd been waiting for me.

Over my shoulder, Junior inhaled tightly. "That's my book," he said. "She found my book."

40

But despite all I'd learned on the road with the "Miracle Babies," my true crisis of faith occurred when I was forced to contend with rumors of a tenth pregnancy, one that my father was allegedly not involved with. If a true "virgin birth," then this tenth pregnancy obviously threatened to upend my father's legacy. While there is no doubt that the original nine Girls are the results of my father's work, this tenth pregnancy apparently happened without his oversight or involvement.

Conveniently, the tale of Lily-Anne's pregnancy was one that nobody else could corroborate. The woman who relayed this story to my companions was too ashamed of where she came from to share the history with her own daughters. In light of this, I had to ask: Is it possible that she was inventing things?

Whether the woman is lying out of malice or simple confusion, I'm not sure, but I couldn't help but think of alternatives. What if this tenth pregnancy was not a virgin birth at all, but rather a traditional pregnancy, caused by some nocturnal visitor? I can understand why the shame of such a liaison would lead the pregnant woman to lie about her condition and the reasoning behind it. History has been scattered with so many women who lie about "virgin birth" in order to save their honor and reputations, or perhaps through simple ignorance of biology, that my father had to work uphill against these rumors when his own experiments took place. Ironic, then, that his detractor could be using the very same lies to attack my father's legacy.

41

"I can explain."

"I don't think you can." Cate sounded bitterly exhausted, as if all the other times she'd quieted her doubts had led to this. "There's no excuse for this . . . this *book* you've been scribbling away in secret all this time. Let's take a look at some choice excerpts, shall we?"

Junior ran his hands through his hair. A familiar gesture, but one that belonged to somebody else, to Tom, and I had a sensation as if Junior had stolen it from a friend of mine. He was frantic and resigned at the same time. We'd retreated into Cate and Isabelle's room.

"I was just brainstorming that chapter," Junior said, voice strained. "I wasn't going to necessarily leave it in. I realize that it's not fair. I never knew Lily-Anne. Or Barbara. I shouldn't have accused them of lying." He clasped his hands between his knees.

Only Isabelle was calm, sitting on the bed and switching languidly through channels like a kid ignoring her parents' fight, Delilah's stolen diary opened up on her lap.

Cate flipped through the pages, pausing. "Okay." Her tone turned arch: "'Like her mother, Josephine Morrow is beautiful. Long brown hair, even longer legs, high cheekbones, and eyes that seem to be evaluating you at every turn. She is driven to a fault, though her cool demeanor cracks a little when you get to know her. Making her laugh,'" Cate read, shaking her head, "'feels like a triumph.'" She lifted her gaze from the page, eyebrow raised.

I turned to Junior, my cheeks and neck hot with chagrin, and he wouldn't meet my eyes. Hearing myself rendered in third person was jarring, like I was being lifted outside of my own body and flattened and smoothed into a paper doll. "I asked you to stop writing this," I said. "But you never were going to stop. You didn't care."

"This story is important to me," Junior said.

"The question is, Junior, are you the one to tell it?" Cate asked. "Because personally, I think our story has been told by the wrong people all along. You don't see anything wrong with having a front-row seat to all our most private tragedies. We're just inventions to you."

"Like light bulbs," I said softly. "Like telephones."

"And who wants to be a light bulb?" Cate asked.

"Just see it from my perspective." Junior's voice hardened, an abrupt energy in his posture. He straightened. "You Girls are the reason that my family was so broken. Don't I deserve a chance to be part of the story? I lost my father as a kid. My mother was never the same after he died. I wanted to at least see that his work was worthwhile. And you, Josie. All of a sudden, you're all over the news, talking about how you're going to finish his work. Just hijack his legacy."

"Hijack?" I said, stung. "I devoted my life to restoring his work and making him proud. That was always my intention. How can you fucking say that?"

"But imagine how it felt for me," Junior said. "Watching somebody else take over my father's work like that. I wanted to be part of it too. I wanted to have a say in his story."

Cate waved one of the pages. "Reading this, I'm just seeing a lot of the same shit that's already been published a thousand times. So he's your father—so what?"

Junior watched her, different expressions flickering across his face: defensiveness, shame, anger. For a second, an almost heartbreaking optimism, like he might still fix this.

"You want a new take?" Cate asked. "A fresh take? Then think about this, Junior." She stepped closer to him. "When your father started out, he was trying and failing to achieve the impossible. He would have tried and failed for decades if Morrow's mother hadn't reached out to him. Our mothers were the ones who did your father a favor. We're our mothers' creations every bit as much as we're his. Now that we know about Lily-Anne, I'm not sure what your father had to do with anything."

The flashing TV screen jangled at my nerves. The truth of what Cate had said seeped in a little deeper. I was my mother's daughter and only my mother's daughter. I was her brainchild, not just her flesh-and-blood daughter. She was my brainmother.

"Look, I'm sympathetic to the Girls of the Homestead," Junior said, struggling to stay calm. "I am. I've found out a lot of things about my father that I don't understand or like. He wasn't the man I thought he was. It's hard to accept that your father might've been a—a—"

"Villain? Liar? Thief?" Cate supplied helpfully.

"A controversial genius. Plenty of great men have had their flaws," Junior said, reddening. "It doesn't mean that my father's entire legacy has to be stolen."

"Stolen?" Cate repeated. "Who stole what, exactly?"

"Maybe it's time for the legacy to decide for itself," I said.

Junior laughed under his breath. "All right, Josie. All right. Then let's talk about this: your mother killed my father." The breath was knocked from my lungs as if he'd hit me. "My life could have been different if he'd lived. It's not just about me and my mother and my brother, because I know you don't give a shit about us. But my father could've continued his work. He would have been able to handle your powers. You would've understood yourselves and what you're capable of—"

"We don't need anyone to *handle* us, we understand ourselves already," I cut him off. "We don't need a Bellanger to do that." As I said it, I experienced a lightness. Not peace, not relief, but a new sense of space inside me. I could sense Cate's watchfulness from the corner of my eye. I felt too nervous to look at her still, like I was trying to pick up our friendship—our whatever-it-was—from where we'd left it.

Junior made a visible effort to steady himself, shutting his eyes and then opening them. "I know we're all upset. I get that. Let's just head to Freshwater. We can keep discussing this, but we shouldn't let this drama throw us off-track."

Cate spat out a disbelieving laugh. "You're not fucking coming with us."

"I've been part of this from the start," he said.

"Junior." She was almost maternal. "There's somebody following us and we don't know who it is because you've misled us. You've been recording private conversations and writing about us as if we're not even real people to you. You're not coming. No way."

Isabelle spoke up: "No way," she echoed, not taking her eyes off the TV screen. "You lost your chance."

He pressed his hands to his forehead, took several unsteady breaths. "Can I have my book back? I've put a lot of work into that."

"Let you run off with these stories that could completely change our lives?" Cate demanded. "Some of these things could really endanger us."

Junior inhaled. "All right. All right. I guess this is goodbye." He rose, moved for the door. He tried to meet my eyes, maybe to telegraph an apology, but I stared into the corner of the room. Let him go, then. Junior had been with me from the start, my whole search for my mother beginning with a lie I hadn't been able to see right in front of me.

"Wait," Isabelle said. She was still watching the TV screen, but her voice held a command that stopped Junior in his tracks. "Leave the car with us," she said.

He scoffed a laugh. "And how the hell am I supposed to get out of here?"

"You'll figure it out," she said, unperturbed. "We need it. We're going to Freshwater."

He made a frustrated sweep with his hands. "You girls want me out of your lives? Fine. Fine, you got that. Congratulations. But now you're on your own. Figure it out yourselves."

Part of me wanted to just leave Tom alone, forget about him as quickly as possible, let this wound of betrayal begin to heal over. But another part of me, closer to the surface, sharper and angrier, wanted revenge. "You took our stories, we take your car," I said.

"You owe it to us." Isabelle turned her head slightly toward him, still sitting on her heels like a little kid. "We're going to find Josephine's mom."

"That's not—" Junior started, but Isabelle stood abruptly, in one fluid movement, and crossed the room toward him. She was swift and sure as a blade, her gaze unwavering. Even Cate and I stepped back, instinctively self-protective in the face of an unruly power.

She reached for Junior, rising on tiptoe to close her hands around his throat, her small, thin hands cupped around the cage of his Adam's apple. Like they'd known each other a long time and Isabelle had complete familiarity with his body. Junior seemed to realize this too, a flush spreading down his neck. Then his face tightened. Blood, red and glossy, seeped out his nose, his ears.

I watched for a second, entranced. There was something beautiful about watching her disassemble a body so efficiently. The opposite of Cate's palms gluing the world back together. When Junior coughed, his skin growing waxy-gray beneath the blood, I stepped in. "Isabelle," I said. "Don't hurt him." But it was half-hearted. I'd thought that revenge would ease my anger, but it only made it grow, bouncing higher like a flame fed with gasoline.

Junior's lower face was brightly striped with blood now. His eyes darted to me, helpless.

Cate was businesslike as she moved over to Isabelle and pulled her away from Junior. Isabelle held on as long as she could, but Cate was strong, certain. Finally Isabelle's hands dropped away, and Junior fell to his knees on the carpet, coughing wetly. "Fine," he muttered, blood staining his teeth. "Take the car. Just don't think you're the heroes in all this."

Walking over, I knelt next to him, looking him right in the eyes. He was breathing hard. All that history shimmered between us. Junior, taking my hand when I was lost, smiling down at me. Junior as my partner in crime, my compatriot. My friend.

"It's our story, either way," I said softly, letting my voice be raw and tender, not hiding my sadness behind the shining heat of anger. "Leave us, Junior."

42

"Well, this is it," Cate said.

We crowded on the porch of a small apartment complex. Concrete-encased yard. Yellow siding. Poorly maintained, but lived-in: fresh oil splotches in the parking lot. Mother Four was the last Homesteader on the list. The final piece of the puzzle. I was one big raw nerve of anticipation.

"If Gina's been reckless enough to be making the news already," I said, low enough that I wouldn't be overheard, "maybe we shouldn't push our luck. Not all the Homestead survivors have been happy to see us. Let's be careful."

Cate and Isabelle nodded their agreement. The idea of all those dead birds, thousands of them, their heartbeats stilled in midair, their feathers scorched. The seriousness of this had grown in my head. Gina might be more powerful than the rest of us. And she obviously wasn't trying to hide her abilities, the way the rest of us had managed to do so far. I remembered that bird on my mother's lawn and something began spinning together. What if, in reaching out to the others, my mother had summoned one of them to her? What if Gina had come to my mother?

With a little show of ceremony, Cate pushed the doorbell, then knocked gently with her knuckles on the door of 1C. We waited. No response. I pressed my hands against the glass to peer inside. It was shadowy in this first-floor apartment. Dishes stacked in the sink, beaded with water. A pair of sneakers by the back door. Men's sneakers, large and ugly.

"Wait a minute—" I began.

The door opened. "Can I help you?" A stranger. He looked at each one of us in turn. He was holding his face in a polite half smile, but his blue eyes were harder, already retreating.

"We're looking for Angela Grassi," I said at once. "Is she home?"

"Never heard of her," he said. "Sorry."

"What about her daughter, Gina?" He started to withdraw into his house, but I kept talking, my urgency like a hand shot through the door. "Do you know them? Do they live here in Freshwater? Maybe you've heard of them—"

"You got the wrong place. I've lived here a long time," the man said. "A long time." He glanced behind him, any excuse to get away from us.

"Look at me," I snapped. I locked eyes with him, digging in, letting that world-tilting sense of vertigo rush through me as I reached inside his brain. "Tell me if you know the Grassis," I said.

"I don't know them," he said at once.

"Tell me if you've met a woman named Margaret Morrow," I said. Phrasing questions like this—commands, not queries—felt more natural to me now. Like people's minds were opened drawers I could rummage through, then close again.

"I haven't met her."

"Tell me if you've heard of the Grassis."

"No. Never."

Cate's hand on my shoulder. "Morrow, this guy doesn't know anything. He's just a tenant," she whispered. "Junior gave us the wrong address. Let's go."

"Shit." I broke the gaze reluctantly, and he shook his head like he wasn't sure what had just happened, inhaling shakily. He was already closing the door, and I suppressed the urge to slip in behind him, run through the rooms screaming for my mother until I made her materialize by sheer willpower and want. But I just stood with Cate and Isabelle until the door was shut, a click so final I could feel it in my bones. My mother wasn't here. Maybe she wasn't anywhere. I'd had weeks to accept this conclusion. It shouldn't have come as a surprise. But I felt that loss, and I realized I'd have to feel it every day if I couldn't find her. I'd never get used to a world without my mother.

We split up and tried every door in the complex. Some people didn't answer; the ones who did had never heard of the Grassis, seeming just as confused as the man from 1C. We returned to the Volvo, connected by a grim frustration.

"What now?" Isabelle asked.

I tried to push my grief aside. "This is the first time Junior's address didn't work." I spoke with an assuredness that became firmer. "He was going to get an address wrong eventually. The Grassis could still be here in Freshwater. Or there's someone who knows where they went next. We're just going to have to look, that's all."

The coffee was stale, the burger greasy and limp. But I was hungrier than I'd realized. All three of us gained a little life as we ate. "I feel like Junior's somehow behind this," Cate said. "His one last grand gesture. His one last fuck-you to the three of us." She swung her middle finger high, then dropped her hand.

"In fairness," I said, "he shared this address with us *before* we kicked him out."

Cate took a long sip of her drink, licked her lips unselfconsciously, a quick glimmer of her tongue. She leaned back. "Do you miss him?" she asked frankly.

I stalled with a long gulp of bitter coffee. "Junior was the first one to help me out. He's like—he's like my scarecrow. So, yeah. I miss him a little. I know it's stupid."

"Like in *Wizard of Oz*? So what does that make me? Who was the second . . . ?" Cate thought for a second, then gave a quick smile. "Right. The one without a heart. And that makes you Dorothy, the girl who's trying to get back home. Sorry that we're ruining that for you. You're farther from home than ever."

"I'm not far from home. Not really." At her quizzical look, I stammered: "I mean—sure, I won't ever return to Chicago. Maybe I won't ever work for a research institute, I don't know. I'm not sure where to go from here. Even if we find my mother tonight, where do we fit in anymore? But—despite all this—I'm home already. I am."

As I said it, I realized how true it was. Even if I was a fugitive. Even if my mother was missing. Beneath all that, being with the other Girls had changed something in me, and I didn't want to go back to the way it was before.

But Cate was silent. Isabelle looked from one of us to the other.

The aggressive air-conditioning in the restaurant brushed cold against my shins. "Are you upset with me?" I asked Cate, ready to get it all in the open.

Sensing something in the air, Isabelle rose abruptly, wandered across the length of the restaurant.

Cate sighed. "Why do you think I came along with you in the first place?"

I knew the right answer, but my heart was in my throat. "Your house burned down. You didn't have anywhere else to go."

"You know that's not the reason," Cate said, narrowing her eyes at me.

"Because you wanted to find out what your mother was going to tell you."

"That was part of it," Cate said, acknowledging this with a tip of her head. "But I also was happy to let her secrets go with her. I liked my life in Goulding. Still do."

"I'm not sure," I lied, and felt my heartbeat everywhere in my body. Cate was sitting in a slant of hot sunlight. Her breasts beneath her thin tank top, her dark curls shot through with caramel, visible only in direct light. Her specificity was so beautiful it almost hurt me.

"Then you're an idiot, Morrow." Hearing that name again, in Cate's voice—even when she was frustrated—was a relief. Everything in me let go in one long exhale.

"Nothing happened between me and Junior that night, by the way," I said. "We just had a few drinks. That's it. If you were wondering."

"Why would I be wondering?" Cate asked, but she looked down into her cup, swirling the coffee inside. I saw a small smile flash over her face. "Poor Junior. He's been panting after you like a puppy dog since the first time I met you two."

"He was never the one I wanted."

Cate waited, still watching her coffee cup instead of me, biting her lip.

"I like you, Cate," I said, letting it out in a rush. "And I don't know exactly what that means. I've liked the men I've been with. Most of them. Some of them. But I—I like you too. I like you *more*. A lot more." It was frustrating and giddy, fumbling to express something that was so big and intricate and yet was delivered to other people in the kind of silly phrases you'd doodle in the margins of a notebook. *I like you.*

I expected Cate to say something back. I expected her to break open with gratitude, to return the sentiment. She was the one who was good at this; she was the one who was practiced in saying the right things to women. It only seemed fair.

"It doesn't have to mean anything more than what you want it to mean." Cate stood. "But if you're going to say things like that, I need to know you're serious." She wasn't accusatory, just focused. "You don't owe me anything at all, Morrow. I just wish you'd give me any of the trust you gave to Junior. You trusted him, no questions asked, no matter how many times he let you down. Don't you see that?"

"I do now. I wasn't thinking of you. No," I corrected, "actually, I *did* think of you, but I've never—and like I said, nothing happened between me and him."

"I'm sorry, but I have to be smart about myself too. Even if I am heartless." She lightly touched her chest. "By now you must know I'm nobody's experiment."

We did not find the Grassis. Not that day. Not the next day, or the next. We stayed in Freshwater, and we tried to cover the place systematically, on foot. All three of us were nervous about splitting up. Somebody was still coming after us, an unknown threat: not Bonnie's attacker, not the Bellanger boys. Our strange specter, a fear that kept changing form. As a compromise, we broke the group apart but stayed close, meeting at the ends of blocks or on quiet cul-de-sacs. We tried not to draw too much attention to ourselves. My mother's face was still appearing on the news, and now Patricia's too. I assumed even I could be showing up in head-lines. Josephine Morrow, vanishing mysteriously at the end of her first year in med school, another echo of Bellanger's own long-ago failure.

Nobody had seen Angela or Gina. There were no friends-of-friends, no neighbors, no colleagues, nobody at the homeless shelter who'd taken them in, nobody at the county jail who'd booked them. The Grassis had dropped right off the face of the planet and, apparently, taken my mother

with them. Some people would talk about the birds when we asked—
strange business—but most of them seemed to treat it with a rote discomfort, a bizarre but unrepeated incident that everyone could put behind
them now. We heard occasional anecdotes about housecats eating the
birds, or disconnected power lines. Nothing helpful to us.

43

"Were we wrong about her?" Cate asked, frustrated. "Was there ever an Angela Grassi at the Homestead? Maybe there were only eight women, not nine. It's been a mass hallucination."

I responded by grabbing one of the many Homestead books I'd retrieved from Junior's car and opening it to a group photo. Angela stood at the edge, arranged right next to my mother in this picture, and Cate leaned forward to look closer, brushing my elbow. My heartbeat grew faster. "Huh. She looks a little like you, Morrow. The hair," Cate said.

I hesitated, not sure if I should say it when we were already stretched thin. "Do you think he already got to them? The driver of the car?"

"God, I don't know," Cate said, throwing her arm over her eyes. "That's a question we can ask him in person if he ever shows up. At this point, I wouldn't even care. I'd just say, *Excuse me, sir, have you seen Angela? Or Gina? Or Margaret Morrow?* Anyone we're looking for. Anyone at all. Fuck. Elvis. Amelia Earhart."

It was the fifth day in Freshwater. Cate and I had returned to the motel room while Isabelle was still out searching. Cate sat cross-legged among the disarranged sheets and covers, the curtains drawn against the sun's glare so that the room felt drowsy. Without thinking, I sat down on the bed too, then realized what I'd done. Cate and I had been careful to keep our distance lately. She always slept in the bed with Isabelle and I took the floor, alone, gazing up at the ceiling tiles and the spider building a home in one corner.

"Sorry," I said to Cate now, rising, but she automatically shifted, making room for me beside her. Cautious, I relaxed back onto the pillows, stretched my legs out long.

"You aren't the one without a heart," I said impulsively. "That would be me."

She laughed. "Okay, Morrow. You've lost me."

"It was a dumb analogy, when I called Tom—Junior, sorry—my scarecrow. I didn't mean to upset you."

"Well, I already knew it was dumb," Cate said. "But thanks for acknowledging it."

I hesitated. I wanted so badly to reach for her. As she lay back on the pillows, her throat was long and bare. Her lips were full and chapped. Those elegant feet, the unpainted toenails. She was beautiful. She licked her lips thoughtlessly, yawned, and my whole body surged. I'd felt it all along, that current running between every interaction, long before she'd kissed me. I hadn't known exactly what to call it and so I'd let it stay there, unidentified and unexamined.

"My mother might've torn the Homestead apart," I said. "She might never have carried out that vision that she and Patricia had of a world of women, conceiving alone. But she did one really good thing. You talked about women in fairy tales and urban legends, the ones who have been conceiving alone all throughout history. But that's the thing. They're all alone. They're roaming by themselves, lurking at the edges of real life." Cate nodded, cautious. "But my mother—and maybe Bellanger too, I don't know—they brought us together. They gave us eight sisters."

Cate didn't answer. She shut her eyes.

I paused, trying to collect my thoughts. "When Bellanger arrived at the Homestead," I said, "I don't think he realized what he was doing. He didn't give a shit what he was doing. Taking that wildness spread across generations, hidden in the bodies and brains and fingertips of women—" and I reached for Cate's hand, and, surprised, she let me hold it, her face blossoming open, vulnerable, her lips parted. "He stole that power; he made it his own. But my mother had already organized us. We lost that for a while, I know, but now we're getting it back."

Cate opened her eyes just a fraction, examined me.

"You are the very best part of all of this," I said. "You are, Catherine Bower. It's not like I wanted to go looking for my mother under these circumstances, but what if I'd just kept on living my life and you'd just kept on living yours and we never met? I was so stupid to never look for you before. I didn't know what I was missing. I didn't even know enough to miss you."

Cate smiled very slightly. She opened her arms, and I leaned against her, feeling every inch of her warmth, the way her muscles were finely sketched beneath her skin, the softness and give of her. I could barely breathe. She smelled exactly like herself. That herbal scent, as if she carried that garden with her everywhere, deep inside, the delicate vines and leaves twisting around her internal organs.

"I think I should kiss you," I said. Cate laughed, then stopped, looking at me more closely. Something broke open behind her expression. She leaned forward, but I held up a hand, stopping her. "I want to be the one to kiss you. Otherwise, I'll never—I won't know how to—"

"So stop overexplaining and just kiss me, Josephine." The slightest flush had risen into her cheeks and her neck. She waited, waited. I leaned in. I kissed Cate.

She was soft, salty, sweet, and slick. I remembered the night she brought me back to life, the way her hands on me had awoken that aching pleasure, stinging everywhere. That same sensation came over me now, concentrated wherever she touched. I gasped against her mouth.

We pulled back what felt like only seconds later, or maybe hours later. Too much and not enough at once. Cate was short of breath, her eyes heavy-lidded, but she managed to smile. "Well?" she asked. "Do *I* get to kiss *you* now?"

When I murmured, *Yes,* Cate slid my dress off my shoulders, tugging the straps loose. Laughing, self-conscious, sparkling all over, I helped her, pulling it free, my hair tousled. I crossed my arms over my chest instinctively, then lowered my arms, letting myself get used to being naked in front of her the way I'd adjust to sudden immersion in cold, clear water. I was pleased and shy to see that Cate couldn't look away from me. She must've caught glimpses of me—camped in little motel rooms, sharing bathrooms. But this was different. This was for her.

Cate reached for me again, and I understood what would happen. My desire was interrupted by a clench of anxiety. "I still don't really know what to do," I said.

She laughed under her breath. "You'll figure it out. Look at the things you've learned how to do, these past few weeks." Her voice changed, huskier. "I've been waiting to do this since I first met you, you know that?" And I smiled, and Cate kissed me.

This kiss. This was not like with any boyfriend I'd ever had. It was the difference between not knowing I had my abilities and feeling them grow inside me, shifting and stretching everything about me, my whole understanding of the world and myself, of bodies and pleasure, sliding apart and then coming back together. With Cate, I was real.

44

A ringing, sharp and insistent. I woke up with my arm thrown over Cate, her body warm and damp against me. I looked around the motel room, at our clothes scattered across the end of the bed and the floor. It was edging toward midday, the light both brighter and heavier. No Isabelle.

The ringing was loud enough to reverberate at the back of my skull. It wouldn't stop. I reached over, scrabbling for the receiver. Cate wrinkled her nose, murmured something. Then her face fell slackly peaceful again.

"Hello?" I whispered.

"Josie?" A laugh on the other end, soft, disbelieving. "God. I didn't think this would work. I'd been calling every motel in Freshwater. I can't—is it really you?"

"Junior." I looked over at Cate, pulling the blanket up over my breasts as if he could somehow see me. "What are you doing, calling here?"

"I'm just so relieved I found you. And that you're fine." A pause. "I mean, are you fine?"

"I'm going to hang up—"

"No," he said quickly. "I did something for you. For all of you. Consider it my way of making things up to you. I know it's probably not enough. We ended on such an ugly note, but I really do want you to find your mother. I always did. Maybe this can—can fix some of the things between us. Please," he added, sensing my hesitancy. "Listen to me."

Part of me missed him too. That part nearly convinced me to hang up.

"You need to know this," Junior said. "After I left you, I grabbed a flight back home. I need somebody else to hear this because I can't believe it myself. I kept thinking about that medical examiner Barbara mentioned, Henley, the one who lied about Lily-Anne's death. It made me wonder what else he was lying about. I reached out to him."

The man who'd spirited away Lily-Anne's body and the body of her second daughter, destroying their place in our story. My chest felt tight. "You did?"

"Leland Henley's his name. He's retired now. He's been living a very quiet life. If my mother hadn't had his information, I'm not sure I would've gotten hold of him at all."

Of course. That explained Thomas Abbott's uncanny research abilities. Marianne Bellanger must've helped Junior find some of the more remote addresses of Homestead survivors. It explained that photograph of my mother and me, moments after my birth. I felt a flare of anger and betrayal again, at how long Junior had been walking alongside me on uneven footing.

"When he heard I was one of Bellanger's boys, Henley shut down. I told him what I knew about Lily-Anne's death. He wouldn't confirm any of it. He told me to stop sticking my nose into things that'd only come back to hurt me. 'Things you don't want to know,' he kept saying."

"So, an asshole," I said. "No surprise there." But my palms were damp with sweat.

"After that call, I went through some of my mom's records again. I'd been using them for research. My mother kept them under lock and key, never let anyone else look at them. Something was bugging me about the autopsy report. My father's and Fiona's bodies after the fire. They were burned badly, pretty much unrecognizable." I understood the effort it took to say this out loud. It had been a specific ache, the brutality of the loss. Wiping away their physical bodies until they weren't merely dead, they were erased. Little handfuls of mineralized bones and teeth glowing out of the embers. "My mother kept a copy of the autopsy report," Junior said. "But I was never able to really look at it closely—he's my—"

"I know. I get it." He was Junior's father. Of course the details hurt. They hurt me too, even now.

"There were only six people on the Homestead grounds when the fire happened and the four of you escaped alive. You and your mother and Patricia and Isabelle. It made sense that the two bodies would belong to my father and Fiona. An adult and a child. But there was someone else making notes on the file—an assistant, I think—and there were all these little objections that Henley ultimately overrode. There's a note that, uh, that the size of the girl's femur suggested an older child. Just a year or so older than Fiona would've been. Does that make any sense to you? Was Fiona big for her age?"

In that film in the Bishops' basement, Fiona had been petite, if anything, small-boned as a bird. My heart caught in my throat. "It doesn't make sense, no," I said. "Anything else?"

"There was a note about how the adult skull had a, let's see, I wrote it down—a rounder 'supraorbital ridge' than expected, more often seen in female cadavers. It can vary a lot between individuals. But it's weird. All these assistant's notes, vetoed by Henley as meaningless."

This tiny difference in the bone that had cradled Bellanger's brain. A woman's skull, lost among the flame-eaten wreckage. But the two adult women on the Homestead at the time had escaped—unless—

Something was building at the back of my mind. I couldn't put it into words just yet. It was hovering on my tongue, hot and dangerous and precious, ready to change everything. "What else?" I asked, urgent.

"Nothing else in the autopsy reports. I know I might be grasping at straws here. Cate was right: I've focused too much on you Girls and not enough on the Bellangers." A bitter laugh. "I want to find out whatever I can about my dad. I don't want to look away this time."

Cate was still sleeping behind me, but she turned, her side profile tipped toward me, her lips parted.

"I went through all our financial records," Junior said. "There's some property and assets my mom has had to sell off over the years. I noticed one particular piece of land was sold off *before* my dad died. About four months before the fire, actually, in February '77. And then I noticed who it was sold to—"

"Henley," I said.

"Exactly. My father sold this land to Henley not long before the fire for one dollar. Why would he do that? They were just colleagues, as far as I know. Barely acquaintances, except for knowing each other in med school. Maybe if I'd seen this a year ago I wouldn't have thought much of it—my father selling off some land, nothing important. But it's too much of a coincidence."

"Patricia mentioned something about your family's land," I said. "Where was that?"

"Do you want to guess?"

"Vermont? No—Arizona, wasn't it?"

He took a moment before he answered. "Utah."

I understood at once. "Fuck," I said. The maroon sedan that had been following us all along.

"I wanted you to know," Junior said. "Nobody else could understand the—" He stopped, unable to put it into words, but I got it. The betrayal, the shock.

The motel room was still here around me. It still existed. I had to reach down one hand and grip the edge of the mattress, the scratchy sheets and quilted comforter. I had to look at each item in turn, the burnt orange of the drapes, the uninspired pink-and-teal abstract blocks framed on the wall. It was all here. I was here. And if I was here, in this motel, then the world beyond existed, everything was the same, every-thing was continuing as normal.

"Junior," I said. "Can you describe to me exactly where that land is? Do you have any kinds of maps? Anything like that? Coordinates."

"Yeah," he said. "I wrote it down somewhere. Hold on."

Beside me, Cate stirred, eyes half-open. I just looked at her. Her frizz-wreathed curls disarranged, her naked body soft and strong be-neath the sheets—and turned away so that she couldn't see my face. But she'd already detected something in my eyes. She was scrambling into a sitting position, sleepiness falling away, face pinched with anxiety. Cate clutched the edge of the comforter, mouthed, *What's wrong?* at me. I shook my head.

"But another thing is—Josie. Listen. Henley wasn't surprised when I called. He mentioned that somebody else had been in touch with him recently, asking about whether Fiona could've possibly survived the fire. It was your mother," he said. "Maybe three weeks ago."

I almost smiled, a strange and painful reflex. My whole life, I'd thought I was following Bellanger's footsteps, that there was no other possible path for a Girl like me, a scientific breakthrough. Now my mother had forced me to retrace every step she'd taken. I'd unwittingly echoed every question she'd asked. Here I was, finally following her footsteps.

"Hello there." The man working the front desk at Fresh Spaces Property Management, just a small office in an apartment complex, was pushing eighty. A faceful of deep lines, a worn-in suntan that contrasted with his white hair. But there was an energy to him that read younger, eyes bright and curious. "How can I help you lovely young ladies today?"

I'd dragged Cate here right away. If Junior could look up records, then so could we. I was only frustrated that I hadn't considered this step the moment we'd talked to the surly man in 1C. There had to be some kind of paper trail, however sparse, that would give us a clearer idea of what had happened to the Grassis after they'd left Freshwater. I wanted to find out they were safe in Boise, or that they'd fled for a remote corner of Australia. I needed to believe they were somewhere. Because if I couldn't prove that, then I'd have to put into words the ugly idea that was already stuck in my throat. I hadn't even been able to share it with Cate yet.

"We're looking for anything you can tell us about Angela Grassi," I said, sunny and calm. "She might've lived here anytime in the past seventeen years. She was in unit 1C at—"

"Of course," the landlord said, beaming as he cut me off. "Angela. Wonderful girl. And her cute little daughter, what was her name? Virginia?"

"Gina," I said, exchanging a meaningful glance with Cate. "You remember them?"

"Do I remember them! Of course I do. They were special girls. Angela was connected to some strange things—but she was a good girl, at the end of the day. She just needed a friend." He leaned forward over the desk, confidential. "I used to watch Gina for Angela if she needed a babysitter. Just let her color some pictures. She was a quiet little thing."

"When was this?" I asked. Gina, Girl Four, was twenty years old by now.

"Oh," the man said. "Many years ago. Many. Hold on." He bent with some effort, slid open a filing cabinet drawer. Cate and I stood silently, bristling with nervous energy, until the man retrieved a paper and scanned it quickly. "Oh yes. That would've been 1977."

The year that was imprinted on my heart, the year I'd lost the only father I'd ever known. The year I was flung from the insular safety of the Homestead into a world that felt too crowded and hostile.

"In '77?" Cate repeated. "You're sure?"

"Of course I'm sure," he said. "Do you know why? Because that was the year of that horrible fire over in Vermont. After that fire, Angela and Gina just vanished. Never saw 'em again. I went to their apartment after they missed their rent. Well, nobody was there. They hadn't had much to their name, but they'd left it all behind. I waited and waited, nearly six months. But sooner or later you got to move on and put the place back up for rent."

"Wait a moment," I said, wanting all the facts to line up neatly in front of me. "The Grassis left right *after* the fire? Could it have been right *before*?"

The landlord scratched behind his ear. "Could be either, I suppose. I just thought . . . that fire was all over the news. Maybe Angela needed to lay low, and that's why she ran."

"But you never actually saw them after the Homestead burned."

"Not that I recall. I would've asked them about the fire if I'd seen them."

"So it's possible they left just before the fire instead," I said, less a question than a statement. The Grassis leaving their new town: the fire a day or two later. A woman with long dark hair approaching Ricky Peters, desperate for revenge. The shape of a skull. The length of a femur. A piece of land in a sun-bleached world, a property title changing hands. The office felt like it was closing in on me.

"Okay," I said carefully. My voice still sounded normal. "Do you have any of the Grassis' things left? Maybe we could look through them. They're old family friends, and we've been trying to get in contact with them for a long time."

"Like I said, they didn't have much. I sold a little of it, threw most of it out. I felt bad, but it was just papers, clothes, things like that." He frowned. "You know, this is the second time in the last month that someone's come around asking about the Grassis and their things. Years without anyone mentioning them, and now—"

My whole body tightened. "Somebody else was asking about the Grassis?"

"Yes," the landlord said. I had the impression he enjoyed our captive interest, that maybe there was a thrill in doling out this useless information, suddenly in high demand again. "I always have tricks to remember. Keeps me sharp. And this was right around the time that those birds came falling down and made all that racket. It all happened right around the same time that somebody was here, asking about the Grassis, poking their noses around—a lot like you girls are doing now. Older fellow. Big beard. Dark glasses. He had a girl with 'im."

"A girl with red hair?" I asked, almost not wanting to say it. My mother had been right all along.

"Yes." The landlord gave me a strange look. "Bright red."

Red like fire. Like open flame. Red hair like the mother she'd lost; red hair like the sister she'd never known.

All this time, I'd been grieving a man who was out there, somewhere, vital and alive. All this time, I'd been grieving Fiona, when I should have been mourning Gina Grassi. So much love poured in the wrong directions. I could hardly pull in a full breath. I was swirling, heart racing, all the oxygen sapped out of my blood.

"Morrow, are you ready to tell me what all that was about?" asked Cate. She tried to sound annoyed, but she just sounded worried. I'd been pacing the motel room for an hour now, feeling like I had to move or else I'd combust.

I had to get it together. I tried to lay it all out like an elaborate equation that had nothing at all to do with me. "Okay, so, the Grassis haven't been in Freshwater since 1977," I said. "Right before the fire. Ricky said that he spoke to a woman with long dark hair threatening to kill Bellanger. He assumed that it was my mother because she was one of the only people there. He didn't realize that Angela Grassi was back in Vermont after she'd already left. Junior said the bodies had discrepancies that Henley managed to hide all this time. Fiona's body was closer to Gina's age. Bellanger's body could've been a woman's."

Cate nodded, face still creased with concern.

"And the land in Utah," I continued. "Bellanger sold the land to Henley, who's been covering for him all this time. That means something."

"What?" she asked softly. "Just say it. Just say it out loud."

"I can't." Something broke inside me, a deep snap. "Cate, I can't say it."

Cate reached for me, and at her touch my whole body stilled. "You can say anything."

I took a deep breath. "Joseph Bellanger is still alive. He's been alive all this time. That fire never killed him. Fiona's alive too, and she must be with him."

Cate pulled me close, surrounding me with her scent, her warmth, the steady pulse of her being. I pressed my face into her neck, and it was only then that I recognized the wetness of her skin against me, her body trembling. No: I was the one trembling. The one crying.

"It's okay," Cate said, her voice aching. "It's okay. I know how much this hurts."

"I'm not—no, I'm not hurt. Just—" But that was what I was running from. Beneath the ache, beneath the shock, there was anger. Rage. A betrayal that could still reach me, even after I knew what he was and what he'd done.

He'd left me on purpose. He'd left us all. For a second I didn't exist. I wasn't Bellanger's favorite and oldest daughter, just a creation he'd abandoned. I imagined my genes unraveling, the nucleotides unspooled, until I vanished.

Cate's skin against my cheekbone, warm and solid. Her heartbeat working its way into my skin. I calmed a little. I was here: I was real. I pulled back and cupped Cate's cheek. "Thank you," I whispered, and I kissed her.

"Of course." She brushed the tears from beneath my eyes.

"And my mother." That was the other thing I hadn't been able to say. The other thing too big to acknowledge.

"What about her?"

"She was looking into all this too. Now she's been missing for weeks. There was a fire. Maybe she tracked them down. Maybe they tracked *her* down." The maroon sedan. The Utah plates. Bellanger's land.

Cate's eyes grew more serious, her thick eyebrows tugged into a frown. "You think Bellanger had something to do with her disappearance."

"I know he did."

"We're going to find your mother," Cate said. "That's what we set out to do." She sounded so confident. Like it was a done deal, no question.

"What if we're too late?" I whispered.

Cate began to answer, but the door opened, sunshine slicing across the carpet and cutting across our bodies. We both flinched.

Isabelle stood in the doorway. She still lived in a world in which Bellanger and Fiona were dead. I envied her, a quick, weary jealousy. She had no idea yet.

"I need your help," Isabelle said, and I realized now that I had no idea what she'd been up to today. "They're coming."

"Who's coming?" I asked, my mind immediately going to Bellanger and Fiona.

"The men from Kithira. I told them we're here in Freshwater," Isabelle said. Because she was backlit, it was hard to see her face, only her calm voice issuing from the halo of sunlight. "We have something they want, and they have something we want. I set a trap for them, but I can't do it alone."

45

We moved along the narrow path that wound around the edges of town. Isabelle walked a few steps ahead of us. Out here, away from the strip malls and chain restaurants, Freshwater was different. Spanish moss draped like cobwebs over tree branches. A river crawled nearby, turning the air lusciously humid. Everything lit with the buzzing of cicadas.

I remembered the way Isabelle had talked about setting a trap for the Bellanger boys in their maroon car, but I'd brushed it off. Now she had led us here, walking deeper into isolation, just the three of us, preparing to confront the men who wanted us dead. I was grudgingly impressed with Isabelle's ambition. Her action. Instead of running, she'd taken her fate into her own hands. Even if it'd get us all killed.

"You know how to use that, right?" I asked, noticing Cate adjusting the holster tucked inside her jeans, ugly against the familiar white of her T-shirt.

"You don't grow up in Arkansas without shooting a few beer cans off a fence," Cate deadpanned. She smiled, although the tension didn't leave her eyes: "Yeah. I'll be fine. At least I know how to work the safety."

I tried to smile back. "I just want you to have a way to defend yourself." Unlike Isabelle and me, she didn't have an inborn ability to protect herself.

"I probably won't even need it," Cate said, and the hopefulness in her voice made my heart hurt.

"You should turn back," I said, speaking softly enough that Isabelle wouldn't overhear. "Seriously. I know you care about Isabelle, but I can handle this."

"So I sit around waiting to hear whether or not you're dead? Not my style. Anyway. Every party needs a healer."

I laughed, surprised. "Dungeons and Dragons?"

"Senior year was lonely for the only known gay kid in a twenty-person graduating class. I took my friends where I could find them."

"Well, I m excited to learn all about your misspent youth." The possibility of that future—an easy future where we caught each other up on everything we'd missed, where we had time to document our tiny triumphs and embarrassing fashion choices—glowed between us.

"We're here," Isabelle called out. "This is where they're going to meet us."

We approached a clearing, the trees thinning out again to show the glass-sharp glimmer of the water, the sloping, sandy shore of the river.

I heard Cate's gasp as we walked into the clearing. The dead birds. Nobody had bothered to remove them from this isolated spot. It remained a little graveyard, the air ripe with the smell of death. There were hundreds of them, scattered between the tree line and the riverbank, in various states of decomposition. Some were nearly whole. Others were just shadows, the silhouettes of outspread wings overlaid with bones and mud-crusted feathers. A few were scorched carcasses, pitch-black arrangements of bones. I shifted back, stepping on the small twisted knot of a bird lying right at my feet. Not the work of Gina Grassi, after all, but of Fiona. Her presence felt stronger here, this direct evidence of her existence, and goose bumps rose along my arms. That dead bird outside my house—a secret signal I'd missed.

Isabelle was scanning the landscape.

"All right," I said. "So we're clear on the plan, right?" My stomach was a tight knot of anticipation. I didn't see anybody here yet—just the swaying branches, the sunlight, the birdsong.

"If they want this diary back, they'll hand over the film they stole from my house," Isabelle said. "I know they have it. They bragged about it to me when I told them to meet me here." She smiled. "We have something they want too."

Delilah's diary. A record of everything. Every interaction. Orange Shirt's real name, right there on the page. What he'd done to her. The growing violence. They hadn't suspected that Delilah would write it all down. Even in all the chaos of Kithira, Isabelle had the foresight to take the book from Delilah's bedroom. All along, she'd been operating on a different level than me, and I hadn't noticed. I thought of both our mothers, trying to bring their dreams to life, always at odds. We couldn't repeat that same pattern now.

"So the men come here, you hand over the diary, they give us the film," Cate said. "Then what? They just walk away and we walk away and we're all copacetic?" Her optimism twisted something tender in me.

But looking at Isabelle's face, I knew the truth. "It's a trap," I said simply. "The diary is just the bait." We were the jaws of the trap, designed to snap shut tightly around them.

"It's for the Strouds. And for my mother," Isabelle said, and all the grief that she'd been concealing beneath that blank layer of control flared to the surface for a second. "These men are a threat to all of us. I wouldn't have asked you two if I wasn't absolutely sure. I'm stronger when the two of you are with me. Haven't you noticed?"

"Yes," Cate said. "Before I met you, I couldn't heal anything stronger than a broken bone." She looked at me, and I remembered the rush of coming back to life. "You've changed me, both of you."

I thought about how quickly I'd learned to use my abilities, how swiftly they'd grown from that first uncertain moment to something that was part of me, automatic and powerful.

"Look at who we are. Look at what we can do. Why are we running from anybody?" Isabelle's face, veiled with the lacy shadows of the leaves, was holy and fierce. "They're the ones who should be afraid."

Cate gazed beyond the edge of the clearing. "They don't look afraid enough to me," she said, voice wavering slightly.

I turned. As if they'd been extracted from my restless nightmares, they were there. Three men came toward us, slow and deliberate, ambling as if they had all the time in the world. Two were strangers, but I knew one of them. Orange Shirt, today not wearing orange. Dressed all in blacks and blues, bruise colors. The man who'd killed me.

Instinctively, I moved closer to the woman who'd brought me back.

The sun hovered hot at its peak, the noise of the cicadas throbbing. The river spread out only a few yards from us, a jewel-bright green. For a moment I almost expected Black Shoes to be here with his gentle sneer. The three of us pulled together, arranged with our backs to the trees. I couldn't help thinking that this secured an escape route.

The men had seen us. They spread out as they came through the trees. Cate was right: They didn't look afraid. They'd come this far to hunt us down, even knowing what we could do. They'd seen what Isabelle did to Black Shoes. The Strouds had struck their entire town—men poisoned in their beds. Still, they looked at us and saw the familiar shapes of those who could be manipulated, tricked, bent and hurt and discarded. Women whose fear was a comforting undercurrent beneath each kiss, smile, scream. They saw what they were used to seeing.

The men paused in the middle of the clearing, the space between us bristling. I realized that all three of them were wearing sunglasses, dark lenses cloaking their eyes, reflecting the hot glare of the sun.

My stomach tightened with a sudden panic. I was reminded of how conditional my power was, tied to my gaze. Were the sunglasses just a coincidence?

I tried to steady myself. I could remove sunglasses. Easy. Drag them off. I just had to wait for the right moment: that was all. I stood there feeling impatient and weirdly hampered, like my hands were bound behind my back. Since that night at the motel weeks ago, my power had become part of me.

"Well," Orange Shirt said. "Look at this. We're evenly matched." He glanced around appraisingly. "Where's your little knight in shining armor?"

Junior. He meant Junior.

"That's not your concern," Isabelle said.

The men hadn't even noticed the dead birds strewn at our feet. They were too focused on the three of us.

Orange Shirt looked at me, and I could see myself captured inside the lenses, small and distorted. "Shouldn't you be dead?" he asked.

"Yes," I said. "I should be." I pulled myself a little taller.

His mouth twitched, and with his eyes hidden, I couldn't tell whether he was afraid or not.

"Hey, I recognize that," Orange Shirt said, and I realized that Cate had withdrawn the gun from her waistband. "That's mine."

"Sounds like we all have things that don't belong to us," Cate said, and one of the men grinned at this. Reaching to his hip, he languidly produced a pistol, holding it casually. The possibility of violence deepened, all of us straightening a little.

"Whoa, calm down," said Orange Shirt. "No need for gunshots in city limits. We're just here for a parley."

"Do you have it?" Isabelle asked. "What we agreed upon."

"Oh yeah, we got it," Orange Shirt drawled. "Your freaky little film? Thing is, I'm not sure we should hand it over. That's the dead girl, isn't it? The little redhead. It's proof of what you really are."

"And we can share Delilah's story just as easily," Isabelle said. "People will know exactly what you did to her. It's proof of who you really are." Her smile was cast with the strange glow of the sky before a tornado. "So why don't we just trade?"

"I know why you're so fucking scared of this movie." Orange Shirt took one step closer. "Because no one will want to be part of your sick bullshit once they see you for the monsters you are."

Cate spoke up, her voice clear. "Better a monster than a man like you. Honestly, you're the ones who are running scared. Because the more of us there are, the less we'll want of your sick—"

"Shut up, freak," said Orange Shirt, careless. The hurt blazed through Cate's eyes. I squeezed her shoulder, and Cate turned her head to lightly kiss my hand where it rested on her shoulder. One of the men glanced at us, staring right at the spot where her lips touched my hand. I saw the knowing disgust in his eyes, tilting on a leer, like he'd caught us doing something dirty and pathetic. Like he understood everything about us. They looked down on us for being fatherless, for being freaks. But the revulsion they'd just shown was well-worn and mapped out. It had just never been directed at me before.

"Are you willing to trade or not?" Isabelle asked, voice direct and almost sweet. "It seems like a waste to come all this way and walk away empty-handed."

The men smiled at this, unthinking, a shared current of amusement. My skin prickled.

"Yeah," Orange Shirt said. "Hand it over. You first."

I expected that Isabelle would refuse. Wait until we confirmed they even had the film. But Isabelle extracted the diary from her satchel and held it up so they could see it. The notebook had a cheerful print of cartoon dolphins, Technicolor and exaggeratedly happy: it tugged at me, this innocent remainder of the dead girl. The witch. Orange Shirt's jaw spasmed slightly, and I wondered if this memory had managed to bring Delilah back to life for a second. The way she must've been to him, once. A real woman, someone he loved.

"Bring it over," one of the men called.

Only three yards separated us, but it may as well have been a vast and hostile desert. Isabelle walked forward, spine in elegant alignment, not a quiver of hesitation in her muscles. The men watched her as she approached, the lenses of their sunglasses dark and blank. Like a herd of deer alerted to an approaching wolf, or lions catching the scent of wounded prey. I couldn't tell which.

Next to me, Cate shifted nervously, clutching the gun with both hands.

I thought Isabelle would head to Orange Shirt, who took a step forward, his hand held out, impatient and authoritative. But at the last second, Isabelle veered away from him and moved to the man with the gun. She stood right in front of him—too close, I thought, too close—and held out the diary. Her posture was obedient, a child with an adult.

The man glanced at Orange Shirt, who shrugged and gave a barely perceptible nod. It was hard to read his expression with his eyes shielded. The man reached out one hand to accept the diary, and Isabelle hesitated. My stomach squeezed. They'd destroy Delilah's words too.

Isabelle dropped the diary to the ground. In one neat, almost casual motion, she grabbed the man by his arm. Both of her hands wrapped around his bare skin. He startled, then laughed, and I understood why. It looked like such a tiny, pointless gesture. She was so small next to him. The sun was starting its descent now, warmer and deeper, slanting into Isabelle's black hair. The insects screamed and shrilled around us.

Then the man dropped his gun.

Orange Shirt said the man's name. Isabelle was bearing down now: even from this distance, I could see the way his flesh blanched white where her fingertips pressed down. She was clutching him, clawing at him with an intensity I hadn't seen when she'd touched the cashier or Junior. The effects were immediate, a small bomb going off in our midst. The man fell to his knees, coughing out an arc of blood that landed on the grass. His skin was glassy white. Isabelle was unraveling him, pulling him apart piece by piece, so quickly that he'd be gone soon. His eyes rolled back in his head.

We were frozen for a moment, watching it happen, and then everything sped up, a blur of movement, everyone driven by instinct. Orange Shirt lunged for the dropped gun. Cate trained her gun on the men, face stoic and ghostly, sweat at her temples. She took a faltering step back and I realized that the third man was charging at us, a bull, head lowered. "Stop!" I shouted, ineffectually, meaninglessly. Cate fired once, a sharp crack through the silence, birds fluttering into the air from across the river.

She'd missed. Suddenly he was right there. He caught her jaw: it was a blunt and dirty attack, sloppy with rage. Her head snapped back on her neck, blood darkening her face so swiftly that it felt like black magic. Her eyes, agonized, caught against mine, and then he'd shoved her down into the grass, his knee braced against her. I watched him hit her again, saw the way he shook his fist, as if clearing away the muscle memory of what had happened.

In the background, yelling. Orange Shirt. Isabelle. I couldn't focus.

I darted forward, not caring about myself. I reached for the man who was straddling Cate. He lifted an arm to block me, but I'd snatched his sunglasses off his face, revealing his startled-looking eyes, pale and blinking and human. Those wide-open pupils. Relief washed through me. I was back on solid ground, I was surging with power.

I locked eyes with him. "Let her—"

Pain exploded in my lower back. The ground rose toward me, a sick rush. I'd been kicked to the dirt, my skull ringing and ringing, the pain an expanding continent across my body. How? Orange Shirt was yards away from me, fighting with Isabelle, and the third man was dead already—we were evenly matched—

No. When they'd first arrived, Orange Shirt had asked after Junior. They'd brought a fourth man, expecting four of us. He had outflanked us from the trees. We were outnumbered.

Gathering all the strength I had, I fought, I screamed, I spat. The man twisted my wrist, wrenched my arm, and bound my hands.

"And her eyes," someone said.

Then the world blacked out. Everything vanished. For a wild moment I thought I'd lost my vision, or dropped into some other reality. I felt the agonizing, tugging pressure at the back of my head. A blindfold. I was being blindfolded. A thick fabric, scratchy, sweaty. I could barely blink, my eyelids pinned by its weight. I screamed, kicked backward, tried to squirm away. The world spun. I didn't know which way was up.

Dimly, I heard the click of a revolver. Nearby. Too close. I was back in that motel room in Pennsylvania, my heart draining out onto the bed, my lungs giving way.

"Cate," I cried. "Are you okay?"

"I'm here," she said. Still close. Her voice faint, breathing labored.

"What's happening? Can you see?"

"Yes," she said. The blindfold was just for me. "There was a fourth, and he ambushed you—" A second later, the crunch of sole against bone. She gave a strangled cry.

I was aware of the chaos behind me as if I were listening to it from underwater. The men shouting, crowing, laughing. Isabelle was silent. The fear was so thick now, like a bad dream, like being chased by an unseen beast that paralyzed with its presence alone. What had Isabelle thought would happen? She was rage-addled, grief-muddled. Cate was a force that could put things back together, not tear them apart. Isabelle was too small to take on all these men. And I was useless: my power thwarted by something as simple as a blindfold.

We needed them all. I saw that now. We needed Soo-jin's wild, world-rending scream, Bonnie's ability to fade into the world itself. Emily's foresight. We needed Delilah and Gina, raised from the dead. We needed Fiona. But there were just the three of us, separated and alone.

Cate screamed and groaned. "Stop," I yelled, my voice not my own. "You fucking—"

A boot to my belly, a dull thud of pain that exploded slowly outward. I keened in pain.

Isabelle's sudden sharp scream.

This was where it would end for us. For me, Isabelle, and Cate. Cate. By the time Cate was forming a flickering pulse inside her mother's body, I was already out in the world, running wild. I'd pressed my ear to Tonya's stomach to listen to the watery echo and to feel the soft, impossible kick of her heel against me. Like stars forming at different reaches of the universe. She'd brought me back to life, but I couldn't protect her in turn.

Birds were singing. The insects' wail rose and ebbed, rose and ebbed.

"Stop," I said again. My voice was thin now, and defeated. Panic beat weakly at my temples, my body chilled with a slick of sweat.

There was so much noise. I couldn't tell what was happening where. There were screams, groans, the men laughing, calling to each other. Isabelle's voice. Cate's voice. The memory of that night brought back. I waited for the shock of pain, the warm, creeping wetness of the wound. Nothing. But Isabelle was crying, somewhere not far, the sound ragged and small. If they realized how much power she held in her hands and found a way to stunt that—and we were helpless now, my powers blinded, Isabelle hurting and hopeless, Cate—

We weren't the trap. We'd walked into one willingly.

I felt something I hadn't felt in a long time. It took me a second to identify it: I missed my mother, the way I had as a child. Her warm, strong presence. Her assurance that it would all be okay. Something I'd carried with me my whole life, even when I was angry, even when I took everything about her for granted.

I'd never see my mother again. I'd come so close to finding her, but at the last minute I'd failed. That loss was unimaginable. I couldn't believe I'd ever accepted my mother as a simple person, somebody to move beyond and outgrow. A woman so one-dimensional and explicable that I could tuck her into the background of my own ambitions. Now, wherever she was, I'd never be able to tell her that I finally knew her.

That message on the Strouds' answering machine, a lonely echo playing to a house where no one lived anymore. It would be the last time I heard her. I remembered standing there in that abandoned home and realizing for the first time how much my mother sounded like me. How much I sounded like her. Her voice still lived inside me. Everything I'd ever said held an echo of her, hidden there, whether I heard it or not.

I drew on that. My mother's voice, wound throughout mine. "Stop," I said, and this time, the weakness left my voice: it rang clear and pure as a struck bell.

But the noise kept on around me, murky and thick, penning me in. Isabelle screamed. Heavy breathing—whose? The violence around us took on a new shape, a roughness that made my belly clench. I was too aware of our three bodies, powerless and hurting.

My mother's face. My mother's voice. Standing on the bright brink of the future. I'd held on to Bellanger's letters for so long, but there'd been a time before my memory was formed when she held me for the first time, my skin damp and waxy, skin designed for another world. And she leaned down to whisper into my ear, *Welcome to the world, my daughter.*

"Stop," I called. "Now."

And the world halted. The rest of the noise ceased and stilled. It was such a relief to be in the quiet that I just lay there, panting, for a small lifetime. I mentally mapped out the pain in my body. The tender softness in my belly, as bruised and soupy as a dropped piece of fruit. The sharper pain at my wrists where they'd been tied together. A hot, raw scrape of pain where I'd fallen onto the ground, my cheek cut by stones or the jutting, delicate bones of a bird.

Into the darkness, I spoke, and I felt their minds out there. Mapped like a constellation. I reached into the nearest one. "Untie me," I said. My mother's voice still there underneath mine, holding it steady when it threatened to crumple inward.

After a second, fingers scrabbled at the knots. It took longer to undo the knots than it had to secure them. I listened for Cate and Isabelle, tried to feel out their specific minds. Cate, wounded and cautious;

Isabelle, blank and smooth as dark glass. The ropes slithered away from my wrists. "Take off my blindfold," I said. My hands ached. I shook them out, feeling the reassuring starry pain of pins and needles as the blood crept back.

Fingers at the back of my skull, pulling at my hair, stinging. The blindfold fell away and I could see everything. I almost wanted to shut my eyes. Not just against the tender brightness of the sun, but the ugliness of what had been revealed to me: the men statue-still or collapsed, Isabelle bandaged and tear-soaked, Cate. Cate.

Cate lay very still, curled into a rough fetal position, one eye bloodied and bruised. The strap of her top was pulled off her shoulder, her jeans unbuttoned, and I went to her, kneeling in the grass. Carefully, I fixed her clothes again, slipping her strap back into place against her collarbone. Just a few hours ago, we'd been in the motel room, and I'd been laughing and hungry as I'd tugged her clothes off.

I looked a question at her, and Cate shook her head, her eyes barely lightening. But coming even that close was too much. The careless greed—feeling like they were owed any part of her miraculous self—

"How are you doing this?" she asked under her breath, where nobody else could hear. "Your eyes. You were blindfolded."

I shrugged. I didn't want to waste words. My power felt stronger here, rooted in my breath, than it had when it was tied to my gaze. I gripped Cate's shoulder once, a reminder that I was here with her, and stood.

Across from me, Isabelle's face was sticky with tears, eyes blotted and swollen. Her arms were bandaged, bulky and white and distorted, spotted with blood—but no. It was the stranger's shirt—the stranger Isabelle had attacked first, now lying in the grass, not moving, his tender, graying skin exposed. Orange Shirt must've ripped it from his back and used it to blunt Isabelle's touch. Just like I'd been blindfolded.

I was rattled by their efficiency. How quickly they'd looked at us and charted out our softest spots. The places where our power could be extracted, muted, and stripped from us.

Orange Shirt stood too close to Isabelle. The other two men were arranged in a loose semicircle, watching me. They didn't talk. They didn't move. Their faces held only a dulled, distant panic, the fear of dreamers. There was a strange silence suspended over everything, everybody just waiting, held still by my voice. Like game pieces waiting to be rearranged.

I went to Isabelle and untied her myself. The knots were harsh and tangled, hard to pick loose. The insects kept keening as if nothing at all had changed. I couldn't tell whether any of the blood was hers.

"I'm sorry," Isabelle whispered. "I thought we were stronger."

"We are stronger," I said, unraveling the last knot. Pulling away the bloodied T-shirt, I examined Isabelle's arms. Unwounded. She flexed her fingers reflectively. "You're okay?"

A quick nod. "What are you going to do to them?" she asked.

"What do you want me to do to them? This is your plan."

"I want to deal with him."

I knew which one she meant. Isabelle turned toward Orange Shirt. His sunglasses were crooked, his whole face out of alignment. He looked so young. I wrapped myself around his brain, held him still for her. "Stay," I said.

Rising onto tiptoes, Isabelle pressed her mouth to his. The kiss seemed to last too long—it wasn't seductive or kind or intimate. I thought of Delilah, her body turned into a means to an end. Proof to these men that their genes would thrive, predictable and safe—and then they'd killed her and the unborn baby anyway. I watched Isabelle as she reached inside Orange Shirt and untied the thin threads holding him together. Let them go.

I watched the life drain out of Orange Shirt almost immediately. He dropped to his knees and his mouth drooped open, the blood glossy on his teeth. He fell forward into the grass and was still, his unseeing gaze fixed on me.

Cate came to us. Isabelle and Cate and I joined hands, interlocking our fingers. The insects and the sunlight and the murmur of the river, the silent trees, the skeletal birds. Everything felt especially real. Full and vivid around us.

"What do we do with these two?" Cate asked.

I considered the two remaining men, who watched me back, darting eyes letting me know they still were trapped in there. I could kill them off. Have them shoot each other. Tell them to walk one by one into the river and stay there until the water filled their lungs. Isabelle had called them here because she knew they would just keep on hunting us down, stalking us, killing us off. Using the proof of Fiona's abilities to rip away our last shreds of privacy and thrust us into the spotlight. Killing them now would end that, at least.

But I exhaled. "Take their weapons."

The three of us let go of each other's hands. Brisk and quick, not speaking, we patted the men down, disarming them. They'd brought rope, duct tape. Guns. A knife that glinted with cruel jagged teeth, in the evening sun. A book of matches—I remembered that scorched clearing, all the life bleached out of it.

I found the cartridge. A square not much longer than a deck of playing cards. So small to hold so much history inside it. I'd once thought this was the only remaining proof of who Fiona was, but now I thought of her—out there, somewhere—still growing, still changing, very much alive.

When we were done, I pulled back. "Turn yourselves in." I raised my voice. "Confess. Tell the world what you did to Delilah, and to Vera, and to Patricia."

The two surviving men hovered there for a second, as if letting the instructions penetrate the surfaces of their brains. Then they began moving out of the clearing, quiet and obedient. The only sound was the light crunch of their footsteps. I watched their forms retreat into the distance until I couldn't see them anymore. The three of us stood alone. Orange Shirt's head was haloed by a creeping pool of blood.

"God, Morrow, I can't believe you did that," said Cate.

"I can't believe it either." My voice betrayed the slightest tremor.

"Where do we even go from here?" Cate asked.

"We're going to rescue my mother," I said. "We're going to find Bellanger."

46

We'd been driving endlessly. The sun through the windshield was so hot and unrelenting that it nearly blurred away my vision, a wash of surreal white. Outside, the landscape was as jagged and unforgiving as an alien planet. All rust-colored rock, serrated cliff edges, ground that was heat-cracked into wide-ranging geometric patterns.

"This should be it," I said.

I slowed. The three of us gazed around, feeling our optimism evaporate in the endless, noiseless glare of the heat. The air-conditioning rattled ineffectually, puffing out a lukewarm breath. I knew I should be sweating, but my skin was sticky rather than damp, the sweat evaporating too quickly. We had our plastic thermos of drinking water, stale and hot, nearly empty. My tongue was heavy in my mouth. I glanced at the Volvo's fuel gauge, the arrow hovering right above E. We were miles from any gas station, and if this wasn't the right spot, we'd need to retreat back to the closest semblance of civilization. Try again tomorrow. Or the next day.

"There's nothing here," Isabelle said softly.

Not quite nothing. Strange rock formations, bubbled archways and sharp wedges, rose from the ground in the distance. It'd been a long time since we'd encountered any paved roads. I double-checked the road map where I'd carefully marked the coordinates Junior had given me over the phone. "This should be the edge of Bellanger's land," I said. "We're going to have to search."

But I didn't move, not wanting to waste a drop of precious fuel. The desert was so empty: a broad scoop of a sky, cloudless. High above us, a bird suspended inside a current, a dark blot. I was surprised to see any sign of life. It seemed like we three were the only ones reckless and desperate enough to be out here, cut loose from the world's natural laws.

"Are you sure we can trust Junior?" Cate said beside me, fanning herself with the notebook.

"He *did* get the Grassis' address right. Just seventeen years too late."

Cate shook her head. "I mean, can we *trust* him?"

"I don't think he'd lie about this." But a spike of uncertainty ran along my spine. After all this, I'd ended up in the middle of nowhere, surrounded by blanched sky, looking for a dead man who refused to appear—

"Look," Isabelle said.

It took me only a second to realize what she was pointing to. In the pale sky, a bright, plummeting arc. The bird. No longer suspended, it dropped from the sky, a blaze like a shooting star. I recognized why: it had caught fire, a flame that began at its tip and then rapidly ate away its whole body. Before the little doomed comet even touched the ground, it was nothing, dissolving into the heat of the day.

"I guess we're at the right place," I said.

After we'd pushed the bodies into the river, we'd gathered our things and left Freshwater. We drove, following the directions Junior had given us. The three of us were bruised and tattered from the fight; Cate did her best to mend our wounds, but she had trouble using her abilities on herself. "It's always been like this," she'd said straightforwardly. Her own eye stayed mottled and swollen, an ugly reminder of what a close escape we'd had. Inside the car, though, we felt alive and vicious with purpose, driving into the future and into the past at the same time.

Lonely farms and abandoned corrals, distant power plants, crumbling barns or mobile homes so dwarfed by the landscape around them that it was impossible to tell whether they were occupied or not. Huge, ominous industrial-looking outposts with no clear function. The towns we passed through fit the definition of "town" less and less easily. Sometimes they were just a grouping of five or six houses, half-finished, tarps fluttering over bare frames. In a way, the very weirdness of the landscape was a cloak of anonymity. I saw why Bellanger chose this place.

I lost track of time, caught inside a strange limbo. I was sure we'd been driving for at least a day, maybe a week, a month. Forever.

The radio stations grew farther and farther apart. We went from having options to getting excited whenever we found a human voice emerging from the static like a drowning person lifting an arm from the waves. Then that stopped too.

The whole time we drove, I thought of finding my mother. I thought of meeting Fiona—Girl Nine, alive again. But there was one person I couldn't focus on too closely because it was like staring directly into the sun. He was just a feeling under my skin. A slowly building rage, burning hotter with each mile.

"Holy shit," Cate said. A laugh came out of her, a bright exhalation of amazement. "For some reason—I didn't think—this is—"

Even though I'd been the one to bring us here, there was something powerful about standing here and actually seeing it. We'd finally arrived at the place that I'd needed to find, unknowingly, ever since I first saw my mother's burned-down house on the news.

The compound stood inside the low dip of a valley, ringed by cliffs. There was a sturdy fence ringing the perimeters. Beyond the shadowed mesh of the chain-link, I could make out pale buildings, beige and stucco, as if they'd evolved to match the stark desert landscape. A few mobile homes were perched, rectangular, next to simple one- or two-story structures. Angular structures, like building blocks scattered through a sandbox.

Wordlessly, the three of us walked down the rocky dip of the valley toward the gate. There was more vegetation here, scrubby and dry, grasping branches and parched clumps of stiff greenery. Eggplant-colored cacti, squat and spiny.

I kept thinking of that bird. Its trajectory arrested, sent to its beautiful and fiery death. I couldn't tell whether it'd been a warning or a welcome. Even as a tiny child, Fiona had been a flame-hot force. Cracking light bulbs, lighting candles. Smashing objects. And now I knew that her abilities had been developing, years and years ahead of the rest of ours. I didn't know what we'd find here. All I knew for certain was that I needed to get to my mother, and I clung to that.

We stood at the gate, stymied for a moment. Prickling loops of razor wire ribboned the top. The place felt even more abandoned than the rest of the desert, the silence highlighted by all those buildings. The wrongness of it struck me deep in my bones. There were none of the noises that usually textured the air—no dogs barking, no birdsong, no human voices.

"What do we do?" Cate asked. "Ring the doorbell?" She spoke wryly, but there was a trace of tension, a wire plucked too hard.

I glanced at the top of the gate, noticing a security camera perched there, its hooded eye trained on us. Before I could fully react to this, Isabelle inhaled. "Do you hear that?"

I noticed it too: a noise at last, a low rattle, growing steadily closer. Every little sound stood out in this empty place. It wasn't coming from inside the gates; we turned, scanning the landscape in the direction we'd just come from. The rattling grew louder, the unmistakable sound of tires against gravel. The growl of the engine. Out beyond the closest formation, a plume of yellowed dust, rising into the air—leaving a suspended trail that slowly, slowly, faded at the edges. The car was coming right for us. There was nowhere else to go.

We waited. The driver must've spotted the anomaly of the Volvo, parked behind a distinctive outcropping of rocks. Whoever it was already knew we were here.

When the car came into view, I wasn't surprised, or even scared. What I felt was the bittersweet triumph of being proven right. The maroon sedan, its color muted with dust. Finally catching up with us. Here we were, unafraid. After so many weeks of being chased down, it was gratifying to be the ones who'd shown up uninvited. We'd found this place, whether they'd wanted us to or not.

The sedan stopped a few feet from us, the dust drifting to us and temporarily engulfing us too. A grit rose against the back of my throat, stinging at my eyes. The creak and thud of a car door opening, closing.

When I opened my eyes, the man had emerged. Tall, a lanky, uncomfortable height, like he'd outgrown his own boundaries accidentally. His hair was sandy brown, bleached now in the sunlight. The last time I'd seen him this clearly, he'd just been a silhouette outside Cate's burning home, that dark, humid night in Arkansas. He moved toward us, not surprised but wary. Something was off, a little incongruity even in the middle of this huge incongruity. I realized that he was meeting my eyes openly. His look wasn't friendly, but his eyes were bare and exposed. He wasn't trying to protect himself from me.

I filed this away: this stranger didn't know what we were capable of. In all his time trailing us from town to town, it was possible he hadn't seen enough to realize what we were capable of.

"I'm looking for my mother," I said, not turning it into a command, falling back onto my old way of gathering information from the world. "Is she here?"

At the mention of my mother, the stranger's expression shifted. He swallowed quickly, the muscles in his face contracting, his gaze dropping. He knew where my mother was. I was sure of it. He glanced backward for a second, as if considering what to do next, and then he began to unlock the gate. The four of us were silent under the heavy glare of the sun.

The gate swung open and the stranger walked inside. He looked back at us, a wordless question: Were we going to follow? Isabelle started forward at once. I almost ran in my eagerness to get closer to my mother, then paused, not sure Cate was behind me. Her fingers slipped into mine, and we walked into the compound.

He fastened the gate behind us. I felt an unease clamping down around me. Watching him lock the gate again—that camera mounted on top swiveling to take us in—I was in the dark wilderness of a fairy tale, the enchanted door vanishing, no way back out.

The stranger led us on a path through the houses, which looked even weirder up close. These fully formed homes perched out here in the middle of nowhere. I noticed another camera balanced on the edge of a roof, its silent black eye facing us. The Homestead had been isolated too, but I didn't remember it feeling this way when I was little. The Homestead had been wild, alive, surrounded by the murmur of the trees, loud with voices and laughter, crawling with animals. Here, there was no warmth. Just a silent watchfulness that stuck to my skin. I noticed Cate rubbing hard at the back of her neck.

The stranger stopped in front of an unassuming building. He pulled open the door and gestured for us to enter, his expression betraying nothing. The interior was dark, the shadows rough with candlelight, a glow of heat emanating from the front of a chapel. I paused for a moment, hit bluntly with the memories that the candles brought along. The Homestead, my mother's burned house, the fire at Cate's. Then I followed Cate and Isabelle inside, and the door swung shut behind us. The heat of the candles was a thousand tiny pinpricks on my skin.

We weren't alone. Rows and rows of benches, bodies lined on them, a rustling and silent congregation, maybe twenty or thirty people. I had the impression they were mostly women: long hair brushed down their backs, wound into intricate braids. My eyes slowly adjusted and more details rose out of the candlelight. Their old-fashioned clothing, rough-hewn, with high necks and long sleeves. They were facing the front of this chapel, not looking at us.

I searched for my mother, automatically scanning for her familiar figure. Nothing.

There was an altar at the front of the room, and over to one side, a simple door. The altar's surface was scattered with flowers. Spiky pink blooms next to long-dried husks, dissolving into dust. A drawing stood in the center of the altar. A pencil sketch, black-and-white. The lines were simple, the shading brusque and impressionistic. Flowing hair, wide, high cheekbones. Her eyes were the only detail that looked wrong. They were blank, no pupil, no iris—nothing behind them. It was Lily-Anne, I thought. No: Fiona.

Beside me, Isabelle's expression was open with wonder, a child waiting for a magic show to start. A man rose from the front row, moving toward the altar. His deliberate self-assurance contrasted with the deference of the people around him. Even the softest noises in the room, the rustling, the coughs, were suppressed, one by one. The man faced the altar for a minute, apparently lost in thought as he looked at the picture of eyeless Fiona.

He turned.

Despite the seventeen years that had worn grooves into his skin and grayed his hair, I knew him at once. It was a face I'd seen over and over again, memorized down to the last detail. The deep-set warmth of his eyes. The strong chin and narrow, aristocratic cheekbones.

We wer caught in the shadows, hidden at the back of the room. He hadn't seen us yet. I was grateful. I needed this time to look at him and accept that he was here and alive.

"Sisters and brothers." Dr. Bellanger's voice carried throughout the small room, disrupting the veil of heat. He sounded louder, rawer than I'd heard on scratchy audio recordings. "These past few months, as we wait to see the fruits of our labor, have been difficult for us all. We are in a time of great flux, on the verge of a future we cannot yet fully fathom. Again and again, I've urged you to see this transition as more than a time of uncertainty. In the right slant of light, it becomes a time of renewal and hope. And now! Now, the world is nearly prepared for us."

Beside me, Cate's breathing had turned tense. The heat of the candles crowded in closer and closer, like curious eyes. For a second everything was tipped over and surreal. *The world is nearly prepared for us*: But the world had been ready for him all along. He'd been the one to leave us.

Bellanger held out his hand. A girl stepped forward, long red hair trailing down her back. She turned around to face the congregation, the pencil drawing an unconscious echo hanging over her shoulder. I had a sudden memory of Lily-Anne at the Homestead. I'd been allowed to come into the room after Fiona was born. Already four years old, considering myself a grown-up, I'd leaned over to look at the last baby born on the Homestead. I remembered her pulpy skin and the animal smell of Lily-Anne's sweat and blood.

Lily-Anne's face was replicated perfectly here—the sharp tilt of a nose and rounded cheeks, framed by hair so bright it seemed to be sapping the blood from the rest of her. Fiona seemed shaken, clutching herself, her expression blank. Bellanger put his hand on her shoulder, transmitting a message that I couldn't decode. She held out her hand, palm facing up, and Bellanger reached into the front of his lab coat. With his free hand, he pulled out a dark glass bottle. He tipped a capsule into her hand, a flash of hectic red, and Fiona lifted her palm to her mouth. She swallowed and shut her eyes briefly. He squeezed her shoulder. Nobody else in the chapel reacted. It had the unthinking crispness of a practiced routine.

I was so transfixed by this exchange that I was startled by the muffled gasp beside me. "She's pregnant," Cate said under her breath, so low it didn't disrupt the stillness of the room.

Once she said it, I couldn't look away. Of course. Fiona's belly was a soft swell between her hip bones. Based on the size, I'd say maybe three or four months. Early. I pictured the fetus, transparent skin, jellied and pink. A budding copy of the sister Fiona had lost. Fiona herself seemed so young to be pregnant. Too young—

"Your trust and patience has been a true gift to me," Bellanger was saying now. "A gift I do not accept lightly, loyal friends. I take my role as guide and mentor very seriously. Fiona's child will be as much a miracle as she is. But you are in the unique position to appreciate that miracles do not occur without miracle-workers. Behind every so-called impossibility is someone who has dedicated his very life to overcoming the limits of possibility. Remember: the goddess Athena leapt fully formed from her father's skull. The goddess of wisdom. I cannot pretend that my path to Fiona was quite so straightforward—" Some gentle laughter here. "But I have dedicated my soul and my mind to not only bringing her into the world, but helping her understand herself. I will do the same for her daughter, certainly—"

But Fiona had found us. Her eyes moved directly through the gloom and the crowds, to land on us, where we stood back against the wall. She rose on tiptoes to whisper something to Bellanger, who stooped to hear her with an attentiveness that caught at some deep part of me, unspooling disgust and jealousy at the same time. His expression changed, tightening, and he looked up sharply now, peering into the shadows.

I didn't wait for anything else. I walked toward them, confident, strong, shoulders back. I'd been six years old the last time we saw each other. It felt like I'd become an entirely different species since then.

The murmur had grown louder now, some people falling silent as I passed, others half rising, faces spread wide in alarm. Isabelle and Cate were right on my heels. Now that the ruse was up, I stared more openly at the women scattered along the pews, searching desperately for my mother. I felt all those gazes creeping in tighter and tighter. I turned, impatient, like I was chasing away a buzzing insect. Each face that wasn't hers felt like a gut punch.

I stopped just short of the altar. Bellanger and I looked at each other. His expression was entirely unreadable to me. I didn't know what he'd do. The decision hung there between us. I held his gaze and I thought: *I could do anything to you right now. I could do anything.*

For the briefest second, Bellanger's eyes flicked past me, to the people waiting. The faithful friends, loyal followers, whoever the hell they were. Now that I was close, I paid more attention to the door right next to the altar. I wondered if it led to the outside, and if I could still make a run for it. The impulse came over me quickly, not so much fear as an instinctive desire to remove myself from this impossible moment. Then Bellanger looked at me and smiled like he'd been waiting for this: looking into a crowd and recognizing an old friend. "Josephine," he said. "Girl One. My oldest daughter."

I couldn't answer. I had so much to say to him. It was pushing against the back of my lips. It was filling me up entirely. Years and years of things left unsaid. One-way messages that I'd absorbed into the echo chamber of my heart, no way to reply. A life spent communicating with him only through dreams and daydreams.

"Dr. Bellanger," I said finally.

He opened his arms and I stepped forward. My breathing steadied as if my body responded to his unspoken command, the authority of its true creator. It was comforting, obeying him on the molecular level—it was a sick shock. Both.

Bellanger pulled me close. I stiffened, unable to move. I smelled an unexpected trace of that old cologne, a sharp, lemony bitterness. Eau Sauvage. It brought along a memory so strong I was dizzy with it. Being so small I fit inside his arms. Staring up at him—way, way up. The safety of him. My stomach twisted. Over his shoulder, I saw that Fiona watched me. She seemed drowsier now, out of it, but I caught the edge of something strange. A dark cloud, swift-passing. I thought of the way that bird had seemed to welcome us here with its death.

"Today, we have the gift of unexpected guests," Bellanger called to the room, not letting me go. "I am sure you all recognize these three Girls. They may not be fashioned from the same cloth as our Fiona, but they are the ones who preceded her. The ones who made Fiona possible. With these Girls returned to us, our horizons have expanded yet again. It's a true gift. The very best of omens."

Something was wrong here. He was surprised, but it wasn't the pure shock wave of seeing three women from his past walk into the room. Bellanger had known we were coming.

I stood there in the candlelight, upended again. The past few weeks, I'd been brimming with rage and frustration that I'd never have a chance to express. I'd felt cheated. But now, staring him right in the eyes, I didn't know where to begin. Until I did.

"I'm here," I said, "for my mother."

He leaned in close, his breath hot against my ear. He whispered, "I know."

47

Bellanger's office felt disorienting. Timeless. Like it could have been early morning, or the middle of the night, or June of 1977—everything held in suspension all this time. No windows, the single halo of yellow lamplight in one corner. Overflowing bookshelves, tables with papers, notebooks scattered widely, some cracked on their spines. If everything else on this desert compound felt functional and impersonal, this space was all Bellanger. I was surprised to see my own adult hands folded in my lap, pressed between my thighs to stop the shake. I felt myself turning back into a six-year-old kid, moony-eyed and hungry for love.

We'd been ushered here, still dusty and tired from the road. Bellanger sat behind his desk with his hands clasped. "My first three daughters." He nodded at each of us in turn. The light from the lamp caught the sides of his face. "Do you know, I remember each of your births? All these years and I can still recall the distinct sound of each of your cries, nine times in a row. Each one a clarion cry. The very world changing."

Cate was brisk and firm, speaking before his last syllable had faded. "We need to see Margaret Morrow."

Bellanger leaned back, a glimmer of surprise, or displeasure, or both. "Of course you'll see your mother, Josephine," he said, addressing me as if I were the one who'd spoken. "Of course. You'll have to forgive us if we aren't exactly prepared for company at this moment."

"What is this place?" I asked, softening my question, making sure he had a choice in responding. I was careful not to overplay my hand.

"This? This is home."

The way he said it, not thinking of the home he'd let burn to the ground. That anger churned in me, so thick I could feel it licking at my throat. "But why are you *here*, Dr. Bellanger?" I asked, and let the question hold all the implications of that. Why was he here? Why was he alive? *Why?* "We thought you were dead. We thought Fiona was dead. And you just let us. You never reached out, all this time? You never wondered about us?"

Bellanger examined me, his eyes steady and probing. Having him right in front of me made me feel like everything else was an illusion. Maybe this strange desert outpost would vanish if I traced my finger along the right seam of it.

"Of course I wondered about you." He sounded almost hurt. "I've followed your paths with great interest. I know all about your lives." He was looking directly at me as he said it, and I realized that Bellanger knew. When I'd appeared on TV, bubbling over with my plans to make him proud, he'd been listening.

"You have to understand," he went on. "In 1977, I watched my miracle fall apart around me. The pressure placed on me was ugly. I'd achieved the impossible nine times in a row, but the world wanted another miracle, bigger and better and bolder. Something they could hold in their hands. They wanted to take what I'd done and package it into a pill, put it on the shelves of drugstores like—like common aspirin. First they ignored me, then they mocked me, and finally they tried to stop me. But when I succeeded, what did they want? They wanted it for themselves. I was this close to handing over my life's work so that my colleagues could play God without earning it."

Bellanger had said similar things in his letters to me. This attitude that I'd always mistaken for confidence, for a maverick brilliance, now sounded petty. I'd always pictured his work as tragically interrupted, but I knew the truth: He'd chosen Fiona over her sisters, over her future sisters. Over everything.

"When I saw Fiona—when I saw that little girl, wielding those powers—I knew what I'd truly accomplished. It may have taken eight attempts before her, but I did it. There she was. A miracle." Bellanger had grown more animated as he spoke about Fiona, gesturing, face flushed, and he rose to his feet briefly, as if to underscore the magnitude of what he was telling us. "I watched Fiona push a glass off the table without using her hands—gravity itself defied by this tiny girl—I saw her slam doors and start fires without moving a muscle. The entire natural world was bowing down to this scrap of a child. And all I wanted was to protect this miracle at any cost."

"What about the rest of us? You never saw the rest of us as miracles?" I asked it partially to test him, but there was a stubborn hurt behind the words. Bellanger looked at me with a faint surprise, as if he'd never seen it from this angle.

"You thought the eight of us were just expendable," Isabelle said.

"Of course not. I merely trusted that you could fend for yourselves."

"What about the Grassis?" Isabelle asked.

Until now, Bellanger had been studiedly casual, but now I watched as he took some time to compose himself. "So you think you've figured some things out," he said. "But I can promise you don't understand the full truth."

Isabelle persisted. "You let them die, and you used their deaths to hide away."

"Let them die? Angela tried to kill me," he said. "You want to know what happened that night? Angela came into my lab uninvited. She drew a gun on me in front of Fiona. She said she'd spend the rest of her life in prison to play out some revenge fantasy."

"Revenge for what?" asked Cate. She squeezed my hand, a signal. I knew that she was thinking of Lily-Anne. Bellanger hadn't mentioned her yet. She was a clear absence in this story.

"For what? For everything. For paranoid fantasies. Angela had always been an erratic woman. Fiona was getting agitated," Bellanger said. "I tried to warn Angela. I was the only one who noticed when the fire began on the hem of her dress. One little flame. Tiny enough to pinch out with my fingertips. But before I knew it, the fire had grown out of control. It was no normal fire. That little flame was ravenous, insatiable, inevitable. The heat was enough to blaze your skin away. When I looked back, Angela was already burning—Gina too. I couldn't save the Grassis or the others, so I fled with Fiona."

"You didn't even warn us," I said, struck by the impersonality of *the others*. "You didn't warn my mother and me, or Isabelle, or Patricia."

"Yet you survived," Bellanger said. "And I found myself in a strange predicament. If I revealed myself to be alive, I might be accused of murder. If I told the truth about Fiona's abilities, she'd be reviled as a monster. *Fiona* had to be my priority. I had to protect her. I had to nurture her unique abilities. And so I went to . . . a colleague of mine."

Leland Henley, who doctored the autopsy reports, who lied repeatedly to cover up Bellanger's obsessions.

"I took Fiona here, a place I knew nobody would search out. I was presumed dead. The media painted me as Icarus, flying too close to the sun. Down I came, in a blaze of fire and ignominy." For a second his face transformed again, twisted subtly: amusement or regret.

The entire story was a lie. Bullshit. Bellanger had sold the land long before the fire. It was all premeditated. With effort, I made my face soft and receptive, the portrait of a good listener.

Bellanger lifted his voice. "I understand why you resent me, Josephine, but I didn't ask for any of this. It's all because of Fiona. You were always my little helper. More than any of the others, you were curious about what we'd accomplished at the Homestead. You grasped its importance, even as a little girl. You grasp its importance now."

I caught Cate's nervous glance in my peripheral vision. "I'm not sure I do," I said. "You don't know what it's been like for us. Out there without you."

"But Fiona is different," Bellanger said. "She needs me more. Each of you was a miracle, of course, but . . ." Words seemed to fail him for a moment. "With Fiona's conception, I achieved perfection. I couldn't bear to see that success overshadowed and complicated by all the pettiness that had grown at the Homestead. I owed it to her and to the world to rescue her from that."

"From our mothers, you mean," Cate said, her voice a low burn. "You were happy to use their bodies, but not so happy that they stuck around afterwards. Is that it?"

I thought he'd be furious, but he didn't even look at Cate. He folded his hands together under his chin, still addressing me. "Fiona does best with individual instruction. The women—your mothers—they meant well. But Fiona could never have truly thrived under their care, not with her unique needs. I know that now, and I assume they'd recognize it too."

"And all these people?" I asked. "Your isolation hasn't exactly lasted, Dr. Bellanger."

"A light like hers can't be hidden," Bellanger said. "Over the years, we've drawn followers. People who crave something deeper in their lives. Many of the women are a lot like your mothers, seeking a certain optimism. Our community has become an oasis of sorts. Look at the three of you," he said. "Pilgrims yourselves. You understand the allure of a place like this."

"We're here for my mother," I said. "You still haven't told me why she's here."

"I blame Freshwater," Bellanger said, and his voice grew heavier, touched with a sigh. He pressed two fingers into his right temple. "That was our first experiment in venturing beyond the limits of this place—to pay respects to the Grassis. Leaving the home we've created here was hard on Fiona. She lashed out. Unfamiliar environments take a toll on her. The world's exactly the way I remember it, hungry to record any irregularity. Pass it around and stare at it. But they've gotten quicker. I wasn't prepared."

Bellanger sounded old. He'd been hiding for seventeen years. He'd missed out on personal computers, VCR players, camcorders, MTV. He probably didn't know about Kurt Cobain's death, or who he even was. The Berlin Wall toppling. The *Challenger* exploding. Joseph Bellanger had once been a household name, synonymous with progress and change, the bright knife's blade of the future. But now he was outpaced. I felt a strange twist of guilt at seeing him diminished like this, as if I were somehow responsible.

"It was all over the news," Bellanger said. "Then I heard from an associate who told me that Margaret had been contacting him and asking after Fiona." Henley, again. It was Henley who'd set my mother up. Bellanger smiled, baring all his teeth. "I know how stubborn Margaret can be when she sets her mind to something. When we visited her, she begged to come with us. She wanted to see what we'd accomplished."

"But she hadn't packed. She hadn't even let me know she'd be gone," I said carefully. I had the distinct impression that Bellanger was looking at me and seeing someone stupid, willing to accept any lie he handed me.

"She couldn't wait. You know that your mother was never fit for a conventional life."

"And the fire?" I asked, keeping my voice innocent and curious, all light, no dark shadows for accusations to hide behind.

"Well. Fiona's nervous habit again. A parlor trick that went a little out of control, that's all." Bellanger gave a brusque laugh, as if in spite of himself. "I'm sorry that we didn't stay for questioning. In our situation, that's not exactly an option. It felt more important to focus on your mother, and on Fiona."

"Of course," I said, offering a sweet smile. "I get it."

My mother had been fucking kidnapped.

"I never considered the possibility that you'd come after your mother, Josephine," Bellanger was saying. "I thought you two were . . . estranged." A weight on this word that made me inhale, defensive. "But one of our brothers stayed behind to ensure there was no more trouble after Margaret came with us. As Mathias followed you, he understood the pattern. That you were seeking out the others, one by one by one."

"Mathias? Mathias tried to kill us in our sleep," Cate said. "Real charmer you've got there."

"You must understand, the people here are deeply protective of Fiona. They worship her, but they see her fragility too. Especially now that she's with child. Mathias made a well-intentioned mistake. He thought that setting a fire, an act of arson with ordinary causes, might conceal Fiona's hand in the first fire. Perhaps police would assume the fires were due to some follower of Ricky Peters."

And it had worked. How much time had we wasted chasing ghosts? Bonnie's attacker. Ricky Peters. Bobby and Junior. All that time, I could've been focused on finding my mother.

Bellanger shifted, cleared his throat. "When I learned that you were contacting the others, I decided that I'd neglected my other daughters long enough. Fiona is precious to me, yes, but the eight of you are still my creations. I was going to reach out to you soon. But here you are already. A welcome surprise." He smiled, a bright tension caught behind his eyes. There was something cloying and appeasing about the way he offered this to us, a compensating brightness. Bellanger was still stuck back in 1977, assuming that the lightning had only struck in one of our nine bodies. He thought we were the throwaways that had finally led to Fiona's spark of magic. "You do remind me of your mother, Josephine. Always one step ahead. Such a sharp mind."

A sudden tug deep in my breastbone, a longing. I'd always imagined what it would be like if we'd stayed at the Homestead; a glimmer of it had sprouted here, in this lonely desert, just waiting for me. "What have you been doing here?" I asked. "Just . . . working with Fiona?"

"Well, yes. Fiona is the raw material. I've taken this girl, an unformed child, crippled by powers she can't understand, and I've helped her grow. Edison didn't create light—he gave it *form*, he brought it into people's homes until we couldn't function without it. He may as well have invented light. I'm doing the same with Fiona."

"Her pregnancy," I said slowly. "Is she—it's parthenogenetic?" I had to ask if she was a virgin, though both possibilities made me feel sick to my stomach. Beside me, Isabelle stiffened slightly, as if she too were considering the implications.

Bellanger frowned, offended. "You didn't expect me to abandon my work, did you? You of all people, Josephine, can appreciate the true scope of this accomplishment. You can't imagine what a special time this is for us, and here you are—you've arrived right in the middle of it. I want you to consider something," Bellanger said. "If Fiona is powerful, coming from an ordinary woman, what will her child be like? Coming from the womb of a goddess."

Isabelle gave a little gasp next to me. The hairs along the back of my neck and my arms rose.

"Well, it's been nice chatting with you, Dr. Bellanger, but we're here for Margaret. We'd like to speak to her now, if you don't mind," Cate said, slapping her hands down on her thighs. Her sudden briskness was startling, like laughter inside a church.

"I do mind." Bellanger finally acknowledged Cate, face chilly and amused, like a parent dealing with a tantruming child. "Catherine, you seem to misunderstand your role here. You've come to my private land uninvited and unannounced. You've intruded on my property, and now you're making demands of me?" His eyes moved to each of us in turn, a calculation that seemed swift and automatic. Like he could reach into us by sight alone and measure our dimensions. Know our worth. I stared right back at him.

"You three could eventually be an important part of what we do here," he said. "But for now, you're strangers."

Worry stirred, dark and slick, in the pit of my belly. A *part of what we do here.*

"So you're not letting us speak to Margaret," Cate said flatly. "How do we even know she's here? How do we know she's all right?"

"No harm has come to Margaret, trust me," Bellanger said, but he'd grown cooler now. He rose and crossed the room. When he opened the door, I noticed the stranger—Mathias, apparently—standing right outside. He was cradling something diagonally across his chest, and when he turned, I realized with a sick jolt that it was a military rifle.

He glanced around as Bellanger opened the door, and the two of them gave each other quick nods, wordless, before Mathias left. I turned around before Bellanger could see me observing this exchange. My heart was wild inside my chest. Why station a guard outside? Could our conversation have gone a different way? But my fear felt borrowed: the remembered fear of the woman Bellanger thought I was, defenseless and powerless.

"Let's continue this conversation later. Emotions are running high. Catherine and Isabelle, my friend will show you to your quarters so you can rest. You've come a long way."

Cate looked at me. "What about Josephine?"

"I'd like to have a quick word with our Girl One," Bellanger said. "Alone."

I smiled, trying to signal to her that it was okay. I wasn't eager for us to be separated, but maybe Bellanger would let me speak to my mother, or to Fiona. It was a little risk I had to take. Cate must've sensed the same thing. She smiled back. Isabelle's expression was complacent, observing everything as it unfolded. I watched the two of them follow Mathias and my heart clutched. They would be all right, I told myself. They could take care of themselves.

Bellanger didn't move back to his desk. He came to sit near me on the couch. I was constantly surprised by his physical presence. Not just the shock of him existing at all, but how much smaller he was now that I was an adult, so different from the towering presence in my memory. He wasn't any taller than me. The room felt more intimate now that it was just the two of us, like I was in his bedroom. Somewhere I shouldn't be.

"You are very single-minded," he said. "Aren't you? I admire that in you, my Girl One. I've received word of what you're doing, and it makes me quite proud. My colleague shared it with me when we spoke. Dr. Josephine Morrow. Born of scientific ingenuity, now changing the world." Bellanger leaned forward, his voice more familiar. "I'm curious to know: Did you keep any of the letters I wrote you?"

I hesitated, not sure whether I should give him the satisfaction. "Yes," I admitted. "I have them all. Every single one." Confessing this was like unclenching a fist I'd been holding for too long, releasing those memorized words from my heart.

He nodded, pleased. "I wrote those hoping that some of my wisdom would pass on to you, Josephine. I often wondered how I would stay a part of your life. I sometimes wondered if Margaret would even allow me a role. And look at you now."

I stayed quiet.

"What have you been studying in school?" he asked.

"Reproductive medicine." Quickly, haltingly, I told him about the zebrafish in Dr. McCarter's lab. I watched his slight smile, and saw it through his eyes: An experiment so restrained and petty. Retreading familiar ground.

"Impatient to get to work. Just like your father. I can see that you've inherited that same innovative spirit: The desire to guide women, to shape them. To help miracles be born."

I'd been waiting for him to say this to me for so long. His brain re-created in my skull. His soul surviving inside mine. But now his influence didn't feel like a triumph. It felt like a sickness I'd inherited, one I'd cultivated instead of curing. I smiled, bland and daughterly. A watered-down version of the smile I always imagined giving him.

"Should you stay here," he said, "you could take your place as my protégée. My successor. There's a beautiful symmetry to it. I was the beginning of this process, and you'll assist me in finally bringing it to fruition."

This managed to startle me. "What do you mean?"

"I want you here with me again as we move into the next round of parthenogenesis."

"The next round," I repeated.

"Not just Fiona's pregnancy. There are other women here who are eager to take part. Women who are . . . most accommodating of any measures we must take. As a scientist, you should understand how precious an opportunity this is. Well beyond the stingy resources and closed minds you'll find out there in the world." He leaned so close he was nearly touching me. "Girl One, you should be with me."

Here with Bellanger. The sole recipient of his knowledge, working alongside him as an equal. The direct transmission of his genius and ambition into my brain. How many times had I imagined something exactly like this? Compared to the slowness of my work back in Chicago, trying to reinvent the wheel . . . this was exactly what I'd hoped for. All these women, empty and waiting and eager.

When I didn't answer, he went on. "In fact, Josephine, I owe it to you," Bellanger said. "Seeing your ambition laid bare like that reminded me that I couldn't hide forever. You inspired me to return to my original ambitions. Without you, I might've forgotten what led me to do this work in the first place."

"It was me?" I asked. "You're saying that I was behind all this?" A memory of the men at Kithira, the way Black Shoes had insisted that it was all my fault. "So were you proud of me?" I asked impulsively.

He looked at me with a faint surprise, eyebrows raised. "Proud," he repeated, turning it over, considering it from all angles. "Well. I'm not sure it was that simple."

"I always imagined you'd be proud of me. That's why I did it. I thought you were dead, Dr. Bellanger, and it was up to me to unlock parthenogenesis again. For both of us. So were you proud of me? Or were you jealous?"

He leaned back. "You must have heard all kinds of things from the others. I'd caution you against paranoia. I'd have thought, with your scientific mind and your understanding of what's at stake, that you'd embrace this opportunity without letting emotions get in the way." His eyes flicked up and down my body. "Although I shouldn't be surprised, you've spent all this time with Margaret. Getting soft. I suppose my influence can only extend so far."

I pressed my lips together. "Sorry, Dr. Bellanger. I'm not your girl."

"Then I was wrong about you," he said. "Clearly. This was a mistake. A gesture of respect that you're too selfish to understand."

"I came here for my mother," I said, sharper now.

"When the time is right," Bellanger said. "I'll show you to your quarters."

I trailed after Bellanger, back through the dusty, drab grounds of the compound. Now that I knew how long Fiona had been here, it felt smaller, tighter, cramped. Like I couldn't draw a full breath. We passed one of the silent cameras, watching from the top of the fence. I glanced at Bellanger to see if he'd explain, or even acknowledge it, but he didn't slow his pace. The place had gone back to feeling deserted. Like the scattering of people inside the chapel had been a collective dream and they'd dissolved the moment we left.

I could stop him, I thought. I could command him to tell me where my mother was. I could make him take me to Cate and Isabelle. Unlock the gates. We could leave right now.

But Fiona. What about Fiona? She would still be here with him.

The two of us passed a small house, barely larger than a shed: a girl, a teenager, was walking out, pausing to stare when she saw us. I looked past her and through the half-open door. What I saw made me nearly stop in my tracks. I forced myself to keep going. Guns: a shiny, spiky clutter of them, leaning against the walls, lined up along the floor. The girl pulled the door shut behind her, expression calm, as if there were nothing strange about the room she'd just left.

I took a deep breath. There was a firearm for every person I'd seen at the compound so far, easily. A calculation that curdled in my stomach. What was Bellanger doing here? *The world is nearly ready for us.* What he had meant was that they were nearly ready for the world. They were preparing for war.

48

After his pitch to me, Bellanger saw Cate and Isabelle in turn. Mathias would knock on the door, escort one girl away, return her after a tense hour. We slept fitfully that night, and when we woke up, the door wouldn't give.

"It's locked," Isabelle said, trying the knob, then falling back onto the bed. She didn't sound surprised, and Cate and I only nodded. Alone in our quarters—a simple, windowless room, outfitted with a couple of mattresses on the floor, a bare bulb, not much else—the true seriousness of the situation clinched around us.

"What did he talk to you about?" I asked Cate.

"He kept bringing up my mother's 'alternative healing.'" She rolled her eyes. "Pretty sure that asshole was trying to convince me to stay. He said I'd be able to look after the women here. Be his little nurse. He was getting pretty mad when I didn't just fold."

I kissed her shoulder, taking in the sweet, almost smoky scent at the nape of her neck. It made me happy to imagine Bellanger faced with the cool wall of Cate's disinterest.

"Yeah, well, he told me that I would be his protégée. His successor." I turned to Isabelle. "What did he offer you, Isabelle? Money? Power?"

"Nothing," she said. "He just asked me about my body."

This managed to shut me up for a moment. Cate took over. "What about your body?"

"He asked me if I had regular periods. How many days there were between periods. He listened to my heart and felt here." She gripped her neck. The spot where her thyroid was tucked.

Cate and I exchanged uneasy glances. The plain physicality of this was more disturbing than Bellanger trying to appeal to my pride or Cate's kindness.

Rising, I tried the door again. "I'm sorry," I said. "This is all my fault." I kept thinking of everything we'd left in the Volvo, now out there in the desert, vulnerable. The guns Cate didn't even have that option to defend herself this time.

"We knew it'd be dangerous. We're here for your mother," Cate said.

"It's not just my mother anymore," I said. "There's Fiona to consider. Now that we're here, we can't leave without her." It was the first time I'd put it into words, and the truth of it sank in. "But I don't think she'll come easily."

"Why wouldn't she?" Cate asked. "Who would want to be here with this creep?"

"I didn't see him as a creep," I said softly. "Not for years and years."

"Hey," Cate said, catching the pain in my voice, and she got up, wrapped her arms around me, kissed the top of my head. "Listen. We'll play this safe if it means getting Fiona out of here with us. If you have a plan, I'm all ears."

"Bellanger doesn't know that we have powers. He thinks we're just eight duds who came before Fiona. You heard him. *Not fashioned from the same cloth.*"

"I noticed that too," Cate said. "If he'd known about our powers, he would've been yammering on and on about them. That's good, though. That could work to our advantage."

I looked to Isabelle; she shrugged. "He never even asked me."

"Mathias never got close enough," I said. "He didn't expect to see our powers and so he didn't even look for them. Just like Junior."

"Then we can overpower them," Isabelle said. "I grab the guard, and Josie, you tell Bellanger to stand down. Simple. We find your mother, we find Fiona, and we leave with them."

"She has a point," Cate said.

"It's not as easy as Freshwater," I said. "There are a lot more people here. There are weapons . . ." I quickly explained what I'd seen. "They're all under Bellanger's spell. Not to mention Fiona. If she's against us, it could be ugly. We didn't have to worry about her in Texas." That bird spiraling toward the ground, eaten by flame; the way her unseen power suffused everything here. "This is my mother, not yours," I said. "I've asked so much of you two. If you want to leave . . . then . . . I understand. If anything happened to you because of me? I couldn't—"

"We aren't leaving," Isabelle said, before Cate could speak. Her voice was assured and steady. "I've been thinking about why I couldn't find my powers. I was trying everything. I put myself through enough trauma, didn't I? And I wanted to be powerful. I wasn't like the rest of you. I *knew* what I could be. I *knew*." The first time I'd seen her: lying in that creek, the water braiding through her hair, lips gone blue from the cold. "That should have been more than enough. So why did my powers only come when I met you and Cate?"

Cate and I watched her, not speaking. My throat hurt with unshed tears.

"You fought those men for me," Isabelle said. "I knew when I called them there that you'd be on my side. I was never afraid because I knew I'd have you two with me. So Cate and I are doing the same for you now. Because you're my power. You and Cate." She reached for my hand. "We can do this. Easy."

There was a knock at the door. It had to be afternoon now, time passing restlessly and sluggishly. All three of us straightened, instantly alert. Mathias stood at the doorway. He beckoned to me. "Girl One." His voice was low, like he had to conserve it carefully. "She wants to see you."

"My mother?" I asked, half rising.

"No. Fiona."

My disappointment was replaced by a keen curiosity. Fiona. My lost sister, the one I'd never expected to talk to again. I had more questions for her than I'd had for any of the others.

Outside, the blue sky was startling against the oranges and reds of the desert. We moved through the quiet labyrinth of buildings. I watched for the particular shed that had housed all the guns, making a small note of it at the back of my mind when we passed.

Then I stopped. Fiona stood just ahead of us with her brilliant hair glowing painfully in the sun. Instinctively I imagined touching her hair, how hot it would feel under my fingertips. She wore a simple white dress, her belly almost concealed by the volume of the skirt. But I looked for the swell, wanting to see proof of Bellanger's next step. When I glanced up, Fiona gave me a small and knowing smile.

"Josephine," she said. "I'm glad you came. Father thought it might do us some good to have a little chat." She held out a hand. I was shaken by the easy way she said *Father*, a possessive term that even Junior hadn't used. "I usually walk the grounds every day for exercise. Walk with me."

I let her guide me as we went behind the nearest building and began walking the ersatz alleyway, the thin space between the buildings and the fence. The whole desert stretched out beyond the chain-link. "Is he coming too?" I asked softly, jerking my head at Mathias, who trailed us a foot behind, a faithful shadow. Close enough to eavesdrop.

"He's just here to offer extra protection. You don't mind, do you?"

The way she spoke. It was uncanny to hear Bellanger's old-fashioned, pretentious talk mirrored in her teenage girl's voice. She'd never picked up the little tics and quickly evolving, snappy slang that circulated through public school hallways, phone calls, cable TV. She channeled one man perfectly, uninterrupted and uncorrupted. His voice in her mouth. "It's fine," I said. "I'm used to that guy following me. Feels like old times." Mathias's expression was unmoved. "What do you want to talk about?"

We walked slowly, past the silent, shuttered windows, our feet stirring the dust. I wondered if my mother was behind one of those windows, and it was all I could do not to stare into each window, calling her name. I took a deep, aching breath.

"I want to request that you stay here," Fiona said. "Father confided in me about your confrontation yesterday. He thought I'd better be able to explain things from the feminine perspective."

"The feminine perspective," I said. "Okay."

"We weren't born to be ordinary," Fiona said. "I know you aren't like me, but you are powerful in your own way. Father is the only one who truly understands what we're capable of. He knew us inside and outside before we were even born. He was the very first to imagine us."

"That's not true. Our mothers imagined us before Bellanger ever got around to it." But Fiona just kept smiling, as if she knew something I didn't. "Doesn't Bellanger ever talk about your mother?" I pressed. "Aren't you curious about her? Lily-Anne. Because I remember her."

"That was a very long time ago," Fiona said, but there was the tiniest hesitation when she said it, a door left cracked open.

"Your mother would've wanted to know all about you," I said. "She was so curious. And she was brave. She wanted you for a long time before you arrived. When I was little, she'd braid my hair and play hopscotch with me, and she'd tell me how much she wanted a daughter of her own. The protesters scared most of our mothers, but not Lily-Anne. She'd scream right back at them if they got too loud. She'd have done anything to protect you."

Fiona's mouth twitched slightly. She blinked. "Father thought highly of her."

"Bellanger always did think highly of our mothers."

I wasn't sure if Fiona was able to detect the sarcasm. Maybe she hadn't learned it yet. But she looked at me sidelong. "Why do you take so much issue with Father?" Then she laughed, half to herself. "Well. Besides the obvious reason."

"What's that?"

"That you're jealous of me." A hot pinch tucked in there. "How close I am to him. You were Girl One for so long, the only one who mattered. Father warned me that this might happen."

I remembered blithely calling Bellanger my *brainfather* in that *Rolling Stone* interview, how easy that devotion had felt, and I wanted to laugh and cry. "You're right that this is a—a big change for me," I said. "For most of my life, Bellanger's just been old letters, and now he's—"

"Oh yes, those letters he sent you. I've heard all about those." Fiona's contempt took on an eagerness, like this was a point she'd wanted to make to me for years. "But you should know, those aren't anything special. He wrote to everyone. He wrote to the Grassis too."

"The Grassis?" I feigned disinterest. "What did he want to say to them?"

"The same trivial niceties he wrote to you, I'm sure. That's why we were in Freshwater, actually. Looking for the letter. He couldn't find it."

I swallowed. The sunlight pressed into my eyes like a headache. Bellanger had been looking for something in Freshwater, then. Not to *pay respects*. What could he have written to Angela Grassi, or to her daughter Gina, that would worry him so many years later? A lifetime later. It wasn't just *trivial niceties*.

I remembered what Ricky Peters had said. The way the woman with the gun that night—Angela, it must have been Angela—had claimed that her daughter was under Bellanger's spell. What if he'd written something to Gina? Or threatened Angela that Gina would always be under his shadow, within his grasp?

Maybe . . . maybe the words in that letter had lured Angela out of the life she'd been building in Freshwater. It sounded as if she'd been happy in Texas, content with Gina, looking for new opportunities. Maybe she hadn't returned to Vermont in a sudden rage; maybe she had been summoned.

"Fiona," I said. "What do you remember about the night of the fire? Bellanger's always told you that Angela Grassi returned that night to kill him, right?"

"She was hysterical." Fiona's mouth twitched, contemptuous. "She started the whole thing. If she hadn't threatened Father, I wouldn't have started the fire. We wouldn't have had to go into hiding. All of this was her fault."

Everything Fiona was saying had the eerie quality of Bellanger ventriloquizing through her. A bedtime story he'd fed her. Angela as jealous and grasping, destroying the Homestead even if she had to burn along with it.

"But what if Angela only came back to the Homestead because she felt like she had to?" I said carefully. "What if that letter was Bellanger making sure Angela and Gina would return?"

"Why on earth would he do that?" Impatient, dismissive. Fiona hadn't moved her hand from mine, and it was starting to grate, that little nagging pressure pulling at me.

"It was a setup." I had to walk slowly, speak slowly, not hurrying ahead with the train of my thoughts. "Bellanger already wanted to go into hiding. It was his plan. He destroyed the Homestead on purpose so that he could vanish more easily." I lowered my voice. "He murdered Angela and Gina in cold blood, and he wanted you to think that you were to blame."

Fiona didn't react. She was so blank that I thought maybe she hadn't heard me, my words just evaporating in the unbearable blaze of sunlight. I remembered Mathias with a sick sinking in my gut; when I glanced back, his expression was implacable. I'd gotten so caught up in the realization itself that I'd forgotten about his constant, quiet surveillance.

Then Fiona spoke. "You're wrong. You don't know him at all. You were only six when he disappeared, weren't you? A mere child. Now you have an idea of him in your head that's built out of lies and gossip. I know the real man. He wept for the Grassis. He'd never hurt anyone intentionally."

Frustrated, I tried to gauge how much Fiona would even understand. All the little calculations that had gone into Bellanger's planning, lost on someone as sheltered as her. "How did he manage to forge the autopsy reports? How did he steal you away to this commune? He schemed and he lied about so many things—about your mother—" *About your sister,* I wanted to say. *About their deaths.* But I reminded myself of Mathias, listening. Not now. I'd already said too much.

"I appreciate what you're doing, even if your lies are quite twisted," Fiona said benevolently. "You want to save me from my guilt, but I made peace with that long ago. Seventeen years ago, I did something terrible. For years, my powers were completely out of my control, but now look at me." She shut her eyes briefly and tilted her head back, as if to give me a better chance to take her in. "Father gave up everything, just to give me a chance to redeem myself. I'm not like you. I don't have to play the damsel in distress and blame him for my weaknesses."

"Your whole life has been in the middle of nowhere, performing for him. He doesn't love you the way a father loves a daughter. I know what a parent's love looks like. Bellanger loves you like a—like a warden loves a prisoner." I remembered the stockpile of weapons. "He loves you the way a coward loves a gun."

We walked. The predictable sharp turn. Another long stretch of alleyway, the backs of buildings, the lonely desert. This was Fiona's daily exercise. Looking out at the same barren stretch of the desert that held her captive, day after day after day. I imagined her in Freshwater, looking around at the wide, wide world, understanding her place in it, and lashing out, stretching into the sky and stopping all those flutter-quick pulses.

"Maybe Bellanger isn't helping you control yourself at all," I said. "Maybe he's holding you back—"

"Holding me back?" Fiona interrupted. Anger and fear compressing her voice into a tight near-whisper. "You have no idea who I am now, do you? I'm— wait."

She turned around abruptly, yanking at my wrist. Mathias paused, caught midstride. He looked from one of us to the other, searching, but Fiona was imperious. "Leave us. Now."

The sudden authority in her voice gave me a prickle of discomfort.

Mathias made a tentative protest. "Dr. Bellanger instructed me to—"

"Do you answer to Dr. Bellanger, or to me? Leave us now, or I can make things very difficult for you."

He hesitated, then stood firm. "My duty is to stay here. For your safety."

Fiona turned away from him. "You need to see," she said to me, a manic light in her eyes. "Of course you don't appreciate what Father's done when you haven't seen proof."

"What are you saying?"

In response, Fiona stepped toward Mathias. Her face changed. Her eyes slid upward, irises vanishing, to reveal a waiting blankness, slippery and fish-belly pale in her face. That picture on the altar, the empty-eyed goddess. Mathias made a small movement, like he was starting to run. All the times I'd let this man rule my imagination, haunt my every move, and now we stood here under the desert sun and he was completely helpless.

Then I was sinking—down, down, into the sand, and Mathias was a dark spot hovering above me. The soles, the heavy black soles of his boot. Fiona was rooted to the spot, head tilted upward. Mathias was rising into the air, a balloon released from a child's hand.

I remembered what Cate's mother had told her: *A girl who didn't have to use her hands the way people did, because her hands were in the air all around her.* Mathias was suspended above us, blank-faced, not fighting. Ten, twelve feet above the ground. Part of the landscape. A fly hanging invisible inside a spiderweb.

A guilty part of me wanted to see what came next. I wanted to see how she'd grown since she was a little girl crying for her mother. But I forced myself to speak. "Fiona, I already know that you're powerful. There's no need for this."

"He tried to kill you," Fiona said. "What do you care what happens to him?"

I couldn't answer. Something was happening now. A small flame, a bright spark shimmering on his shoulder. It looked like a reflection of the sun, a pale dot. But quickly, too quickly, it spread along the seams of his clothing, a blaze hot enough that I stepped back, the warmth touching my skin. Fire. It wreathed his arm, twisting. She was controlling it, a live wire that she was playing with. Then she let go, and the fire spread.

He screamed, an animal cry that wrenched something in me, nausea pushing up my throat. Hanging there, he was as bright as a planet. A star. I thought of that bird, evaporating into nothingness. Into ashes. Mathias's screams were low and keening, outside of his control.

"Fiona, you don't have to do this," I said. The fire that night in Arkansas seemed so long ago now. Ancient, meaningless history. I didn't have any desire to see this man punished, not now. Not standing here on the property of the man who'd kidnapped my mother, stolen my youngest sister, and lied to me.

Fiona didn't seem to hear. "Please," I said. "Please." Then her eyes slid back into place, her pupils startling and wet inside her face, and she blinked several times.

Mathias fell from the sky, the laws of physics returning. He landed with an animal thump, the dull pop of submerged injuries. Bones cracking. But the fire was still spreading, eating away at his arm, crawling up his shoulder. It no longer had that delicate, twisting quality, the visible marker of Fiona's control. It was an ordinary blaze now, hungry and indiscriminate.

"Put it out," I yelled to Fiona. "He's going to die. Put it out—just—control it."

"I can't," she said, looking at me like I'd suggested something ridiculous.

I looked around wildly. There was a heavy, dusty tarp crumpled near one of the houses that hemmed us in. I tossed it over Mathias, yelling at him to *move*. I tried to push at his unfamiliar bulk. He managed to roll, a slow, sluggish movement. When I pulled the tarp away, I was so relieved to see the fire extinguished that the other details didn't stand out right away. The air smelled ripe, that acid smell of smoke and seared skin that had followed me since I was six years old and running—running—

I breathed tightly. The skin of his arm was raw and red, wet-looking, the clothing fused to his flesh in patches. But his chest rose and fell, a rough rhythm of breath. He was alive. For now, he was alive.

Fiona's eyes moved past me, her face suddenly softening. The manic shine snapped away, making her seem younger and more uncertain. Even before I turned around, I knew that he'd be there. Bellanger stood back near the corner of a nearby building. He was smiling.

I stood still, breathing hard.

Fiona moved to Bellanger. She held out her hand, and he reached into his pocket and pulled out that bottle. Neat, perfunctory, he tipped loose a capsule, crimson as a drop of blood, and again placed it in the center of her palm. She brought her hand to her mouth and shut her eyes. Just like they had in the chapel, the first time I'd seen them together.

Those bright red capsules. I watched as a serenity fell over Fiona, like she was just climbing into bed for a long sleep. "What are you giving her?" I asked. "What are those?"

"Fiona's powers can take a lot out of her. We've found that this medication can settle her nerves." He slipped the bottle back into its hiding place.

"But she's pregnant." I swallowed against the sourness in my throat. "You have to be careful about contraindications. Those pills aren't—"

"Don't you think I'm careful with my own daughter?" He took a step toward me. Just a step. But something in his face made me step back. A clumsy, primal retreat that I instantly regretted. My heart pounded in my chest. This raw anger wasn't exactly a shock to me anymore, but it hurt to see it in his face, directed at me. I'd loved Bellanger once.

Over his shoulder, Fiona watched us, her face expressionless.

When I returned to our room, Cate rushed for me, grabbed me gently around the waist. I hadn't felt faint until she touched me like that, and then abruptly my knees slipped and I realized I was shaky. "Jesus, what did Fiona say?" Cate asked, close in my ear. "You look like you've seen a ghost."

"We might be in over our heads," I said, leaning into her. "I couldn't get through to her. Fiona was so little when she came here. A baby. Bellanger has done everything he can to keep control over her. And if he'd treat *her* this way, I have no idea what he's done to my mother."

When Cate and Isabelle were both silent, I pulled back to look at them. Their expressions held a strange determination, grim and excited at once: Isabelle's eyes were shining, while Cate's forehead was creased with worry. I knew that face. She didn't want to tell me something, her reluctance as bright as a beacon. "What?" I asked, urgent.

"Listen, Josie," Cate said. "Isabelle's figured out where your mother is."

A hard jolt of hope pulled me upright and out of Cate's arms. I wondered if the hope would ever stop feeling this fresh, so new it was painful.

"We were passing the little chapel," Isabelle said. "The guard was taking me back after I spoke with Bellanger. We passed by the place with the altar and the candles. I saw someone walking out of it with a tray of food. Half-eaten food."

My heart clenched. "Okay, that could be something. But we don't know—"

"There's more," Isabelle said, and I fell silent. "I heard your voice. It confused me because I thought maybe you'd escaped and followed me. But when I looked around I didn't see you anywhere. It must've been her. Your mother."

My voice, conjured out of my mother's throat in the middle of this strange and lonely place. "What did she say?" I asked.

Isabelle hesitated. "She said, 'Please.' Just that one word. 'Please.'"

The chapel. I'd stood only a few feet away from my mother and not even known she was there. Maybe she'd caught a trace of my voice when I spoke. Maybe she'd called out to me and I hadn't heard her. Hidden in plain sight. *Please.*

I looked at Cate and Isabelle, these faces I'd come to love so much, reminding myself what we were capable of. Being here and hiding our true selves had started to wear me down, but now I was reminded of all that power brimming under our surfaces. "All right," I said. "Let's get my mother the hell out of here. It's time."

Isabelle broke into a grin, but Cate was more cautious. She squared her shoulders back. "What about Bellanger's little army? You know how much I want to get out of here, but we've got to plan this carefully—I don't want any more loss."

"I have a plan." It had spun in the back of my mind, held together with thin, shining threads of hope and recklessness. "It's time to show them what we can do."

"Then I'm in," said Cate.

"Me too," said Isabelle at once.

"Fiona can start fires. We know that much. But what I learned today," I said, "is that she can't put them out."

49

We'd waited until late at night, or as close to late night as we could gauge in the windowless limbo of our room. I knew we needed to hold off until only a few people were still awake. The hours crawled by with agonizing slowness. Every time I thought it was late enough, I made myself wait, counting down the minutes in my head.

When I was reasonably sure it was past midnight—the noises outside had settled, the darkness at the edge of the door had thickened—I'd listened at the door for footsteps passing by outside. I didn't want to attract a group. My target was just one person, walking alone. I waited until I heard light, faltering footsteps and then gestured to Cate and Isabelle, my pulse taking off. We were going to get out of here.

Isabelle had volunteered to be the bait. She banged the soft side of her fist on the door. "Help," she yelled, mouth close to the door. "We need help. I'm bleeding." She sounded tear-stained, ragged with fear. I had to fight the urge to rush to her side even though I was in here with her, able to see her whole and unhurt. "Can someone please help us?"

The three of us waited. Seconds ticked by, broken only by the convincing shudder of Isabelle's faked sobs. Maybe it wouldn't work. They didn't care if we were bleeding. Then: keys in the lock. The door swinging open, tentatively, revealing a wedge of silky black sky, punctured everywhere with stars. A woman with her gray-blond hair tied into an elaborate braid. She peered inside, face creased with concern.

Reaching for the woman's mind, I spoke. It was a wild relief to become this version of myself again, like stretching a sore muscle. "Walk inside," I said. "Give us the key. Don't make any noise," I added, as her mouth twitched against my order.

The woman walked into the room. Mutely, she handed the key to Isabelle. Isabelle grazed her hand against the woman's wrist, the lightest stroke of her fingertips. The woman's eyes rolled back; she crumpled to her knees. "Don't worry," Isabelle said to us. "I was gentle. It was just enough to knock her out for a while."

"You can do that?" Cate asked.

"I'm getting better," Isabelle said.

Without being asked, the two of us hurried over, lifting the woman's body between us, carrying her to the bed, and laying her down gently. Isabelle had been telling the truth. The woman still looked healthy, cheeks flushed faintly, chest rising and falling.

I peered outside, looked left and right: nobody. The compound was dark, peppered with only a few lit windows. We went outside into the surprising coolness. The air was so dry that the heat of the day slid right off, dissolving into a chill. Isabelle locked the door behind us. We stuck close to the shadows as we moved toward the chapel.

Near the center of the compound, I paused abruptly. We were right between our targets now. To the due east, the chapel and my mother. To the west, the shed with its arsenal.

"We split up here. Don't argue," I said, over Cate's protest. "It's the best way to do this. You don't need to wait with me while I rescue my mother. It will be quicker if the distraction is already happening when I've got her. By the time they even realize my mother is gone we'll be halfway out of this state." I could already feel the wild pull of freedom in my bones. "You have them, right?"

"Yup." Cate reached into her jeans pocket and pulled out the plain little book of matches. The matches that Orange Shirt had intended to use to burn the evidence his violence left behind.

"You two go ahead, start the fire while the coast is clear," I said. "We'll join you as quickly as we can." Using the plural noun gave me a sudden bloom of optimism. My mother and me, finally back together. One unit.

"I don't like splitting apart, Morrow, you know that—" Cate said.

"I know, and I'm sorry. But we've got to take some risks to pull this off. We don't have much time." I lowered my voice. "This is the last time, Cate. This is the last time we're going to have to do this, and whatever happens next, we'll be together. I swear."

Cate's resistance softened. We kissed, deeply, everything compressed into the points where our bodies met. "Just hurry," she whispered.

When Cate walked ahead, I grabbed Isabelle's elbow and pulled her closer. "Listen. If we don't come back soon enough? Burn this place to the ground and then get out, and get Cate out too. Please, Isabelle." I locked eyes with her. "Leave him with nothing."

"Of course," Isabelle said, like any other option was too stupid to entertain.

I watched the two of them as they walked away from me. Cate with her confident lope, head held high even at a time like this, like she'd rise up into the sky on the next footfall. Isabelle hurrying to keep up with Cate's long stride. I watched until they vanished around a corner. Then I turned. For the first time since Kansas, I was totally alone. I was going to find my mother.

Bellanger's house loomed out of the shadows. As I walked past those darkened windows, I could almost feel his presence right behind them, my whole body on high alert. I could only hope he was asleep. Dead to the world, complacent in his belief that he had us trapped. Fiona was in there somewhere too, swaddled by pills. My stomach cramped. She seemed so incredibly alone.

The chapel was different. It looked smaller now, as if Bellanger's presence inside the space had made it physically larger. I tried the door; unlocked. I slipped inside. Most of the candlelight was extinguished now, only one votive candle standing alone at the far end of the space, sending its bright, tattered shadow up the wall and against the ceiling.

There was one other person in the chapel, leaning his back against the wall, half drowsing. A young man, face shadowed from the candlelight. Like Mathias, he wore a gun slung over his chest. I approached the young man without hesitation. Like I belonged here. The guard barely had time to react—he scrambled upright, glancing around like he expected to see somebody with me. His face stuttered into confusion when he realized I was alone.

"I'm here to see Margaret Morrow," I said.

His eyes darted to the door next to the altar. "You're not—did he send you? Nobody's supposed to talk to her until—" He stopped, his mouth tightening. "You shouldn't be here."

"Unlock that door," I said, soft yet authoritative. Instantly he turned, fumbling in his pockets for a key ring. He was young, barely my age. Rabbit-like features and dark hair. I wondered why he was here, in a makeshift chapel in the middle of the desert, giving up sleep to watch over a prisoner. Was he drawn to the mythology surrounding Fiona? Or the promise and authority surrounding Bellanger?

Cate and Isabelle must've already reached the shed. Its secret stockpile of guns and ammunition, a dormant explosion that could be nudged along by the single swipe of a match. "Tell me if you have the key to unlock the main gate," I said.

"Yes," he said. "I have it."

"Then you're going to wait here," I said. "Wait here, until I'm ready for you. Stay quiet." I walked into the darkness that held my mother.

"Mom?" The air in this little room was warm and sour, twice as thick as normal air. No windows.

"Mom?" I called again. By now I'd arrived at so many doorsteps, crossed endless county lines, always half believing my mother would be waiting on the other side. I'd been chasing the scraps of her left behind on notebook pages, on answering machines, trapped in other people's memories. I stood inside this sweltering space. A small room near the back of the chapel, the door to the side of the altar that I'd barely noticed before. My hand shaking, I held up the votive candle I'd stolen from the altar, the glass burning my palm. The guttering flame revealed piles of boxes, blankets, dust-frosted and haphazard. Maybe she wasn't here either. Maybe Isabelle had been imagining things. My mother was gone, and I had to get out of here—

From the back of the room, she rose. Margaret Morrow. Mother One. My mother. The last time I'd seen her, she'd stood on our porch and waved goodbye, both of us awkward and uncertain as I stepped into Bellanger's future. She was different now. In the dreamlike lighting, I could see that her face was older, hollowed and thin, her hair threaded with gray at the temples. Her lower face was distorted: I realized that she'd been gagged, a dark cloth tied tight around her mouth. I set the candle down, trembling too hard to trust myself with it.

She began moving toward me, uneven. Her hands were tied too. I hurried toward her, reached behind her to grapple with the knots. My own hands trembled so hard I could barely work the knots loose, but then they gave. I pulled away the gag, and something in my chest unclenched too. My mother drew a deep, trembling breath. "Josephine," she said. Her voice. My voice. "My baby."

I pulled her into a tight embrace, and we stood there, the same exact height, our heads nestled onto each other's shoulders, our bodies shaking as she cried. I swallowed back my tears; I couldn't stop smiling. My gratitude was fierce and huge and it filled every part of me. Our identical heartbeats were pressed together. As I'd gotten older, my mother and I had become more and more distant. By the time I'd left for Chicago, we'd rationed our physical contact to a quick peck on the cheek or a functional, fleeting touch to catch each other's attention. This felt like making up for lost time.

Of the nine women who'd given birth at the Homestead, only three were still alive now, my mother among them. I wanted to drink her in. It was the first time I'd met Margaret Morrow as she really was.

"You're a fucking idiot, Josephine." My mother pulled back too soon. She grabbed my face in both her hands and shook me. Her tearstained face was terrified. "You shouldn't be here. You have to get out now."

My mother's fierceness scared me. The sheer desperation on her face. "I was hoping—I was praying every day—that he wouldn't bring you here," my mother said. "The things he plans to do to you—"

"But I came here to find you," I said.

"—And then you show up here by yourself. Just saving him the time." She glanced toward the door, her face haunted. "Why are you here? He refused to let me talk to you. Did he change his mind, or . . . ?"

"I'm here to get you out. But you have to tell me, Mom." The word

Mom felt so right, clicking my world back into a recognizable pattern. "What was he planning to do to us?"

She searched my eyes. "He didn't tell you. Of course not. That fucking coward." She exhaled heavily. "Joseph wants to find the others. All of you Girls. Bring you back together again, on his terms. He's fixated on the fact that you're returning to his work, Josie. It hurts his pride to see you getting all the attention. I don't think he predicted the possibility that you would displace him. He thought we'd just vanish once he abandoned us. And now he wants you to be the next phase of his experiment."

My blood ran cold. Not the scientist, then, but the guinea pig.

My mother continued, "He's been trying on the women here and it hasn't worked. There've been so many losses. So much blood and pain. Terrible problems. He can't do it."

My lower belly cramped, an awareness of my dormant uterus. The size of a fist. His offer to make me his successor had been an empty ploy—his brusque examination of Isabelle, sizing up her body, was closer to the truth. It'd been a long time since I'd been the subject. That Bellanger would do this to me—that he saw me as a means to an end, saw me no differently than the men in Kithira had—

"But Fiona," I managed. "She's pregnant. It worked with her." Half a question.

"Yes," my mother said, urgent. "Exactly. Fiona's pregnant, and only Fiona. He's convinced that he can only create virgin births in certain bodies. *Our* bodies. The nine bodies he lost. And how does he get those bodies back? Through—"

"Through the daughters," I finished for her.

"Exactly."

I'd seen our mothers' past resurrected in our identical bodies over and over during the past few weeks. The heartbreak and disgust hit me so hard that for a second my own body was heavy around me. Bellanger hadn't wanted my brain or Cate's heart. He only wanted what lay inside us, all the tangled hope and beautiful fearsomeness of our interiors. I knew how much people wanted to control what we held inside ourselves, and how much people feared it running wild.

I'd feared it too. I'd wanted to control it too.

"Why did you never tell me about him, Mom?" I heard my child-hood self creep into my voice, that old sadness and earnestness. "I know everything now. If you'd just trusted me sooner—"

"Joseph had such a hold over you. He was cradling you in his arms before the umbilical cord was cut. That was the first time I really thought: *What have I done?* I was so naïve." Her voice dropped lower. "I hurt those women. The Mothers. I brought a wolf right into our midst. The guilt nearly drove me crazy sometimes. What he did to Patricia Bishop, especially . . ." In the flickering light of the votive candle, she flushed. "He was so cold to her. He was jealous of her, knew how im-portant she was to me. Bellanger took every opportunity to make her feel excluded."

"Why didn't you tell me about you and her?"

"Back then it wasn't so easy to be open about loving another woman. But Bellanger knew. He dangled it over my head that he could always tell the press about our relationship. It could've made it much harder to fight his custody claims, if he decided he wanted you or Isabelle. I just learned to keep quiet. I didn't want to expose Trish like that."

"But you could've told me," I said. "He was dead, as far as we knew."

"You were just a kid, and it was hard on you, and I—I felt so guilty for abandoning her. I could barely let myself think about it. Then years pass, and it's easier to just let things lie, and suddenly you're turning into a young woman who's starry-eyed over Joseph. Just like watching a younger version of myself brought to life. When I pushed back, I came across as bitter. I'd done so much to have a daughter of my own, and here I was, with a child who loved her fake father more than me."

I began to protest, then realized how flimsy and insulting it would sound. Any time my mother had even brushed against a disapproval of Bellanger—even her silence, the absence of praise—I'd been a little more willing to see her as resentful, sour, unable to appreciate his glow-ing greatness.

I fumbled in the dark for her hands and traced the hinge of her fingers.

"Even your name," my mother went on. "He asked me to name you after him, and how could I say no? He'd helped us. So you were

Josephine. His namesake. I'd wanted to give you the name Trish and I loved the most."

"Isabelle," I said softly. At some point, I'd have to tell my mother about Patricia's death, but not now. Not while she was this vulnerable. "But in the end, he never wanted any of us except Fiona," I said.

"His want is a dangerous thing," my mother said.

"I thought you were the one who killed him. I thought you burned the whole place down." That image of my mother that had haunted me for weeks: her eyes shining as we ran, that wild joy.

"I wanted to," my mother said. "I could see a future where all nine of you belonged to him. Destroying the whole damn place seemed like the best way, but I couldn't do it in the end. It was a relief when the fire happened anyway. We could start over. Anywhere at all. I thought I was protecting you by never revisiting the past, but my silence only protected Joseph. Josephine, I failed you."

I shook my head, throat thickening with tears. "No," I managed. "No, I—"

From outside, a sudden, muffled shout. My mother flinched. I stayed very still, listening, holding up one finger—another shout, a rise of voices. Then one word resolved from the fray, shouted again and again. *Fire.* My heart jumped: They'd already done it. Isabelle had lived up to her promise.

My mother spoke in a strained whisper. "Are they coming for us?"

"There's a fire," I said crisply. "We have to go now."

"Oh god, Fiona—" My mother shrank back deeper into the cramped room, moving automatically, as if her body had memorized every inch. "We can't upset her, Josie—"

"No, no, it's all right," I soothed. "It wasn't Fiona, it was us. It's part of our plan. We're getting you out of here, okay?" Grabbing the votive candle, I started toward the door. I was eager to take a full breath again. The air in here was like a cloth clamped over my face.

"It's too dangerous," my mother said, and the fear in her voice broke my heart. "Have you seen what Fiona can do? I never forgot what she was like as a child. I used to dream about it." I paused, breath catching in my chest. "I thought whatever it was—whatever was different about

Fiona—went with her. When you were growing up, I watched you for hints of it—I almost wanted—"

Slowly, I turned. My mother had been just like me. She'd been waiting quietly for some spark of magic to manifest in my blood. The two of us yearning for the same thing without ever speaking a word about it, carrying out our lives of homework, leftovers, card games.

I made a swift decision. "I've seen what she can do. But you haven't seen what I can do."

It took a moment for her to understand my meaning. My mother stared at me, searching my face, something opening up behind her eyes. Relief. Wonder. Fear. "Does Joseph know?"

I shook my head. "We have a plan. You'll have to trust me."

I held on to my mother's elbow, unwilling to lose the physical contact. In the main chapel, the darkness expanded and changed shape, huge and cool compared to the prison. My mother stumbled at the doorway, like she wasn't accustomed to even this much space. I caught her, silently counting the days since she'd vanished. Three weeks of captivity.

With my free hand, I held up the candle in its glass shell, throwing a wavering wedge of radiance along the empty pews. Out here, the chaos swelled louder, the shouts and screams cutting more sharply. I imagined that trail of flame slowly eating its way up the walls of the shed. The anticipation of the explosion was a hard bubble in the pit of my stomach, rising and rising. I started toward the front of the chapel. "We need to get to—"

Something was wrong. The guard. The guard was gone. I'd told him to stay right here.

Before I could fully react to the implications of this, the room was illuminated in a swoop: all the candles that ringed the edges of the room flickered to life, one by one by one, a glittering wave. It only took a few seconds, barely the space of a blink. A part of my brain stood back and recognized the simple magic of all these flames springing to life without a source. Beautiful.

The chapel was blazing with brightness now, my own candle useless in my palm. I kept clutching it anyway, as if it could anchor me to something familiar. A shout crested above the noise outside. Too close.

Beside me, my mother tensed. "You're here," she said, and she didn't sound surprised. Her voice was stretched with a resigned fear, well worn.

Bellanger stood at the back of the chapel, a half smile on his face, staring right at me. His gaze was so pointed, cutting right through everything, through the heat and the haze, that I almost didn't notice Fiona standing right beside him.

50

"Dr. Bellanger." Instinctively, I stepped in front of my mother. "We're leaving."

He moved forward, unhurried and almost friendly. "That little trick out there—is that you and your friends? You want to take everything away from me, is that it?"

"Only fair," I said. "You've burned down two of my homes now, by my count."

He smiled without warmth. "Other people live here. You're taking their home too."

Sudden, hollow echoes of gunfire: bullets cooking in the heat. "Shouldn't you be with them, Dr. Bellanger?" I asked. "Maybe you should help your faithful followers instead of wasting your time with us. We can let ourselves out."

Fiona watched us.

"But where *will* you go?" he asked, as if he really wanted to know. "Margaret, will you return to your life of TV dinners and shelving books? Josephine, will you keep playacting as a great scientist, clinging to my coattails?" I didn't even flinch. "Or perhaps both of you will run off and tattle, like spiteful children. You'll come charging back with a self-righteous cavalry and attempt to take what's left of my work. Throw me into a prison cell. Have your grand trial and your tawdry headlines. Revenge at last."

My mother and I were both quiet. I could feel both of us trying to calculate how to get out of here as quickly as possible. Fiona's eyes on us were so intense that they seemed to be the source of the heat growing in the chapel.

"Neither of you will spare a thought for me, but think what this is doing to Fiona," Bellanger said. "You already took one refuge from her, Margaret."

"What did I take from her?" my mother asked.

Bellanger laughed, swift and pitying. I watched Fiona gauging his reaction, molding her heart to his. "Don't downplay your own hand in destroying the Homestead. You girls were more interested in fighting each other than in letting your vision unfold. Women will always blame their troubles on men. You can't take responsibility for the ways you hate each other too. Maybe if you hadn't fostered such bitterness between your so-called sisters, Josephine could have grown up with the Homestead instead of merely reading about it. We could've been together."

"Together," my mother repeated. "As long as we did exactly what you wanted, handed all nine Girls over to you eventually—"

"Even before the fire, you girls were scattering far and wide. You've avoided each other for years. What's kept you from your little utopia? All these years that I've been gone."

My mother was silent. The triumph in his voice stung me too. He was right. I'd only been thinking about Dr. Joseph Bellanger when I set out to unlock parthenogenesis; I'd forgotten the other women involved. I'd been blind to my own arrogance, or—worse—I'd looked right at it and mistaken it for virtue. Now it seemed impossible I could've even lasted these past seventeen years without knowing the other Girls. But what mattered was what we did now.

"We're leaving," I said, "and Fiona's coming with us."

Fiona's eyes flickered to me, a flash of genuine surprise. I understood just how completely we'd abandoned her. We'd left her to become exactly what I'd thought I'd wanted to be: Bellanger's favorite. Powerful and stunted, all at once. Everything about Fiona showed his fingerprints. She was light trapped inside a bulb, illuminating only him.

"What can you possibly offer Fiona?" Bellanger said, contemptuous. "What can you offer the child she's carrying?"

I made a decision that barely felt like a choice, the words pushing irresistibly into the room. "I can offer her the truth. I can tell Fiona what happened when her mother was pregnant a second time." I looked right at Fiona, those startled and startling eyes. "I can tell her about the tenth Girl. Your little sister, Fiona. Before she died, your mother conceived alone without any help from Bellanger."

He laughed softly, as if his derision alone could erase my words. My mother was staring at me, her realization spreading, tugging heartbreak in its wake. I saw Margaret Morrow in another life, a woman who'd walked away knowing that the Homestead had created the future she'd wanted so deeply: a woman conceiving on her own. The two of them, Lily-Anne and her incipient daughter, a perfect and closed system.

"Joseph?" my mother asked. "Is this true?"

"Of course not. You were there, Margaret. Don't you think you'd remember a tenth pregnancy?"

"No, no, no. I was there, but . . . things were strange. Lily-Anne was sick. Those last few months, she was so sick we never saw her. I thought it was her heart. I never imagined. I wish we'd known. I wish she'd trusted us."

"Lily-Anne died in childbirth," I said. "Bellanger and his friend worked together to hide the evidence, and they threatened Barbara— the only woman who knew—into silence. You couldn't have known. Bellanger made sure of that."

"This is ridiculous," Bellanger said. The simple authority in his voice nearly shook my conviction; I steadied myself. "Nothing has changed. It's still impossible for women to self-conceive. Where are all the miraculous births now, if it's really so simple? I'm disappointed to see that you're no better than the women who came before you, Josephine. Stubbornly fixated on cheap superstitions." His voice was dry with contempt.

"You can't re-create the original experiment," I shot back. "You've tried with other women and you can't do it. So you want to use our bodies now—mine and Cate's and Isabelle's. We're finally worth your time again."

The smoke was thicker now, creeping in under the door. The shouts had thinned out, but the ones left were louder and more desperate. The fire must be spreading, hopping from building to building. I fiercely prayed that Cate and Isabelle had found their way to safety already.

Bellanger began to speak, but I lifted my voice over his. "Fiona," I said to her. "This pregnancy—it's yours, isn't it? *Only* yours. Not Bellanger's at all. You wanted to make your father proud, and you couldn't watch him try and fail. But this pregnancy has nothing to do with him. You did this alone, like your mother."

Fiona's eyes on mine were a steady flame. She gave no sign of agreeing or denying. It wasn't until I looked at Bellanger that I realized what I'd done. The ugliness there transformed his entire face. He looked bruised, exposed, and I knew now that he'd worried about this too. Lily-Anne's influence had extended past her death. He knew what abilities Fiona held inside, and he would always wonder, looking at her pregnancy, whether it was really his. That kind of doubt could drive a man mad.

"We have to go," my mother said, low in my ear. "Please. Josie. I won't lose you."

"I can't leave until Fiona comes with us," I said, but her face was immovable. I needed time. I was undoing a lifetime of cruelty and tenderness in a few sentences. I thought of the zoo animals released back into the wild, unable to survive in the unpredictability of the world.

I needed something more—I needed to show Fiona who Bellanger really was. As I thought this, something pooled at the back of my brain, an oily awareness that didn't take specific shape just yet. I looked at Fiona, the heavy blankness of her eyes. Those drugs that Bellanger kept slipping her. The easy way she'd swallowed them down. Barbara Yoon had mentioned Lily-Anne's medications, administered during that second pregnancy. Bellanger had been desperate to get her under his control.

What had he been feeding Lily-Anne? What was he feeding Fiona now?

"What about the drugs?" I asked Bellanger. "Why do you give her those pills?"

"Fiona's medication is important for her. It's all that stands between her and another disaster. Don't pretend to understand her needs," Bellanger said.

"What's in them?" I asked.

He didn't answer. Bellanger began to reach into his jacket, a slow movement, as if he hoped I wouldn't notice.

"Is that what you spent all your energy on?" I asked. "Not focusing on finding a way to spread parthenogenesis, but on a way to get us under your control."

"You don't know what you're talking about." His hand shifted under his jacket.

"Then take one yourself." I locked eyes with him, and that rush of dizziness came over me: no longer disorienting, now as clarifying and clean as waking up after a long sleep. "Take one of the pills, Dr. Bellanger." A direct command, the first one I'd used against him.

The world felt too silent, shrunk down around the two of us. My mother tensed. I knew that to her ears, my command sounded like ordinary words put out into the world. Hopeful but inadequate. Reliant on the other person's obedience. She didn't know that my voice was worming its way into his brain, taking his choices and handing them over to me instead.

Bellanger stood very still. Nobody spoke. For a moment I wondered if it would even work: What if I couldn't control him? His brain had made me. His words had formed me. Could I reach into his mind, or was he too familiar, still holding my very genes in thrall—

Then Bellanger's hand was moving again. He pulled the bottle free and unscrewed the cap, tipped out a palmful of the blood-bright pills. A pause, long and heavy. I could feel the hovering shock of Fiona and my mother, wondering whether he'd go through with it. He pressed one pill into his mouth, his lips opening, and after a moment his throat bobbed.

"Take another," I said.

Bellanger's lips moved. It took me a moment to realize he was saying, *Please*. I thought he'd try to turn it into his decision, but this was naked fear and rage. He didn't understand why he was obeying me. A body he'd ignored, suddenly turned powerful. Then he slid another pill between his lips.

Fiona looked from Bellanger to me and back again. Something had cracked along her expression, like she was seeing him for the first time. I grabbed on to that hope. She was the least predictable and most important part of this equation. I had to get through to her.

I walked forward until I was right in front of Bellanger. He staggered, caught himself. I was met with the sour brush of his breath. A hint of that same cologne. I reached out to steady him, and he grabbed at my arm, grudgingly grateful. Wordlessly, Fiona watched Bellanger struggle to stay upright, his muscles slurring out of his control. "How?" he asked. His pupils were widening pits, big enough to slide a finger right through. "How, Josephine?"

God, how I'd imagined this moment: Telling him who we really were. Showing him what I actually was. This power that was supposed to be a testament to his legacy. That little girl on the garage roof, thinking that Bellanger would hold me up if I let go and flew into the air. "We're all like this," I said. "Every last one of us."

"No. No. I would've known. I watched you—"

"All of us," I said, "except the one you murdered." But Gina would've revealed something impossible too, if she'd been given the chance.

Bellanger shook his head, low sweeps, back and forth.

"It's inside all of us. Isabelle can stop a man's heart with her fingertips." I held up my hand, my own fingers hovering close to his skin. "Cate? She brought me back to life. And when I speak, you obey me."

His breathing was labored, as if each pump of his lungs hurt him.

I addressed Fiona now. "He's taught you that your powers are his too. But he abandoned us, and we found our power on our own. You lose nothing by leaving him, Fiona. You have a whole world to gain." I lowered my voice. "I'm afraid for you. I'm afraid of what Bellanger is planning to do with you, and I'm afraid of what he'll do with your daughter. What will he do if he decides he wants her more than you?"

Fiona touched her stomach, and I imagined her responding to a submerged kick and flutter.

"You can't take her," Bellanger whispered.

"I'm not asking you—"

"No." He cut me off, a sudden burst of ferocity. "I mean that it won't work. This girl has never known anything but this place. She's never known anything but me."

"We'll be with her," my mother said, almost surprised by her own stridence. "She won't be alone. She'll have us." We smiled at each other, an understanding passing between us. My mother knew who I was now. She knew what I was capable of.

Bellanger coughed out a laugh. "You? You can't manage your own daughter."

I saw the wince pass over my mother's face. There was grief there: I felt it too. My mother and I were both part of Bellanger's legacy, always, forever, implicated in the world he'd created. "You don't know anything about what's between my mother and me," I said to him. "All this way, I fought to find her."

Bellanger was retreating, eyes clouding. A man half caught inside a dream. From outside, the screams spiked and rose, the fire surely pulling closer to us.

"Josie—" my mother said, a warning.

"I know. We're leaving." I looked right at Fiona. I'd given her everything I had—every reason that she should walk away from him—but it had been just the two of them for so long. Their bond ran so much deeper than whatever I'd spun in my own head. "When we first arrived, I saw that sign in the sky," I said to her. "The bird. I didn't know what it meant at the time, but I think you sensed that we were here." Something fluttered behind her gaze. "That was a warning, wasn't it? You know what Bellanger's planning to do to us. And I think you understand, deep down, how dangerous he can be if he wants something from you."

Bellanger's eyes shifted, a quiet witness as we decided what would happen next.

"Mother Eight told me that Bellanger was giving Lily-Anne medications," I said. "Your mother died not long after that. It's no coincidence. Bellanger killed your mother."

It was the first time I'd said it aloud, and I had to stop for a moment, letting the words expand. I'd felt it for a long time—but I hadn't understood it with this confidence until I'd seen Bellanger standing next to a reincarnated version of Lily-Anne, young and pregnant and under his spell. Her death hadn't been summoned by a heart issue, and it hadn't been childbirth.

Fiona's face broke, a deep grief and rage beneath the surface. She looked at Bellanger, who didn't move. Around us, the candle flames spiked upward in long, ragged stripes, escaping the neat confines of the glass holders. "Is it true?" she asked Bellanger.

He was silent.

"Is it true?" she asked, and I heard the desperation for it to be a lie.

"Answer—" I began.

"No," Fiona said, and it took me a second to realize she was talking to me. "He needs to tell me himself." I hesitated; lying to Fiona had been Bellanger's natural state for the past seventeen years. But the intensity in her eyes convinced me. Slowly, I released my grip over Belanger, like relaxing a clenched fist. I felt him slip from my grasp, opaque to me again.

"Did you kill my mother?" Fiona asked.

Bellanger turned his gaze toward her, slowly, painfully. "You have to understand—it was for you. It was all for you. Your mother was—she couldn't give you a good life—"

"You killed her," Fiona said, her face too still. "You killed her and my sister."

He had a look of sour astonishment, like this was a shock to him too. I wondered if he'd ever admitted it to himself this openly, or if he'd wrapped it under layers of justifications and half-truths. "She was standing in the way of everything," he whispered.

The candle flames spiked higher again, too high, nearly reaching the ceiling now before receding. My mother flinched. "And the Grassis?" Fiona asked. "The fire?"

"Everything I did was because of you—" His voice dipped lower. "I'll make it up to you. I'll spend my lifetime making it up to you. I promise."

Fiona didn't answer. Her expression was almost peaceful now, like she hadn't heard him. She stood there, half swaying. I knew what she was experiencing, everything twisting out of her understanding, taking on a new shape. I flashed between triumph and guilt, triumph and guilt. I'd gone looking for the truth. She hadn't. I'd brought it to her, thrust it into her arms.

The candle flames pulsed upward, slowly, slowly. This time, they didn't retreat. The flames twisted together, braiding and intertwining like fingers. They crawled up toward the ceiling, more and more strands joining together. The flames edged overhead, spinning together deftly until the entire chapel was wreathed all over in this frozen fire, flickering above our heads. For now, the flames were suspended, but I knew what would happen when Fiona let go. The blaze would devour this place in a second, join up with the fires slowly building outside, and eat us alive.

My mother called my name. "If we don't get out of here now . . ." she said, not finishing the sentence, letting it hang there as a frantic warning.

Bellanger was struggling to remain standing, his face ashen, skin slack, as if something integral had been siphoned out of him. If the pills could kill Lily-Anne, if they could subdue the sheer power of Fiona, then I wondered how they would affect Bellanger. "I want you to come with me," I said to Fiona.

"Tell me to go."

I hadn't expected this. "What do you mean?"

"Tell me," she said fiercely. "Tell me to leave him. Make me. Or else I won't go." Her voice dipped to a whisper. "I can't leave him. You know that."

The flames twisted slowly overhead. I opened my mouth, the words ready on the tip of my tongue. Fiona was right. I could force her to escape. The smoke and the heat distorted everything—the world too clarified one second, smudged the next—and all I could see was Lily-Anne staring out at me, a ghost enduring inside her daughter's DNA.

"No," I said instead. "If you leave here, it's going to be your choice." For most of her life, Fiona had been under Bellanger's control. I wasn't going to take away her decisions again. Around us, the wall of flames spasmed and cinched like a sudden muscle twitch.

I turned. I took my mother's hand. We began walking out of the chapel together, and I didn't let myself look back. Would Fiona follow us? I was so intently aware of Fiona behind me that I was confused when I heard my name shouted—not behind me, but in front of me.

It was Cate. Cate. Running into the chapel, her gaze fixed right on me. I was furious at her for returning, and then I was overwhelmed with joy, because of course she came back. Of course she wouldn't have walked out of the flames without me. But Cate's glance slipped past me, and she was pointing, her face wide open with horror, and I turned, thinking Fiona was in danger—

Everything happened too fast. A series of images and impressions.

Bellanger was on his knees, but he held a revolver, aimed at me. His face was so pale and distant that he barely seemed conscious. His hand didn't shake. The revolver. Orange Shirt's gun. That's where it'd ended up. I acknowledged this in a flash of quick, instinctive understanding, realizing that I'd let him out of my control. And then—

The gunshot cracked through the noise. Instinctively, I looked down at myself, searching for the blood. Nothing. I turned around to Cate, who wouldn't look at me, her face pulled tight with shock. Confused, I turned to my mother. She wasn't there. I had to look down. I didn't want to. I couldn't, I couldn't, I couldn't: a drumbeat in my head.

I did. I looked down.

My mother on the ground, crumpled. A single red blot in the center of her forehead, her eyes glassy and unseeing. I'd just gotten her back. I'd just gotten her back and now she was gone. The shock of it brought me to my knees, my stomach hollowed out. I reached for her, hand shaking. I pulled her into my lap. I could feel how empty she was, all that stubborn life gone, the brilliant brain I'd barely understood already sinking into blackness. I put my hand on her stomach, imagining myself nestled there, decades ago, the impossible product of her impossible dreams. Safe inside her.

"You take something from me," Bellanger said, and he didn't even sound triumphant. He sounded exhausted. "I take something from you."

I opened my mouth and nothing came out but a wail of grief and anger. I had to tell him to drop the gun, and I couldn't find the words. As I watched, the revolver was yanked from his hand by an invisible force, sent spinning across the floor, out of anybody's reach. Fiona looked to me and my mother, her eyes wide, fattened with flames.

Cate knelt beside me. I thought she'd reach for me, and I couldn't bear to be touched right now. I didn't want to be reminded I was still here. But she reached for my mother instead. Gently, she ran her hand over my mother's forehead, like she was smoothing back her hair. Cate's eyes fluttered closed, her lips drooped open. The rhythm of her hand kept up, steady, her skin vivid and alive against my mother's quickly fading flesh. I watched, heartbeat dull against my temples, waiting for something. Waiting for my mother's eyelids to flutter. Waiting for her to gasp for air.

Nothing. Blood was smeared on my mother's forehead now, matted through her hair. The shot had been so direct. My mother didn't have any thin threads connecting her to the world anymore. She was already gone, and even if Cate thrust her hand through the layer separating life and death, my mother's fingertips were too far down to reach hers.

"Cate—" I said, my voice broken. "It's hopeless."

She didn't answer. I could see in her face that she was hurting, sweat beading her forehead too thickly, lips gone bluish. She'd end up killing herself too if she kept this up.

Movement behind me. I realized that Fiona had approached. She stood over Cate, face blank, watching. Watching. I wanted to shout at her to get away, but I didn't have the energy. Fiona reached out a hand. Delicately, she touched Cate's shoulder. I saw Cate twitch slightly, like she'd been brushed by a cold breeze. Her face loosened for a second, then she drew a deep breath. Her hand stilled. She pressed her palm hard against my mother's forehead. They stood arranged like that: Cate connected to my mother, Fiona connected to Cate.

All three of their faces were glowing in the firelight, but it seemed to come from inside their skin, a buried source of radiance.

I looked back at Bellanger. I wanted to see him seeing them. Watching them undo what he'd done to my mother. His eyes were wide with awe.

My mother opened her eyes. She gasped. Cate fell backward as if she'd been pushed, but she was half laughing, catching herself on her elbows. I said my mother's name and she turned her head immediately, seeking out my voice. She looked perfect. The gunshot wound had been absorbed back into her skin, and she was glowing, the fatigue scrubbed away from beneath her eyes, her cheeks flushed and eyes alert. As if she'd had the past few weeks erased from her body's memory. "What happened?" she whispered.

"Magic," Cate said, her whole face alive. "It was magic."

My mother repeated the word silently, tasting it in her mouth. Fiona looked from one of them to the other, and I couldn't tell what she was thinking. It seemed impossible that she wasn't responding on a bone-deep level to the sheer power of this: a Mother lost, a Mother brought back.

But I couldn't forget where we were, the fire pulling closer, danger still lapping at our heels. I turned to Bellanger, crouching on the floor. He'd escaped a fire before. He'd walked out of the flames, remaking himself, starting over, and he'd do it again. Rising, I walked to Bellanger until we were only inches away. I knelt and took his face in my hands, his beard scratching at my palms, his skin beneath it feverishly hot. He flinched, began pulling back, and then he relaxed into my grasp. My palms were wet with my mother's blood.

I remembered looking up at him as a child. Watching him work. His intensity and concentration. His wisdom, his willingness to change everything we knew about the world, whatever it took. I had wanted that wisdom for myself. I had spent a lifetime steeping myself inside it. It was wound through me now, impossible to escape.

The lives he'd taken: Lily-Anne, dying alone; the tenth Girl, gone before she even started; Angela and Gina, dead and unnoticed, their bones standing in for more consequential deaths. Fiona and the thwarted, half-formed life he'd given her in exchange for her mother and her sister.

My mother.

He spoke so quietly that only I could hear him. "You can have the world, Josephine. You can take it. Everything else is yours. Just let me have her."

There was a renewed blaze of heat against my back. Fiona had let go of the flames, and they roared to life now, unrestrained, eating away at the ceilings and the walls. The fire was out of her control. It was the same as the fire outside, just as hungry and just as wild. This place would burn too quickly, surrounded by miles of dry, merciless wilderness.

I looked deep into Bellanger's eyes. Milky brown, swollen irises. The very first eyes to look at me when I emerged into the world. His face changed. He was reverent, like he was seeing me for the first time. "Girl One," he whispered.

I said, "Get up. Walk into the flames. Stay there."

My hands fell from his face. He rose; I rose. Mirrors of each other. I turned and went back to the three of them, pulling Fiona tight against me, feeling her fine bones. Her skin was sheened in damp sweat. Cate had her arm looped around my mother's shoulders, steadying her. We turned in the heat, and we began walking toward the door. I held on to Fiona. I didn't let her go. Behind us, the sizzling crash of the roof collapsing. We walked, Fiona's steps matching mine.

At the doorway, I couldn't help it. I turned once. Dr. Joseph Bellanger walked in the opposite direction, deeper into the flames, only the white of his coat shining for a second before he was lost to us.

The world was fire-streaked and smoke-darkened. We followed the people running, running, everyone fixated on their own private escape, ghostly silhouettes darting through the haze. Seventeen years of Bellanger's life vanishing. Fiona leaned against me, half stumbling. The shed was the bright center of the blaze, the heart of the destruction, with sparks hopping to the surrounding buildings and carrying the fire along the arteries of the compound.

The gate hung open, barely discernible from the blur of smoke and the mesh of the fence. It was nothing now, barely a barrier, and I walked through, following my mother and Cate. Fiona hesitated for just a moment, the fire at her back, everything else before her. She stood with her head ducked, her sweat-slicked hair curled against her neck. I thought for a moment that she couldn't step into this future without him. Then she gripped my hand, and we walked out of the compound.

Our heads down, we kept moving. Even here, the smoke was a veil hanging over the compound. I imagined how it would look to anyone watching from a distance: the frosty silver of the desert in the moonlight, and then the explosive spray of heat and noise and chaos. People were crowded at the edges of the gates, some of them walking farther out, most still clustered close, watching the compound burn as if they could still sift through the ashes and find enough there to rebuild their lives. I felt an instinctive pity for them. I remembered the sensation of running into the black woods with my mother, already understanding in my gut that I'd lost something I could never replace. But I knew now how much I gained when I was torn from Bellanger, running into the future with my mother's hand in mine.

He hadn't wanted us to run from the flames but we'd run twice now, emerging into a different world each time, remade.

Nobody else approached the four of us. Some of them ignored us, their eyes glassy with the reflected flames, their bodies sagging with defeat and shock. An older woman hugged a younger woman, their pale hair mingling as they leaned into each other. A man stood alone, arms hanging limp. I looked around, searching for Isabelle, and anytime I accidentally made eye contact with a stranger, they'd look away, dropping their eyes. As I led Fiona farther from the heat and the smoke, I realized that a path was clearing for us. They were afraid. Of her; of us. I breathed deeply, letting the dry, sparkling night air reach deep into my lungs.

I scanned the desert for Isabelle, my anxiety growing. Isabelle could've run into trouble without us. The fire—the explosion—any strangers who didn't yet know to fear us—

"Over here."

Isabelle stood underneath the outcropping of a cliff, the thin moonlight and the wash of firelight just illuminating her. She stepped out, raising one hand in the air. My whole body lit up with relief at seeing her safe. Letting go of Fiona, I hurried toward her.

"What took you so long?" she asked.

"Thank you," I said, taking both her hands in mine.

She shrugged, though a small smile played at the corners of her lips. She looked past me to my mother, and I glanced back, seeing the way my mother had slowed, her face suddenly stricken. "Hello, Isabelle," my mother said.

"Hello," Isabelle said softly. "Mother One."

Isabelle and my mother together. For a second, time slipped and slid, and I saw that old photograph of Patricia and my mother sitting close together. The two of them resurrected, on the edge of everything, nothing yet decided, all of it possible. Then I blinked and Isabelle was the motherless daughter who carried our mothers' favorite name. The one who'd lost her mother so that we could find mine. Guilt nudged at my edges. My gaze slipped to Fiona, who tilted her head, eyes shut in the moonlight, as if she were praying. She held her stomach with both hands. Outside of the confines of the compound, she looked so young.

"You did the right thing," my mother said, following my gaze.

"I hope so," I whispered.

A roar, a crackle. The fire was devouring everything, a patient beast finally unleashed. I pulled back from my mother and I turned, fascinated. All those times I'd seen footage of the Homestead fire on the news and felt the sharp echo of that long-ago loss. Here it was. Happening right in front of me.

I stood next to Cate, and we threaded our fingers together, palms held close, all that power concentrated between us. We waited together, the five of us: my mother and Isabelle standing close, Fiona clutching her belly. We watched the fire blaze, the hectic flames like a sunset. Like a sunrise. Like the world was remaking itself, right here, just awaiting our arrival.

51

December 1970

Dearest Trish,

You said we weren't talking enough lately, so here's a nice old-fashioned letter from me to you. I never ever *ever* mean to neglect you, please believe me. What I've been doing with Joseph has taken up my time, but it's all for you. For us! For our future daughters. I wake up every morning feeling like I'm holding the entire future inside me.

Your turn will come too. I'll make sure of it. I care for all the wonderful girls here, but you're my favorite in all ways, forever. My sweet, serious girl. The first to ever believe in me. Even when you barely knew me, you could see into my soul and you knew what this would mean. Not just for you and me, but for every woman.

The baby is fine and strong and healthy, and I'm practically glowing with life. I know you laugh at me, but that's how I feel. Like the sun herself. Joseph wants us to be careful about telling the world until we have a more "certain outcome" (his words). And I'm trying to be good, Trish. But the secret is bursting out of me every day. If I could stand up and shout it from the rooftops, this is what I'd say: that in April of 1971, my child will be born, and I already know two things. I knew them the first time I felt the baby kick.

One: she will be a girl. Two: she will change the world.

ACKNOWLEDGMENTS

First of all, thank you to my agent, Alice Whitwham, for always taking my wild ideas so seriously and for helping guide me from the wobbly beginnings to a clear and steady draft. And my gratitude goes to the whole team at Elyse Cheney Literary Associates. Endless and massive thanks to Daphne Durham for instantly seeing the best version of this novel and giving the most incisive (and fun!) feedback to help the story arrive there. It's been magical to see Josie and friends develop with your guidance. Thank you so much to Lydia Zoells for sharp and amazing feedback, and to the entire wonderful team at MCD for giving this book such a welcoming home.

This idea was originally sparked by a book called *Making Sex*, by Thomas Laqueur, and I owe a lot to Laqueur's work for making me think about the history of reproduction and the ways women's bodies have been treated as afterthoughts in that whole process. I also found incredible insights through Aarathi Prasad's *Like a Virgin*. The historical accounts of searches for a child born of virgin birth inspired some of the tests in *Girl One*, including the skin graft operation. I learned a lot from reading *The Genius Factory*, by David Plotz, which is about the emergence of sperm banks and the resulting "fatherless" children, and *My Life as the World's First Test-Tube Baby*, by Louise Brown. *Utopian Motherhood*, by Robert T. Francoeur, gave me insight into the views of the changing reproductive landscape in the early 1970s.

I have to thank Franklin Sayre and Janelle Barr Bassett for being patient friends and early readers as I agonized over parthenogenesis for . . . years! Thanks to Franklin for answering some of my med school–related questions (any mistakes are very much my own).

Much love to my parents. Dad, unlike my protagonist, I'm lucky to have a good father who's always encouraged my love of reading. Mom, I could never have written a book about mother-daughter relationships without our wonderfully complex and supportive relationship. Thanks to all my siblings-in-law and siblings. To my mother-in-law, Karen, thank you in particular for helping with childcare so that I was able to write!

Huge thanks to everyone who's taken my writing seriously over the years, including one of my most enduring mentors, Kathryn Davis, whose belief in me as a writer has carried me so far. Thank you, thank you, to everyone who supported my debut. You have my eternal gratitude, and I'm so honored to have such generous readers.

To Miles and August: you've never made my writing process easier, but you make life infinitely weirder and sweeter. And finally, my everlasting thanks to Ryan, for being a tireless source of support and insight, for reading endless drafts, and for always being just as curious about the world inside my brain as I am. Having a partner who loves reading, writing, and plotting is a gift I won't take for granted.

A Note About the Author

Sara Flannery Murphy is the author of the novel *The Possessions*. She grew up in Arkansas, studied library science in British Columbia, and received her MFA in creative writing at Washington University in St. Louis. She lives in Utah with her husband and their two sons.